empty cities
of the
full moon

ACE BOOKS BY HOWARD V. HENDRIX

LIGHTPATHS
STANDING WAVE
BETTER ANGELS
EMPTY CITIES OF THE FULL MOON

empty cities
of the
full moon

howard v. hendrix

ACE BOOKS, NEW YORK

To Laurel

EMPTY CITIES OF THE FULL MOON

An Ace Book
Published by The Berkley Publishing Group,
a division of Penguin Putnam Inc.,
375 Hudson Street, New York, New York 10014.

Visit our website at
www.penguinputnam.com

First edition: August 2001

Library of Congress Cataloging-in-Publication Data

Hendrix, Howard V., 1959– .
Empty cities of the full moon : a novel / by Howard V. Hendrix.
p.   cm.
ISBN 0-441-00844-5 (alk. paper)
I. Title.

PS3558.E49526 E47 2001
813'.54—dc21
00-050230

Printed in the United States of America

10   9   8   7   6   5   4   3   2   1

ACKNOWLEDGMENTS

First, thanks to the usual suspects: Ginjer Buchanan and Carol Lowe at Ace, and Chris Lotts at Ralph Vicinanza, Ltd.—all of whom pushed me to make this thing of plot and character live up to its ideas and ideals. Thanks again to my friends Bruce Albert, Mike Lepper, Art Holcomb, Barbara Wallace, Dirk Vander Elst, Lisa Weston, and Matt Pallamary, for volleying ideas back and forth with me over the years.

Thanks, too, to some new suspects: Harold Gross and Eve Gordon, Rob and Barb Kline, Mike Clifton (for our conversations on the gothic), Edward Garcia (for Morrison materials), Jim Freund at WBAI, Stephen Spusta at UCSF (for trying to keep me honest on prion biology), Elmarie Anzelmo (for insights on South Africa), Gerald Gaylard of the University of Witwatersrand (likewise), and the organizers and participants of the Eaton Hong Kong 2001 conference. Thanks also to a line of physicists (most recently David Deutsch) for their work on parallel universes and the multiverse—ideas which I've been toying with in my fiction for years and which they have made more fun by making them more plausible. (Note: None of these theorists are to blame for the "parallel universe processing" concept described herein. Responsibility for that strange creature is mine alone.)

I suspect the world will find all of you innocent of blame for these pages—and worthy of your share in any praise they might receive.

Prologue

**What the Past Will Be
1966**

THE WESTERING SUN TURNS THE DRY AUGUST GRASS TO GOLD ON ALL THE hillsides around Lake Falmouth. The boy's father waves him into their blue 1955 Nash Rambler. The boy's mother stays behind at the vacation home with the boy's tired younger brother. The boy's father promises her that he and their son will be gone just a few minutes.

**1999
Universe A**

THE WESTERING SUN TURNS THE DRY AUGUST GRASS TO GOLD ON ALL THE hillsides around Lake Falmouth. The boy's grandfather, a mathematics professor recently gone emeritus, waves his severely immune-deficient grandson into the classic 1955 Nash Rambler his family calls Ol' Blue. He has kept it mothballed in the garage since 1966, when it hovered around the 100,000-mile mark. The boy's grandmother stays behind at the family vacation home with the boy's already sacked-out parents. The grandfather promises her that he and the boy will be gone just a few minutes.

Not far away, beneath a spreading oak in the yard of a house on a hilltop overlooking the Ohio River, guests depart a wedding reception. Earlier that afternoon, Everett Colton married Marian Halverson. The JUST MARRIED red Ford Taurus of Ev and Marian follows a rented white GEO Prizm. In the Prizm sit two young couples: Marian's sister Emma Halverson and her husband, Hisato Yamaguchi, and Ev's sister Grace Colton and her husband, Charles Drinan. The Prizm, driven by a more than slightly drunk Charlie, blares its horn like a herald and spins gravel from its wheels, skidding loudly ahead of the newlyweds' Taurus.

For a time, the boy's grandfather drives the blue Rambler over the twisting backroads, no apparent destination in mind. Like his grandfather, the boy in the isolation suit is on vacation. Destinations aren't too important. The boy sees, however, that his grandfather's eyes dart repeatedly to the old-fashioned dials beyond the steering wheel. Vaguely the environment-suited boy recalls a story his father once told him—about a trick Grandpa played on him when he was a kid. The boy wonders if the same trick is about to be played on him.

In the white Prizm, Charlie Drinan speeds up, swerving over the centerline and rounding off sharp curves. The newlyweds in the Taurus can't keep up with their relatives as the Prizm screeches down the twisting two-lane road. Drinan hits the horn less frequently now, unable to concentrate on both driving and honking at the same time.

"Come over here, kiddo," the boy's grandfather says, pulling the boy in the earthbound spacesuit closer to him as the car heads up a hill with blind curves. Reaching around the steering wheel, Grandpa directs the boy's attention to a dial he taps with his finger. "That's the odometer. It measures the number of miles this car has traveled. It only goes up to five places, see? 99998. 99999, now. In a minute this car will have traveled 100,000 miles. Watch."

They watch. Suddenly it happens: 99999 goes to 00000—not one digit at a time, but all at once, in the same instant.

"Look! There!" the grandfather says. "Did you see it?"

The boy smiles up at his grandfather, a seven-year-old convinced that numbers are magic and his grandfather is a magician. His grandfather laughs as the two of them watch the odometer click over to 00001.

"This old car is new again," his grandfather says, "at least by the numbers."

A white car, blaring its horn too late, almost slams into them. The boy's grandfather swings the old Rambler out of harm's way just in time to avoid a collision. As the old man brakes the Rambler to a stop, a red Ford slips past them at speed.

"Damn fools!" his grandfather says, shaken. "Lucky they didn't kill us all!"

1999
Universe A Prime

REACHING AROUND THE STEERING WHEEL, GRANDPA DIRECTS THE BOY'S attention to a dial he taps with his finger. "That's the odometer. It measures the number of miles this car has traveled. It only goes up to five places, see? 99998. 99999, now. In a minute this car will have traveled 100,000 miles. Watch."

They watch. Suddenly it happens: A white car, blaring its horn too late, slams into them. The boy's grandfather swings the wheel of the old Rambler reflexively even as the Prizm hits them, but he is too late to avoid the collision. Both cars go off the edge of the narrow road. Flipping and tumbling, they roll down the hillside on separate arcs. In the seatbelt-less old Rambler, the boy is tossed about, then ejected through the open passenger's-side window, hurt but alive. When the Rambler comes to rest, the grandfather lies in the wreckage, dying, the steering column skewering his chest.

In the Prizm, all four passengers are dead. In Universe A, Emma Halverson Yamaguchi is pregnant with the son she and Hisato plan to name Seiji. The same is true in Universe A Prime, but here Seiji Robert Yamaguchi is never born. His younger brother, Jiro Ansel Yamaguchi, will also never come to be. In Universe A Prime, Charlie and Grace Drinan do not live to raise the family that, in Universe A, includes their son, John Drinan. In Universe A, John decades later helps his cousin Seiji find Seiji's lost brother, Jiro. In Universe A Prime, however, Jiro Yamaguchi is more truly lost. Having never existed, Jiro never goes insane, never dies and experiences his machine-aided resurrection. Jiro's gnostic apotheosis never shapes the human future, in Prime.

Dying in the wreckage of the Rambler, the boy's grandfather hears his grandson crying. The old man is relieved at the sound. At least the boy is alive. The grandfather thinks of when he first performed this odometer trick, a third of a century earlier, with his son, the boy's father, the grown-up Wall Street wizard. The dying man thinks of a phrase he used long ago with the boy's father and hoped to use again this time: "This old car is new again, at least by the numbers."

On the road above, the red Taurus screeches to a stop. Witnesses to catastrophe, Everett and Marian—he in tuxedo and she in wedding gown—leap from the car and begin making their running, slipping, staggering way down the hillside, toward where the dust of the disaster has not yet settled. Behind them, rhythmic chimes sound a subdued warning from the Taurus, its doors left ajar.

By the numbers, the old man thinks. Is that why this tragedy has been visited upon them all—because he cheated some god of sums? Because, given the odometer-watching Zeitgeist in this year of nines, he couldn't resist the temptation to turn back the odometer, to share with his grandson what he had once shared with the boy's father?

Which offended god visited that other, earlier tragedy upon them—the boy's severe immune deficiency? In the tiny chemical miscalculation that doomed the boy to life under protection of drugs or marrow transplants or isolation suits, what design had governed? Had that environment suit born of misfortune now *saved* the boy?

In his mind as he dies, the boy's grandfather has a final vision: Of numbers, underlying everything, latent substrate to blatant reality. Of atoms decaying, clocks ticking, stocks jittering graphwise, odometers turning over. Mathematical processes, functioning somehow like proteins: the simple equations linear, the more complex proofs folding back upon themselves in strange sorts of higher-order dimensionality, shaping patterns, traces, memories. In that final vision's compression of all the data of his life, his existence in time, the dying man sees the patterns of subtler, higher orders. Whatever predictive powers ordinary dreams might possess, his final vision possesses vastly more, his mind building upon already detected patterns. He sees the future laid out before him, far clearer than the past. . . .

"Dead," Everett Colton mutters to himself. Just like Hisato and Emma and Charlie and Grace. He turns from the old man and walks toward where Marian sits in her wedding gown on the dusty ground. She holds a bleeding, sobbing, sniffling young boy seated in a half-upright position and dressed in an odd astronaut costume. The boy's blood has made a wine-dark spot on the white gown, over Marian's heart. The boy quiets as Ev approaches.

"Son, can you hear me?" Ev asks. The boy nods weakly. "Who're your folks? What's your name?"

"Cameron. Cameron . . . Spires."

Ev nods. He pulls from the inside pocket of his jacket the matte-black parallelepiped of his cell phone—there all day, switched off during the wedding ceremony. With a sigh he turns the phone on and dials 911.

1

A Boy and His Dog Who Fell to Earth
2032
Universe A

"YO-HO, YO-HO, A SPACER'S LIFE FOR ME!" JOHN DRINAN SANG TO HIS big mastiff dog and constant companion, Ozymandias. "Drink to that, Oz m'boy?"

Ozymandias cocked his jowly head quizzically at John, who laughed, whipped off his suit gauntlets, and scratched the big dog behind the ears. John brought a half-full bottle of Belgian lambic ale to his lips and drained it. He'd already celebrated enough so that he couldn't tell, without looking at the label, whether the flavor of this particular bottle was *peche* or *framboises*. No matter. More of both flavors waited in the pressure locker, anyway.

Taking off his maroon knit cap, he ran his free hand through his longish, greasy dark hair before allowing it to scratch and settle in his thin beard. If he wanted to celebrate around other people, he'd have to clean himself up once he reached the orbital habitat. *Bathe once a year, whether I need to or not*, he thought with a smile.

Looking at his reflection in the glass of the bottle, he saw a distorted image of a young man with deep-set eyes behind archaic wire-rimmed glasses, his features made all the sharper by the glass's convexity and the gauntness of his face. As always, his thin frame was dressed in bulky gray spacer's coveralls and heavy space boots—the whole uniform overlaid with a Jackson Pollack drip-camouflage of paint and stains.

"This place is a mess," John muttered, shaking his head. Around Oz stood archaeologically stratified clutter. The work area in the cabin of his

Solar Harvester Travel-All, the *Helios*, doubled as a long-time bachelor apartment. "But at least we're a *rich* mess."

Less than an hour had passed since he cashed out his completion bonus. He'd gotten the robotic asteroid miners trained in time and delivered them to the big mass-driver tug *Swallowtail* right on schedule. His seldom-seen bosses had to shell out the full amount—good pay, but the time had been lonely, even for a solitary guy.

A flash from the port side caught his eye. Then a second flash. John hunched forward. Fireworks? To celebrate the impending launch of the *Swallowtail* and the opening of the two new habitats? No, not in the airless void. The location—low Earth orbit—was wrong, too.

Half a dozen bright points of light were flashing into view now, from around the other side of the Earth. Unlike fireworks, those lights were staying on, not guttering and dying.

Voice-activating the main viewing screens, John picked out the distant gleam of the two new space colonies and the shine of the asteroid tug behind him. The first of the orbital habitats shone nearer at hand. Earth stood partly in darkness; those points of light rose away from it. Between Earth and the orbital habitat flashed dimmer glints: the necklace of X-shaped structures he'd heard the media calling X-sats, when he hadn't been too busy to pay attention. He gathered the X-shaped satellites were causing heightened tensions between Earth and its first space colony.

John called up the location of one of the X-sats in its ring-around-the-planet necklace. He sat back as the viewscreen's optics zoomed in on that location. At first he thought it was a wobble in the optics, but he soon saw that something about the X-sat was changing as he watched. The X-shaped satellite was canting over, altering its orientation. It began to slowly separate into halves that reminded John of "greater than" and "less than" signs.

He had the screen pan back until four of the X-sats hovered in his field of view. They too were separating into halves and drawing apart, like chromosomes moving from metaphase to anaphase in some enormous dividing cell.

He zoomed in on the bright points moving up from Earth. Magnified, each of them was a stealthy blue-black above its burning engines—and all of them looked entirely too much like United Nations and Corporate Presidium troop shuttles. The thought occurred to him that they might be ships of an occupation force, perhaps part of an armada headed toward the orbital habitat. He whistled softly.

"Hoo, boy. What have we gotten ourselves into, Oz?"

A brief but intense flash of light made John blink and Oz bark. When John opened his eyes, he found he had not been blasted out of space. The nearer group of half Xs, however, were much closer to each other—and much closer to him. He ordered *Helios*'s navigation computer to plot a track for the divided X-sats. In a moment more, however, even before the ship announced it, John saw that the nearer of the halved X-sats were reeling in, directly toward *Helios*—a cloud of less-thans pulled along invisible spindles, left-arrows fired along lines of force.

John had only a moment to wonder why his ship was the pole toward which these spindles converged—to wonder who or what might be at the other, "greater than" pole, to wonder who might be behind it all—before paths of light spiked along the spindles and all around him. In his Iambic bottle reflection, a lambent knot of flickering fire danced above his forehead until his eyes began jittering so fiercely in his face that he became blind to his immediate environs.

That, however, did nothing to decrease the inner visions flooding through his mind. He saw crowds of people, their eyes remming furiously in their skulls for the instant it took this Light to blast into their heads. He saw Earth from every side clasped in wings bright with a billion billion lightpath pinions. He saw the face of his lost cousin, Jiro, and heard, months after death, that cousin's voice, which he had never heard in life, calling the X-shaped structures information refractors and using even stranger words to describe what was happening.

The boundary between outer and inner vision, between external and internal reality, vanished. The Light seemed to be opening a vortex around him, a whorling ring of light. In it he saw all times at one place and all spaces at one time. Was his ship moving and the vortex standing still, or the vortex moving and his ship standing still? No way to tell. Around him, all time was one time, the standing wave and traveling catastrophe of the present bent round itself into the shape of eternity, of innumerable nearly parallel universes branching off each other at every instant, forming a vast plenum less branched like a tree than webbed and woven like an impossibly complex tapestry—

2032
Universe A Prime

JOHN CAME BACK INTO NORMAL SPACE WITH MEMORIES—DIM BECAUSE OF their overwhelming number, yet also deeply interfused with the impression that his cousin, Jiro, had something to do with that Light. But how? Jiro was dead; had been for months. John had been right there in the orbital habitat with Jiro's older brother, Seiji, when the death had been announced in a phone call from Seiji's mother.

He shook his head and rubbed his eyes, then checked his ship's screens. Everything seemed in order. The nearest orbital habitat was still there, the *Swallowtail* was still there—though they were both receding a good deal faster than they had any right to. Where were the X-sats and troop shuttles? They had disappeared as completely as if they'd never existed.

The ship's optics showed Earth growing—too big and too fast—on the screen before him. Alarms began to sound. John checked his ship's velocity. Nearly 220,000 kilometers per hour? But that was impossible! What could have kicked up *Helios*'s speed this way?

Helios was too near Earth and going far too fast to pull out of Earth's gravity-well without tearing herself apart. John voice-activated all ship's retrorockets and ran the trajectory of a catastrophic braking maneuver. It would cut their speed down, but the ship would not survive. He slammed on his suit gauntlets and took up the space helmet he wore as seldom as possible.

"Into the escape pod, Oz!"

The dog bounded awkwardly away toward the pod's open door and John made his decision. He commanded the ship to initiate the braking maneuver. *Helios* began to shudder. Locking his helmet over his head, John saw the ship's status readouts come on in the visor's heads-up display. In the next instant he dove into the escape pod, then strapped himself and Oz into their crash couches in the mindless blur of his moving hands.

The shuddering of *Helios* grew steadily from tic to palsy to spasm. The braking and breaking maneuver appeared to be working, though. Ship's velocity fell to 100,000 clicks, then dropped still farther. Trying to ignore the ship's seismic shuddering, John waited an endless white-knuckled moment longer. Then at the last possible instant, praying he hadn't waited too long for clean separation, he blew the explosive bolts, jettisoning the escape pod.

The escape vehicle departed the dying *Helios* with a velocity less than one fourth of the speed the lost mother ship was clocking when John sent it into catastropic braking. Good, but not good enough. If they were to survive, he would have to step their velocity down still more, before the atmosphere around them thickened much further.

Less a pod than a smooth-edged isosceles triangle—a lifting body with crash couches in the nose at its apex and stubby winglets at the far ends of the triangle's base—the jettisoned spacecraft plummeted Earthward. And whoever called this thing a "lifting body" was dead wrong, John thought as he fired the craft's all too puny engines. A falling body was all it really was—but hopefully one that would fall slowly enough that he and Oz might survive the impact.

As best he could, John steered the craft in a long, falling suborbital trajectory. The tiled underside of the escape pod began to heat and flare. Orbiting means falling all the while, he reminded himself. The way that walking, too, is falling, and catching yourself from falling. They had taken a giant step. He hoped this falling star caught itself before they stumbled fatally.

The cabin grew hot. Damn! Their speed and angle of entry were right up against the red zone, but that wasn't the real problem. With luck they wouldn't burn up in the atmosphere. They might even slow down enough so that the big rectangular drag-airfoil wouldn't rip itself to shreds the instant it deployed. No—the problem was that they would overshoot both the Rosamond and Rogers Dry Lakes at Edwards. Scanning the map in his heads-up display, John had no choice but to shoot for the much smaller Cuddeback Dry Lake and try to drift-steer the falling pod around Fremont Peak.

The crashpod came in through the last glow of evening twilight. John wondered if he was giving a long meteor-streak of a show to people in the Channel Islands and Oxnard.

Just when the tiny cabin had grown noticeably cooler, a jerk yanked the falling craft so hard it made Ozymandias yelp, even strapped into his crash couch. The drag-airfoil had deployed—at spec altitude, but significantly above spec speed. They were falling through darkness, swinging and buffeting heavily. Stabilizing at last, the crashpod whiskered past Fremont Peak. The ground rose toward them. The falling pod's structural integrity was going to get quite a test. . . .

With a noise like a one-ton oil drum shot from a rail gun plowing into a sand dune, the crashpod gouged a long groove into and across the length of Cuddeback Dry Lake. Ozymandias howled and John ground his teeth. After booming sand and shrieking metal had nearly deafened them, the crashpod at last ground to a halt. John knew he was still alive because he heard Ozymandias whimpering, felt his own blood running from his nose into his mouth—and smelled smoke.

Ignoring the grinding pain from his ribs, he freed himself and Oz from the crash couches, then lunged at the hatch above the nose. The emergency door creaked and clanged open. Together John and Oz fell out of the battered crashpod and onto cooling desert sand. Beneath a stardusted night sky, they limped and staggered away from the burning crashpod. Collapsing at the base of a rock-strewn hillside, John and Oz watched as flames transformed the escape pod into a pyre.

Their lifeboat never really exploded. It just burned higher and more brightly for a time, becoming a whirling column of flame, until the little spacecraft had consumed itself down to a broken skeleton of scorched and melted airframe. John and Oz walked back toward the remains, once those had at last gone cold and dark.

"Looks like a total loss," John said quietly to Oz. He thought of making a tired joke about drinking and driving and crashing and burning, but he just couldn't find the strength to say it. His rib cage hurt and his back felt stiff, but at least his nose had stopped bleeding. He turned away from the debris. They began walking through the starlit desert toward the bustling burg of Red Mountain.

Coming over a small ridge, John saw in the distance lights to the north and west. Some of the nearer ones appeared to be moving—vehicles making their way along a lonely stretch of Old Highway 395. Heading toward the lights, John pondered why it was no one had come out to investigate their crash. True, they had come in through falling darkness and might have been mistaken for a meteor, but someone's radar or satellite must have spied them. Maybe no one had gotten around to on-site investigating yet.

John's head cleared as he and Oz walked toward the highway. His pain subsided enough that he remembered the commlink on the left gauntlet of his suit. Wondering who to inform of his debacle, he decided against emergency services or any agency that might entangle him with the authorities. Checking a map readout on the link, he remembered his brother Greg lived in Palmdale. Closest living relative, John thought with a slight smile.

The FreePhone commlink called up Greg's number from its index. John waited for the connection but when it came, it was a wrong number. Odd. He punched up area code information. When the roboperator answered, John pronounced the name of the city and his brother's full name. The synthetic operator came back with "No such listing. Please try again." Had his brother gone to some sort of high-privacy status on his personal comm access, without telling him about it?

As he and Oz picked their way by the light of the stars and newly risen moon, John discovered that the desert terrain here was surprisingly uneven—not only pocked by more scrub brush, but also cut by washes and dry-creek ravines. Sitting down in a sandy spot in yet another dry wash, he began systematically punching up numbers for all his brothers and sisters. Every one of them came back as wrong numbers or "not in service." When he tried to go through Information, he just got different wrong numbers: people with similar names, but who either had no brother named John or whose brother John didn't match *him* at all.

"Aw, come on!" he said at last, frustrated. He stood up and began walking toward the highway again. Oz tagged at his heels as John set a pace calculated to relieve his annoyance. When he had calmed down enough, he decided to call his uncle Ev and aunt Marian. Attacking the problem from a different angle, he ran a search on them. This time he found the party he was looking for, though not in the city he'd expected. He stopped walking, pondering the names. When he placed the call and made the connection, at least the voice on the other end *sounded* like his uncle.

"Uncle Ev? It's me. John. Your nephew."

"I'm afraid you have the wrong number. I don't have a nephew named John."

"Come on, Uncle Ev! John Drinan, remember? Is this some kind of practical joke? I know I haven't been good about keeping in touch, but jeez! Did everybody get together and decide to change their numbers—to teach me a lesson or something?"

"Young man, I have no idea what you're talking about. If anybody's playing a joke here, I suspect it's you, and I don't find it very funny. My sister Grace was married to a man named Charlie Drinan, but they died in an auto accident years ago. Is that what you wanted to hear? You're a damn Web-tweaker, aren't you? Your kind make me sick. You must have a pretty twisted sense of humor to try to pass yourself off as their son."

John's uncle Ev—if this *was* his uncle—abruptly broke the connection. John considered calling the number again, but then thought better of it. He picked up his walking pace once more, Oz following close at hand in the moonlight. The highway was nearer. He could hear the cars.

What about Seiji? They'd spent time together, for the first time, just a few months back. If this was some kind of joke, or punishment, or tough-love treatment, John was pretty certain his family wouldn't have gotten all the way to Seiji in the orbital habitat, a cousin distant in both space and blood relationship.

When he tried the commlink, however, there was no Seiji Robert Yamaguchi in any of the public databases. No one by that name resided in the orbital habitat or was employed by High Orbital Manufacturing Enterprises, if John remembered right what HOME stood for.

He stepped up and over a guardrail and onto the shoulder of the highway. Oz leapt the rail and joined him on the shoulder, only momentarily disoriented when his master, preoccupied, began walking backwards along the road with his thumb stuck out. John, though, was not just preoccupied. He was more disoriented than his dog would ever be capable of knowing.

Punishment is treatment, he thought. Treatment is punishment. Okay, so he *had* never been much contented with the cog-logic of "finding his place" in the mighty machine of The World. He was the black sheep of the family, all right, but he never thought they'd go *this* far.

Using the commlink, he tried to access his credit and funds accounts, but all requests came back "Unknown Account." He'd always had enough money to pass as eccentric rather than just plain crazy. No longer? If he figured this right, all he had now were his phone (thank heaven for the FreePhone system) and his skills—if he could manage to keep his wits about him.

Hitchhiking along the moonlit desert highway, he struck on the idea of trying via commlink to find proof of his own parents' existence in the world's databases. Was such a brainstorm proof of his sanity, or of his madness? When his search turned up news items from before he was born, however, he lost all track of his surroundings. Articles described a tragic automobile crash in which a car carrying Emma Halverson Yam-aguchi, her husband, Hisato Yamaguchi, Grace Colton and her husband, Charles Drinan, collided with another vehicle on a hilly road near Lake Falmouth, Kentucky. The other car was driven by one Jacob Spires, and the collision resulted in the deaths of Spires and all the aforementioned. The Drinan and Yamaguchi couples had, moments before, departed the wedding reception of Everett Colton and Marian Halverson.

John's eyes grew hazy and vague. The implications of this discovery overwhelmed him. Unthinkingly, he began to drift into the road. A hov-ertruck with an old pickup-style bed in back whipped around him and whirred to a stop on the highway shoulder not far from him, rousing him from his torpor. He and Oz broke into a jog.

"You look like you've been walking awhile," said the driver, when John came up beside the hovertruck's passenger-side window. The man looked to be about John's age or maybe a little younger. "Hop in the back with your dog. I can drop you at either Red Mountain or Johannesburg. Got a preference?"

"Whichever's more convenient for you. Thanks."

John and Oz went around to the pickup bed and climbed in. John banged once on the roof of the truck's cab. The driver gave a small wave of his hand and set the truck to hover before shooting off down the highway. In the moonlit desert John saw no sign of human habitation until they passed a blank but still lit billboard which some A-V graffitist had appropriated, smartbombing it with a shifting shouting agglomeration of letters and images that spelled and spoke the word "NAZREZ." Shivering against the meaninglessness of the graffito as much as the night's wind and cold, John patted Ozymandias repeatedly on the head, finding no small comfort in the dog's presence beside him in this world which felt somehow so much like—yet no place like—home.

"Looks like we're not in Kansas anymore, Oz."

2

Hour of the Wolf-Woman
2065

A SHIVERED LADDER OF DIAMOND LIGHT FLOATS ON THE QUIET WAVES, stretching away toward the full moon that falls down the sky toward the horizon. Overhead the ocean of stars glows.

The moon dances the ocean in the tango of tides, thinks the woman in the wolf's-head mask and wolfskin robes. *But the ocean also dances the moon. Someday they will dip and kiss in cataclysm, though not yet.* She is grateful to be the coxswain, who calls and steers, and does not have to row. Taking a deep breath, she begins.

"Before the jeweled fog of cities and towns dissolved into darkness, the moon was only an island in the night sea, not far offshore. The Oldfolk swam out to it in fiery machines. The glowing fog of light their cities made had wrapped tendrils so thick about their world, the stars themselves were dimmed by it. When the Oldfolk looked back and saw that Earth was a heavenly body too, they were stunned by the reminder."

She sees her shipmates—shapeshifting Werfolk all, in ceremonial skins, woven leaves, glistening feathers—nodding. They look around them at the sea, at the sky, at the other small craft loosely roped together in their five-boat flotilla. Rowing steadily, the men and women at the oars in all the crews listen to the wolf-woman's words, their oars pushing aside the quiet sea in the steady rhythm of their labor, the rowers muttering among themselves.

The woman in the wolf's-head mask knows what they're thinking: What grim powers the Oldfolk once had, to turn light into a deeper kind of darkness. Swimming to the moon in strange machines makes even this present journey—over the salt sea in long dugout canoes and older boats with dead engines, jury-rigged sails, salvaged oars, often-patched hulls— appear a minor feat by comparison. All in the flotilla fall silent for a time. The silence stretches out long before the wolf-headed woman, standing in the stern of the lead boat, speaks again. In the swelling, carrying voice of the holy tongue she addresses them all.

"Their world is *our* world, now. But it was not yet our world then. We had not yet become what we are. Once the night took back what the bright fog had veiled, then we also came to be. The moon and stars are clearer now—and farther away."

Her shipmates and the crews in the other boats smile. They know. All the stories of the old world slouching toward Bedlam so that she and all her fellow rough beasts might be born. All the tales of the Time Before and the Time After.

"The few Oldfolk who were left there in the sky, looking over from the distance of the moon, when the dark fell once more—how they must have wept, fearing that the source of that bright fog had disappeared too! What else could they suppose, but that their fellow fog-makers had gone dead with their fog machines?"

The wolf-headed woman looks about at her audience, at the five crews rowing steadily toward the first distant hints of dawn. She sees some of them nodding in understanding. They know that Oldfolk, too, have survived, much reduced in numbers, lingering on in ways none of their ancestors could have predicted.

"Everybody dies—just not all at once. Not even the Oldfolk could make *that* happen. They came close. *Too* close, when the cities went mad, then dark. We, born of the Death they made for themselves—*we* live lives that are still too short, all these years after!"

Her shipmates, and the women and men of the other crews too, nod more fervently and grumble. That bane of shortened life is why they have again gathered together from a dozen clans, to risk this journey over the sea. To raid once more the islands of those "true people" forever trapped in their one history, their one physical form. Those isolatoes, too small of soul to ever change their shapes—much less leave their physical bodies behind and voyage afar through the subtle and unseen air, as the wolf-woman has.

No surprise such a stiff-necked and stubborn style of humankind also holds truest to the machine-haunted ways of that other age. The Oldfolk of the islands are still sad dreamers of the dream they call history. *Before* the time of many names—the Last Pandemic, the Madness Plague, the Collapse, the Great Death—set all the captives free.

They see it so differently than we do, the wolf-headed woman thinks, recalling those names. For us, that is the time of legend, the coming into time not of the "Great Death" but the Great Shift: Nearly all humankind, their souls passing through the bestial so that, like droplets of water reuniting with the sea, they might return to the divine. The time of the sacrifice that *made them sacred*—

A creature leaps from the water nearby. Everyone stiffens, the rhythm of their oarwork breaking for a moment. Only a dolphin, the wolf-woman notes with relief. That relief is strangely tempered, though. Dolphins, porpoises—they are just too much like the islands' Merfolk guards for any raider's comfort.

Their soulless "home watch," the wolf-headed woman thinks, shaking her head. Biotech mermaids and mermen created by the same science that destroyed the civilization it had built. How do *those* fluked abominations imagine the Time Before—if they imagine anything at all? Is the Old-folk's "history" only the time of myth, to them?

"Their islands are much closer than the moon," the wolf-headed woman says to her comrades, over a sea grown too quiet. "That is why they hoard their secret of Longlife. The Oldfolk there will not share it— not even with those of their ancient kind who live on the mainland. They have vowed never to share it with Werfolk, though we want but a little. They fear our numbers will grow as their own did, in the old days, so we are denied. Is that how it must be? Must we *die* for *their* fears?"

A few of the rowers shout "No!" but the wolf-masked woman gestures them to silence. She looks over her companions with a deep, almost maternal fondness. Most of the raiders are in their twenties or early thirties. She is old enough to be the mother of almost any one of them. Calling her Mother Lupe started out as a joke among them, but now that name suits her more than her given name of Guadalupe Sanchez ever did.

"We will not make the same mistakes they and their machines made. We will not jumble together living and nonliving things as they did. We remember the great commandments they in their islands have never learned: Thou shalt not suffer a human being to exist in the manner of a made thing! Thou shalt not suffer a made thing to exist in the manner of a human being!"

The voices of the five crews rise in assent. The rowers row harder through the waves. The moon sinks, yet the sky, paradoxically, lightens further. The Hour of the Wolf, the woman thinks with a sly grin. That period of morning twilight when dreams have the greatest power to shift the shape of reality.

Looking at her companions, she realizes they are too young to remember the vanishing words and ideas she still knows, the names and concepts—like the beliefs of ancient Romans—that her own poor but educated parents remembered and taught her. These young Werfolk cannot remember how the rich were always the first to be immortalized in words and stones and statues. How eventually it was not only their deeds that were recorded and preserved, but their lives too. How the rich were the first not to die at all, but rather to have their lives go on, only differently—as constructs in machines, or as flesh whose end might be endlessly postponed through replacement parts.

Though these fur-, flower-, and feather-clad young people may recall childhood stories of long-lost empires and monsters and other atrocities, they can never know the full import of "ancient Romans" or "machine intelligence" or "biotechnology." They cannot remember, as she does, the trembling beauty of the world that was lost. How, after sunset, the cities brought the heavens themselves down to earth, as if the stars in the roof of night's cave had dripped pure shining geometry, light-encrusted stalagmite towers dreaming of impossible reconnection, rising skyward layer by layer, bright-blindly groping with the disappearing stars. . . .

Yet the young Werfolk, born since the pandemic and its accompanying collapse, have rediscovered so much. They have already circled back much of the spiraling distance toward a beginning both old and new. Young though they are, they have remembered truths which, through a hundred centuries, the Oldfolk in their cities and towns forgot—with disastrous results. Even without the formalities of history, these brave young people understand these raids are their dark inheritance from that lost past, when the rich and powerful began to live without that fear of mortality which the poor and powerless must needs always face too soon. More so, now, than ever before.

"We seek their Longlife treatment for ourselves. We do not seek to live immortally, as they do. That would be to exist in the manner of a made thing. We ask only for the chance of the 'three score and ten' years our ancestors once hoped for. Yet the Oldfolk will not even give us that much life. While their lives go on and on, we are supposed to mourn our young dead and comfort ourselves with 'Life goes on.' Yes, life goes on, but then it doesn't anymore! Life goes on, but death goes on *longer*! They have left us no choice but to take from them our fair share of life—and take it we will!"

The voices of assent grow into full-throated cheers, rising into the reddening dawn light that tints what remains of the setting moon. Then they fall silent as all see—long and low on the horizon before them, hazed with a mist dissolving with the early light—the distant outline of their island destination.

The raiders' oars cut more deeply into the water; the rhythm of their rowing intensifies. They unrope their boats one from the other. The small craft quickly spread out in a wedge. In a few moments more, the raiders hoist sails into the freshening dawn breeze, their speed surging still higher. They race toward a cove they know awaits them, somewhere ahead, amid the palms and mangroves and Caribbean pines of the shoreline.

The wolf-woman watches the shore with a sharp eye as the last dark of night struggles against sunrise. From the old maps she knows the landmarks. They are speeding south, past West End, toward Eight Mile Rock and the back side of Freeport. Toward the inlet where, according to the maps, the Old Road runs closest to the north shore. Between the cove and Freeport Harbor lies only a narrow neck of land.

Another raiding party, coming from the west, will land at the Harbor, and a third, coming from the south, will land east of Freeport. The landing parties will make their way toward the islands' administrative centers. In the west they will strike toward what the pre-plague guide books called the Grand Bahama Beach and Golf Resort. The landing party in the east will attack that area the laminated maps, four decades old, call the Bahamas Princess Resort and Casino.

At the thought of the names, the wolf-headed woman gives a toothy grin. The islands may be the last abode of the old rich and their endlessly extended lives, but the new poor keep coming. One day—today, maybe—a raid on these leftover places with the leftover names will take either the Longlife treatment or the islands' criminal ruler, Cameron Spires. Either outcome is all they'll need.

Even as the last remnant of the full moon sinks beneath the horizon, the battle fury comes upon the wolf-woman. She shrugs off her robes and tears the wolf's head from her brow. Whether from the work that strange proteins or tiny machines or phases of the moon are supposed to be doing in her blood—or from the slashing rhythm of the oars, the feel of mask and skins—it does not matter: The magic is returning. She feels her jaws lengthening into muzzle, her canine teeth growing. The scents in her nose, the sounds in her ears, all grow more intense, more acute.

The cheering that breaks out now is roars and howls and gibbering glossolalia. Around her, the faces of the Bear people pass through swift changes, their hands becoming paws darkening with thick fur, their nails growing into claws. In the Panther clan, eyes flash golden, irises lengthen and narrow to slits, bodies stretch with feline grace.

The dark communion of the Shift is upon them all.

The world spread before them seems peaceful and civil. Instinctively, the wolf-woman knows such seeming will prove to be a lie. If the raiders' arrival is detected by the Merfolk guarding the islands, then bloody work lies ahead. Whatever happens, however, for good or ill, it will become the stuff of songs and stories—if any of them survive this raid. No stories to tell without survivors. No survivors without stories to tell. That is what the world amounts to, now.

The Thing of Shapes to Come
2032

TOMOKO HATED THE TUBE WHEN IT WAS CROWDED LIKE THIS—THE ancient and glacially slow Circle Line most of all. Such close proximity to the rest of coughing, sneezing, perfumed, cologned, body-odoriferous London humanity aboard the Underground made her think of it as the "Test Tube."

At least they'd gotten seats in this car, she reminded herself—and only halfway to their destination, too. Beside her, Simon seemed not at all bothered by the press of humanity. That, at least, had not changed over the years. He stared off into some middle distance where his unfocused, civilly inattentive gaze was sure not to offend anyone.

Tomoko looked more closely at him. With his reddish hair, and features that made him look perennially young and untried, Simon was still a boyishly handsome man. Even now, she could see why she fell for him when they first met, at Cambridge. Part of it was Cambridge itself, she supposed. Gothically grand colleges along the main street. The spring-flowered Backs running down to the River Cam in broad lawns behind them. May balls and bumping boat races. The place struck Tomoko as what the University of Utopia might look like—if it had been designed jointly by Walt Disney and Pope Innocent IV as a pastoral theme park.

In the end, however, it had proven to be both a good place to do science, and to fall in love. Like herself, the shy yet drily witty Simon Lingham already had an M.D. when they met. Like Tomoko, he too was pursuing a Ph.D in biochemistry and medical microbial ecology—with an eye toward work in epidemiology, in his case. Tomoko, then as always, hoped to establish her own biotechnology company. Their whirlwind postgraduate courtship was a wild flight. Only her sensible and efficient scheduling of the requisite formalities re-anchored their lives. They managed to squeeze the wedding in before exams. They put off the honeymoon until the break between terms.

That willingness on both their parts to sacrifice a romantic relationship to career goals was something of a harbinger, as it turned out. After their schooling ended, Simon's flourishing career with the World Health Organization had with surprising speed taken him away from Tomoko and their London flat to long days and then weeks at WHO's Geneva headquarters. Despite being an astute physician-scientist, however, Simon could and did prove surprisingly obtuse in his relationships with other human beings. Tomoko's annoyance with the situation had been largely unspoken. Still, Simon should not have been nearly so surprised when, on that morning five years into their marriage, she presented him with the *fait accompli* of the incorporation of her biotech startup, Protean Pharmaceuticals—with herself as founder and chief scientist.

"The name's a private pun," she tried to explain that morning, "on the words 'protein' and 'protean'—from Proteus—with maybe a distant echo of 'prion' as well."

Yet, month after month afterward, Simon showed only the same blank disinterest in her work that he displayed that morning. At last she grew angry enough to say what she'd been thinking for too long.

"I fell in love with you and married you because you're a genius. I want a divorce because being a genius is the *only* thing you're good for."

Not the nicest thing she had ever said to him. Despite that, their divorce two years ago had been surprisingly without rancor. Their parting wasn't about infidelities with other people (there had been none) but about fidelity to their own respective career goals. When scientific conferences took Simon to Seattle or Tomoko to the UK, as now, they were still friendly enough that they looked each other up and spent an evening or two together.

"I really don't know why you chose to locate in Seattle," Simon said as their train pulled into Westminster. Uncannily he seemed to read her thoughts, as he had done so many times when they were married. "Seems to me that town is still more Silicon Valley than Petri-dish Ridge."

Tomoko had been to the California originals of both those historic function-places—outside San Jose and San Diego, respectively—when she was trying to decide where to locate her firm. She had considered her hometown of Kobe, too, as well as two prominent Science Cities in Japan, before settling on Seattle. Simon wouldn't understand the aesthetic selling point of the fact that the 360-degree panorama from her office—above Lake Sammamish, atop what the locals nicknamed Cat Peak—gave her views from the Space Needle to Mount Rainier, on any halfway clear day.

"A gamble," she said, nodding, as the train mercifully disgorged riders. "I've got the best mix of infotech and biotech workers around, though. Paid off more than I expected."

Even that was an understatement. She was wealthier than she'd ever dreamed. Not far from her office, and sharing much the same magnificent view, stood the new home her investors built for her: A place of travertine floors and upholstered walls the color and pattern of cream in coffee. Cabinetry hand-carved and antiqued to resemble woven wood. Stout interior columns and arches. Master bathroom modeled on a Roman *balneum* at the moment the barbarians took possession. Heavy black iron faux-flambeau medieval-castle light fixtures, from which hung big rough chunks of quartz crystal as pendants. Laser-mown Corsican mint outdoor "carpet" growing in patches over tilework, like lawn over a ruined abbey's floor. Japanese gardens and a mosaic-floored swimming pool watched over by a statue, 3D-puzzle-constructed from rough-hewn horizontal slate slabs into the semblance of a Buddha or meditating pool guard whose identifying features had all been eroded away by time, whose crossed legs were surrounded by a circle of loose slate chips, and at whose back a standing stone of the Avebury style fanned up and out like the hood of a minimalist cobra.

All in the best Pacific Rim Gothic style. The tech, too—like the floor-to-ceiling windows programmed to opaque instantly at the uttering of the words "Privacy, please." The most embarassing thing about an embarassment of riches, Tomoko thought, is realizing that the wealthy live in the future before anyone else gets there, and gets theirs. And that now *she* was one of them, getting hers.

"So you're happy? With the way your company's growing, I mean?"

Tomoko pondered the question as the train pulled into Embankment Station.

"The name has turned out to be more prophetic than I thought. We've got a couple of products coming to market that utilize the capabilities of conformation-altering proteins."

They stood up together and disembarked from the tube train.

"You mean prions? Like scrapie? Mad Cow disease? Doesn't sound like a very promising start for therapeutic uses."

The crowds around them thinned somewhat in the station and on the station stairs.

"Oh, but it is! Look at how thoroughly bovine spongiform encephalopathy, or fatal familial insomnia, or kuru, alter brain chemistry. You know kuru?"

They walked from the Underground and joined the evening crowds headed toward the Hungerford footbridge. Simon stopped to turn up his coat collar against the biting wind from the Thames.

"Heard of it. Found among cannibals in the South Pacific, wasn't it?"

An old, rare disease like kuru was outside Simon's bureaucratic bailiwick, so he was giving this conversation only half his attention at best. Tomoko tried to protect her hair from blowing about in the wind as they started up the bridge stairs.

"Right, Dr. Epidemiology. The 'laughing death,' they used to call it. A disease of the Fore Highlanders of Papua, New Guinea. They honored their ancestors by eating their brains—well into the twentieth century."

"Charming."

"Maybe not, but it appears that kuru initially began as CJD—Creutzfeldt-Jakob disease."

"I know what CJD is. So, kuru is what happened when a rare, spontaneous genetic mutation in a tribesman met with the cultural practice of eating the brains of the deceased—that's how it spread, right?"

"Presumably. CJD occurs spontaneously in humans. I wondered how amenable *other* human proteins might be to having their shapes warped and bent by *synthetic* conformation-altering proteins. So I hired some of the best ontogeneticists I could find and we set to work."

"Wait a minute," Simon said, and the two of them actually did stop walking for a moment, before continuing to the top of the stairs and onto the footway beside the train tracks. "Ontogeneticists? Why? Prions are proteins altering proteins, *without* DNA or RNA."

Before Tomoko could answer, she and Simon had to run a silent gantlet of homeless people. Mostly young men shapelessly bundled against the cold, they sat partway out of sleeping bags, moths unable to emerge far enough from cocoons to dry their wings and fly, half-resurrected dead unable to shed their body bags and join the fully living. Some of them stroked and muttered to pet dogs or cats huddled beside them, but most just hunkered down, unspeaking and immobile, cups or hats or hands out, too cold and disheartened to ask for alms.

Before they had cleared the last of the homeless, Simon and Tomoko were halfway across the Thames. Tomoko looked away, troubled. The lights of the city sparkled brokenly on the dark river below them.

"I can see why they call this place *Hunger*ford."

"I'm sure that's *not* how it got its name."

"No? Too fitting to be an accident, if you ask me."

"Look, you don't want to give them money. You lived in London long enough to know that, Mokie. Most of them suffer from mental illnesses that are treatable, but they won't stay on their medications. Give them money and they'll just self-medicate with illegal drugs and legal alcohol."

A Chunnel-bound maglev train whooshed loudly past, close at hand. By the time it was gone, Tomoko had brightened considerably, struck by ideas and possibilities. They started down the stairs from the footbridge, toward the esplanade running from the bridge to the National Theater and beyond.

"What if there were a way to make them stay on their medications? What if it might be possible to develop an artificial prion, a 'prionoid,' that would work as a one-shot, get-it-and-forget-it treatment?"

"Good luck. You'll need it, if you're hoping for a magic bullet to take down poverty *and* insanity in a single shot!"

Tomoko said nothing more about her hypothetical idea—neither during the quick dinner they grabbed before the show, nor during the National's performance of Shakespeare's *Troilus and Cressida*. At that point during the play, however, when Achilles complained of the other Greeks that "they pass'd by me/As misers do by beggars," Tomoko gave Simon a sudden, piercing glance, which he pretended to ignore.

The idea she had formulated there on the bridge would not leave her head, however—not during the conference, not when she left London, not when she flew home to Seattle, not when she returned to work. Within hours of her first day back, she proposed the basic concept of it to Leeza Gitlin and Anita Wellek—the brace of brazen redheads who headed her two best research teams. Tomoko outlined to them the possibility of developing a new pharmaceutical: a neuromodulating prionoid. Perhaps one altering the shape of a neurotransmitter-synthesizing enzyme—like tryptophan hydroxylase, for instance, which converted dietary L-tryptophan to serotonin. Leeza and Anita, once they understood and shared her vision, went back to their labs and got their teams fired up about Tomoko's idea, too.

Serotonin synthesis was a good pathway to start with, Tomoko thought later in the day, after making only slightly different presentations to the full complements of both teams. There were undoubtedly many other pathways that would bear exploring. Prionoid analogs for neuropeptides like enkephalin and endorphin would be a good area to investigate next. . . .

Sitting in her office, she remembered the homeless ones hunkered down on the Hungerford, and the purposeful ones walking purposefully past them. Trolls and rams, or sheep and goats, on the same bridge. Maybe, just maybe, she and her co-workers might be able to give a new ending to certain old myths and fairy tales.

4

Brave New Island
2065

STARING THROUGH HIS BINOCULARS INTO THE EARLY MORNING LIGHT, Simon Lingham has already seen parrots and white crowned pigeons, more proof (if any were still needed) that species long extinct on Grand Bahama are returning, spreading here from the other islands, particularly from Andros and the Abacos.

In the old days such a find could make his morning. Not today. From the moment he woke he's been apprehensive, yet with no discernible cause. Taking the binoculars from his eyes and setting them down on the railing of the widow's walk, he stares past the bushes and shrubs surrounding his house—yellow elder, hibiscus, bougainvillea, and poinsettia.

Beyond lie his groves of avocado, custard apple, mango, and lime. His home is surrounded by a productive and well-ordered landscape. He should be happy. Instead, he sighs with a weariness unfit for this early in the day.

Widow's walk. A spouse left alone. Yet there is no widow or widower here. His kids are all grown and gone. No wife—he and Sulima have been quietly divorced for almost a year now, the end of the fourth marriage for both of them.

The same longevity treatment that freezes people's aging processes between twenty-five and forty (on average) has put nearly every plague survivor in the islands into a kind of permanent midlife crisis. Numerous divorces, fast-forward serial monogamy. A side effect of the treatment no one anticipated.

Or maybe it's been brought on by something else, something having little to do with the treatment? Some delayed effect, some aftershock of the human species' great die-off? Somehow fostering the belief that human numbers having been so devastatingly reduced by the pandemic, it's selfish of both men and women *not* to spread their genetic material around and broaden the gene pool—raising families early, and late, and as often as possible?

Maybe all those are just good excuses. Socially acceptable ways of moving on to a new "commitment" as soon as the old "commitment" begins to grow stale. Absently he lifts the binoculars again to his eyes and is amazed by how far away the parrots have strayed—until he realizes he's looking through the wrong end of the field glasses. With a frown he turns them right way round, thinking *that* is exactly what the pandemic did—turned everything wrong way round, upside down, inside out.

People used to come to these islands to escape civilization, for a retreat in a wild paradise. In the decades since the plague, however, the islands of the New Bahamian Polity have become the most civilized place on Earth. Everywhere the cities of the continents reverted to barbarism, blood, and fire. For nearly a third of a century they've been abandoned to legend: to the slow twist of vines and branches, to the quiet push of roots into the concrete and steel of a lost world eroding slowly in wind and rain.

Not that civilization is all that stable *here*, he thinks, staring through the early morning light at the flock of white-crowned pigeons. In these islands too, the plague's aftermath has turned things topsy-turvy. For four hundred years before the pandemic, the Bahamas were the haunt of shipwreckers, buccaneers, slave traders, rumrunners, offshore money-launderers, data-napping switchdoctors. The outlaw traders and pur-veyors in the island markets long stood as shadow to the upright daylight of the less-free and less-enterprising mainland techonomies. That, too, the pandemic has turned inside out.

Now it's the islands that are the upright daylight world. The mainland is the great shadow, out of which comes the sporadic trade of foodstuffs and handicrafts from other scattered enclaves of unaltered humanity. And, more grimly, the Werfolk raiders too, shapeshifting marauders of the new Dark Ages, crossing the sea to attack more and more often.

Simon takes the field glasses from his eyes. The inside-outness of things isn't just about these islands and the mainland. All the spaces and places of the world have been everted by the pandemic and its aftermath. In the years before the plague, urban technological society reigned tri-umphantly from center stage. Untrammeled nature and traditional hunting-gathering cultures were banished together to the wings, to the farthest margins and peripheries of the planet—when they weren't destroyed outright.

The pandemic changed all that. Center and margin, figure and ground—they're all reversed. Before the plague, Simon used to disappear each year for weeks at a time into whatever wilderness he could still find on Earth. His hiking and backpacking in remote mountains and jungles perplexed his parents, his friends, his colleagues. He was never able to explain to them his need to disappear, fearing they might be obscurely offended by what he would say.

His first wife, Tomoko, had at least understood his desire to disconnect from the matrix of human things in order to reconnect, in wilderness, with the world itself. With the sun and moon and stars. With waterfall and birdsong. With grasshopper buzz and thunderstorm. With the wind in the trees and the trees in the wind. With the trout swimming through the stream and the stream swimming through the trout. With all the news that never got old. She understood—even if she seldom joined him on those trips.

At one time and another before the plague, he sent postcards to her, with sentiments that now seem naively mystical. "Only deep in wilderness do I hear the music never played, the music that has no musician, yet is always playing"—for one. "The more I lose myself in wilderness, the more I find myself waiting there for me"—for another. And even, "The further outside I go, the deeper inside I get." Simon remembers believing all of that—devoutly.

How quaint such sentiments sound now. Wilderness is resurgent over all the Earth. A third of a century ago, when the pandemic swept through humanity like fire through dry grass, the vast majority of urban civilization and of the world's population became only so much smoke and broken mirrors, sudden ghosts in sudden ghost towns. The natural world is powerfully, even frighteningly, on the rebound. To feel nostalgia for wilderness now, Simon realizes, is as misplaced and anachronistic as nostalgia for city life would have been before the pandemic.

Yet, anachronistic or not, this morning he feels civilization is too much with him. These islands are no wilderness. He longs to escape the weight of all the many human affairs that are his responsibility here. To travel to the savage heart of that savage continent just over the horizon to the west.

What might he find there now? Before the pandemic, there were nearly nine billion people on Earth. Now, decades into a radically depopulated postpandemic world, his most optimistic data and models suggest that, worldwide, perhaps twenty-four million unaltered humans survive, along with perhaps thirty-eight million shapeshifting Werfolk. The few hundred ocean-dwelling Merfolk that Cameron Spires has managed to create barely figure into the equation anywhere, except in the waters around these islands.

Sixty-two million surviving humans—and even that estimate may be wildly hopeful. The only close precedent for such a devastating depopulation among anatomically modern humans is the massive volcanic eruption of the Toba caldera on Sumatra, seventy-five thousand years ago. Its ensuing decade-long global winter killed off at least ninety-nine percent of the global human population too.

At least when Toba hit, the survivors could still continue their hunting and gathering lifeway. When the pandemic collapsed twenty-first century society, though, people who had lived all their lives in the penthouse of the technological skyscraper suddenly found themselves wandering dazed amid the debris of that toppled edifice, back at ground level, having never hunted nor gathered in their lives. The very plants and animals on which they might have subsisted were in many cases already extinct—a result of the success of that previous technological civilization.

The human survival rate of one percent in Toba times would translate to eighty million or so survivors out of Earth's pre-pandemic population. Given the added components of deep technological collapse and culture shock, the survival rate might be much less, even now. But how much less? One in 1,000? One in 10,000? Simon runs the parameters in his mind yet again, drifting into memory and abstraction, not really seeing what his eyes are looking at through the field glasses.

Numbers put a distance both comforting and disturbing between him and the realities of those deaths. From the rarefied heights of statistics, tragedy threatens to cease being tragic. For all their potential truth, too, numbers can also be the shortest path from a faulty premise to a foregone conclusion, as someone—Tomoko? Mark Fornash?—once reminded him.

Thoughts of those two call one image after the other out of Simon's memory, the second remembrance flashing through the sky of his mind fast on the heels of the first, one meteor after another, as if God were chain-smoking shooting stars. He remembers Tomoko, brushing her bangs back from her forehead with a touch of her hand, graceful certainty in her every movement. He sees Mark Fornash again, a short man with long wild graying hair and goatee—and even wilder gray eyes.

Time and again Simon tried to make them see the pandemic process the way he himself still thinks of it: an unexpectedly shapeshifted protein, shifting in turn the shape of brain enzymes into conformity with its own warped and warping form, setting off a brain chain-reaction, a "seeding" of the sparking cloud forest inside the skull, until brainstorms whip and twist through the trees, bend the stems and trunks, knock down the lianas of that forest, a great electrochemical storm plaguing one mind after another, roaring silently among them, until the insanity explodes into the world, again and again, all the paths and roads and streets and alleys and hallways of human settlement running with blood, glittering with shattered glass, homes and high-rises and skyscrapers burning, exploding, toppling, pipes bursting, transformers raining sparks, power lines going down, bridges collapsing, rivers choking on corpses, boats and ships slipping under the waves, aircraft and spacecraft falling from the sky as madness sweeps the world. . . .

Leaning hard on the railing of the widow's walk, Simon takes a deep breath and shakes his head. Best not to go back into those memories. Best not to look for reasons beneath all that unreason. Yet he cannot help himself. Maybe that's why he thinks of Tomoko and Mark now: Neither of them was ever fully satisfied by any of the explanations put forward for the pandemic and the global collapse.

Deep down, neither is he. Oh, the science of it is right enough, as far as it goes. The problem is that it doesn't go far enough. What prepared the ground for the black blossoming of the pandemic and collapse? Was it that there were so many people? Was it that everyone *wanted* so much?

Why is it that now, three decades later, so much is still left to be discovered about the pandemic? Origins? Mechanisms? Exact epidemiology? He reminds himself that even in the pre-pandemic world, with its armies of physicians and biomedical scientists, diseases such as the Machupo and Ebola hemorrhagic fevers, or the highly virulent Sanger strain of Valley Fever, were still not fully understood years and decades after their initial outbreaks. He tries to comfort himself with the fact that far greater resources in the past were just as stymied as his in the present, but it's a hollow comfort.

Tomoko and Mark are among those gone to seek their answers on the mainland. John Drinan was the first to leave, but he was easy to write off, at the time: self-proclaimed once and future astronaut—fled to seek his crazy grail in the swamps and scrublands around the old Cape spaceport. Yet, over the years, the people who have departed for the mainland have been more and more respectable, not only eccentrics but also some of the islands' finest minds—thinkers Simon misses talking and arguing with, even now.

Simon has not left. He wonders if he would be willing to risk death to get at the truth, as his friends in exile have. He thinks of those uncomfortable truths Fornash often hinted at—with his self-taught suburban shaman rants about ecstasy and consciousness, masked sorcerers, and the "hundred-horned Lord of the Animals" and Life as "Gaia's hallucination." Of course, everything was shamans and hallucinations with Fornash—and complexes:

"shamanic complex" *this* and "prionoid-nanomechanical complex" *that* Nothing ever simply what it was.

He shakes his head again. Why is he remembering all this? His memories of the days before and during the pandemic are strangely telescoped of late. He remembers moments decades in the past, but can't remember what he had for breakfast yesterday morning. If he wasn't certain the Telomerid Longevity Treatment put the brakes on his aging when he was forty, he might be inclined to think he's beginning to suffer from some sort of mental derangement related to senescence. He is seventy years old, after all. Even if he is an unnaturally young seventy.

Why do those memories of long gone days so concern him now? Is there in fact some link between the longevity treatment, the human brain, and what happened to billions of minds during the pandemic, as some of his research suggests? But whether the Empire of Reason was overrun by hallucinating hordes, or the System of Logic carried within it that which was destined to prove them all fools—what does it matter now?

Simon is suddenly aware of the eerie, resounding tones of conches trumpeting shrilly in alarm. Sounds of roaring split the early morning quiet. The birds he's been watching scatter and disappear in a burst of wings. He looks about, disoriented. One of the atmospheric buzz saws—a hurricane or tropical storm—coming on to ravage the islands yet again? But no, the sky is blue, free of cloud, and the season is all wrong for cyclonic storms.

There—thick smoke rising from the south, in the direction of Freeport Harbor. Gunshots. Movement draws his gaze toward the nearer bay, little more than a cove really, to the north of his house. That's where the gunshots came from—and also where his son Phillip is on patrol this dawn. Scanning the beach to the north with his field glasses, Simon hears more conch-trumpeting, the alarm signal of the Merfolk home guard. Then more gunshots. The treasured guns and their even more treasured ammunition are used only in extreme emergencies. Something big is happening.

He looks past the scrub and sea grape and scattered palms, to where the pale beach slips into waters of blue, turquoise, and ultramarine. Then, through the binoculars, he sees it: Merfolk like dolphin-human hybrids surging through and vaulting from the beautiful water, sounding their conches, lifting their stout tridents against Werfolk canoes and antique fishing or pleasure boats as those craft race toward shore. The tridents upset the boats, send the shaggy-headed raiders with their contorted faces tumbling and plunging into the morning sea.

The waters are shallow there, however. At least two of the raiding craft have made it all the way to shore. Those raiders whose boats were caught and overturned now regroup as well. Moving through the waist-deep water, the raiders flail about viciously with war clubs or fire off arrows against the Mer guards, the drenched raiders fighting a rear-guard action as they head onto the beaches to join their already-landed companions.

As Simon stares in stunned and paralyzed silence, the chaos and carnage worsen. From what little shelter the scrub, pines, and palms afford, a squad of perhaps a dozen defenders—Simon's redheaded son, Phillip, among them—open fire with gun and crossbow on the invaders. The raiders nonetheless press forward behind flights of arrows and spears. The outnumbered defenders slowly pull back.

Simon thinks he sees his son go down, but cannot tell amid all the smoke, the disorienting movement of weapons and bodies—a confusion only worsened by the field glasses, which turn every twitch of Simon's hand, every movement of his arm, to a mad bounce. Letting the binoculars drop to his chest on their thong, Simon breaks from the paralysis of observation and dashes off the widow's walk, through the door into the master bedroom. He plunges down the stairs and out the front door, pausing only to grab up his best handmade bow and quiver of hunting arrows in the entryway as he charges out.

Leaping down the two front steps, he forges ahead through flower gardens and groves. At the end of the latter he runs down a sandy path between a stretch of marsh and drier scrub, toward stands of lignum vitae and pine copses woven with poison wood.

Either he has run faster than he thought or the battle has moved inland, for suddenly Simon finds himself surrounded by the noise of the melee. He nocks an arrow to his bow only an instant before a naked, gray-headed crone leaps from a pine copse and lopes half-wolfishly forward along the path. Leering maniacally and wielding a massive double-bladed axe she should not be able to lift, the crone slashes at a pair of island patrollers—a girl who has tripped and fallen, a youth who is still standing.

With a single stroke the roaring crone cuts the face off the young man, who collapses in a splatter of blood and pulsing brain.

As the crone turns toward the young woman, Simon looses an arrow at the naked berserker for what he hopes is a killing shot to the heart. The crone bends away and takes the shot in the upper part of her chest, between collarbone and shoulder. With a shriek she turns her attention to Simon, charging toward him as he clumsily tries to nock another arrow. She is only a few strides away when a shot rings out at such close range it almost deafens him. As he nocks the arrow, Simon realizes the fallen girl has fired. Still the wolfish old harpy comes toward him, wobbling now, having taken a bullet in the right leg. She lifts her great axe for the death stroke as Simon, with agonizing slowness, tries to bring his bow up.

Another shot rings out and the ravening woman falls to his right, losing her grip on her axe as she hits the ground. Simon looks and sees it's Phillip, dirty and blood-smeared, who fired the second shot. Father and son exchange a brief smile.

All too brief. In the next moment Simon can only stare in horror as the point of a spear juts out of his son's chest and Phillip topples forward. The spear-thrower, a young berserker of perversely feline grace, stands reaching behind himself, into the band of the loincloth at his waist, pulling forward his war club.

Without a thought, Simon looses the arrow he's already nocked. It takes the young raider in the throat. At the same time a shot sounds from where the girl, fallen a lifetime ago, has risen to a sitting position. The bullet from her pistol explodes into the raider's left eye and brain and out the top of his head, knocking him off his feet backwards.

Simon stands, numb and unmoving. The fallen girl still sits, legs akimbo, as Island Patrol reinforcements rush up from behind them and flood forward, yelling. They charge into the trees after the few remaining raiders, who are now retreating toward the cove from which they came. In the bright morning sunshine of a beautiful day, blood from the newly dead and wounded soaks slowly into the pale sand of the path all around Simon.

The wolfish crone, still alive, moans and curses and grinds her teeth as she tries to drag herself on her elbows toward where her axe has fallen. The young woman slowly stirs from where she sits. Weeping loudly, she crawls to where her young comrade lies dead, face down, faceless. When she reaches him she begins to wail furiously, her lost comrade clearly much more than just a comrade.

Rousing himself from his stupor, Simon approaches the axe toward which the still defiant crone is bent on dragging herself. Taking up the great double-bladed weapon in both hands, he is about to fling it as far away as he can, but then thinks better of it. Breathing heavily, he turns and walks to the place where his son lies dead, the shaft of the spear rising into the sunlight like a gnomon from Phillip's back. Gently he turns Phillip on his side. Less gently, he raises the heavy axe and brings it down on the shaft of the spear, snapping the shaft. Gently again, he rolls Phillip over to face upward, and cradles the young man in his arms.

Simon looks into his dead son's face, brushes a lock of dark hair away from his son's eyes. Phillip is only thirty years old, seven years younger than Simon was when the pandemic began. Phillip just started longevity treatments a few months back. He is still boyishly slim, still has a full head of hair—darker red than his father's coppery thatch ever was, with none of the gray that crept into Simon's during the Plague Year. The stubble of his son's day-old beard is still growing, even now, he knows. A useless fact.

Simon tries to ignore the gnashing and convulsing of the wolf-woman where she lies upon the ground. If he could only ignore the blood and the gory spearhead sticking from his son's chest, maybe he could imagine that his son is not dead, only sleeping. He devoutly wishes it were true. Neither his imagination nor his capacity for denial is up to such a task, however. He knows too well that the longevity treatment is a bulwark only against aging. Not against mortality itself—especially mortality brought on by murder, mayhem, mischance.

So unfair, he thinks. So against the way of nature. Sons ought to mourn departed fathers, not the other way around. Simon presses his lips to his son's forehead. Sitting back, he lets his hand creep down toward Phillip's blood-drenched chest, to come up short against the spearhead and haft section that protrude there. Resting the young man's shoulder and head against his own left thigh, Simon brings his left hand to join his right on the haft, below the spearhead. Getting as firm a grip on the slippery, bloody haft as he can, he pulls at the trapped weapon, tears coursing silently down his cheeks. He pulls so hard at the spear, it feels as if he's trying to remove it from his own body. Drawing it forth from his own flesh and blood. The pain is the same. Quietly sobbing now, he draws the last section of the truncated spear free of Phillip's body and tosses it weakly aside.

Simon rubs away the tears from his eyes, succeeding only in replacing the tears he cries for Phillip with Phillip's blood, still damp and sticky on Simon's own hands and, now, on his face as well.

Mothers and fathers burying sons and daughters has grown too common on these islands always at war with the raiding Werfolk. Young men and women have killed, and been killed in turn through twenty years of raids, yet still Simon knows no one who has grown inured to it. It all feels terribly wrong—people still killing each other, when the dead of this century already so vastly outnumber the living.

Medical corpsmen arrive. The girl still wails piteously beside her dead love, the crone (when she isn't coughing up blood) still raves. Taking his son in his arms and rising to his feet, Simon distractedly listens to the naked, bleeding old woman. Her ramblings punctuated by odd laughter, she is even now feebly trying to fend off a medic's attempt to treat her wounds.

"Oldfolk kill Werfolk for being what Oldfolk themselves created! Your Mer people are just were-dolphins—shifted like us, only more so! Forever!"

The old woman, overcome, collapses into a coughing fit. Simon wonders. Is she right? Do the years of killing make any sense anymore? They haven't brought any of the dead back. More killing in the future won't bring his son back—won't bring back any of the billions who have died during his lifetime.

With Phillip's body in his arms, Simon walks over to the medic.

"My place is up the trail here. Bring the girl up there, if she needs some quiet. If you can get this crazy old woman on a plank or a stretcher and up to my house, you can work on her there."

Simon heads forward, the weight of Phillip's body keeping his pace slow. Before he gets home, he hears footsteps in the sand and over the limestone cobbles behind him. Two medics and the girl are following him. One of the medics bears the faceless body of the dead island youth in a fireman's carry over his shoulder. The girl and the other medic carry a stretcher on which the unconscious woman is strapped down.

Simon lays his son's body down gently on the sofa in the living room. The girl and the medic he spoke to set the stretcher down on Simon's dining table and loosen the straps. The old woman, her eyes still closed, is making an odd humming sound. Simon bends low to hear more clearly, but as he does so the old woman lashes out, blindly yet unerringly, with her right arm and catches Simon firmly about the temples and forehead with her hand.

Into his head flashes one image after another: the spearhead bursting from Phillip's chest like a meteor bursting into the daylight sky. A bone-handled Inuit knife with a blade of meteoritic iron. An ancient stone tool next to a piece of moon rock. The earliest tools made from silicon nodules in chalk. Human beings using tools to make tools to make war—

The medic and the girl pull the crone's hand from Simon's head and the three of them restrain the old woman, but the contact has been made. When all is quiet within the house, when the medics have done their cutting and bandaging work and tied the crone into the hammock on the porch, the medics and the girl at last depart, carrying the girl's lost lover inland, leaving Simon alone on his porch to guard the old woman and mourn his son. He ponders the vision the old woman caused to form inside his head, a waking dream assembled from his memories of time spent in a great museum of that other world, that world so lost it might as well be a dream.

As the day grows old, there isn't much to see from the porch—just more patrols, coming and carrying away more bodies toward Freeport. His daughters arrive, to mourn Phillip with him and spell him in his guard of the captured crone, but Simon cannot shake off the numbness that has settled on him—not even for them. He thinks of the old woman calling the unaltered humans of the islands "Oldfolk." As wrong as what Cameron Spires always encourages the islanders to call themselves: "True Folk," or "Trufolk" as it has become in common parlance. Better to call them Urfolk, as *Ur* means "out of," the parent stock from which later variants arise.

With all the hatred between Ur and Wer, though, who here would welcome even such a small change in terms? Life on these islands suddenly feels very empty and lonely to Simon. Looking to the west at sunset, he finds himself searching for the shadow of the mainland, into which so many people of his time and years have already departed. Retiring at last to his bed, he falls into a sleep troubled by dreams of lost children, and lovers, and friends.

5

Tidescape
2032

WHEN THE HOLOPLAY BOMBLET WENT OFF IN FRONT OF HIM, MARK FOR-nash realized he must have stepped through a motion detector of some sort. Too late. Although the last chunk of the sun hadn't yet dropped beneath the distant western waves and he hadn't thought it dark enough yet for this kind of display, apparently he was wrong. Nothing for it now but to wait until the Narrator in his white tie and tails, and the other characters—apparently drawn from old black-and-white film footage wrapped around computer-generated wire frames—had their say.

NARRATOR
In a movie I never managed to see, Charlie Chan asks, rhetorically—

CHARLIE CHAN
If sand makes oyster grow pearl—
If fern makes planet grow diamond—
If noise makes message grow signal—
Then what makes cookie grow fortune?

NARRATOR
To which Number None Son replies—

NUMBER NONE SON
Very funny, Pops, but today's nonsense
Is tomorrow's meaning, so imagination
Is the answer.

CHARLIE CHAN
(*bouncing his eyebrows, leering like Groucho*)
I'd never accept a philosophy
That would accept me as a philosopher!

NARRATOR
And promptly disappears from the screen
In a movie I've never seen.

Out of light then solidified the message "This Public Surveillance Announcement presented by Lemming Balm Meaning Simulators"—along with a feedback Web address and pay-line. In the next instant the whole production disappeared.

Probably put together by some adfotainment whiz kids over at USC, thought Mark. It had all the earmarks of a student research project, anyway: ambiguously serious and seriously ambiguous. Hard to tell which here on Ocean Front Walk in Venice Beach, among the buskers and knickknacksters and fakefood vendors, the jongleurs and streetcorner illusionists and fetish bodyshapers. That, however, was the great thing about Ocean Front and, further on, the Promenade through Ocean Park to the Santa Monica Pier. This entire section of beachfront strip was at the edge of more than just the continent. It was a cultural subduction zone, where a panhandler could in all seriousness refer to himself as a funds transfer agent. Where a lone busker could be so MIDIsized, she sounded like a full symphony orchestra.

Lemming balm. He'd often thought he and his fellow Californians, running up and down their maze of highways day after day, were like lemmings who'd forgotten their way to the beach. Balm was needed, no doubt about it. *Got to know where the shores are*, he thought, *if you want to catch the waves before they crash.* That was why he made the pilgrimage down here every Halloween, for this night of special wyrdness.

Between Ozone and Navy Streets, the shaman's drum under Mark's arm began to resonate in sympathy to a music he recognized, that brand of Hmong-Mex country ska blues called the "Fresno sound." The quartet—Latina singer/lead guitarist, ditchbank blond fiddler, Hmong drummer, and black sax player—pumped out a strange deep groove he found hard to resist. Standing in the small crowd and listening to the words of what was apparently a lament in a language he didn't understand, he thumped his drum slowly and softly in time to the band's beat.

Mark had always believed in speaking the truth with as kind a heart as possible, but that was no easy task when it came to the city these kids were from. Whenever he'd passed through Fresno, that place struck him as ten thousand years of agriculture-based urban civilization *gone wrong*. Yet listening to the band, he realized something beautiful had come out of there, nonetheless.

When the song ended, Mark reluctantly forced himself to move on. Behind him the next song slowly faded as he made his way past Marine, then into the gap between the north end of Ocean Front and the south end of the Promenade. The big Halloween moon crept over the video-sheathed buildings of Santa Monica and their endless advertisements, to shine down on the sand in the small freezone between Venice Beach and Ocean Park. He heard bottles breaking against stone, smelled cheap beer and burning driftwood on the breeze. Gyrating figures hove into view, dancing around a beach bonfire to a beatbox thudding with the retro urban cowgirl music of Pink Bullets.

Mark tsk-tsked as he walked on, absently scratching his short gray goatee with his left hand. Relying on recorded rhythms reduced the power of any drum experience by at least half. He was more of a trance-dance purist, himself. A disciple of the Big Beat, he'd made rhythms both sacred and profane with his own hands and feet, drumming in Buddhist temples as eagerly as in bar bands.

Nearby, oceanward as he walked through the sand, he saw his first costumed revelers—a team enacting a sandworm, with little plastic action-figures riding atop the three-person alien annelid. Watching the worm, he thought of his own costume. Looking down at his moccasins, his buckskin leggings, and his fringed vest, he concluded it was time to put on his antlered headpiece. Although he only dressed this way on Halloween, more and more he felt that this was who he really was.

Once he'd hit his mid-twenties, Mark had moved away from his old bar-brawling and street-fighting warrior ways. He began studying shamanism instead, in a less painful attempt to get back in touch with his broken and buried Native American roots. Not that he'd limited himself to Cherokee heritage alone, though. He favored the pan-tribal approach. Over the years, he'd volunteered at half a dozen excavations throughout the once and future Aztlan. During the course of ethno/entheobotanical seminars, held amid Mayan ruins at Uxmal and Palenque, he had ritually ingested most of the local "power plants." He had become quite the autodidact in archaeology and anthropology.

Walking over the sand, he reminded himself that academic knowledge wasn't the goal—ecstatic experience was. The journey *to* that and the goal *of* that were the same. In becoming a true ecstasy technician, the only way to *do* that experience was to *be* it; the only way to *be* that, was to *do* it.

"Do-be-do-be-do," he sang softly, thinking of Sinatra, and laughing.

Mark had learned and practiced the shaman's Four D's of ecstatic technique: Drumming, Dancing, Dreaming, Drugging. In the process his experiences became more far-reaching. He had whirled with Sufis and wailed with swing dancers. He trained himself as a lucid dreamer over half a dozen years. He consumed mind-altering substances, sometimes in the manner prescribed by ancient traditions—and sometimes not.

That "sometimes not" was what could get him into trouble. The idea that a deep archetypal shamanic complex lay at the origin of human consciousness—his best insight into the whole subject of shamanism— *that* had come to him while he was in an altered state of consciousness himself, after ingesting some dearly bought sporeless *Cordyceps jacintae* mushrooms. Sad, really. Any mention of *that* context would inevitably discredit his insight simply by association.

Walking from the beach onto the promenade proper now, he saw that the impromptu Halloween parade was much further underway here. Joining the costumed promenaders, his heart jumped as he was forcibly, claustrophobically, reminded of his height—or lack thereof. He always felt it in crowds, but even more so here, where so many of those around him wore tall masks and more than a few sauntered along on stilts.

At least his antlered headpiece made him *feel* taller.

He moved through, with, and sometimes against a tide of dancing skeletons drumming on skulls and xylophoning rib cages, then past knife-in-the-skull "murder" victims. Around him flowed period-clothed people in wraparound celebrity videomasks and full-body celebrity skins. Next came astronauts and scuba divers, surfers in the mouths of sharks, Frankenstein monsters and witches and insectoid aliens, bull-headed bipedal Minotaurs, multi-legged Chinese dragons, winged faerie-folk, furred and tailed catwomen, werewolves growling and laughing, masked and leotarded superheroes, Dracula and a host of later vampires showing their fangs—even one young man with a stag-horned head, a glowing cross between the horns, the rest of his body done up as the label from a Jägermeister bottle. Mark wondered if the costume was original, or some kind of corporate product-placement sneaking into the parade.

He watched the Halloween parade of the masked and the marvelous pass around him, relieved that the Jägermeister man's costume was by no means a duplicate of his own. Stag of Saint Hubert, he thought, recalling the history behind the trademark icon and wondering at the persistence of animal powers throughout history. Lions of Saint Mark. The White Stag of King Richard. American eagles and Russian bears. Shamans as were-jaguars in Olmec artifacts. The long-tongued and antlered Chu shamans of ancient Chinese art. The myth of Proteus. Actaeon transformed into a stag and destroyed by his own hunting dogs. The Old Testament story of Nebuchadnezzar's madness transforming him into a grazing animal . . .

The paraders flashed past, a phantasmagoria of persistent images from both ancient hunting-gathering times and contemporary unconscious-nesses individual *and* collective. Whatever might link them all, it was obvious that popular festivals like this Halloween parade had come back—with redoubled force—since the Christian States of America had relinquished its hold over California. The ban on such celebrations of dream and nightmare was lifted so completely it was as if it had never happened at all.

The booming of an amped-up voice caught Mark's attention. A long-haired imitation Cyberite street preacher, face and body video-tattooed with religious images and mathematical equations shifting over him at flashcut speed, addressed everyone in his vicinity.

"As Nineveh was once the omphalos, as Jerusalem was once the omphalos, as Rome was once the omphalos, screenspace is now the omphalos, the navel and center of the world. Gazing at the screen is omphalos-gazing, gazing at the navel of the world, the center that is every-ware and the circumference that is node-ware."

Manager of a connectionist network for UCLA-Harbor General Medical Center, Mark had a professional interest in such ideas, even if they were being parodied here. He slowed his steps and lingered at the edge of the small crowd surrounding the Cyberitic performer, trying to get a better look at this illustrated manifestation as he worked himself into a thundering, soothsaying frenzy.

"What do you see when you gaze at that navel? I see node-weights in neural networks. I see individuals evaporating into social relations and social relations condensing into individuals. Incarnation versus virtualization! I see Nature realer than Culture and Culture hyperrealer than Nature. I see numerology and mysticism, pushed to enough decimal places, become mathematics and physics—and physics and mathematics, pushed enough decimal places further, become mysticism and numerology again. I see the superego of sociology, the ego of psychology, the id of biology. I see -ologies everywhere, to the Left and the Right, each seeing what they're believing and believing what they're seeing—because observation calls forth the minimal program, the collapsed wave function, from the cloud of possibilities."

A few in the small crowd laughed and clapped, Mark among them, at how perfectly the parodist had captured the essential Cyberitic rant. The Halloween ranter, on a roll and in his role, continued without a break in time or character.

"In electronic networks, memory is impossible without resistance to change. In social networks, resistance to change is impossible without memory. No memory without resistance, no resistance without memory! Remember and resist! Stay conscious! On the big screen of the whole wide world—inside the theatre of your head—you are the movie always watching itself being made! Own that process, or that process will own you!"

The pseudo-Cyberite gave the slightest bow as Mark and those around him applauded. Walking slowly on amid moon- and sun- and bird-masked revelers, Mark wondered if he'd really gotten the point of that parody. How could a movie watch itself—much less watch itself being made? Especially if it was the movie of your life.

Could parody also proselytize? He'd heard some of this stuff before. Albertian conscious disurbanism and Zerzanian philosophical Luddism had been in the air for years. Despite Mark's personal familiarity with connectionist networks, though much of the illustrated pseudo-Cyberite's sermon was over his head. What wasn't made more sense than he expected it to.

The next scene he encountered featured paraders videomasked with the faces of prominent Christian States preacher-politicians and other sanctimonious hypocrites doing a Busby Berkeley stomp and chanting:

> *Don't be a druggie! Don't be gay!*
> *Don't be what we do—do what we say!*
> *Don't you know only our way is true?*
> *And don't sass back when we're talking to you!*
> *Don't be uppity! Don't be eco!*
> *Don't act like a Jew or a liberal freako!*
> *Don't you know only our way is true?*
> *And don't sass back when we're talking to you!*

Pretty rude, Mark thought, joining in shocked laughter with those around him. He supposed shock was the point, a counterblast to the hyperliteral Football Bible Warehouse Churchers who had ruled the country—and ruled out Halloween—for far too long. As understandable as the motivations for such backlash vitriol might be among the revelers, the chorusline and its chant-song still made him more than a little uncomfortable.

Ahead, the long line of lights on the Santa Monica Pier stretched away seaward. It was good to see the old pier still standing. The world's ever-weirder weather had taken out the smaller pier that once jutted into the Pacific from Venice Beach, but here the pier—repaired and rebuilt as often as the legendary bombed bridges of Hanoi—still stood, an enormous bioluminescent marine creature, frozen in place in the shallows on the brink of submerging.

As he approached, the pounding polyrhythms of the big drum circle sounded even closer at hand than the pier itself. Mark made his way around an enormous man costumed as a red-capped mushroom and accompanied by a dancing ring of diaphanously dressed fairy-women. Ahead, he saw myriad percussionists thumping nearly in unison as they generated their great waves of sound. In the center of the drum circle masked women and men danced lithely, younger ones among them flashing in flying leaps over the bonfire burning at the drum circle's heart.

Stepping down onto the sand, Mark walked over to the circle and took his place in it, adding the rhythm of his vintage one-sided drum to the beat already thrumming and crashing around him, joining the rest in their search for that elusive, consciousness-altering variant on the 2 hertz pulse.

For a moment Mark thought how strange it must seem that a techhead like himself would join this circle. Yet drumming, here and now, he was not just a short, graying bachelor, a curly-haired and wild-eyed infogeek fighting off the ravages of time and gravity. He was in his own element, and powerful.

As Mark watched masked trance-dancers leap and spin in the firelight, the image of the dancing "masked sorcerer" filled his head. At 15,000 years old, the great cave-painting at Les Trois Freres was arguably one of the oldest "realistic" depictions of a human figure. Mark thought again of his own costume, and the long association of shamanism and shapeshifting. He wondered just how realistic that painting might actually be.

He let the drumming carry him into trance. The journey was exhausting and took hours, but—when the Halloween revelry intensified around him to the point of aching clarity, when the drumming filled all space, when the moon itself became a giant gong resonating in the sky—he realized he'd already arrived where he had hoped to go.

This is the one thing that makes all the pain and suffering of being conscious *worthwhile*, he thought as he looked out at the drumstruck moon shining on the water. All religion is an attempt to explain this vastness of ecstasy I feel right now.

Ecstasy, he thought. A word cheapened and worn by use, tagging everything from illicit drugs to explicit chocolates. A word frightened out of its right sense, needing to be coaxed back to the greatness of its original meaning. Like love. How did the Cyberite parodist put it? You're the movie of your life always watching itself being made? Maybe he was right. Maybe that's what consciousness is. How to reconcile that with ecstasy, though?

Something about the moon shining on the ocean caught his attention and would not let go. Somehow he knew that consciousness and ecstasy were related, just as the moon and the sea were related, despite their oppositions. The simple, singular moon, high and dry and bright. The complex, manifold ocean, low and wet and dark. Yet each, consciousness and ecstasy, a different state of the same thing. One, self-awareness; the other, an awareness that isn't about the self.

What he was feeling now—was it the influence of the moon on the ocean, or the influence of the ocean on the moon? The bright moon passing over the dark ocean, lifting up the shining surface of the tide? Or the shining surface of the tide calling the bright droplet of the moon to drown itself in the deep?

Surface, surf face, he thought. The bright droplet of the moon fell into the shimmering night sea. Experience overwhelmed explanation. Mark Fornash passed out on the sand.

When he came to, the darkness had begun to pale in the east. What he distinctly heard in twilight sleep as the sound of someone playing "Silent Night" on steel drums in the New York subway turned out to be the backup beeping of a robotic coffee cart nearby. A young black woman dressed as an old-time peace-sign activist and a thin, sour-smelling man in coveralls were helping him to a sitting posture.

"No time to be sleeping," said the woman. "The beach patrol is starting to make its morning sweep."

"You don't want to be cited for vagrancy," said the thin, bearded man.

Mark smiled. He wanted to tell them that he hadn't been sleeping. That consciousness is as much an altered state of ecstasy as ecstasy is an altered state of consciousness. Instead, he just nodded.

Standing up, he brushed the beach off his hands, then absently patted it off and out of his clothes. Shaking his head and running his hands through his hair to dislodge the sand still clinging there, he remembered his antlered headpiece. Quickly turning around, he reached down and snatched it up off the sand. Shaking the headpiece out and brushing it off, he watched the young woman and the man in coveralls (accompanied by an enormous buff-colored dog) continue around the circle, rousing those who had passed out or fallen asleep.

Joining them in that work, he helped raise up his share of the unconscious. Some of them, he noticed, woke up startled and embarrassed. He wanted to tell them, *Don't be ashamed—be proud!* but figured that might disorient them still further. Instead he woke them with the message that he had been roused with himself.

They got everyone up and moving onto the promenade before stepping onto the broad walkway themselves. The slowly roaming automated coffee cart he'd heard earlier now appeared—with the yellow, balloon-tired Beach Patrol vehicle not far behind, its electric motors almost inaudible against the background of the surf. Mark wondered how the man and woman who had wakened him knew it was coming.

"Either of you up for a cup of hot joe? My treat . . ."

His companions, hunkered down against the chill of the early morning, nodded and shrugged. From their awkwardness with each other, Mark gathered that the pair had also just met in this dawn. With a wave of his hand in front of the coffee cart's motion sensor, Mark stopped the JoeBot, which was shaped like an oversized ancient percolator. As he and his companions ordered, it occurred to him that the stylized coffeebot looked nothing at all like the actual coffee-brewing apparatus in the machine's innards.

They took seats on benches facing out to sea. Mark tried to figure out what the silver slogan on the young woman's black T-shirt—"Nuclear Winter Cures Global Warming"—meant. He learned her name was Malika something, and that she was finishing up her undergraduate double-major in Physics and Biology, with an eye toward graduate work in what she called QBC.

"What's that?" asked the thin, bearded man, absently stroking the big head of his dog with a grime-blackened hand. He was dressed in splotched and grease-smeared gray coveralls and a maroon knit hat—authentic enough as a down-at-the-heel spacer's costume, Mark thought, but the guy really ought to retire it. Halloween was over. Then he looked at his own buckskins, and thought better of that idea.

"Quantum biocode," Malika said. "Complexity gap-filling. *Q* is for scaling up from microscale quantum theory to macroscale relativity. *B* is biological, filling in the gaps between microscale DNA and macroscale developed organisms. *C* is code, information-based cosmology theory from microscale infobits to macroscale physicality."

Mark wondered why someone with her interests was drumming in the big circle on Halloween, but he didn't know the woman well enough to ask. Instead he raised his warm coffee cup to his lips, smiling.

"Sounds like major heavy-lifting."

"Not really. All strings and things—strings of vibrational energy, strings of base pairs, strings of numbers, and the things that elaborate from them."

"Maybe you can help me out," said the man with the dog. The guy's name was Drennan or Brennan, if Mark had heard right.

With no warning at all, this street guy in his grimy spacer coveralls and heavy space boots (which he wore with too much familiarity for it to be just a costume, it seemed to Mark) started talking about how something he called the Light blew him out of his own universe into a closely parallel one. The grimy spacer even produced crumpled documents from his ample pockets, records he claimed all confirmed the fact that his parents and some other relatives *here*, in this universe, were killed together in a multicar accident—before any of his cousins or his own siblings or he himself could be born. According to the guy's papers, his name was Drinan.

In this universe, the homeless spacer contended, he and his cousins had never existed. Those few people who in his home universe were his close friends had no knowledge or memory of his existence in *this* universe when he phoned them or tried to meet them. To top it off, one of his cousins—nonexistent in *this* universe but merely dead in the other—had somehow been responsible for the Light that catapulted the spacer and his dog into this universe, with such speed and disorientation (he claimed) that their spacecraft had suffered a fiery crash in the desert between Barstow and Ridgecrest.

Mark was tempted to shout Stop! and put an end to the wild ride of this guy's ramblings, but the man with the dog was up to speed now. Mark supposed he was harmless enough, so he didn't interrupt. Discovering neither you nor your siblings nor your cousins had ever been born, that your parents and your aunt and uncle (or great aunt and great uncle, or whatever) had died as young couples—that no one in the world knew you nor had any record of your existence—Mark thought all that, if true, would be enough to drive even the sanest of people to madness. The problem was that he doubted Brennan or Drinan or whoever he was had ever been numbered among the sanest of people. His doors of perception must be seriously unhinged, if he truly believed this Rime of the Ancient Spacefarer shtick he was putting out.

Mark tried to write him off as just another streetcrazy for whom everyday is Doomsday, every night is Halloween. Malika, however—maybe only out of politeness?—seemed to be listening objectively to the spacer's story, even taking parts of it seriously.

"The universes are not parallel in the geometric sense, but parallel in the computing sense?"

"How do you mean?"

Knowing something about connectionism, Mark figured he might as well humor them both.

"A connectionist network. Like all the neurons and the connections among them in the brain. Parallel lines don't meet or connect in space, but a parallel processing system does."

The spacer thought about it, then nodded slowly. Malika, however, was off and running in a burst of undergraduate theorizing.

"Parallel lines don't meet in *Euclidean* space, you mean. The branching system of all possible universes, the plenum, is also *acausal* or *quantum* connectionist system. Not machinelike. Quantum events are not related by causation. Think of the Uncertainty Principle, Bell's Theorem, the Aspect experiments. Einstein's 'spooky action at a distance.' The English astronomer Eddington said 'Our universe looks less like a great machine than like a great thought—'"

"Whoa," Mark said, thinking about the previous night's experience. "Okay. I'll buy the idea that consciousness shows itself in the network connectionism of the brain. Are you saying it also pops up in some bigger 'quantum' connection, involving the whole universe?"

"Not universe—*plenum*. Not just this universe, but the system of all possible universes. I never really thought of it that way, but maybe so.

Why shouldn't it manifest itself in the plenum as a whole? If a single universe is a great thought, then maybe the plenum of all possible universes is the great mind capable of thinking all possible thoughts. Maybe *human* consciousness reflects that larger plenum consciousness, through fractal self-similarity across scales."

The spacer said nothing to that, just patted his dog on the head and smiled. Hearing that "self-similarity" stuff, Mark wondered if shamanism, maybe most mystical systems, might be attempts to synch individual human consciousness with this far vaster thing, this "plenum consciousness." But no; that was just too far out. For strangeness to be fun it had to have some plausibility. Despite Eddington or whoever, there was just no solid proof the universe might "think" or that this plenum thing of parallel universes might do that—if it even existed.

Glancing at Mark and the guy with the dog, Malika suddenly laughed. Mark laughed too, but the spacer just arched his eyebrows. She knows how weird all this sounds, Mark thought, but the guy with the dog—he believes it, like he's already encountered it. Going around talking about "parallel universes" and his "nonexistence" problem might not be wise if he wanted to stay clear of lock-down in a psychiatric ward.

"You won't get invited to the best parties, talking that 'I'm only visiting this universe' kind of stuff."

Refusing to get the message, the spacer stared at Mark. Malika nodded and frowned, trying to explain.

"Mention 'parallel universes' to most people and they think of their evil twins with goatees. Even Deutsch's photon proofs of the multiverse were mocked as photons with goatees."

"Hey," Mark cut in. "I've got a goatee *here*. Does that mean my evil parallel-universe twin is clean-shaven?"

Malika groaned at Mark's joke, but the spacer seemed to still be thinking about that earlier "parties" comment.

"The great thing about being a pariah is that the kind of people I don't want to talk to don't want to talk to me."

Mark nodded. Not much he could say to that. Finishing his coffee, he recalled the v-mail he'd read about the joint project between Protean Pharmaceuticals and the hospital. Clinical tests of those new prionoid neuromodulators. If he remembered correctly, the physicians and neurophysiologists running the testing program were looking for "appropriate trial subjects"—schizophrenics and deep depressives, paid volunteers to serve in limited experimental trials. This spacer seemed like a good candidate.

Mark handed each of his companions one of his Talking Book smart business cards. The cards—crammed with his résumé, interests, photos, full text of several of his favorite books and movies, computer access links, as well as high-limited phone access to his home, work, and road numbers—probably gave them more info on him than they'd ever need.

"I'm starting up a small drum-and-trance circle at my place. Here." To the spacer he added, "Get in touch with me. I think I might have something for you at the hospital where I work, if you're interested."

The spacer gave him an uncomprehending look, then nodded. The thin, bearded man called his dog to follow him and moved off slowly, preoccupied, toward the pier. The young woman muttered something about needing to get to her seat in a live-audience class—before she fell asleep. She waved and jogged away.

Walking slowly down the early morning Promenade, abandoned but for a few cyclists and runners, Mark mused about the way the night had slipped away, and the fascinating folks one met on Halloween Night at the beach.

6

Isolation Suit
2065

REACHING UP UNDER HER SHORT REDDISH-BLOND HAIR, TRILLIA SPIRES ejects the dataneedle, turns off her headplug in frustration, and removes her viewshades. "Entheogeny recapitulates phylogeny"—that was what the man on the screen said. What on earth was *that* supposed to mean?

Trillia shakes her head. Sometimes the contradictions of that Other Age overwhelm her. Its motorized warfare and high-speed carnage. The smells the oldsters are always recalling: sparks and concrete, oil and rubber, gas and plastic and burning bodies. Twilight highways pulsing with that world's power: veins and arteries of stone flooded with bloodcell flows of innumerable vehicles, headlight white and taillight red, corpuscles moving through vast transhuman bodies. Cities of golden towers by day, jeweled pillars—sapphire and emerald and topaz—by night.

Increasingly, cities of flashcut diamond, near the end. A shining cancer of skyscraper signage spreading from the great urban crossroads of the world, sheathing older buildings too in an unsloughable skin of giant videoscreens and holonics. All of it pushing products via a multifaceted dazzle of images, the empty light of advertising expanding to fill all space not specifically denied to it. Then, when the power went down, the flat bright hollow life of all those endless acres of screens and projectors ended too, leaving behind on the dead skin of the cities only a pallor of ashes, as if the inhabitants finally resorted to warming themselves by burning their diamonds.

The very forces that reared and lit the towers, that pumped in the hearts of the cities, also brought them low and dark, wiping out so many human lives and all their potential in so very short a time that (as the survivors told it) there were too few of the living to bury the dead, too little lime in the world to mask the stench of all the rotting corpses.

A civilization whose intelligence was perfectly clear, but whose soul was mad—long before the pandemic made it official. The idea of it is so alien to Trillia that, sometimes, she thinks the great dead megacities were built by enormous (and enormously sophisticated) social insects—and not at all by the kind of human beings she's familiar with.

Determined to understand this stuff despite its strangeness, she slips the viewshades back over her tired eyes, turns the headplug back on, and slips in again the *Religious Responses to the Prionoid Pandemic* dataneedle she was viewing. Not wanting to face the same frustration as before, she quickly scans to a different selection. She stops at a man dressed in a dark suit, speaking in a booming, amplified voice. His white hair, coiffed into a sort of soft helmet, seems impervious to the wind that ripples over the dais around him, onto the crepe-draped podium, and through the crowd in the skyscraper-flanked square before him.

"I hear people saying, 'Who has done this terrible thing to the human race?' I hear them asking, 'Why does the Grim Reaper—who used to be pictured with a scythe—come at us now with a combine harvester?' I'll tell you who, and I'll tell you why! The Dark Prince of the Air, who owns this world, revels in his triumph at what we have done *to ourselves* at his bidding! Don't think ol' Satan has pulled one over on God, though—not a chance! This great plague, too, fits into the divine plan. God is destroying the human race in order to save it. In order to prove yet again His power and save us all from the demonic, soulless future we've been making for ourselves: a spiritually impoverished future, a machine-run future devoid of free will, a future of oblivious zombies! You've seen it already in our so-called arts and letters. Entertainments whose 'psychological realism' is just another name for salacious gossip, whose 'characters' are little more than spectacles of emotion and unholy confession—thinly veiled autobiographies not of humans but of creatures equal parts sick monkey and sensual machine. This Plague is in reality the salvific horror, the saving holocaust, the fortunate fall! God is erasing all the failed words and equations so we can start again, clean, in *His* kingdom, which shall indeed be 'on Earth, as it is in Heaven'!"

With two rapid blinks of her eyes Trillia pauses the display in the middle of the testifying Amen!'s and applause. In records of only a few months earlier, she's seen this same well-coiffed wolf in shepherd's clothing describe some sufferers of the plague as "possessed by Satan" while others are "moved by the Holy Spirit"—the distinction between the two resting largely on whether or not they chose to join his flock.

Life in the world she's grown up in somehow doesn't seem like the thousand-year kingdom of God on Earth, either—

Someone flicks off her headplug switch, snatches off her viewshades, and puts hands over her eyes.

"All time working and no time free-a," says a male voice, "makes out of this girl a very boring Trilli-a."

"A very poor rhyme, Ricardo," Trillia says with a laugh as she grabs his hands. Coming around beside her, the dark-haired, gray-eyed Ricardo Alvarez brushes her cheek with a kiss, before he sits down opposite her, still holding one of her hands.

"I scan as many of the old documents as anybody, but spend too much time studying history and you'll miss out on making your own."

"With you, I suppose?"

Ricardo laughs and sits back.

"Not just with me. You Spires people! *Always* so preoccupied with those headplugs of yours."

Trillia looks out from veranda toward palm fronds moving slowly in the evening breeze.

"I had no choice in the matter. Sometimes I hate having this stupid plug in my cranium—not to mention the microphone in my tooth, the audiophone in my mastoid bone. My parents and grandparents say it's one of the 'family burdens.' "

"Rank hath its responsibilities, I suppose. Simon Lingham has a headplug too—because he's your grandfather's top science guy, maybe? He doesn't use it much, though."

"The plug's been in my head as long as I can remember. That's why I use mine more than someone like Lingham, say. He got headplugged as an adult. It's the ultimate in intimate hardware, but it's probably easier to get used to if you can't remember a time without it."

"All the 'descendant-advisors' to the islands' 'founder-ruler'—you all have to be headplugged?"

Trillia looks down to where her fingers drum the rattan tabletop.

"Grandpa President himself decreed it, for everyone in his bloodline. Installed at birth. While my umbilical to my mother was being removed, this one was being installed—the OUR, Occipital Umbilical Receptor. My very own wireless ghost machine. The keyhole into the haunted house of the world that once was."

Ricardo leans forward and grabs her drumming fingers to silence them.

"Now, don't you poor-little-rich-girl me! Those ghosts are light as electrons."

"Maybe, but there are so many of them, they weigh me down sometimes."

Ricardo glances away, growing momentarily more serious.

"What if someone were to offer to remove your headplug and all the tooth and bone peripherals? What if *I* offered to do it?"

Trillia feels uncomfortable, not because she hasn't considered the possibility before, but because she has.

"Most likely, I'd turn your offer down."

"Why?"

"I don't know. For me, it's like a world memory, joined to my personal memory. If I were to lose that memory, I'd feel diminished somehow. Almost as if I'd lost my sense of smell or taste."

"Then, just as taste and smell sometimes pick up unpleasant sensations, so too you will just have to tolerate occasional unpleasantness in what your machine-aided memory gives to you."

Trillia laughs, Ricardo's mock-pedantry reminding her more than a little of Dr. Lingham's manner of speaking. Ricardo drops out of pedant character and into his own voice.

"Your electronic ghosts aren't as bad as the living ghosts. All the spry longlifers who founded our 'island oasis' here—*they're* more burdened by that history than we could ever be."

Trillia glances into his eyes, then away.

"I know. They can't escape the guilt *and* relief that *they* survived when so many others didn't. Trapped in their own memories, like bugs in amber. Every time they tell me stories of that Other age, it's like they're trying to get me to feel what they feel at having survived the Great Death. How can I possibly feel that? It all happened years before we were born!"

Ricardo nods, then begins ticking off on his fingers the sins of the fathers.

"Bloated population, bloated consumption, irreversible environmental damage. Their mistakes, not ours. And everybody ended up paying for them."

He stands up and stretches, lazily cracking his knuckles—a habit Trillia would like to break him of. He glances down at her.

"As distracted as you are by that headplug, those raiders could have taken you hostage in the big raid yesterday and you wouldn't even have noticed. They almost got old man Cameron himself—" Then, in a lower voice Ricardo adds, "Not that *that* would have necessarily been a bad thing."

Trillia grimaces. Both she and Ricardo have felt the sting of her grandfather's tenacious and irrational opposition to their love. Trillia's parents—and Ricardo's family too—continue to bend before Cameron Spires' will. The only reason ever given by any of them is that Trillia, at nineteen, is too young for such an involvement, and Ricardo, at twenty-four, is too old *for* her! Ridiculous, in both directions. Still, it's not reason enough for Ricardo to talk that way about her grandfather.

"That's not an appropriate thing to say about our President. No matter how much you may dislike him, he's still my grandfather. It's not polite for you to wish his capture and death, not even in joking."

Ricardo begins to pace around her table.

"That's the history I was talking about before! Happening right now. I just saw Simon Lingham. He's got his daughters bearing a stretcher with his son's body on it. They're headed toward Golf Parliament. President Spires, the Great Pontificator, is almost done with the day's presiding there. Lingham's got an ancient-looking werwoman in a chair, too—and a crowd following them! Looks like ol' President Bubble-Boy is about to get a surprise."

Sometimes Ricardo can be just plain rude, Trillia thinks. "Bubble-boy billionaire"—that was how the press had disparagingly referred to her grandfather when he was young. More often than not they neglected to remind people that her grandfather was born with Severe Combined Immune Deficiency, half a dozen years before it became readily curable.

Trillia remembers the stories. As a kid, her grandfather Cameron was more accustomed to interacting with machines than people. According to family legend, that was the source of his wealth before—and his survival after—the pandemic: familiarity with machines, and with disease. His ability to read meaning into vast amounts of machine-generated data supposedly helped him understand the future shape of the market, build new mountain ranges of wealth, create new worlds and ecologies of stocks and industries. Her parents have suggested, too, more quietly, that living in dread of disease all his young life helped him see what was coming in terms of the pandemic, sensitized him to the shape of the great plague, before most people had any idea what it would mean. . . .

Trillia looks up and sees Ricardo still looking at her. In her woolgathering he undoubtedly finds more proof that she's too distracted from the physical and real. Remembering what he said earlier, she knows trouble when she hears it. Simon Lingham is indeed her grandfather's "top science guy," as Ricardo put it—his chief advisor on biomedical matters. His son Phillip was one of the fourteen islanders killed in yesterday's bloody raid. A split between the President and one of his top advisors would not be a good thing for anybody on the island. Trying to maintain a calm outward appearance, Trillia pops the dataneedle out of her plug set and puts it in its carrying case.

"What's that to me?"

"What's it to *you*? A chance to catch history in the making, like I said. If we hurry we might just be in time to see some of it."

Despite her misgivings, Trillia rises slowly to her feet—too slowly for Ricardo, who has already danced his way to the veranda's front steps.

"Come on!"

"I'm coming."

Ricardo, half-walking and half-running, pulls Trillia along by the hand behind him. The way to Parliament slips past them in a blur of evening sky, flower-lined streets, rattling palm fronds. It seems to her they will arrive too soon for her to gather her wits about her.

Twilight is moving toward dark by the time they join the crowd milling among the market stalls of the Open Forum courtyard. One of the many post-pandemic additions to the offices and chambers of the Parliament, the courtyard, like the rest, grew out of the old hotel and golf resort.

Angling his way through the crowd, Ricardo leads her forward, the better to see and hear what is going on between Cameron Spires and Simon Lingham. When at last they reach the front of the crowd, Ricardo and Trillia see Dr. Lingham clad in black and standing beside his veiled and black-garbed daughters. His four daughters wear their hair drawn back tightly against their skulls and falling straight behind. Each one holds a lighted torch.

By that flickering torchlight Trillia also sees her grandfather, wearing his softly glinting environment-suit like robes of state. At the top of the broad stone stairs above Lingham and his people, the President's entourage stands bunched about him too, where they have stopped at the sight of unexpected petitioners.

Trillia sees what stopped them: Lingham's murdered son on a flower-strewn bier, and a woman—older-looking than anyone else on the island, yet possessed of sharp, glittering eyes—heavily bandaged and seated in a wheelchair, with a woven robe thrown loosely about her. From the buzz in the crowd around them, Trillia gathers that the old-looking woman is

Werfolk. She's either in Lingham's custody, or under his protection, or some combination of the two.

"I hear he's on the brink of a cure for the pandemic," says an African woman in a yellow-and-black kinte cloth dress and yellow turban, gesturing toward Lingham.

"After thirty-some years?" asks a red-faced, red-mustached man, the trace of an Australian accent just audible in his voice. "It's about time!"

Several people around him laugh, until a bespectacled, dark-complected man—South Asian by his accent—speaks up and catches their attention.

"But what he was working on destroys the effectiveness of the longevity treatment too. He's stopped working on it—"

The crowd quiets, for Lingham has begun speaking.

"—end these decades of raids and battles, costly in terms of our slow material progress and even more costly in lost human lives. More war cannot bring back the many we have lost; it can only cost us the lives of more sons and daughters, more fathers and mothers, more sisters and brothers. I therefore propose we end this endless bloodshed by negotiating with the Werfolk some reasonable means by which we might provide them with limited access to the treatment. Only in that way can we bring this long violence to a hopeful end."

Murmurs run through the crowd. Around Trillia, several people either accept or reject Lingham's proposal outright. Most of their comments obviously reflect the speakers' already established opinions. Others (like Trillia herself) weigh Lingham's words quietly, keeping their mouths shut and their minds open.

Environment-suited President Spires raises his hand for silence. Tall but slightly stooped, dark-haired but a bit gray about the temples, he still looks remarkably hearty for a man who has seen a very eventful life of more than seven decades. When the noise of the crowd abates, he speaks in a loud, clear, suit-amplified voice. Beneath her grandfather's measured tones, Trillia hears a persuasive rhetorician trying to turn the situation to his advantage.

"Simon, accept my deepest condolences on the death of your son. We have all lost loved ones in our efforts to secure in these islands a better future for ourselves and our posterity. You were among the first to join me here. I have not forgotten that. No one has forgotten that. From the devastated world of the Great Death we came away together, you and I and all the founders, in order to preserve—against the further ravages of the pandemic—the true humanity we had known.

"We were like Shakespeare's Prospero, who also survived shipwreck on a desert island. One where the beast-man, Caliban, already dwelt. Our case was in some ways the opposite, however. When we first came here, the whole of the human world was the shipwreck. This island was a stone life raft, always under threat of invasion from without and within by the Calibans known as Werfolk."

Trillia hears muttered agreement, sees heads nodding at the words. President Spires looks around him, taking in the whole of the crowd. His words draw everyone to him, the Great Father of the islands and his children. Yet it is hard not to note the sneer of distaste on the President's face when his eyes fall upon the bandaged but bright-eyed woman in the wheelchair. The thought flits through Trillia's mind that if the old woman ever needed Lingham's protection, it is now.

"We are too well aware that the number of True Humans surviving worldwide remains perilously small. Were-creatures twisted by the lingering effects of the plague keep appearing among True Human populations at an alarming rate. Thank heavens the plague that still twists them also still shortens their lives—even if not nearly so drastically as it once did.

"Now you would have us give them longevity, Simon? I must admit, I've sensed this coming from you for a long time, but I cannot agree. No, my good old friend, increasing Werfolk longevity in any manner would be a foolish and short-sighted appeasement. Look at that old creature you brought with you—her life has been plenty long enough already."

Everyone in the crowd glances toward the wounded woman, but she seems not at all daunted by their staring. She is probably not yet sixty-five, but from her aged looks she strikes the islanders—especially the younger ones like Trillia—as an ancient.

"She doesn't seem in need of any increase in *her* life span. Yes, yes: I know her age is a rare exception, that she's probably one of the oldest of her kind—but she proves the rule. We can't afford such appeasement. Not when the world's climate is still hung over, from both the binge-burning that fueled the old megacity world and from the cities themselves afire, sometimes for years. No appeasement. Not when our small outposts of light, our tiny seeds of possibility powered by wind, wave, and sun—the tattered remnants of our lost civilization—are still so few and far between. No appeasement. Not when these islands themselves, the most hopeful of such seeds, are constantly under threat from high seas and hurricanes—and raids by plague-debased creatures bent on taking from us all we have made!"

Scattered applause and shouted assents rise from the crowd, but the President has not yet driven his point all the way home.

"No appeasement. Out of that shining tapestry of everything that once was, only a few threads remain, all of them too thin and fragile to bear the burden you propose. If we were to give the shapeshifters our longevity treatment, *we* would soon be swamped and overwhelmed by their plaguey hordes. In their promiscuous rutting and knotting, like the half-animals they are, they would drown us in the tide of their numbers—driving True Humanity itself to extinction!"

Cries of "No!" and "Never!" and much else in the same vein erupt from the crowd, until the President quiets them again.

"I put my faith in our own resolve and in the strength of the Merfolk we have created. They join us in vigilantly guarding our way of life here, standing between our island sanctuary and these banned shapeshifters who would destroy it. Though the Merfolk are few as yet, their numbers will grow. Together with us, and with our Trufolk brethren struggling in enclaves throughout the world, we will someday take back what we have lost. We will build anew the world civilization that fell to ruin—build it better this time, build it to last forever! Never again shall human beings fear the moon and the madness and the fire!"

Loud and persistent cheering spreads through the courtyard. Lingham and his daughters slowly raise their torches and move them in small circles over their heads until at last the crowd quiets. When the torches stop moving, Simon Lingham speaks once more.

"Cameron, you've always been good at speechifying—and even better at casting our life here in a grand romantic tradition. Allusions to your much-beloved Shakespeare! So be it. But we are less Prospero than Dr. Moreau, fled from the wider world to these islands in order to create a new race of—what? Anthropomorphic animals? Zoomorphic humans?

"We have a right to be proud of the Merfolk, I suppose. They are a great advance, the result of years of round-the-clock work by many of us. Ultimately, though, they are your creation. Your vision. The product of all the billions you spent, when that sort of money still meant something. Your final 'investment.' We all *think* we know about them, but do we? In their radically altered 'human' form, the Merfolk are less akin to us than they are to the shapeshifters! The Merfolk, permanently shapeshifted by us before birth, are more were-creatures, *were-dolphins*, than the Werfolk themselves!"

In the crowd, whispers of annoyance become angry mutterings.

"Yet, because the Merfolk recognize us as their creators, because they serve us with dogged devotion, we do not kill them as we do the Werfolk. Our mermen and mermaids need ask us for no longevity treatment. They are already essentially immortal in their physical bodies. If long life is one of the measures of 'true humanity,' then it follows that the Merfolk are more 'truly human' than we are ourselves!"

Murmurs of unease and displeasure, growing and working their way through the crowd as Simon speaks, now burst out in a chorus of rebuttals.

"What then is this 'true humanity' you wish to save?" Lingham continues, shouting down the babel of objections. "At least three types of humanity exist now, or none at all. We cannot exist cut off from the Werfolk world. Any enclave of unaltered human beings can only become a dead end if it isolates itself from the rest of the human world and what remains of the human future.

"Why is it that we have been able to greatly extend our own life spans and even to bio-engineer aquatic human forms—but have yet to overcome the continuing effects of the pandemic? It's true, as you said, that the Werfolk's lives are not shortened as drastically as they once were. Nor, according to my informant here, does their madness come upon them nearly as often, nor so uncontrollably and fatally as it once did. What factors affect its onset? Strong emotion? The phase of the moon? We need to learn from the Werfolk as much as they need to learn from us. Dialogue between ourselves and them will kill far fewer of us than the murderous silence between our two cultures already has. I swear upon my son's memory that I will work to open that dialogue. I implore you to appoint ambassadors to the Werfolk, and to allow me to serve in such a role."

In the crowd many turn their gaze to the President, whose own gaze shifts from Lingham to the werwoman and back again. In his forceful reply he seems to speak *for* the people in the crowd as much as *to* them when he answers.

"Never! You do dishonor to your son's memory to even suggest such a thing. You must be mad with grief. Only a madman—or someone entranced by one of these mainland witches—would wish to be an 'ambassador' to the Werfolk and their moon-mad world. We will not allow you to serve in such a role because we will not appoint any such 'ambassadors.' "

Spires and his entourage turn to go. Lingham sighs, then takes a deep breath.

"Then you leave me no choice," he says formally, in a loud clear voice, "but to reject all the benefits of these islands, renounce my citizenship in the New Bahamian Polity, and demand the right of outcast."

A stunned silence falls over the crowd. Outcast! Simon Lingham, an abjurer? Trillia can barely conceive of those words occurring in the same sentence. In the entire post-pandemic history of the islands, only forty-three islanders have found life here so unacceptable as to turn abjurer and flee into self-imposed exile. Their mere existence is a blot on the post-pandemic history of the islands—one seldom spoken of in public.

Spires turns slowly toward his now much-disfavored advisor.

"This is a grave decision indeed," President Spires says, not just to Lingham but to everyone listening. "Only those who dwell in these islands receive the longevity treatment and the prolongation of youth which accompanies it. Those who leave the islands begin to grow old again, quite soon after their leave-taking. Those who abjure, who seek the right of outcast, pass the sentence of death upon themselves. You ask for that?"

"I do," Lingham says flatly. "Mr. President, we used to joke that we had created the fountain of youth that Ponce de Leon once imagined he would find somewhere between here and Florida. We prided ourselves on the idea that the old explorer had a premonition of what *we* have brought to fruition. Now, after all these years, I see that the more we isolate ourselves, the more our fountain of youth turns into a stagnant pool. I therefore ask, as is my outcast right, that I be granted a week's time to settle my affairs here. That none of my kin be held legally tainted by my decision. That I be provided with transport to the mainland. And that this outlander woman accompany me on my journey, as my hostage."

President Spires shrugs, the gesture betraying a hint of disgust and even anger at this betrayal.

"Until you come to her people, and you become her hostage? Granted."

The President and his entourage hasten away, glad to leave such matters behind them. Guards come forward to escort Lingham and the aged werwoman. Together they move in procession with Lingham's daughters and the dead Phillip on his bier, all of them headed toward the cemetery outside Freeport.

The crowd, and Trillia and Ricardo in it, is slow to break up—as if their lingering together might somehow help them heal the wound made by this sharp and sudden breach between two of their island-world's founders.

7

Abnormal Conformers
2032

ONCE HIS OVERSEERS HAD GOTTEN OVER HIS NONEXISTENCE, JOHN thought, the only real problem with the program at the hospital was that he had to keep Oz tied up outside. His "situation" had been less chaotic since he started the program—no doubt about that.

He'd had to reach a pretty low point in his life before he could bring himself to take the Talking Book smartcard Mark Fornash gave him and jam it into a datalink. Cost him nothing to do it—the business card's telephone and computer access function took care of the charges—but he had to dive into some personal dark depths before he reached the point where he could turn to a stranger for help.

Living in a world of *nothing but* strangers got to him more and more. That this world which possessed no record of his existence was also so familiar only made it worse. Things he'd planned to do—like returning to the crash site for proof the crash had happened, or making the visit to Uncle Ev and Aunt Marian to learn their side of what happened to his parents here—he'd never been able to bring himself to do any of that.

"In this universe," he joked to Oz, "it's like I'm Superloser! Made of pure *deleterium*! Rare entropy-enhancing element that makes everything I touch fall apart, come to naught, turn to shit!"

The joke became less funny and more real the longer it went on. In despair he sold or pawned all the electronics and telecom gear off his coveralls. For money and credit to buy food for Oz and "antidepressants" (mainly cheap booze) for himself. Even that hadn't helped. In that other universe he'd grown up in he had been taught that the present was inevitable. Now he found it wasn't. He had always believed he was unique and valuable, but here he found himself just another disposable person among the other throwaway people: a replaceable cog in the social machine, a social placeholder who had lost his place in society. He found himself walking the pier aimlessly, thinking more and more about his own suicide—dreaming about it at first, then planning it. He might have done it, too, if he hadn't had the big dog to take care of. They'd been together so long, it would have been a shame to leave Ozymandias a stray here on the sand.

He thought about calling Malika, but she hadn't given him her number, much less a data-stuffed smartcard with comp phone privileges. Besides, she might get the wrong idea or something—the whole sex and dating thing. Mark Fornash seemed the better bet, since John didn't feel anything toward him, that way.

"Something is wrong with me," John said at last over the phone, his voice shaking. "I don't know what it is, but it is."

"Stay right there," Fornash said. "I'll get some people and we'll come help you out."

That was how he got drafted into the trials of Protean Pharmaceutical's neuromodulator treatment, run locally by UCLA Harbor General. Mark and a couple of nurses—one male, one female, both unnecessarily burly—took John and Oz to the hospital and into the program.

John told the clinicians about the Light and the crash in the desert and his discovery that he didn't belong in this universe. He told them what he remembered in detail only later: how his dead cousin Jiro was mixed up in it along with some vast alien mind, the Allesseh (which struck even John as loony, but there it was). His story convinced the white lab coat types he was an appropriate test subject. In a matter of hours they set him up in a small apartment inside an assisted-living complex not far from the hospital grounds. Other participants in the program soon joined him there.

All of them posed different problems for the program staff, John supposed. Some of the others were more genuinely nutty or suicidally depressed than he was himself. None of the others had dogs, however, and all of them were traceable through valid identification documents, bank accounts, and government records—which made them easier to put on the program's payroll than John proved to be.

When John gave his name and then insisted there were no records of his existence, the program's pencil-pushers at first believed he had amnesia or was simply lying. The documents he possessed—driver's permit, spacecraft navigation license, social security tattoo—all showed no matches in their databases. That, however, just made the low-level bureaucrats suspect he might be not only an amnesiac and pathological liar but a brilliant forger as well.

No matter how hard the program administrators searched, however, they could find no trace of his existence prior to the date John gave for his crash-landing in the desert. Still, they stubbornly refused to send people out to the crash site to search for any remaining physical trace of his ship. He volunteered to take them to the exact location if they'd provide transportation, but they always turned his offer down—as if granting his story even the slightest possibility of a basis in reality would pose a threat to *their* precarious sanity. His inquisitors, so careful to avoid toppling into the vortex of his delusion, were soon as frustrated with his story as he was annoyed with their refusal to believe it.

On his fifth day in the program, his latest caseworker informed him sharply that nowhere in any accessible databank could they find fingerprints that matched the ones on his hands, nor retinal prints like those in his eyes, nor vocal prints matching his voice. Hearing the usually sedate blond woman complain about her frustrations drove John into his worst bout of despair since coming "inside."

"Why don't you accept that what I've told you is true?"

"Because it's just too improbable!"

" 'When you have eliminated the impossible, whatever remains, however improbable, must be the truth.' Sherlock Holmes said that. Or maybe it was that barber, Occam."

Such learned allusions did not make the caseworker any happier with him. She contented herself with latching onto the perverse synchronicity whereby John, in the same place and within the same hour in that other universe, had learned of the deaths of both his cousin and his own mother. Surely such coincidence must be either the cause or effect of some deep-seated trauma. . . .

Who knew what story the program authorities told themselves now? Last he heard, they theorized he was a spy of some sort, whose records had all been destroyed by one side or another in the recent religious wars: a shadowy figure who had his memory wiped so he would never recall whatever it was he was supposed to have done during those dark days. More believable to them, he supposed, than that his story of the Light and parallel universes might be true.

At all events, his historical nonexistence ceased to be a problem for them after a week or so. As long as John allowed them to keep taking stool and urine and blood and cerebro-spinal fluid samples from him, they seemed content enough. He would allow them to keep doing all that so long as they provided him with room and board and a "salary" of sorts. Soon enough they found ways to identify him and document him to their satisfaction. Traces of his existence at last began showing up on the record-keepers' radar.

Maybe having his memory wiped wouldn't have been so bad. His problem (one of them, anyway) was that he *remembered* his strange story. Felt compelled to tell it again and again. Maybe he was just too stubborn to admit telling his truth would only get him labeled crazy—long before it set him free.

At least he was making some progress convincing Mark Fornash. Whenever one of John's mandatory appointments with the program's body-fluid vampires and one of Mark's work-breaks coincided, the little shamaniac left off Webspidering various of the hospital's many networks and stopped by to say Hi. Dressed techie-casual in his work uniform of Escher-patterned shirts and natural-colored jeans, Mark had begun to ask him pointed questions when they met, trying to punch holes in John's story, rather than just dismissing it out of hand.

"Hey, John! They tell you yet?"

"Tell me what?"

"The meeting, bro! With To-mo-ko. Dr. Fukuda. Chief goddess of Protean Pharm, you know? She's on her way down from the headquarters in Seattle to do a walk-through this afternoon. I've met her twice myself. She's got some powerful female energy, that one."

"So?"

"So she's going to be on hand when they shoot you up with their new prionoid, that's what."

"They've taken enough fluids out of me the past few weeks. It's about time the program put something back."

When he met Dr. Tomoko Fukuda that afternoon John didn't know whether to feel anxious or relieved. With her dark hair cut in blunt bangs across her forehead, Fukuda looked younger than he'd expected. Dressed in an off-white suit, she moved with a dancer's grace. The possibility that she might have a dancer's body under that suit flitted across John's mind, but his erotic daydreaming was quickly quashed. Dr. Fukuda, preoccupied with the nurses prepping his left bicep for an intramuscular injection, was all business—and her business was all science.

"The staff here has explained to you how this testing procedure works, I presume?"

"They tried."

Dr. Fukuda held up her hand slightly. In so doing she stopped the nurses and their prepping process, just before the hypodermic spray gun was about to make its grand entrance.

"You don't understand it?"

"Not fully. Too much talk of 'ligands,' 'alpha helices,' 'beta sheets,' and 'proteolysis.' "

A fugitive smile, quick and quiet as distant lightning, flashed across Fukuda's face and was gone.

"You understand the basic experimental setup?"

"I know one group of us gets the actual therapy and one gets a placebo. Not even you know which gets which, at this point."

"It's a bit more complicated than that, but yes, that's basically correct. It's the nature of the therapy itself you don't understand, then?"

"Bingo."

"DNA serves as a template for various RNAs, and the RNAs translate out to various proteins. Among the most important of those proteins are enzymes."

She walked behind him to examine the injection site the nurses had been prepping, continuing her explanation as she went. A real multi-tasker, John thought.

"Prions are proteins that propagate themselves without DNA or RNA involvement. They were first discovered in relation to neurodegenerative diseases in mammals, but they're much more widespread in nature. They appear sporadically. They can be inherited. They can also be transmitted. They provide the basis of some inherited characteristics through non-Mendelian genetics."

" 'Non-Mendelian'?" John asked, vaguely hoping to stave off, through talk, the inevitable injection. Fukuda gestured to the nurses.

"The efficient transfer of characteristics from mother cell to daughter cell without the involvement of chromosomal genes. Through cytoplasm, from cell to cell alone. More generally, prions bind to other proteins similar to themselves and convert those other proteins into actual *copies* of themselves. Through this binding and conversion, they alter the conformation—shift the three-dimensional shape—of those other pro-teins. Usually it takes place in the endocytic pathway, particularly the endoplasmic reticulum. In cell types like neurons and astrocytes."

"Yeah, I sort of got that part. Like vampires in the tunnel of love."

Dr. Fukuda looked at him quizzically, then understood, that quick smile flashing across her face again.

"The endoplasmic reticulum, the ER, as a tunnel of love. Hmm! Only it's not about love or sex. It's not even about replication. It's about conver-sion by altering conformation. This 'Dracula' only has to hug you or grapple with you—not bite you—to turn you into another vampire, an exact Count Dracula copy, and then you, in vampire form, grab someone else, who becomes another vampire, who grabs someone else, and so on. Pretty soon only Draculas are coming out of the tunnel of love. 'Abnormal conformers' is the technical term."

Fukuda made a comment to one of the nurses, an instruction of some sort, then turned back to him.

"I think of a prion as a protein whose altered shape is contagious to other proteins. Sort of like a cross between the games of Go and dominoes. Each protein, once altered, can now alter the shape of those other protein molecules it was itself originally shaped like. A cascade effect."

John stared at the hypospray in not-so-mock horror.

"And you want to shoot me up with something like *that*? A contagious protein?"

"Not at all. You may be getting 'shot up' with a placebo, remember? In any case, we're several generations beyond the original prion types. We use the conformation-altering capabilities of *artificial* proteins for therapeutic purposes."

"Such as?"

"Years ago, a noted biochemist looked at the proteins that cause Alzheimer-type amyloid plagues. By the time I was a postdoc working in his lab, he was using a manufactured protein to shift those amyloid proteins into shapes that could be cleaved and broken down by the nervous system's proteolytic enzymes. Oops! I used 'proteolytic,' didn't I?"

"That's okay. I'll pretend I didn't hear it. Go on."

"By using the conformation-altering capabilities of the artificial proteins we've developed—what we call prionoids—we've found we can modulate levels of enzymes involved in synthesizing neurotransmitters in the brain."

John stared at nothing in particular in the examination room.

"How do you make these 'artificial proteins'? Run them off *E. coli* or something like that?"

"Not quite. On computer simulators we design a protein structure we want to try. Then we insert the gene sequence for creating such a protein into insect SF9 bacculovirus or mammalian cell lines. The SF9 or mammalian lines make that protein for us. We don't use a bacterial production system because we want proper protein folding—technically for post-translational alterations like glycosylation, adding sugar moieties. Getting that wrong could induce unexpected prion formation, and we wouldn't want that."

"No, I suppose not."

"Using artificial peptide prionoids, we can directly intervene in the release, binding, and uptake of the neurotransmitters themselves. Both the enzyme-modulation and the neurotransmitter-intervention approaches have worked well in cell culture. We've already had success with species-specific prionoids developed for mice and monkeys. In humans, we're looking at this approach for treating disorders like schizophrenia, depression, and bipolarism."

Although he was interested in what she was saying, John found that he could not turn his gaze from the hypospray resting near his bare flesh.

"I thought all those were being handled through the genes."

"Some significant progress has been made in that direction, yes. Unfortunately, many neurological disorders seem to result from multiple genes in combination with whole ensembles of nongenetic factors. Mind-numbingly complex. We come at them from an ontogenetic approach, further up the developmental ladder. That's where volunteers like you come in."

She jabbed him with the hypospray. He felt almost nothing at all.

"There. That wasn't so bad, now was it?"

John thought *that* time-tested medical mantra was just a meaningless cliché. In point of fact, however, it *wasn't* that bad. He rubbed his bandaged arm as Dr. Fukuda spoke with the nurses about "monitoring his progress." If this was as bad as it got, then his "employment" in Protean's program might prove to be a sweet deal after all.

8

Thinking Like a Landsman
2065

FROM DEEPER SEAS NEREUS SWIMS RAPIDLY TOWARD THE AQUAMARINE shallows surrounding Grand Bahama. His interviews with Cameron Spires are few and far between, but always momentous. What else could they be? Such conversations mean contact with his own creator, the maker of all the Merfolk.

His thoughts also move deeply, though neither so swiftly nor so effortlessly as he swims. For someone who by nature lives fully in the present, it is hard to think himself into those places and spaces of future and past where Trufolk and Werfolk spend so much of their time. Still, he tries. With the type of intuition Merfolk are not supposed to possess, Nereus wonders if this call from Spires has something to do with the most recent attack by the were-creatures.

In the end, the origin of the long war between Trufolk and Werfolk, and all reason for it, is beyond him. Try as he might, he can never fully comprehend either the physical tragedy of the Trufolk's Great Death, or the spiritual transcendence of the Werfolk's Great Shift. For Nereus the pandemic is neither the Trufolk's "vast catastrophe" nor the Werfolk's "global epiphany." It is merely the larger circumstance surrounding the creation of his own kind.

The ways of both Trufolk and Werfolk are alien to him. When he was younger and spent more of his time trying to think like land-dwellers, Nereus wondered about gods and religions. They are such a big part of the human record. Yet Christ on the Cross, Buddha beneath the Bo tree, Muhammad at the Merkabah—none of them seem to reflect Nereus's experience in life, no matter how much he stares at depictions of them. What Trufolk see in these figures has never taken with him. He remembers one of the Trufolk, Sister Vena, long ago trying to help him see it. Imagining Jesus speared by harpoons, or Buddha beneath a brain coral, or Muhammad in an undersea cave helps a little, but not much.

With X-ray clarity, his ultrasound senses show him the skeleton beneath the skin, the bones beneath the flesh of all folk around him. Everyone in Nereus's world is naked to the bone. He can no more understand Trufolk or Werfolk ideas of the sacred or mystical than he can fathom their conceptions of modesty.

Like all Merfolk, he is, at any rate, not destined for death. "Those not born like mortals are not fated to die like mortals," as his creator puts it. Cameron Spires is as close to a god as Nereus has ever known—yet he is a god who does not believe in gods, or sacredness, or mysteries. All the light and sound that leak from the teaching machines in the natatoria are, in Spires' words, intended to "demystify." The screens are not holy oracles—only machines. The call for this interview with Spires, sounding in Nereus's own head, is not the voice of a god but only a mechanism to which his reflexes have been conditioned.

Through aquamarine shallows Nereus speeds on, effortlessly as an angel flying through a blue-green heaven. His passage makes silver schools of fish flash and flicker, shifting direction before him the way an angel's passage would part a starling flock in midflight.

He takes a quick spy-hopping leap from the water into that higher ocean, that sea mostly blue and white when he sees it, but also black and stardusted, or gray and cut by lightning flashes at times—that sea along whose floor the other types of human being creep. For a suspended instant Nereus feels its sunlight sharp and bright on his skin, and the breeze of *their* world—a ghostly current in the air—before he slips with a loud splash into the water again.

Dappled light shifts through the water around him. Against his skin, temperatures vary with every change of depth or swirl of current. As his strong flukes propel him into shallower water, he feels the ocean warm slightly in waves over his slipstream flesh. The sensation fills him with joy. He hears seascapes near and far: the songs of whales and dolphins; swirl, crash, and clatter of storms and waves on distant shores; innumerable fish noises; the clicking and popping of crabs and shrimp, of mussel and clam and oyster shells. He tastes the salt of the ocean along the length of his body. He swims in ancient seas, ancient seas swim in him.

Flashing into Freeport Harbor, Nereus gives thinking a rest. It's much better and more natural just to feel. To live inside all the richness his senses bring him each moment. He homes in on the natatorium off the bay where Cameron Spires is waiting for him—his creator seated beneath the waves, in a sealed and pressurized dome rising out of the bottom, free from his environment suit for once.

As Nereus approaches the communication screen, Spires waves at him. Though Nereus can hear and understand spoken language at the surface well enough, he and his creator have long since realized that this screen-mediated translation, converting Trufolk vocal tones to the water-piercing whistle speech of the Merfolk and back again, is more accurate and effective for both parties.

"Nereus! Hello! Good to see you again. I was wondering about something, Nereus. Have you ever thought why I named you that? Ever looked it up on the machines here?"

"Yes, I have."

"And?"

"A marine deity. He used his shapeshifting ability to avoid revealing his power of prophecy."

"Do you think that name is appropriate for you?"

"I can't shapeshift. I do not have the power of prophecy. As to being a deity, landsman religions have never been my strength."

"Of course. What need have Merfolk for such things? You are not for death, and death is not for you."

Searching through the remembered present of his thoughts, Nereus agrees in silence. Yes, there are dangers for Merfolk—sharks and barracudas moving like killing machines carved from pieces of the night ocean, even the stray toothed-cetacean with poor manners—but all of these are known and can be anticipated. He can avoid death indefinitely, if he's careful. Spires coughs, catching and redirecting the merman's drifting attention.

"Though that may not prove as true as we thought. You called us landsmen before, Nereus. What do you think of us—the Trufolk and the Werfolk? Be honest, now."

Before Nereus can stop himself, he says it—and by then it's too late. He might as well say it all, now.

"I feel sorry for you. When I think of the way you live—with no sea to buoy you up, and no echolocation either—it's no wonder you dream of blue heavens and winged angels and invisible gods. Or create artificial paradises in your heads. Maybe I just don't understand. Maybe you don't live as much in what you feel, as we do. It's hard for me to think the way you do."

"How is our thinking different?"

Nereus floats before the screen, trying to put such odd thoughts into words. Spires looks so puzzled, Nereus hopes he hasn't offended his creator.

"You're always remembering the past and planning for the future. Maybe what your senses bring you of the present moment is not enough to fill your minds."

"Oh, I see what you mean! Our landlocked senses are so impaired we have to distract ourselves with abstractions. We have to escape to unknowable futures and unrecoverable pasts. To heavens before birth and hells after dying. Hmm!"

Nereus finds it hard to think as they do, but the only way to communicate with the landfolk is to try to think into that empty space which all their words never fill. He forges ahead, mentally swimming through thick seaweed.

"Yes. Maybe you suffer and war because you grow fond of the things you hope will end your suffering."

"Nereus, you've become quite the philosopher! So, we literally *live* for all those devices and distractions we use to fill up the, er, 'impoverished' moments of our 'limited' lives—is that it? Our consciousness as a nostalgia for the present moment, which we can never possess, which always eludes us, is always past by the time we're aware of it. I hadn't expected so subtle an analysis of the human condition from you. Thank you."

Nereus wonders why he is being thanked. He shakes his head. If the gods and demons of Trufolk and Werfolk dwell in the world beyond the sky, then he supposes the Trufolk and the Werfolk themselves should somehow be *his* gods and demons, since they dwell beyond the sky of his world—beyond the tense, rippling, yet permeable surface where the roof of the sea merges with the floor of the sky.

Yet every time he tries to think like them, as now, Nereus pities them. Strange, the way their very weaknesses have led them to develop tools and words and machines—all their great powers and abilities. Stranger still that gods and demons, once pitied, cannot long remain either gods or demons. They become just other types of human beings, even if almost miraculously powerful ones.

"Your name is important for another reason. You see, in the ancient myth, Nereus revealed to Hercules the way to the place in the west, the Garden of the Hesperides, where Hercules could obtain the golden apples. That 'fruit' granted the wisdom of soul, which makes possible the attainment of true immortality. You're going to go west for me, young Nereus. Perhaps many times. If we're lucky, your efforts may some day reveal how I can obtain those 'golden apples.' "

Nereus cocks his head, puzzled at the need for such journeys.

"I thought we already were immortal."

"As far as I know, you are. Since you're bioengineered for an aquatic existence, your respiratory system keeps you safe from the airborne protean pandemic. When we made you, we also protected you from every other biological threat we could imagine. Your resistance to mortality is much more complete and much more powerful than even our longevity treatment bestows upon us. That completeness, however, may prove a problem. Over the years I have maintained contact with some machine-intelligent 'gnomes' on the mainland. They suggest there may be similarities between our programming of biological immunity in you Merfolk, and the virus-protection programs once used in computers. In computing, no virus-protection software can detect *all* the possible viruses that might alter a given system, without the software itself altering that system and thus *becoming* the thing it is intended to protect the system against."

"But we're creatures—not machines."

"True, true. But, by creating in you an increasingly complete program of protection against mortality, it's possible we may run up against the same constraints. The more complete the defense, the more likely that defense will go on the offensive and alter—or 'attack'—the organism it was intended to defend against alteration."

Nereus finds it both strange and appropriate that he should be in this place, speaking for all the Merfolk.

"But what does that mean for us?"

"My advisors suggest that there can be only one ultimate outcome: Any biotechnical approach to immortality, designed to defend against all possible biological causes of mortality, must itself become a biotechnical cause of mortality. Any truly complete form of protection against death must in fact become a *cause* of death."

"Then it's not truly complete."

"Nor ever can be," Spires says quietly. "Goes back to a mathematician of the last century and his incompleteness theorem. Frankly, I think it's rather a long stretch from the mathematics of set theory to the functioning of immune systems in living organisms. My advisors, since they are partly descended from *machine* intelligences, may just be exhibiting a mechanistic bias, an obsession with issues of completeness and consistency. But it does concern me, and should perhaps also concern you."

Nereus doesn't begin to understand all the new paradoxes and high abstract thinking his creator is forcing on him, but the possible ramifications for his people are clear enough.

"Yes. What can I do to help you find out whether this danger is real or not?"

Spires smiles from his pressurized chamber.

"I appreciate your eagerness. I won't need you for a few days yet. One of my former advisors here has been plunged into a rather late midlife crisis by the death of his son. He will soon be gallivanting up and down the mainland. I will grant him the use of one of our solar-engined sloops. Along with two of your fellow Merfolk, you are to accompany him and his hostage until they give up the use of the boat. Then you and your companions will tow the sloop back to Freeport and report directly to me all that happened during your passage. Everything I've discussed with you must be held in strictest secrecy, between us two alone. Go now, Nereus. I'll call you again when I need you."

In his dome beneath the waves, Spires stands and waves goodbye. Nereus leaps up, breaching, then slaps flukes against the water's surface as he reenters it, his signature way of bidding farewell.

As he swims out of Freeport, Nereus cannot help being perplexed. His brain feels raw. To think the way landfolk do—living a life filled with innumerable moments, each never quite full enough in itself. For Trufolk— and for Werfolk too, he supposes—their presence *in* the world is always at the same time marked by an absence *from* it, by gaps and breaks, like a sea-roof and a sky-floor that somehow cannot merge. The gap or space, which *allows* them to think the way they do, is peculiarly airless and empty to Nereus. After talking to his creator he always feels as if he has leapt so forcefully from the sea that he has arced clear out of the world, into that weightless and airless void the Trufolk reportedly visited, beyond the atmosphere, if not beyond the sky.

All this thinking has made his head pound. Too landish by far. He's happy to be headed home. Soon enough he finds a group of his fellow mermen *lekking*. Joining them, he sings along in the massed choir in an attempt to attract females—a trick learned from male humpback whales. Between choruses, his friends Delphinus and Triton joke about blue whale penis size.

Even as he sings, however, his peculiar landish thoughtfulness will not quite leave him. Listening to the song around him and seeing mermaids approaching, he thinks of how strictly the Merfolk are schooled in the old Trufolk ways. Yet his people have begun to bend those ways into a way of their own.

Incompleteness, he thinks. Maybe Spires himself has not anticipated the way Merfolk might yet develop. Despite his loyalty to his creator, Nereus is glad of all those ways in which the Merfolk are not only Spires' creatures but also themselves. Yes, on his trips to the mainland he will be his creator's eyes and ears—but his will be Merfolk eyes and ears *first*. Others among his people need to assist in this too. Perhaps one of these mischievous young mermaids he leaps with here—Amphitrite, say—will help him see and hear what even his creator cannot.

9

Salvation and Obsolescence
2032

LIKE ALL NUNS OF HER ORDER, SISTER VENA HAD LONG PRAYED THAT HER work with the homeless, the terminally ill, and the poorest of the poor would someday cease to be necessary. It hadn't happened. The work of the Missionaries of Charity was at least as necessary here in Calcutta now as it was when the Missionaries were founded by Mother Teresa eighty years back—more so even, given the numbers of poor and homeless on the streets this morning.

Walking into the precincts of Nirmal Hriday, Sister Vena sighed. This edifice was an abandoned Hindu temple before the nuns took it over. The great reformers and world-saviors—Buddha, Jesus, Mahavira, Muhammed—had long since come and gone, each remodeling religion's sanctuary against pain. The human suffering they so deeply yearned to end remained, however. Nirmal Hriday was an emblem of the persistence of that suffering.

For Sister Vena here, the suffering was personal. Her own heritage was, like this remodeled temple—in which niches that once held dancing Shivas now held saints and Blessed Virgins—also Hindu, overlaid by Christian. Or at least a secularized Brahmin lineage, overlaid by vows of poverty and religious humility. In Vena's personal pantheon, the Holy Trinity of God the Father, God the Son, and God the Holy Spirit ranked foremost, but another trinity—Brahma, Vishnu, Shiva—was also part of her upbringing and memory, despite her parents' worldliness, their scientific rationality. The cosmic snake, the ocean of milk, the butter-churning creation of the universe, lingam and yoni symbols—they were all as much a part of Vena as crucifix and Eucharist, Adam and Eve, or the lives of the saints and history of the popes.

With such images drifting through her mind, Vena barely noted the cool stone floors and time-worn pillars of the halls she walked through on her way to Mother Mary Corona's office. She thought instead on how her double history lingered even in her name. Officially, she was Sister Dolores Srinagar, "Dolores" being the saint's name she had taken on completing her novitiate. Everyone still called her Vena, however. Her Order—not strictly enclosed, and trying to be flexible given the largely Hindu population with which she worked—allowed that living fossil of her former identity to persist.

She stepped up to the voice and retinal-print analyzer outside the heavy office door and announced her presence. As always she was struck by a momentary sadness that this was a world where even convents had to impose strict security measures. More than a few radicals considered the Sisters' work the latest form of neo-neo-colonialism. As the door opened,

Vena's thoughts returned to why Mother Mary had called her away from her daily work on the streets of Mumbai and old Bombay, to meet with her here in Calcutta.

Mother Mary was a ruddy-faced woman of middle years, dressed in a habit the same as that worn by all the Sisters of Vena's Order: a simple white cotton sari with blue-striped border. As Vena came into the room, she snatched the briefest of glances around the thoroughly businesslike office. Only the presence of a large crucifix on one wall and a discreetly placed picture of the current Pope, surrounded by a phalanx of nuns, suggested the religious nature of the work overseen from here. Mother Mary glanced up from the paperwork and retractable computer screen on her desk.

"Come in, Sister. Sit down."

The young nun took a seat in the hard wooden chair before Mother's large but unadorned desk. Although nothing in her dress distinguished Mother Mary from any other Missionary of Charity, when she looked up at Sister Vena the Reverend Mother's demeanor possessed an aura of serenity, self-assurance, and command that Vena found daunting. Mother Mary's clipped, slightly Spanish-accented English only strengthened that impression.

"What if I were to tell you we've been presented with something that might restore many of the poor and suffering we work with to a healthier, more livable state?"

"I'd welcome that—if it proves to be true."

"Yes. That's the question, isn't it? It's the question I intend you to answer for us, Sister."

"How would I do that? This is the first I've heard of such a thing."

"Not a thing. A proposal. From a company called Protean Pharmaceuticals. A local representative of a much larger concern, Spires Biotechnologies, contacted us about it. I'm no stock-trader, but I suspect Spires Biotech has a growing interest in this Protean concern. Be that as it may, they wish our help in conducting a series of trials. They're working with new treatments for neurochemically based mental disorders. An array of 'prionoid neuromodulators'—that's what they call them."

Mother Mary paused, peering at Sister Vena, looking for some reaction. The young sister's head was already awhirl with questions.

"How do these prionoids work? What's the action in the nervous system?"

Mother Mary smiled slightly. She raised her hand in the gesture that, in a statue of Shiva, would have meant "Rest assured" and signified the unquestionable power of divinity overseeing and underlying all things. The impression that Mother Mary was momentarily incarnating an aspect of Shiva was so strong, Sister Vena had to blink it away.

"I don't pretend to understand the biochemistry. The long and the short of it is that they believe these prionoids could, as the result of a single injection, provide lifelong correction of a number of mental illnesses. Protean Pharmaceuticals—with, I gather, backing from Spires—is prepared to make a very generous donation to our work around the world."

"In exchange for . . . ?"

"In exchange for our help in locating likely test subjects for the trials—and the use of our hospital and hospice facilities, here and in Mumbai, for establishing 'baselines' and such. I believe we'll accept their proposal, despite some misgivings I still harbor about this."

"You don't think the treatment is dangerous, do you?"

Mother Mary glanced off into a meditative middle distance.

"Not in a biological sense. In a larger sense, though, perhaps it *is* dangerous. Science and technology as panacea, yet again. Technological solutions for all human problems. Just look at this morning's news—the latest superintelligent biocybernetic system, with however many millions of times the processing power of the human brain. Frankly, I find the idea that machines will save us by making us obsolete just plain *pernicious*. Is there no value in compassionate service to one's fellow human beings? Where is God in an injection? Human problems require *human* solutions. From all sources—not just the technological."

Sister Vena nodded in agreement, though she did not completely agree. If the divine influenced all things, couldn't God also be found in an injection? She said nothing, sensing that Mother Mary, holding her chin thoughtfully, was not yet finished.

"Still, I would be loath to impede any procedure that might genuinely alleviate human pain and suffering. That's why I want you to coordinate with the Protean and Spires people. I want you to realistically evaluate their treatment and its potential."

Sister Vena glanced away.

"I'm honored at the appointment, but—why me?"

The Reverend Mother frowned slightly as she called up items on her screen.

"According to the records I have before me, you trained as a nurse-practitioner and counselor before you joined our Order—isn't that right?"

Sister Vena agreed that it was.

"It says here your studies focused particularly on the 'biochemical bases of neurological and psychiatric disorders.' Is that also correct?"

Sister Vena nodded. Mother Mary gazed fixedly at her.

"What led you to abandon your studies in that area of the health sciences, Sister?"

"I came to believe that many disorders of consciousness were just not reducible to chemical imbalances in the brain."

Mother Mary gave a small, somehow self-congratulatory, smile.

"Could you be a critical yet unbiased observer of these trials I've mentioned?"

Vena balanced her objectivity in scales visible only to her.

"Yes."

"Then you see why I think you're perfect for the job, don't you?" Mother Mary said, handing Vena a smartcard. "This contains an executive summary of the proposal and project, along with the full proposal itself. It also contains links to sites that describe the work in greater scientific detail, as well as all the contact numbers and addresses you'll need. I will expect weekly reports from you by virtual mail. Now, if you have no further questions, I think we should both get busy with our work."

Mother Mary turned back to another stack of documents on her desk and Sister Vena humbly took her leave. Striding through the former temple precincts, she tried to sense the divine ecstatic presence underlying the stones and mortar, but couldn't. In the smelly, grit-blown streets of Calcutta, she walked numbly along, amid the poor with their hands out to her, under a sun hurtful to her eyes after the dimmer light of Mother Mary's office. Clutching the smartcard, she made her way toward the personal rapid transit depot, contemplating the virtues and vices of obsolescence.

10

Seeds Blown Over Water
2065

SIMON LOOKS OVER AT THE SLOOP-RIGGED MOTORSAILER *SEA ROBIN* THAT will take him and the werwoman Guadalupe to the mainland. Bobbing quietly beside the dock, the motorsailer is a dinghy compared to the President's oceangoing yacht *Derceto*, anchored nearby. Still, it's probably bigger than they'll need.

Lupe carries nothing with her—just the clothes Simon's daughters gave her. Did he see a look of disdain flicker over her face as he manhandled his backpack into the boat? He doesn't think he overpacked. In his head Simon runs over again the list of basic survival items he's packed: solar-sheet tent and cookstove, manual water pump/filter unit, lightweight sleeping bag, cooking gear, matches and igniter-drill; telescoping fishing rod and small box of lures, compound bow and hunting arrows; rainwear, a couple of changes of clothes, animal-proof food canister filled with an assortment of dried food; compass, rope, maps of the Intracoastal Waterway and the old highway system; insect repellent, medical kit, an antique Swiss Army knife.

Switzerland. Before the pandemic he traveled there often, particularly to Geneva, where he bought that knife. For a moment he remembers blue sky, white clouds, peaks like gray and black stone teeth dusted with snow, sapphire lakes—some crossed by ferries not all that much larger than *Sea Robin*. What is that country like now? Cities and mountains both empty? Perhaps a few herders or hunters still scratch a living from its mountain valleys and high meadows. Or are those meadows gone? Has the lingering hangover of global warming decimated them? He hopes not. Thank heavens the sunspot-cycle "plateau" or "minimum" kicked in not long before the pandemic. Otherwise, that hangover would have changed the world's climate far more than it already has.

The clearing of someone's throat behind Simon brings him firmly back to the dock, the salt air, the subtropical present. He turns around and sees his daughters—Ruth, Claire, and Vida—with their husbands. Behind them a scattering of their children, his grandchildren, mill about. Farther back is Teyana, his youngest and favorite, with her lover, Brenda.

Behind them, he sees others come to bid him farewell, too. Most are old friends and acquaintances, bearing fruit or flowers—and brave enough to withstand the censure they might incur from being seen in the company of an abjurer. The only real surprise in the small crowd is the presence of Trillia Spires. Then he sees she is accompanied by young Ricardo Alvarez, one of Simon's informal protégés. Simon recalls rumors that the two of them are intimates, despite the President's objections.

Simon reads the looks of sadness and frustration on his daughters' faces. Although they rarely agree about anything, his children are united in their opposition to his self-imposed exile. Not wanting to argue the matter further, Simon opens his arms to his daughters and is inundated by tearful farewells. He half walks, half swims his way backward through the small crowd, shaking hands, giving and receiving hugs and pats on the back, until the human tide washes him back down to the end of the dock once more, beside *Sea Robin*. Teyana wipes away a tear, yet still tries to put a brave face on the situation.

"What are your plans? Where will you go?"

That's the question they've all been wanting to ask, he supposes, but which they have waited until now to bring into the open. His youngest daughter has apparently been designated speaker for the family—and thus for the small crowd of well-wishers, too. Gesturing toward the wer-woman, Lupe, where she sits in the sloop, Simon speaks loudly enough that everyone in the crowd can hear him.

"First I plan to meet my companion's people. Depending on what happens with Guadalupe's people, I hope to visit some other old friends who've gone west over the years. Tomoko Fukuda, for one. She said she was headed for Atlanta. John Drinan, too. Last I heard, he was living near the abandoned spaceport at the Cape. I don't know which of them I'll go see first, if I do, but after that I think I'll head north, up the Atlantic Intracoastal Waterway."

Teyana nods, scribbling down notes on a little pad computer.

"Why there?"

"Before the Collapse, the inland waterway was maintained against rising sea levels and weather chaos by a system of sun-run robotic dredges. They kept the channels clear and shored up the barrier islands. Like the dredges we have here, only more autonomous. No human oversight needed. Some of the older folks here might remember Mark Fornash and Vena Srinagar, too. They planned on using the waterway to go north, after they left these islands—"

"How far north will you go?" Teyana asks suddenly, as if worried her father will just keep heading north until he disappears into the snows around the pole. Simon thinks of references he's heard Cameron Spires make over the years—to Wall Street. To powerful biocybernetic intelligences he hinted might still linger on Manhattan Island. GNOMES— Gödelian Market Evolution something or other. Worth investigating, at any rate. Simon reaches out and clasps his youngest daughter's hand once more.

"No further than what used to be New York City. Don't worry. I'll find my way. Maybe find a nice place to live—maybe an abandoned mansion in the Hamptons—How about that? Things might even change enough that, someday, I'll be able to come back here. Who knows?"

"We look forward to it," Teyana says, eyes shining. "In the meantime we'll do everything we can to make that change happen!"

A murmur of assent spreads through the small crowd—a sound that gladdens Simon's heart. He is caught up once more in tearful goodbyes and farewell embraces. By the time he comes back to himself again, he is half-turned from the wheel of the boat as it eases into the harbor. Looking back through the blur of his pent-up tears, toward an anemone forest of hands and arms waving farewell, he calls "Goodbye!" until he is hoarse, and waves until his arm is sore.

Turning away at last, Simon and his—hostage? passenger?—move out of a harbor grown silent around them but for the occasional clang of buoy bells disappearing astern, and the low whir of the motorsailer's little solar-electric motor. As *Sea Robin* moves onto the open sea, three mermen, coming from the east, leap from the ocean—once, together—then take up positions about the bow, swimming in arrowhead formation where the sloop plows a clean furrow through the water. Lupe frowns.

"What are *they* doing here?"

Simon startles at hearing her voice again. During all the final preparations and farewells at the dock, Lupe said nothing.

"Our escort. They're supposed to help guard us against capture, then tow this boat home once we're in sight of your homeland. I suppose Cameron sent them to keep an eye on us, too."

Lupe gives an indignant sniff. Soon the wind rises and the water grows choppier.

"We should get these sails up," she says, rising to her feet. "We'll make better time with the breeze."

"Right," Simon agrees. The two of them work the rigging and crank up sail. "Thanks."

He wonders a moment at her reasons for wanting to make better time. Is she in a hurry to return to her people? Angling to make the mermen work harder to keep up? Both? Whichever, *Sea Robin* is soon scudding along, toward the Florida coast.

Lupe falls silent again. Simon contents himself with manning the ship's wheel, watching *Sea Robin*'s passage over the waves and the movements of the mermen beneath those waves. Despite his disagreements with Spires and the questions raised by their transgenic modification out of human stock, Simon must admit the Merfolk are a marvel. Much of the work that went into their creation was based on animal models: dozens of species of fish, as well as porpoises, manatees, orcas, great whales. From the almost vanishingly small seeds of "aquatic ape" traits humans possessed from their evolutionary history, Cameron's vision of "genetic and embryonic engineering for improved aquatic bio-efficiency of the basic human form" has caused something quite spectacular to unfold in the Merfolk. Lupe clears her throat as she turns slightly toward him.

"Those were brave words you spoke to your President."

"Which words in particular?"

"About the fountain of youth becoming a stagnant pool. About how there are now three types of humans. Do you really believe that?"

Feeling the ship's wheel against his hands and the wind and salt spray in his face, Simon glances at the compass heading and wonders what he actually *does* believe.

"I suppose I do. Cameron seems to think I've been bewitched by you."

"Have you?"

Simon gazes ahead, moving the ship's wheel lightly in his hands, steering toward the only visible sign of the mainland—the haze of broken clouds floating in the sunshine above an invisible land mass.

"I don't know. I mean, when you gripped my forehead that day, *something* happened, though I can't say exactly what."

"Would you like to try it again?"

"No, thanks. Not while I'm driving."

Lupe's laugh is both childlike and a crone's cackle, at one and the same time.

"Come now! Science is about experience, right?"

"In the proper time and place, yes."

"It's not so different from shapeshifting, then."

"Just the opposite. Science is about *not* shapeshifting. It's about *repeatable* experience. Not about what you believe, or what you hallucinate."

Lupe nods, then shrugs.

"Shapeshifting is not about faith or belief, either. It's about experience. Like science."

"Prove it," he says, taking his hands from the wheel—a gesture his companion immediately misinterprets. Moving faster than he would have thought possible, Lupe appears beside him and catches his forehead in that viselike grip of hers once again, plunging him into the museum of his memory, with all its facts and exhibits.

Yet, even among the facts and exhibits, the strange and hallucinatory persist and will not disappear. Fossil belemnites called Zeus' thunderbolts. Fossil gryphaea shells called devil's toenails. "Ruin marble" patterned like a ruined cityscape, though it has nothing to do with either ruins or cityscapes. The "third eye" space of frontal sinus shared by humans, chimpanzees, and gorillas. The whole loopy feedback relationship between context and content, environment and creature dreaming together new dreams through coevolution—yet opals still dry out, lemmings drown, whales are stranded. No living system is foolproof, not even a hallucinatory one—

Simon finds he has fallen onto the deck. Lupe, her hands no longer on his head, stands staring down at him. Behind her, the ship's wheel stands abandoned for the moment, steering itself without need of a steersman. Simon rubs his eyes and shakes his head.

"Did I lose consciousness?" he asks. Lupe nods and glances away. "How did you do that?"

"Werfolk know a lot about where the soul is, and where it goes."

Simon gets unsteadily to his feet. He knows Werfolk can be fantastically agile—like warrior-monks in the Hong Kong martial arts films he watched as a boy—but he didn't expect it from someone Lupe's age, who is still supposed to be "on the mend" after near-fatal wounding. Taking the wheel once more, he turns their course northwesterly, annoyed that she knocked him out with whatever hoodoo trick it was she played on him.

"What do you mean?"

"The Great Shift. Billions of individual ecstasies—"

"—resulted in global catastrophe. Unprecedented death tolls."

Lupe laughs. Simon glares at her.

"Death is the shift everybody has to do, someday. Many took their last soul-flights during the year of the Great Shift."

"What are you saying? Death is some kind of 'final frontier' of shapeshifting? That's preposterous."

"You old-style folks have never been very understanding toward shapeshifters. Always trying to pin us down, drive stakes through our hearts, shoot us with silver bullets, nail us to crosses, whenever we arose among you. But it's hard to keep a good shapeshifter dead."

"I hardly think Jesus—"

Lupe cuts him off with a sharp look, staring at him before turning to look out over the sunlit sea.

"Don't blame the Shift for death. You old-style people wanted the Big Death for thousands of years before it happened. Apocalypses, Armageddons, aliens and big rocks from the sky wiping out everything. But you were always your own worst nightmare."

"Oh?" Simon asks, losing sight of his compass and its directions as she turns her aged and weathered gaze toward him. "Is that so?"

"You were all waiting for something to go terribly wrong. You weren't disappointed, were you? Overcoming your worst enemies, you *became* your worst enemies—especially on the islands."

Simon remembers the days before the pandemic—too well. Might what she's saying be true? Some unwritten law of extinction karma, by which any species that succeeds by destroying other species must, necessarily, also destroy itself in the end? Must any culture that triumphs by driving other cultures into extinction also inevitably drive itself into extinction?

"Why do you say 'especially on the islands'?"

Lupe walks toward the bow, glancing down at the waves where *Sea Robin* cuts through them, perhaps also at the mermen swimming there.

"That's where the worst of the old ways still hold sway. You islanders endlessly refuse the shapeshift of death—the one we come to know *too soon*. We raid you only because you withhold longevity from us. There is *no war* between us and the Oldfolk who live on the mainland! They have nothing we would want to kill them for. We have nothing they would want to kill us for. What need to kill, when there are already so few human beings, and so much world to share?"

"So few? Even if only one in one hundred survived, there might still be as many as eighty million people left in the world."

Lupe's face draws tight in a quizzical frown.

"Eighty million? The world's a big place, but if people are as sparse everywhere as they are on our shores, I doubt there are *eight* million in the whole world, much less eighty. You've been on those islands too long. You need to get out into the rest of the world and look around."

"That's what I'm attempting to do."

Somehow he doesn't sound like the heroic explorer when he says it—not even to himself. Watching her as she sits there, silent and still but for her hand trailing in the spray off the bow, Simon thinks of Tomoko, the only other woman he has ever known who possessed this much poise and self-confidence.

At the wheel of *Sea Robin*, Simon wonders if perhaps it all began there, on that night, with him and Tomoko passing by the homeless on the Hungerford footbridge. That seems far too tiny a windblown seed from which to reap the whirlwind of the Great Plague and the crashing, overwhelming death of all the world that once was. Still, he cannot help wondering. After all these years, what might Tomoko think of that—if she is still alive, and he can find her?

11

Predator-Prey Relationships
2032

POLICE LIEUTENANT LEIRA LOSABA LEFT JOHANNESBURG'S MAIN POLICE station and crossed Bezuidenhout in early evening light. It had rained earlier that afternoon. The city was scrubbed clean, the dust of a long dry season washed away. Slanting shadows and growing golden twilight around her made the deep canyon of Market particularly beautiful. This evening the city seemed to be living up to its local nickname—"Egoli, the City of Gold"—as if its very streets and towers were made of precious metal flowing in strange sheets and rising in great crystals from the Earth itself.

Lieutenant Losaba's mood, however, was neither golden nor beautiful. Much preferring the analytical challenge of criminal investigation, she detested being assigned duties of an administrative or political nature. Her current duties—entirely political and administrative—were not at all to her liking.

The politics of it was straightforward enough, she supposed. Muggers had been busy around the Carlton Centre, the Garden Court, and Rand International Hotels for so long they had become part of the city's folklore, if not one of its institutions. Recently, however, their activities had spread westward. Tourists (mostly older, wealthy, and white) were being disencumbered of their valuables by robbers (mostly younger, poor, and mixed race) in the very shadow of the Supreme Court building. Thus the need for a younger, up-from-the-streets, mixed race officer like herself to head the anti-mugging task force.

Thinking about what the night would likely hold in store for her, Losaba sighed. Between Becker and West, she stopped to buy hot nuts from a vendor standing behind an elaborately decorated cart. On a flatscreen video just over their heads played the usual noise of talk show junkies confessing their ills, game show monkeys professing their skills—all the poor, sad hypes who had mistaken the needle of publicity for the drug of fame. Only when a newsreader interrupted the chatter to say something about researchers from the University of the Witwatersrand did Lieutenant Losaba give the screen a measure of genuine attention.

"—the most recent Early Man excavations at Sterkfontein," said the Afro-Indian newsman. "Paleozoologists, archaeologists, anthropologists, and graduate students have completed a decade-long research project tasked with determining whether *Dinofelis*, an extinct Big Cat, specialized in killing and eating humanity's ancestors. The researchers' findings, published in today's *Web Nature*, indicate that *Dinofelis* was in fact an obligate 'people eater,' preying upon humanity's ancestors between two and three million years ago."

"From who's extinct and who's doing the excavations," said the co-anchor, a blond woman, "I guess we know who won *that* evolutionary contest."

Lieutenant Losaba tuned out the adfotainment chatter and thanked the street vendor. Continuing along Market, she munched nuts in lieu of the more wholesome dinner she had no time for. Turning onto Diagonal Street, she passed an elderly woman putting away bright clothing and folding down the awnings of her sidewalk shop. A remnant of the *old* Diagonal Street, the lieutenant thought. From her childhood Leira Losaba particularly remembered the shops of the herbalists and traditional healers here, *inyangas* and *sangomas* with their *muti*, counters and walls and ceilings displaying animal hides and tree-bark scrapings, dried flowers and tubers, places dark and rich with earthy smells.

Old days, she thought. The days before the international banks and transnat megacorps bought up all the property for blocks around the Stock Exchange. That newscast, on the latest work at the Sterkfontein Caves—oldest of old days. As a teenager she and her History classmates made trips to the caves at Sterkfontein, Natal Drakensberg, and the Southern Free State. Their teacher was fascinated by the art of the San people, the hunter-gatherers later called Bushmen. Cave paintings depicting tranced-out shamans metamorphosing into eland—and what such art said about San notions of the relationship between spirit world and ordinary reality—had not meant much to young Leira, but at least it was better than another annoying field trip to the Voortrekker Monument.

Halfway along Diagonal, she glanced up at the big Business News sphere, three stories tall and hovering several stories above the street. Breaking news from world markets flashed over and within it, while a silver-haired anchorman, alpha male tribal elder of the global village, narrated the day's events in reassuringly bland style.

"—Fukuda publicly announced today the acquisition of her company, Protean Pharmaceuticals, by Spires Biotechnologies. Protean stock has soared of late, amid rumors that worldwide clinical trials on its patented prionoid technology will soon be successfully completed. The startup has been a prominent takeover target for several of the larger biotechs ever since word of its prionoid research became public."

Print headlines—"Rogue Proteins: From Terror to Therapy" and "Medical Maverick Molds New Cures From Old Killers"—flashed up behind the newshead's narration, along with clips from Tomoko Fukuda's "Profile" in *Scientific American Online*. Watching the image of Fukuda smiling and blushing like a bride at the betrothal of her company to Spires, Leira Losaba shook her head. *That woman's got good reason to smile*, Losaba thought. *I'd smile too if I were far richer today than I was a week ago*.

On the sphere, a box labeled Local Connections opened up, to remind her that Protean Pharm had a presence here in the land of *Protea* and springboks. Not in the botanical gardens or game reserves, but in a program overseen by the University Hospital at its Eton-Rock Ridge facilities. Watching images of socially dazed streetpeople receiving injections in a hospital clinic reminded the lieutenant that police and social welfare agencies had both provided "volunteers" for the Protean program. Coverage of such cooperation and coordination was, unfortunately, sadly missing from the all-too-brief Local Connections report.

Walking beneath and past the hovering news sphere, the lieutenant turned right on Pritchard, headed toward the Supreme Court, thinking about the pharmaceutical program. From what she'd overheard in the staff room, Protean was testing some kind of super mind-straightener. She doubted the myriad problems of this world and its madness could be solved by a shot, in the arm or any other location. Everyone else had tried to solve such problems over the years, though, so why not give the biotechnologists their chance? Their solution couldn't be that much worse than the rest.

By the time she reached the old Cuthberts Building, the lieutenant had concluded that such biotech advances were no threat to her job security. Most criminals she'd encountered, though usually not the brightest lights in a dark night, had been sane and rational enough, in their limited ways. No, it was unlikely in the extreme that anyone would find a cure—prionoid or otherwise—for lawbreaking anytime soon.

"Stop! Dief! Help!"

The words came rapidly in what struck the lieutenant as a stiff and rather oddly accented mix of English and Afrikaans. A tourist? Farther away, Losaba heard police whistles. At the sound of swiftly running feet heading her way, Lieutenant Losaba stepped back into an entryway, out of the runner's direct line of sight. A dark-complected man, young and slight, appeared in the glare of a streetlight, legs and arms pumping hard. Just as the man was almost past, Losaba stepped out and, bracing her feet, thrust her left arm into the runner's path, catching him between chin and throat in a perfectly executed clothesline maneuver.

The thief sprawled onto his back, a woman's purse breaking free from his hand and spewing its contents across the sidewalk and into the street. Almost before the thief had time to know what or who had hit him, Losaba had flipped him over. Locking up both wrists behind the man's back and handcuffing him with plastic zipcuffs, the lieutenant calmly informed him of the nature of the charges against him.

Two young officers—one white, one black, both male—pounded up breathlessly. With their help, Losaba lifted the prisoner to his feet, then turned him over to the tender care of the young officers. They took the captive into their keeping, grave and sheepishly respectful toward their superior officer—and with a bit more pushing and shoving about of the prisoner than was absolutely necessary.

"Egoli is bad Karma, me brud!" the prisoner said to the black officer. "Remember dat!"

The junior officers gathered up the purse and its contents for evidence and headed off in the direction of the mugging victim. Leira Losaba glanced across the street, toward the monumental pile of the Supreme Court building.

Thirty percent of the planet's gold charted its way through this city, she reflected, yet the poor were still mugging the rich in the shadow of the temple of laws. Yes, Johannesburg *does* have some bad Karma to work out, my brother. What need for big toothy cats to prey on us, when we can always be counted upon to prey on ourselves?

Under a moon both rising and waning, the lieutenant felt both disturbed and relieved that her job was only to enforce the laws—not to understand them in all their labyrinthine complexity. She wondered, nonetheless, if she might somehow be squandering her talents. Shaking her head slightly, she walked on, thinking of black miners tunneling beneath the city of gold.

12

On the Horns of a Divinity
2065

FROM HER SEAT NEAR THE BOW, LUPE SQUINTS HER EYES AGAINST THE noon-sharp sun.

"Hey! Ahab! We're coming up on the coast, if you hadn't noticed."

Simon sees it's true, and nods. In moments they are close enough to see that Simon has missed both his possible destinations. He planned to come ashore at the Space Coast cape, where he might still find John Drinan, or further north—the St. Augustine area, from which Lupe and her comrades sailed on their unsuccessful raid.

"If you were intending to hit St. Augustine, then you're too far south. Daytona. See all that white sand?"

Simon checks his map, cursing himself for not packing a smartmap pad instead of this ancient paper foldup. He has managed to arrive at a point almost exactly halfway between his planned destinations. At the densest concentration of old hotel towers, he turns the wheel hard to port and sails into what was once the Daytona Beach municipal yacht basin.

The sleek recreational sailcraft once harbored here are now little more than tangle-masted hazards to navigation. Abandoned hulks broken and piled haphazardly by weather and wave, the once glamorous boats disintegrate crusted plank by crusted plank, half-submerged against the barnacled and musseled remnants of tumbledown piers and rotten docks. It takes all Simon's skill to avoid running aground on the sunken yachts, tugs, and channel boats as he picks *Sea Robin*'s way through the basin and along the channel, toward the inland waterway's land cut.

At least someone showed some forethought before the end: All the drawbridges over the channel have been left to rust in the Up position. Some sort of automatic default setting? The result of human planning?

What that plan might have been Simon cannot guess. Sailing north into a land-cut stretch, Simon realizes they are now fully within the system of the Atlantic Intracoastal Waterway. The signs designating it as such have long since rusted or rotted away, but those etched in stone or concrete can still be deciphered.

Sea Robin skirts sunken craft now and again as they continue up the waterway, but the waterway itself seems to be in remarkably good shape hereabouts, despite decades of neglect. Not much silted up beyond its initial minimum depth of twelve feet. At more than ninety feet wide, there's still room enough to maneuver around the occasional abandoned wreck.

The engineers who restructured the waterway before the plague did more than just rely on the robotic dredges. They made plenty of room in their calculations and projections for barrier-island and wetlands damage, as well as the more general coastal flooding linked to the lost economy's global heating—fading away only now, under the twin cooling effects of civilization's collapse and the sunspot-cycle's low plateau.

Looking outward from the waterway, Simon sees patterns in the way things have decayed. The older asphalt and gravel roads have broken up and grassed over in many spots, but many of the abandoned highways and bridges look passable. What escaped fire in the last days of the old world looks dusty, grimy, and not so sharp at the corners. Concrete *does* rot, cement *does* erode. Structures built for government and commerce are most intact, while those built for private use have not fared as well. Concrete-and-steel government and corporate buildings, hotels, and condominium complexes appear more or less structurally sound, though marred by broken-out windows, by streaming rust and patina stains wherever metal was exposed, by grass and weeds thatching balconies and roofs. Vines and spindly trees clamber up lower levels of façades. Vivid splashes of lichen daub weathered stone with explosions of gray, green, orange, and yellow. Where fire and explosion swept through, broken bones of rusting rebar slowly bleed red dust into daylight.

As *Sea Robin* passes into the sprawling miles of ruined housing developments around Palm Coast, Simon thinks the entire area must have been hit by whirlwinds of fire—and at least one hurricane with associated tornadoes. Rusted or burnt-out remains of cars and trucks stand in unusual resting places, twisted and overturned. In the least damaged of the houses, paint and glass are a hollow wind-whipped memory amid graying or blackening boards riddled with rot and the incursions of termites, ants, and woodborers. The few intact and upright homes passed over by fire or wind are roofed with grasses and weeds and bearded with vines. More homes in the ghost-tracts lean precariously or stand half-collapsed. Broken-out windows stare from them—hollow, empty eyes. Bush and tree canopies poke up between the gapped ribs of exposed trusswork.

Still more houses, utterly collapsed, are little more than vine- and weed-covered mounds. What were once yards and driveways have long since reverted to saltbushes and spartina grass—even mangrove, studded by cypress and palm, in the wetter areas. Other houses, burned or blown away or both, have disappeared down to the weedy slab.

When *Sea Robin* passes out of the land cut and back toward the sea proper, the mermen at the bow brighten, leaping from the water and surfing the boat's bow wake. Simon offers Lupe some of his water—she has drunk all of her own already—and some smoked fish he brought with him in his pack. They eat their spare late lunch as Simon tries to determine their location.

According to his map, *Sea Robin* now stands only a few miles south of the Matanzas inlet. The site is labeled "Marineland" in one of his older maps—an identification confirmed when they pass a rusted plaque. Even now, the area seems curiously rich in sea life—particularly porpoises and pilot whales. Maybe that's what captured the interest of the mermen.

They enter the Matanzas inlet, passing amid storm-battered mangrove and flooded cypress and sabal palms. Simon sees sea turtles and then alligators and—the biggest surprise of all—something he believes is a sea cow, a manatee. If he remembers correctly, the last wild manatees died out not long before the plague. Did Marineland have some captive breeding pairs? Did they escape? Did someone release them, as the severity of the plague became evident? Tomoko, he remembers, was among those people "repatriating" zoo animals, during the chaos of the final days. Whatever the history, Simon is sure there are now manatees in the Matanzas.

They pass what the map labels Rattlesnake Island. Lupe recognizes the bleak, weather-worn stone structure of Fort Matanzas. Sailing through golden late-afternoon light, they follow the Matanzas River through marshy country. The pelicans and cormorants of the coast give way to wading herons and egrets. Further on they are surrounded by swarms of agile, acrobatic birds—swifts and swallows, flashing and flickering, darting and diving in circles and spikes around the sloop. Pursuing the insects rising with evening, the nimble predators are oblivious to the boat, its passengers, and its outriders.

Where the Matanzas River meets St. Augustine Bay, a great ancient fort stands, with high parapets and battlements. Square in shape, it unfolds to arrow points at the corners. From the water, it seems star-shaped somehow.

"Castillo de San Marcos," Lupe says, standing near the bow in sunset light. "The walls are thicker than any two men are tall. My people should be waiting for me here—if they haven't already left."

Within moments, fires appear atop the Castillo at its four arrow points. As the boat draws closer, Lupe lets out a long ululating call. In a moment her wail is answered by several others in return. Hands wave to them from the sections of the walls nearest the fires.

"Your mermen won't get a very friendly welcome. You probably ought to leave them out here."

"Yes. I gather their orders are to stay with the *Sea Robin*. We'll take the inflatable dinghy ashore."

Taking in what little sail they still show and killing the electric engines,

Simon and Lupe coast *Sea Robin* to a stop one hundred yards off the sea wall below the Castillo. One of the mermen—the leader?—spyhops near the stern of the boat. Simon thinks he recognizes the merman as Nereus, one of the first successful merfolk somatotypes, but he isn't sure.

Simon formally tells the merman what he plans to do. The aquatic human nods and dives back into the water, rejoining his two comrades. The three of them wheel together toward the stern and remain there as Simon inflates the dinghy. He and Lupe put it in the water together.

The mermen steady the dinghy. Simon and Lupe load his pack and their oars and themselves into the small boat. Releasing their hold on the dinghy, the mermen vanish. Simon and Lupe take up their oars, paddling toward the shore and the fire-topped battlements of the Castillo as night falls around them.

When they land beside the south edge of the sea wall, the drumming has already started. A torchlit procession of people drumming and clapping gathers on steps leading down to the beach. Two young men run, then wade out to them, pulling the dinghy the last few feet onto shore. Lupe, greeted and hugged by the people on the steps, converses with her folk in a rapid-fire patois that blends English, Spanish, and French, as well as a smattering of words from other languages Simon does not recognize.

He gathers she's telling her side of what happened during the raid. She also seems to be describing Simon's mission to the mainland—and encouraging the others to hold off on any final decision about her hostage until after tonight's welcoming celebration. It's hard to tell, however, because the patois conversations are all shouted over the sound of four drums weaving an intricate, polyrhythmic beat through the night air.

Caught up in the beat, Lupe and the rest of the Werfolk never stop dancing as they move onto the top of the sea wall, then up more steps, to the overgrown parkland surrounding the Castillo. The small mob of Werfolk dancers are dressed in clothes old and new—fabrics and jewels salvaged from the lost world, skins taken from animals alive until quite recently. Although her people are all far younger than Lupe, Simon notes that she dances as energetically as any of them. Together they pass over first one and then a second drawbridge above the Castillo's moat.

Ahead, Simon sees the broad doorway that leads into and through the Castillo's massive limestone walls. He is almost to the doorway when a young dark-skinned torchbearer, dressed in salvaged shorts and an intricately woven feathered cape, sidles up to him from behind. The face-painted young man, jittery as the sensitive flame of his torch, dances nonstop to the rhythm of the drums moving ahead of them.

"Friend, you aren't hearing the spirits of the drums! Here, drink this. It'll help their voices speak to you!"

The young man hands him a calabash aslosh with a liquid Simon can't identify. The idea of swallowing anything that might also in its turn swallow *him*—and perhaps refuse to spit him back out, no matter how thoroughly he vomits the stuff up—holds no small measure of fear for Simon.

"What is it?"

"Soul vine wine! A great aid to our dancing. Tonight we celebrate Guadalupe's return, and honor the spirits of those who died in the raid."

The young man's eyebrows arc up expectantly. Simon gets the message: Drink, or dishonor your hosts and their revered dead. Feeling the fellow's eyes sharply focused on him, he drinks—trying to swallow enough so that he won't offend local custom, yet reluctant to risk imbibing too much of the unfamiliar stuff. It tastes surprisingly sweet and cool. Simon drinks a bit more than might be necessary for custom's sake alone. The initial sweetness of the "wine," however, is deceptive. It has a lingering aftertaste—spicy, then alkaline, then bitter enough to make him cough and squint.

The feather-caped man laughs and slaps him lightly on the back before dancing away down the tunnel. From what Simon can see by torchlight, once through the wall the passageway empties into an open courtyard beyond. Left alone, he hesitates. He could still run back to the safety of the *Sea Robin* and its mermen guards, turn out to sea, and sail home, or at least away from here. . . .

Simon forces down his fears. Taking a deep breath, he follows the man in the feathered cape, or at least the sound of his footsteps dancing away through the passage. Whatever it was he drank, it has no immediate effect. He has not been seized by any sudden overpowering urge to dance, certainly.

When he emerges from the passageway Simon finds he is standing in an inner courtyard or central keep open to the sky. The first stars of evening flicker overhead. The courtyard itself is very nearly a perfect square, except for the broad stairway in the southeast corner, which angles up from interior ground level to the top of the broad east wall and its battlements.

Drumbeats echo from the walls. Lupe's people have lit a bonfire. By its growing light Simon sees that the walls surrounding this inner yard are not quite as featureless as he first thought. Doors and windows open onto the inner yard from all the surrounding thick stonework. A single tall tree rises from the center of the inner yard's weedy lawn. From a stout branch of that tree hangs what looks like a pair of vines or ropes, twisting in a double spiral to the ground. They are joined to each other by rough, stout sticks laid crosswise like rungs. Near the top of the spiral ladder, a rough wooden platform stands wedged into the tree.

With a bounce in his step—the "soul vine wine" must be having *some* effect—Simon makes his way closer to where Lupe dances with snaky, languid movements. His own movements growing more rhythmic, he asks her about the spiral ladder and its platform before she dances away.

"That ladder? That's how Caribs fly into the sky!"

The drumming grows louder and the dancing more frenzied. The effect of the soul vine wine is working on Simon. He's getting caught up with the other participants in the dance—entranced and entrained with the pulsing sound, like them. Somewhere between pure noise and pure music, the rhythm of the drums opens a space into which his body can move—a space into which his body *must* move, in which it cannot choose *not* to move.

None of the drums, however, are as loud as his heart pounding in his ears. Loud, too loud. When he tries to maintain control over what is happening to him—when he tries to hold onto the person he is in his everyday life—his heart beats harder and harder. The tighter he holds on, the more it batters toward oblivion.

The only way he can save himself is to lose control, to let himself go. One moment he desperately fears his heart will give out on him; the next instant he laughs like a child, overcome with rapturous pleasure at what he's experiencing. How did he forget how to laugh like this? His laughter calls him beyond himself, yet still he finds it so hard to let that person go.

Even through the deepest darkness, Simon thinks, some people laugh like children all their lives—which is annoying to those of us who are trying to sleep!

His laughter at the strangeness of that thought overwhelms him. Laughter and dance, drumbeat and heartbeat—all one. His laughter is the wild dancing of his heart, the clapping of his hands, the pounding of his feet to the drums.

If I save myself, I lose myself, he thinks as he convulses smilingly toward the ground. *If I lose myself, I save myself.*

Waves of motion and emotion flood through him as he lies on the ground. Smiling against the powerful pounding of his heart and slow writhing of his body, he remembers what Lupe said about where the soul is, and where it goes. He remembers Mark Fornash, many years ago, telling him individual consciousness rises out of ecstasy, and to ecstasy it returns. Yes, just that.

Bird and animal people stare down at him from increasingly distant heights. He sinks into the earth in a hole the shape of his body. Past roots, past innumerable strata of sand and stone, he sinks. In a cavernous chamber deep underground, the young man who gave him the soul vine wine to drink bends over him. The man in the feathered cape is strangely transformed: left half plumed birdman, right half robustly robotic, muscularly mechanical.

Helped by robotic gnomes, the mechanical birdman whistles and hums as he works on Simon's paralyzed flesh. He severs Simon's arms and legs from his torso, then his head as well. Satisfied with this strangely painless torture, the birdman hangs Simon's head from the ceiling of the underground chamber, in such a way that Simon can view all the gruesome particulars of his own dismemberment—the careful stripping of skin and fat and muscle from bone, of viscera from body cavities.

In a process that is equal parts surgery, alchemy, and metallurgy, the torturer tosses the flesh of Simon's severed limbs and the viscera from his torso into bubbling vats aswarm with biomechanical life. While this strange stockpot simmers, the bodysmith dips Simon's bones one by one into the molten center of an electronic crucible, transmogrifying the bones' blood-streaked whiteness into chrome-glinting metallic alloy and superconducting ceramic.

As Simon disconnectedly watches, the torturing bodysmith and his micromachine helpers reassemble him piece by piece, knitting together his body electric, weaving micromachined circuitous flesh onto glinting cerametallic bone. When at last they come for his head, the torturer grabs it up by the hair and plunges it into vat and crucible.

Simon loses consciousness completely.

When he wakes, Simon hurtles upward out of the ground, past bird and animal people dancing in the firelight. The moon shines above him. *Let's swim to the moon*, sings a voice in his head—lines from an old Doors tune his father loved. *Let's climb through the tide.*

A strange fish, he swims effortlessly through the stream of space and time. Reaching out, his fish fins transforming to amphibian and reptile limbs, to feathered skin, to fingers long and thin, he half flies, half climbs an enormous twisted Carib ladder into a vast tree above the walls of an ancient fortress. The more he climbs up and out of himself, the more he climbs down and into himself. The platform at the top of *this* world is the bottommost floor of the next.

Gazing at the moon over the sea beyond the walls, he flings himself from the tree into the air, into the sky. The winds hold him up, racing beneath him. He speeds across the ocean, climbing through one heaven after another, heaven upon heaven. A moonlit meteor, he shoots across the firmament, coming to a shore and landlocked sea he knows from long ago, then to mountains rearing white in the night. There, in a flower-flooded Alpine meadow of purest springtime, Simon sees the hundred-horned Lord of the Animals, were-stag with a glowing white orb over its forehead between its horns, bright cosmic egg on the horns of a divinity.

He looks into the light, and wonders: Why are ecstasy and death so close together? Then, as if an immense wave rolling just beneath all the blatant surface of things has caught him in its flood, he understands how his plans must change, where he must go, what he must do. And then it isn't he who is understanding, or wondering, or looking, anymore.

13

The Man in the Very High Office Building
2032

THE SPIRES BUILDING IN MIDTOWN MANHATTAN HAD BUT ONE SPIRE, AND Cameron Spires was the only human being who had ever permanently occupied its highest chamber. A graceful soap bubble nearly three stories in diameter, the spherical chamber hung transfixed midway up the building's final spike. The floor of its central living space ran exactly along the equator of the sphere. The walls of that space were thick, weapons-proof polymerized glass extending deep into the mid-latitudes above and below the sphere's equatorial floor. From northern mid-latitudes to north pole, the sphere was opaqued for privacy in the sleeping quarters and master bathroom. From southern mid-latitudes to the south pole stood the equally opaquable kitchen, service, and utilities areas.

Beyond Cameron's virtuality sunglasses the 360-degree panorama of Manhattan towers, Central Park greenscape, and the rest of the New York City hardscape spread fungally away, over the flat world trapped between sea and sky. Cameron couldn't help feeling a bit smug. The view from the highest permanently occupied human residence in the world's tallest building was grand indeed. True, people lived at higher elevations on mountainsides in the Himalayas, and there *were* those space habitat people in cislunar orbit—but he doubted either of those groups could look about them and see so much that was so humanly grand.

Bubble-boy billionaire indeed, Cameron thought, frowning slightly. The media hung that tag on him when he had first put forward the consciously retro plans for this building, the world headquarters for his varied enterprises. The editorial pages had caricatured him as a bubble-helmeted Earth-astronaut, with slicked-back hair and thin mustache, faux-cigarette holder passing in and out of the admission membrane at the front of his headpiece. Cruel and cartoonish.

Those were the only times he wished he'd bought more heavily into the adfotainment media. Not that the adfotainers explained—in terms of

T- and B-lymphocytes, ducts in the thymus glands, or lack of ADA or PNP enzymes—his accident of birth and *why* he preferred isolated environments. No: Far easier to slot him into the "reclusive germophobe rich weirdo" niche. Cameron was in fact not a recluse. He loved to throw great parties, even if he rarely made his presence known at them. That, however, only made him "Gatsbyesque" in the eyes of the media opinion-shapers.

Cameron shook his head. Ah, well—"There is only one thing in the world worse than being talked about . . ." He was the last of the bubble-boys, transitional figure from a world where Severe Combined Immune Deficiency was incurable to one in which it could be cured. Yet *he* tacitly refused to come out of the bubble, to leave the world of isolation in which he'd grown up. That was what really bothered the opinion-shepherds. He had transformed his disease into a lifestyle choice—a change too confusingly individualistic for the herd-thinking masses of humanity to cope with. Most of them never considered that by living in the final high bubble of this sphere above all of them, he was parodying their perception of him—thumbing his nose at it.

Why *should* he come out of the bubble? Yes, he could have. Before Cameron was ten years old, life in aseptic isolation was medically unnecessary for patients with SCID. Yet first his parents and then he himself had persisted in maintaining his "medically unnecessary" isolation. His life was the family experiment—and it had worked.

Cameron's machine-mediated, medically isolated condition sensitized his father, Randolph Spires, on how best to ride first the infotech, then the biotech bubbles, before either of them burst. That had made Dad a millionaire and paved the way for his son—via biocybernetic booms and busts—to eventually become a trillionaire.

"You've got the touch, Cam," his father said, in their last real conversation. "Your success is as much your own as what you learned or inherited from us."

True, he did have the "touch." Unlike the millions of unfortunates caught in the great pyramid scheme—the online "democratizing of investing"—Cameron was never beaten by the market. He could look at almost any mountain range of data and instantly grasp the locations of its peaks and valleys, understand its overall topography. He had not relied on his quirky talent alone, however. In a machine-mediated age (as his father had liked to remind him), many of the best traders in the marketplace were agoraphobic, a term that originally meant "fear of the market-place"—and maybe there was something to fear.

"Paranoids see patterns that aren't there, stock analysts see patterns that are," his father said, "but the step from the latter to the former is a short one. There's a difference between 'betting with the house's money' and 'betting your mortgage on it.' "

Cameron was not above seeking help in seeing the shape of some of those things to come. Help materialized most powerfully in his GNOMES, Gödelian Nonstandard Optimized Market Evolution Systems. A Spires Biotech subsidiary had originally developed such colonies of cellular automata, evolving in biocybernetic habitats, for the purpose of simulating world economic markets. Over the last several years, however, they had grown and fused with quantum biocomputers into something far less prosaic—something unusual enough that even the Tetragrammaton Consortium had expressed considerable interest in it.

Yet—despite all his caution and all his aids, all his investments in pharmaceuticals and nanomedical technologies, in diagnosis and prognosis—his "touch" had not became a healing one until after his father's death, when he was forced to think in that direction, and then put more and more of his considerable resources there. Despite the best that could be obtained from the biotech and nanomed sectors, his father had been dead more than a year now. In the end, the old man had grown tired of the endless organ transplanting and regrowing. He had refused to have a model of his mind transferred to a machine, maintaining (perhaps rightly) that such a construct would not be *him* anymore.

In his father's last days, Cameron had moved both his parents up here, into this high, private aseptic chamber where Cameron felt comfortable enough to shed his environment suit and just be a son to aged parents. Letting them in, however, had let other things in that no environment suit was proof against—events, emotions, memories. The memory of his father's last moments, not least of all. A memory that would not leave Cameron, even now.

Dad's eyes were wide open when they walked into the room Cameron had caused to be partitioned off for him. Through many small sips, his speechless, heavily anesthetized father drank the full container of apple juice Cameron's mother gave him, as if to please her—and it did, very much.

Moments later, the terminally ill man began to make a bruffing sound. Was he trying to say something? Was he aspirating the apple juice and choking?

"I guess we need to be more careful giving him fluids," Mrs. Spires said to the hospice nurse when she came to examine Cameron's father. "So he doesn't choke like this."

"That's not what this is," the nurse said to Cameron and his mother, simply but with the force of urgency. "He is dying. He's going. Come up on either side of him: Now. Hug him. Pray for him. Say goodbye to him as he goes."

Cameron and his mother hurried forward. They hugged his father and held his head. Across the bed his mother cried, "We love you! We love you!" Cameron said, "Love you, Dad." The nurse muttered a steady stream of prayers, in which "Jesus" was the most often repeated word. As they prayed their goodbyes to Randolph Spires, Cameron closed his own eyes and pressed his head to his father's.

Into his mind flashed images of a silver-haired but healthier Randolph Spires, proclaiming the family motto—"The only sure thing is, there's no sure thing"—and laughing. Images of the automobile crash that claimed his grandfather's life (and very nearly Cameron's own) a third of a century back. Images of his own ten-year-old son, William, living *outside* the bubble, and being raised at a distance by his mother.

Then it was done. Cameron and his mother stepped back in silence. When the last breath was gone, there was only open-mouthed, slack-jawed death. His father was there, yet he was gone.

Even now Cameron could not really make sense of what happened to his father—and what would happen to him, if mortality continued to have its way. His ability to read the patterns in the Big Flow of the human infosphere might not have enabled him to make sense of his father's death, or the eventual prospect of his own, but he could not deny that he was well-acquainted with mortality.

After his father's passing, Cameron began to invest heavily and directly in the more exotic longevity technologies—an investment strategy that was at last paying off. The ability to greatly extend human longevity lay within his grasp—and it was a terrible burden. Looking out over the vast city and its enclosed garden of parkland, he knew he would have to make a decision.

The larger object of his wealth and power, Cameron thought, was to help get humanity back to the garden. Restoring to them the immortality they had supposedly lost there, however, would also paradoxically drive them farther from the garden than ever. Where humans go, extinction and desertification follow—anyone with a sense of history could see that.

He knew his fellow mortals all too well: squabbling about which should come first—the wealthy consuming less or the poor having fewer children. About "whose rights?" and "whose choices?" Consoling themselves that despite the continuing increase, in absolute terms, of human population and global warming, the *rate* of increase was dropping. But Cameron had the best deck chair on the *Titanic*. From where he sat it was clear the big boat was not being steered away from the big berg fast enough. The hull-ripper was coming for this ship of fools.

Cameron knew a thing or two about booms and busts. A large generalized increase in human longevity would only shorten the time to tragedy. High population levels *plus* high birth rates *plus* high material consumption *plus* greatly increased longevity could only equal catastrophe. That equation had to be changed. One or more members of that Unholy Quaternity would have to be removed from the left side of that calculation. If not, then the ensuing catastrophe would cause incalculable human suffering, perhaps even the extinction of the human species. How much suffering *now* would be worth it to stave off that greater suffering—even that permanent oblivion—later?

That was the great question. Looking away from the windows and into his virtuality shades, he had the personal archival system in his headplug play back the section of his memoirs he was working on before his thoughts wandered past the boundaries of his ensphering bubble and into the larger world:

"Progress, in human affairs," he heard his tooth-miked voice say softly, "consists of abolishing a manifest atrocity and replacing it with what will eventually be seen as a more subtle atrocity. Cultures dependent on slavery, for instance, give way to cultures dependent on wage-slavery. Societies, composed as they are of imperfect human beings, will likely never achieve the perfect or ideal ethical state. That, however, should neither prevent nor excuse us from trying to create societies that are better and better approximations of that ideal state. The point is not that we will not fail along the way, but rather that, along the way, we will learn to fail better."

That "fail better" part was good. He once heard one of those orbital-habitat idealists say something along those lines, but in a *very* different context. Of course. He thought such idealists naive fools—as surely as they considered realists like him selfish Machiavellis. Thinking of idealists reminded him of Tomoko Fukuda, and of the "obvious good" offered by the prionoid technology from her company (and his recent acquisition), Protean Pharmaceuticals. Pondering it, he realized that prionoid tech might offer the potential of a non-obvious good as well—to those who thought long range, as he himself did. He was not the only one anxious about the prospects for humanity as a whole, after all. Others too were concerned with the long-term survival prospects for the species, Tetra-grammaton's Dr. Vang not least of all.

Still, good doctor Vang's work with the wheels-within-wheels of Project Medusa Blue and the Tetragrammaton program was rather old-paradigm, Cameron thought. Only to be expected, given Tetragrammaton's roots in the ancient days of the Cold War and the depth-survival studies performed by the intelligence agencies of that time. Dr. Vang was rather old-paradigm and Cold War, too. In his mind's eye Cameron saw that little man, well into his eighties, his thin gray hair and spectacles making him look rather like a doddering grandsire. Having on occasion run afoul of the old man's shrewdness and tenacity, however, Cameron knew nothing could be further from the truth.

Over his tooth-mike, Cameron Spires commanded the wireless Web access in his headplug to display in virtual space summary records regarding Ka Vang. The audiophone in his mastoid bone purred a narration to match what Cameron saw in shadespace.

Yes, Cameron thought as he watched and listened to it. Vang was indeed the fullest embodiment of what Tetragrammaton and Medusa Blue were about. A living fossil—and damned persistent, just like those organizations. Tetragrammaton, first as "program" and now as "Consortium," took a different tack on the Unholy Quaternity problem than Cameron did. Provide essentially unlimited space for human numbers to expand into, the Tetra types reasoned, and then it wouldn't matter how many people there were, or how fast they were breeding, or how long they lived, or how much material they consumed—so long as they could always get away to somewhere else at greater than the speed of light.

Tetragrammaton's attempts to create a seamless mind/machine interface, and thereby make human and machine intelligence co-extensive, were quite laudable in their way, Cameron supposed. The program's larger design, however—to create, through that intimate entangling of human and machine intelligence, an information density singularity, a gateway into and through the fabric of space-time—*that* was a long shot indeed. When it came to coping with matters as grossly physical as the mass movements and migrations of human bodies through deep space, Cameron had his doubts about that approach. He suspected the speed of light limit would remain an unbreachable wall.

Still, it pays to hedge one's bets. That was why he kept in touch with Vang and the old depth-survivalists. Tetragrammaton had some interesting human intelligence assets, too. He called up several of their "humint" profiles—particularly the more exotic and esoteric types—into his shade-space virtuality: Martin Kong, a.k.a. Phelonious Manqué, Web wizard of the Myrrhisticinean cultists, long since imprisoned in Silicon Bay for causing the Black Hole Sun disaster at Sedona. Michael Dalke, a.k.a. Hugh Manatee, livesuited brain-damaged crime victim, floating manatee-like in a neutral buoyancy tank beneath one of Retcorp and Lambeg's corporate buildings in Cincinnati, his reconstructed neurophysiology locked directly into the infosphere in the fullest integration of human and machine yet achieved. Roger Cortland in the orbital habitat, keeping an eye on things there for Tetra—especially on Marissa Correa's longevity and anti-senescence work. Dr. Lydia Fabro of the Page Museum and La Brea Tar Pits too, who claimed to have unearthed a uniquely advanced form of microtechnology—in an artifact considerably older than human agriculture, cities, or civilizations. . . .

Cameron Spires smiled. Quite a rogues gallery. Tetragrammaton talent scouts were adept at patrolling the bleeding edge and fraying fringe to find such people. And *things*, too. Into his shadespace he called up recent

Tetragrammaton reports. For some time now the Consortium had been all aglow about a class of biochemicals—"supertryptamines"—isolated from an obscure South American fungus. Maybe Tomoko Fukuda's conformation-altering prionoids could be of help to the Tetragrammaton people and their mind/machine jiggery-pokery: Trick the brain into generating its own supplies of supertryptamines, pump up mental energy to the point where mind could effectively communicate with machine—something like that.

He owed Tetra something, at least. His Tetragrammaton connections had clued him in (via Roger Cortland) to Marissa Correa's promising work in the orbital habitat. On his shadescreens Cameron called up his extensive and graphics-laden file on Correa's efforts. Her work with telomerases, with telomere stabilizers that didn't induce cancer, with extra engineered copies of so-called Methuselah genes, particularly DNA sequences for making free-radical absorbers like superoxide dismutase—all very innovative. Of course, Correa's work on a delivery system for her antisenescence factors—"finding intron and pseudogene locations" where her *"viral vector* could safely splice in manufactured coding"—*that* was way behind the curve.

"Viral vector" indeed. How very like a biologist to think in terms of such an outmoded approach. Specialists so often missed the point, especially when the point was to swap advances among different disciplines. It's all about permutations and combinations, he thought. Discoveries from biology and chemistry, hooked up with synthesis and fabrication tools from engineering and physics. What those in the know called *binotechnology*—tech "bio" and "nano" and deeply "info." When he first heard the term Cameron thought it sounded like something done *by* or *to* very pale people with pink eyes, but he'd soon enough grown used to it.

If he could only foster in more minds what he so prized in his own: the ability to think outside the accepted disciplinary confines and methodological boxes. All the best work comes from transgressing the accepted boundaries, Cameron thought. The transgressors were the first ones who went transgenic, rejecting entirely the notion of species as anything more than bundles of genes. When they were the first to put fish genes in tomatoes or squid genes in corn, their opponents had thought them Frankensteinish, but it was true pioneering work.

Just as his own application of Correa's mortality and longevity ideas would also prove pioneering. In a fitting tribute to his father's memory, Cameron had set a research team to "adapting" an idea from one of Vang's pet companies—Crystal Memory Dynamics' quantum-size-effect binotech, its "self-assembling crystal memory matrix." The Tetra types hoped to use that for mind/machine communication, but Cameron's team hijacked that same tech for medical repair at the DNA level. The life extension possibilities were enormous.

No honor among thieves—or mad scientists, Cameron reflected with a wry smile. Using Fukuda's prionoids to get around the protein-folding problems, to scale up from quantum-level to macro effects, would be even more daring. He spoke a quick sotto voce note to himself, to avoid losing the insight.

Sitting back, he pondered the dangers inherent in his syncretic and synthetic approach. A dark potential lurked there, unavoidably. But how much risk now would provide how much benefit *later*?

That question, again. Somebody had to think long-term and globally about humanity. Think realistically about how long Earth's ecosphere could sustain human impacts before it reordered itself in a way that didn't include human beings. Not even Tetragrammaton was doing that. If "somebody" turned out to be him, so be it. If large numbers of people had to die, it would still be worth the cost if he could ensure a more sustainable long-term prospect for the human species—and a longer life for himself.

I'm far-sighted enough to want to save the human species from itself, he thought. And short-sighted enough to think the human species actually matters in the grand cosmic scheme of things. My blessing, and my curse—if either "blessings" or "curses" have any reality.

Cameron composed a virtual mail to Dr. Vang, with information about Fukuda's prionoids and their possible usefulness to Tetragrammaton. Once he'd completed and sent the v-mail, he dictated, in a quiet undertone, more material for his memoirs.

"Progress consists merely in having to go down to finer and finer resolution to discern human evil."

He sat back thoughtfully in his chair, pondering at what degree of resolution the distinction between good and evil became impossible to detect, and therefore irrelevant. "Evil" and "good" were just bundles of ethical questions dependent on context, the way "species" were just bundles of genes dependent on environment. Such categories had no intrinsic reality. He wondered when the rest of humanity would get around to realizing that fact.

In the city below him, the lights of evening and Christmas were coming on. The days had grown so short, now. His gaze traveled around his bubble once more. Bubbles and bundles. Booms and busts. Something tentative about all of them. Even this impaled bubble, solidly made though it was, sometimes felt as if it had only paused here before flying higher into the sky.

Bubbles are always full of surprises, he thought with a smile. The most surprising bubble, though, would be the one that never burst—and only flew higher, endlessly.

14

New Variant
2065

TRILLIA CAN SCARCELY BELIEVE HER EYES. PROTESTERS' BOATS CUT HAPhazardly back and forth across the harbor, beneath a deceptively peaceful blue sky. The ragtag crowd on the pier ahead of her carry placards reading AMNESTY FOR ALL ABJURERS and NO MORE DEATHS FOR LONGEVITY! Still others bear banners saying WAR AGAINST THE WER GETS US NOWHERE and OPEN NEGOTIATIONS NOW! Trillia feels disoriented, as if one of her dataneedle historical records has come to life and she has become trapped inside that life.

What's worse is seeing how prominent a role Ricardo is taking in all this. His lean, dark-haired form moves everywhere throughout the crowds, organizing them and whipping up their enthusiasm. He calls chants on one of those portable amplification devices which—for reasons she has yet to fathom—were once called bullhorns. Where did he manage to find such a thing? Trillia has never before seen one, except in media from the lost days.

Standing on the periphery of the protest with other interested observers, Trillia realizes with a pang that Ricardo is now a leader among the small (but increasingly vocal) group of islanders discontented with her grandfather's rule. Though it's happened fast, still she wonders why she didn't see it coming. Grandpa Cameron's disapproval of her relationship with Ricardo is at the center of her blindspot—but there's something more, too.

Since Simon Lingham's departure, Ricardo has been spending a lot of time with the rest of the Lingham clan. Jealous, she suspected Ricardo of having an affair with someone in the family. Watching him with the bullhorn now, however, she realizes Ricardo's mistress is a newfound passion for politics. Trillia is not as relieved by this realization as she might have hoped.

"Look!" Ricardo calls over the bullhorn, field glasses to his eyes, "The Merfolk escort Spires sent is returning! They've just entered the harbor, towing the boat Simon Lingham was aboard when he went into exile—see? Let's let them know we haven't forgotten him, or them!"

A shout goes up from the small crowd, and from the protesters' small flotilla of boats. Soon the crowd's roar, guided by the bullhorn-wielding Ricardo, becomes a chant of "Report to us! Report to us!" The crowd moves as a body, reaching the *Sea Robin*'s docking slip at the same time the mermen guide the crewless motorsailer into it. Four protesters' boats hem in the motorsailer, but the mermen slip away from the crowd and boats as if oblivious to their presence.

Teyana Lingham gestures to Ricardo for the bullhorn. He passes it to her.

"The Merfolk won't come to the surface and talk to us but our questions are surfacing anyway!" Teyana announces. "My father raised a few of them: Why—a third of a century after the pandemic—do we still remain cut off from the rest of the world? Why do we act as if the plague is still rampantly contagious and infectious, when that's not the case? Why is it we can greatly extend our own life spans, even bio-engineer the Merfolk, but can't overcome those effects of the pandemic that still linger? We need answers. I say, let's march to the Golf Parliament to get them!"

Like children of Hamlin following a bullhorn-toting Pied Piper, the small crowd cheers and chants as it follows Teyana. Ricardo is temporarily reduced from general to foot soldier in the line of march. Trillia approaches him, touching him on the shoulder, hoping he will stop to talk with her. He turns toward her, slowing but not stopping.

"Ricardo, how much of this sudden political fervor of yours is personal? You and me—and Grandpa's opposition to you and me?"

Ricardo gives her a searching look for a moment, then glances away. He strides along to keep up with the march, forcing Trillia to do the same. He almost has to shout to be heard over the chanting.

"It's bigger than that now. Simon Lingham was right. He said what a lot of people were already thinking. It's time for a change."

"What kind of changes do you want?"

"Amnesty for the abjurers. Negotiations with the Werfolk. A longevity-for-peace deal, to end the raiding. You're the headplugged historian, Trill. 'Cold wars' and 'low intensity conflicts' can't go on forever."

She's tempted to correct him with instances of the Thirty Years War and the Hundred Years War, but then thinks better of it.

"You can help us, Trill."

"How?"

"Talk to the President. He's your grandfather—and you're his favorite."

She stares at him, annoyed.

"And if I pressure him to consider amnesty for the abjurers, if I nag him to negotiate with the Werfolk, how long do you think I'll stay his 'favorite'?"

Ricardo tries to shrug indifferently.

"How far you're willing to go is your call. The least you can do for us, for these islands, is pump your grandfather for any information or speculation on Simon Lingham's travel plans. Simon was his chief lieutenant for a long time. Maybe the President was privy to his lieutenant's thoughts about the mainland."

Trillia comes to a dead stop, forcing Ricardo to do the same.

"And my grandfather will also just *happen* to be the one who gets the report from the mermen he sent to escort Lingham. Which is what you just *happen* to really want to know."

Trillia turns away from Ricardo, shaking her head, infuriated that he could think of exploiting her family connections this way. She hears Ricardo breathing quietly behind her, hears him inhale as if to say something, but then hears only his footsteps turning and striding away to catch up with the other marchers.

Fine, she thinks as she begins walking home. *He's made his decision. I've made mine.*

Still, she doesn't stop worrying, not even when she gets home. Over the next several hours, Trillia can't help following Island Net's coverage of the march's progress, and then of the protest outside the Golf Parliament. Most of the camouflage-clad security forces setting up a perimeter around the Parliament are Island Patrol officers—trained to fight raiders from without. The swiftness with which they are reassigned to address this perceived threat from within, however, makes Trillia uneasy.

When the marchers attempt to breach the perimeter, the security forces on horseback wade in among them, striking out with nightsticks and batons. Other officers, on foot, begin firing wooden dowels into the marchers, then smoke, gas, and tangleweb grenades.

Trillia shuts off the net and its images of chaotic melee. Fearing for Ricardo's safety in that mess, she cannot bear to watch any more of it. The nightmare of history has come around again, waking these islands up to madness, as it last woke the whole world during the pandemic.

Numb, she sits in the denlike mediary of her family's home, silent among all its records—its books, tapes, disks, cards, needles. Staring at the racks and repositories of all that history, she wonders again and again what makes a dream become a nightmare. Wonders if she can wake from this nightmare into anything other than death. Wonders if there might be a different type of waking life, one that doesn't include these ignorant armies clashing in broad daylight.

Her personal phone chimes in soft alarm at her shoulder. When she answers, it's Ricardo, asking if she'll come down and bail him out of the holding pen set up for those arrested in the riot, in a square not far from

Parliament. Thank God he's not hurt, she thinks, even if he does sound more nervous than she expected.

Trillia's trip to the temporary holding pen and infirmary is a blur. Somehow she arrives at a scene of waiting, punctuated by reunions both tearful and shamefaced. The newly released prisoners seem lost, disoriented by what has happened to them, returned to a familiar world they no longer recognize.

After interminable bureaucratic wrangling—far more than that involved in the release of the other prisoners, it seems to Trillia—Ricardo is at last turned over to her. In silence they walk along the street, away from the square. She guides him toward the nearby restaurant district for coffee. Ricardo is so downcast—at once so anxious and depressed—that Trillia feels she must comfort him.

"Hey, cheer up. There'll be other riots—I mean 'protests.' "

"No. Not for me."

"What do you mean?"

"You remember when I had my regular physical exam the other day? The one I kept putting off and you kept nagging me about?"

His digression annoys Trillia. By island law everyone has to get a full medical exam every six months.

"So?"

Ricardo pulls a computer printout from his pocket and shows it to her.

"The guards processing me happened to spot a brand-new red flag in my records. My cytology results. According to which I have begun 'manifesting initial signs of the Wer.' "

Such news, if true, would be devastating: Under New Bahamian law, those unfortunate enough to show Wersign must suffer banishment or execution. But no—it can't be true. "Latents" possessing only partial immunity to the plague are rare enough in these islands. They *always* show increased prionoid numbers in their blood and cerebro-spinal fluid by the time they reach their early teens, too.

"What? That's impossible. You're too old."

"Not according to *this*. A new variant, they call it."

"There has to be some mistake—"

"If it's a mistake, then it's a *convenient* one, don't you think? I wonder if this is how your grandfather will get rid of *all* his opponents."

Trillia steers the morose Ricardo through the flower-decked front gate of a coffee shop and onto its tiled patio. Above them, sunset paints wisps of cloud pink and orange.

"I refuse to believe that. It's a mistake. We'll get it taken care of."

As they sit down at a table together, Trillia squeezes Ricardo's hand and stares deeply into his eyes, hoping she looks and sounds more self-assured and reassuring than she actually feels.

15

Thoughts of a Rainy Sunday Morning
2033

GLANCING OUT THE SLIDING GLASS DOOR ONTO MARK'S SCREENED-IN patio, John saw Ozymandias, quiet but alert, his head on his paws. Behind the big dog, four young drummers—two male, two female, all in their late teens—still managed to twitch out staccato, percussive rhythms, despite their closed eyes and more than eighteen hours' drumming. Beyond them lay Mark's privacy-fenced tract-house yard, tan winter-dry grass just starting to green up with the arrival of the long-awaited rains to SoCal. A pair of struggling citrus trees stood sentinel above wilty roses in the light of a gray and dripping morning. Mark Fornash gestured at the wall screen above the couch where Malika Hardesty lay sleeping, calling John's wandering attention back into the house.

"See? I know I'm good at shamanizing, but I *told* you the drum circle was growing a lot faster than I expected. Faster than my most *optimistic* expectations. Not just here, either. Look at this stuff on the news."

From where he sat slumped in an old rocking chair, John paid more attention to the wall screen. Trance drumming seemed to be spreading like crazy all over the world. Mark's eyes were fixed on the screen.

" 'Rhythmania' is what they're calling it. That's just a name, though. Not an explanation."

"Some kind of fad? A craze of some kind?"

"More like an obsession. Been building every week for almost a month.

I don't know if you took a count, but we had over sixty people out there drumming last night, before the police came. If that emergency call hadn't interrupted their visit, we'd be in jail, like as not—"

John remembered the police coming by. The two officers who banged on the door were still in the macho chest-thrusting stage, harassing Mark about the noise from the Drum Circle, when their shoulder-radios blared. One of the cops gave a ritual curse about the "damn full moon" before he and his partner swung inside their vehicle and sped away. John saw it was true. The moon behind them was bright enough to read by. The clouds hadn't come in yet.

"—least twenty people crashed on floors and beds and chairs all over the house. Hey, look at the screen! I know that place! It's right near here!"

Mark clicked up the sound enough for them to hear. A reporter narrated how, last night, "masked hooligans" swept into a twelve-block area and smashed every surveillance camera they could find. Records from various scenes of attack showed masked figures carrying ladders and step-stools, drumming with axes and hammers on cameras and audio-video bubbles before the much-abused machines recorded their own demises. Judging from the footage, minimarts and convenience stores were particularly hard hit.

No looting was reported. The motive for the destruction was "apparently political." Someone had taped a hand-lettered sheet to the front door of a minimart whose heavy concentration of surveillance gear had suffered particularly extensive damage. SMASH THE SURVEILLANCE MACHINES! ABANDON THE CITIES! LIVE YOUR OWN MYTH! read the note. No Web, phone, or street contact address, John noticed. The people who had carried out the machine-smashing must have been seriously anarcholuddite. Or seriously spontaneous.

"Hope their own myth includes bow-hunting and fly-fishing."

On the screen the reporter speculated as to whether the wave of machine-smashing was related to the severe damage at PUERCO, the firm up in the center of the state that specialized in surveillance cameras and monitoring devices for police and security forces—or to a fire in a drug-testing laboratory much nearer at hand, at about the same time. Mark brightened.

"Maybe that's what pulled the cops away from our doorstep. The timing would have been about right."

The scene on the screen switched to coverage of the local drumming mania, with percussionists pounding everything from doumbeks and gongs and slit drums to pots and pans and antique plastic Tupperware bowls. Drum Circle spokesfolks busily denied any connection with vandals or vandalism. Mark grew positively gleeful.

"I wouldn't bet on *that*. Maybe no direct connection, but drumming and damaging are up, in all the big cities. It's a percussion epidemic!"

Mark lowered the volume on the wall screen again. John shook his head. His own life had finally begun to return to some sort of order. Thanks to the testing program, he had a roof over his head. He'd traded in his grungy spacer coveralls and heavy boots for civilian slacks and shirts and walking shoes. He still wore his maroon knit cap, but both the cap and his hair were a good deal cleaner now. Denying all that old parallel-universe alien-mind weirdness had been working better and better for him lately, thank you. He didn't know how long the support would last into this new year, but he was already grateful to the program. It had helped him clean up his act and get his head screwed on straighter than it had been in years.

And now Mark, the same guy who had hooked him up with his new life, was telling him that just when he'd started to go sane, the world had chosen this time to go crazy? He didn't want to hear that kind of noise. Not right now, and not any time soon.

"The only 'epidemic' I've heard about is the usual flu coming out of wherever it is this year—Asia or India or Australia. Nothing unusual about that."

He recalled the visit of one of Tomoko Fukuda's esteemed scientific colleagues, Dr. Robert Wong Tung-Shing of Spires Biotech, who'd come to the clinic to look over the prionoid trials. John didn't know who gave what to whom, but by the time Dr. Wong flew back to Hong Kong everybody in the program was down with some bug, including Yang. A nasty one. Made people puke and shit for twenty-four hours—even made them pass out, albeit only for a few seconds at a time. Poor T. S. Wong probably spread the little beastie to more than a few of his fellow passengers on the flight home.

"Maybe the epidemics are related . . . ?" Mark suggested, half seriously. They stared at the wall screen, which now showed coverage of an enormous religious revival featuring Christian pop music. The audience swayed, eyes closed and hands raised, fervently whispering "Amen!" and "Thank you, Jesus!" Moved by the spirit, others in the crowd spoke in tongues, quaked and shook, fell swooning to the ground. A lot of his peers in the program had gotten religion of late, so John watched the report with interest—until Mark, muttering, clicked the wall screen off.

"Yeah, yeah. God is my favorite special effect too."

John tried to return to their earlier conversation.

"Last I heard, wanting to bang a drum—or go to church—wasn't a symptom of flu or the common cold."

Mark stretched his arms toward the ceiling and turned his back to the wall screen.

"Behavioral epidemics have happened before. Mass psychoses. Great Fears. Great Awakenings. Witchcraft hysterias, dancing manias . . ."

"Caused by bad rye bread."

"Ergot poisoning of grain, you mean? That explains some of them, I suppose. I think this may turn out to be different, though."

"Oh?"

"I've been studying shamanism for a *long* time—"

John rolled his eyes.

"The Four D's again? What is it with you and that stuff? Too many after-party nights, where *every* vehicle you see on the way home is a police car?"

Smiling despite himself, Mark sat down on the edge of the couch where Malika slept.

"More than that. More than just drumming, or dancing, or dreaming, or drugging. That's all part of something deeper. A shamanic complex, at the root of human consciousness. An ancient, psychophysical pattern. A deep archetype, if that doesn't sound too mystico-simplistico for you. It's been lost to us for a long time, but it's still there, in all of us. Maybe this percussion epidemic is the chance to 'come out and play' it's been waiting for."

In his time he'd been crazy, and maybe he still was, but John thought he recognized self-serving nonsense when he heard it.

"Wait a minute. You're saying 'rhythmania' is part of this 'complex'? We're all going to be drumming, then dancing, then dreaming, then drugging?"

"Maybe not in exactly that order, and maybe not all the steps, but something like that, in the early stages."

John shook his head.

"Sounds like what the psychs in the program call 'projecting' your experiences onto the entire world. Just because *you* may be suffering from some kind of 'shamanic complex' doesn't mean everybody else in the world is, too."

His wild-eyed, gray-haired, goateed friend laughed and jumped up in a brief satyr's dance before settling down again.

"If I be shammin' when I say I'm a shaman, that'd be shamin' to my mom and dad's memory! My personal shamanic complex notwithstanding, though, the Four D's are important because they lead to the Two Big S's."

Mark Fornash plopped down cross-legged on the floor, smugly crossing his arms. John fought the temptation to make a low joke.

"Okay, I'll bite. What Two Big S's?"

"Shapeshifting and soul-flying."

"*What?*"

"The more I've studied hunting-gathering cultures, the more I see links between shamanism and shapeshifting."

"You mean like werewolves? That kind of thing?"

"Not the low-budget horror version you're thinking of. Dracula and Batman and the Wolfman are all just distant echoes of the Shaman and Hu-man thing. Ecstasy technicians who talk to animals, become animals, leave the body and aerial-voyage. Shapeshifting, Shamanism, and the Origins of Human Consciousness!"

Mark got up and strode over to one of the floor-to-ceiling shelves that lined two of the room's walls, housing media from books to dataneedles. John looked at him quizzically.

"And you think this shamanic complex is inside *all* of us?"

"Always has been. The way we were . . . wolves, were . . . jaguars. Were-bear berserkers and Beowulf. Were-bats and were-elk. Here, I'll show you."

From a shelf he selected a tall, thin, time-worn book. As Mark opened the volume and paged through it, John saw it was called *The Shamans of Prehistory*. His friend shoved the book at John, pointing to a photo and accompanying caption on page 69.

"This is it. At least 15,000 years old. From Les Trois Freres Cave in France. Everybody agrees it's a figure of a shaman. The archaeologists and anthropologists call it The Masked Sorcerer but that's just wrong."

"How so? 'Masked Sorcerer' describes it pretty well, to me."

"It's not 'masked' to look like a stag or an elk. It's *transformed* into one, into something half-human, half-animal. Look at the hands, the legs. They may be moving in a dance, but they're also *paws* and *haunches*. Look at the face. Not the antlers and ears—the oversized, spooky eyes staring out at you, see? The artist who made that fully believed the shaman, in ecstasy, *became* a were-elk. It may well have been the shaman who *painted* it, too."

Mark snatched back the book, turned pages quickly, and gave the book back to John.

"Most images of 'masked' shamans are depictions of were-creatures. Try this one. Page 46. From the same cave. It could almost pass for a straight painting of a bison—except that it's walking on two legs and playing a musical instrument. 'The small sorcerer with the musical bow' is part human, part bison—a were-bison. Paleolithic Europe, the Kalahari Desert, the Australian outback, all over Old Siberia and the New World—it doesn't matter where. You find this link between shamans and shapeshifting all over the planet."

John stroked his beard and leaned back farther in his chair, glancing off into the space of speculation.

"Okay, but even if shamans *could* transform themselves into these, um, human-animal composite beings, what makes you think this 'shamanic complex' applies to everyone—and not just to the shaman?"

Mark, finger pointing skyward in emphasis, was obviously ready for just such a question.

"Because the vast majority of shamanic cultures also have a tradition that, in a bygone era before the world fell into decadence, *all* members of the tribe were able to do everything only the shaman can do now. *Everyone* used to be able to talk with animals and become animals through shapeshifting. Anyone could leave the body and aerial voyage in this world, or visit spirits in the lower and upper worlds."

The fervor he heard in his friend's voice surprised John.

"You believe their myth is actually true?"

"I believe the past leaves traces. Since I met you and Malika on Halloween, I've been thinking a lot about the fractal self-similarity stuff she mentioned."

John did not see the connection.

"And?"

"The old biologists may not have been exactly right in suggesting 'ontogeny recapitulates phylogeny,' but the course of an individual organism's biological development may still represent, in some data-compressed or fractal form, the evolutionary development of that organism's entire species."

"What's that got to do with myths?"

"In the same condensed manner, I think mythology recapitulates actual prehistory. Put Freud's and Jung's ideas together, and the growth of the individual psyche bears a fractal self-similarity to both that individual's ontogeny *and* the mythology of the surrounding culture."

"So?"

"So, if those, in their turn, recap the development of *both* the species before the individual came into time *and* the prehistory of the culture before it came into history, then every human mind bears within it a fractal self-similarity to the entire prehistory of life and thought on this planet."

No matter how hard John tried to follow those ideas, he still didn't have much luck. Why was it everyone he'd been spending time with lately seemed, well, so damned *intelligent*? Or was it *crazy*? Whichever, it was undeniably frustrating.

"If all this is already in our minds somehow, then why do I have to think so hard to understand it?"

"Because it's a *data-compressed* record of our origins. Maybe it contains even more than biology and culture. If consciousness is a sort of interface between instinct and ecstasy, then maybe what everyone used to be able to do was *decompress* that data, through ecstatic techniques. Scale up and down that fractal. Shift shapes through all the animal ancestors, until their souls flew, entheogeny recapitulating phylogeny, and they *became* the god they sought. Maybe what I'm trying to describe isn't just an after-shock of something that's already happened—but a foreshock of things to come, too."

Snatching off his maroon knit cap, John laughed. He shook his head and rubbed his scalp—hoping perhaps to improve the blood flow to his brain by so doing. *He* was the ex-spacer, the guy who'd seen the solar system, yet he was way out of his depth here.

Malika groaned audibly. They had completely forgotten her presence. She sat up, throwing aside the red coverlet to reveal a green blouse and black pants rumpled from her having slept in them. Grumpily, she rubbed her eyes.

"Déjà vu of coming attractions. Jeez, I know it's Sunday morning, but you think you could scale back on the heavy spiritual and metaphysical stuff? At least until I've had my first cup of coffee?" She stood up, stretched, then turned to Mark. "Speaking of which, do you . . . ?"

"In the kitchen. Two pots already brewed up. Can't you smell it?"

Malika mumbled something about a head cold, then wandered off toward the kitchen. John took that as a cue, too, and joined Malika there. Mark, absently scratching his goatee, was deep in thought when they rejoined him. For a time they sat in silence, sipping coffee and pondering the gray day. Putting down her empty blue coffee mug, Malika looked up, knitting the fingers of her hands and stretching her arms and shoulders.

"Now that we've leveled the mental playing field a little bit, I don't know that I buy your idea of ecstatic techniques as data-decompression algorithms."

"I didn't think of them as algorithms, but I see your point. Might sound too stepwise. Too mechanistic."

"Right. You might want to think 'dynamical system,' too—instead of 'fractal' or 'data compression.' "

"Sounds more active? Gotcha."

Finding himself at the edge of yet another conversation poised to lift off into an intellectual stratosphere quite unfamiliar to him—and into which he doubted he could follow—John was put out a little at Malika.

"Just how much of our conversation did you eavesdrop on, anyway?"

"Enough to get the gist of it. You know, Mark, no matter what kind of ecstatic or esoteric realms it ultimately hooks into, your 'shamanic complex,' if it exists, would probably have to be initiated by something physical in the brain. Some trigger that allows for the creation of a mental state *meaningfully related* to physical changes in the brain, without exactly being 'caused' by those changes. Something to pump up the neural 'gain' enough to shift around the state-space attractor inside your head. Something that brings on a quantum mental event powerful enough to allow your shamanic archetype-thingy to flow in from wherever it is that it's been hiding out."

"Something such as—?"

"How should I know? Ask a biochemist. A neurophysiologist. Somebody who specializes in that sort of thing."

"I think I know just the person. I'll bounce her a virtual mail with my theory about this global rhythmania. Send her a few predictions about what to expect in the next stages. That should grab her interest. Follow up by asking her if she knows of any physical change in the brain that might bring on your 'quantum mental event.' "

John knew, without knowing how he knew, that his friend was thinking of Tomoko Fukuda.

"She might just think you're a lunatic with a crazy theory."

"Maybe, but it's worth a try. Who knows? It might even turn out to be important."

"Let me help you draft that v-mail," Malika said. "It'll read better if we both work on it."

Mark agreed. He and Malika disappeared into one of his workrooms, leaving John behind to stare out the sliding glass doors and ponder the strange words and phrases that still hung in the room, or at least inside his head.

Neural gain and quantum mental events and shamanic archetypes. Weird stuff. On the screened-in patio, the drummers and their drumming had grown loud enough again to drown out the sound of the rain on the roof. John thought he heard other rhythms growing in volume, too, but whether they were echoes of this circle—or other, *fractally self-similar* drum circles "meaningfully related" *to* this one but not "caused" *by* it—he could not tell.

16

Parting
2066

THE NEW YEAR HAS DAWNED, GRIM AND WITHOUT FANFARE, AT LEAST FOR Ricardo. Nothing changes, except to grow worse. Sitting with Trillia in the anteroom to President Spires' chambers, he remembers how poorly he slept last night. The pre-pandemic decor of the Executive House guest room where he spent the night—"guest," but perhaps no longer "citizen," of these islands—was not very calming. Matching curtains and bedspread, tan expanses covered with stylized, luridly colored knots and spirals and helices, thick wavy lines with partially attached spheres along their lengths. Like ribosomes, DNA, and proteins from the nightmare of a student passed out after cramming for a final examination in cell biology.

The dream he himself had, too. The twilight streets of one of the great pre-pandemic cities, canyons lined by cubes and clashing cubist planes and the wavy billowing funhouse walls of morphogenetic architecture. Tall screens sheathing those buildings, and holographic images projected from them, overlooking a central square or crossroads. The skysign programs, even the streetlights, pumping out social weather, crystalline purple and yellow fog flooding out of them, filling all the streets. The people disappearing into the fog, morphed by it into crystalline cloud mechanisms, dully shining purple and yellow phantasms dispersing and recondensing, utterly at the whim of the wind blowing from the fog-making machines, and himself running and running, panicking as the purple and yellow fog mounted higher and higher, above the tops of the tallest buildings, blotting out the stars—

Ricardo shakes his head. Since learning of his prionoid death sentence, he has begun to take himself too seriously. Given his not-yet-apparent condition, however, it's only natural that he should be obsessed with the pre-pandemic world—and how the global madness destroyed nearly everything that once was.

How can his dreams *not* be influenced by his current fears and obsessions? Key questions all too relevant to him are still unresolved more than thirty years after the Great Collapse: Who was responsible for the pandemic? How exactly did and does the "prionoid schizophrenia" create its effects? Those answers that have survived the maelstrom of the collapse fall far short of satisfying.

Decades *before* the collapse actually happened, there were already those who believed the pre-pandemic world was ripe for catastrophe. Ricardo has been scanning a great deal of the work of those pre-pandemic thinkers who, more or less accurately, predicted the end of global civilization— philosophers whose works strongly influenced residents of the lost space habitat, and more than a few of the early abjurers of these islands, too.

Philosophers of disurbanization like D. B. Albert, who savaged the materialists, social-ontologists, chatterers, and privacy-destroyers of the pre-pandemic world. Decrying the thoughtless "Age of the Body" into which his American homeland had fallen by the turn of the millenium, Albert predicted the collapse of global civilization because it had "sacrificed the reality of the individual to the abstraction of 'society,' and thereby cut human beings off from their own greatness." For him, techno-dependent and media-saturated societies trapped their individual members in the mindless grip of a "social psychoid process," an anti-archetype drawing its energy from the conflict between individual consciousness and the strictures of social conformity. According to Albert, such a soulless and dispiriting "social order" was too rigidly programmed and programming to ever adapt to the arrival of that contingent and unanticipated event which must inevitably destroy it.

Ricardo wonders if Albert might have considered the pandemic of prionoid schizophrenia part of the "healing sickness" needed to turn humanity around. No, wait. Although Albert believed urban civilization was doomed, the disurbanist philosopher also believed the alternative to urbanism's pernicious effects lay not in the contingent event of plague and pandemonium, but in reasoned population reduction. This the philosopher hoped to see achieved through attrition over a period of fifty to one hundred years: People *choosing* to reduce the rate of reproduction, allowing mortality itself to reduce populations naturally over time, eventually abandoning their old urban centers for lives lived out in small-scale communities.

Certainly nothing as abrupt or radical as NeoLuddites and techno-reversalists like John Zerzan, who felt that the root of technological humanity's malaise lay in civilization-addiction and technology-dependency itself. By the late twentieth century he had called for a return to hunting-gathering lifeways. His followers later yearned for an apocalyptic reversal, an immediate restoration to the hard paradise of the pre-agricultural world, whatever the cost in human lives and suffering.

Having read so much of such taboo thinkers lately, how can he *not* think of that lost world, its god-voice calling from billions of burning screens, singing its one long hymn of greed and desire, billions of flashing electronic altars demanding sacrifice, demanding holocaust? Was the collapse the inevitable failure of that civilization's Buy More Be More faith, or its ultimate success—the world built on salvationist consumerism at last consuming itself? Ricardo is not surprised at having dreamed what he did, though why in purple and yellow he cannot say.

Trillia squeezes his hand and he turns toward her. For a thin young woman, her grip is surprisingly strong, forthright, even fierce. Glancing past her pixie-cut red-blond hair and looking deep into her eyes, Ricardo sees she still has hopes for the proceedings. Despite the way her parents and all Ricardo's and Trillia's friends have knuckled under to the "rule of law"—despite that law's decree of banishment or death for all those in Ricardo's condition—despite even his own cynical resistance, Trillia's hope is contagious. Looking into her eyes, Ricardo finds himself beginning to catch it.

Until Cameron Spires opens the door to his office.

The unguarded look on the pinkish, slightly jowly face inside the environment-suit head-bubble is cold and hard. Ricardo realizes this interview is going to be an exercise in futility. Trillia, however, plunges ahead, standing up and walking toward her grandfather, who embraces her and smiles like a backdated cherub.

"My dear girl! Come in, come in! What can I do for you?"

Ricardo lags behind. Trillia waves him forward. Together they enter the indirectly lit confines of the President's office, a realm of dark wood and dully gleaming brass fixtures. They take seats before the President's desk.

"It's about the Wersign policy, Grandpa. The cytological cut part of

Ricardo's latest medical examination says he is Wer-prionoid positive. For someone born after the pandemic, that just doesn't make sense. It's unheard of that he should turn out to be only heterozygous-resistant so many years beyond adolescence."

"Such a case *is* unprecedented. I can't deny that."

"The doctors have told him he's got some kind of 'new variant.' They admit it might be what they call a benign polymorphism, but they say the consequences of the Wersign policy apply anyway. Banishment or death! When they don't even know whether he will ever become infectious—or even manifest external symptoms of the Wer!"

"Trillia, Trillia. Please calm down. What would you have me do? I can't change your friend's diagnosis."

"But you can change the policy!"

"No, I'm afraid I can't. That's an issue for the legislative branch of this government. The executive branch has no power to meddle in that area. There's no legal precedent."

"But you said yourself that Ricardo's case is unprecedented! Please, Grandpa. You're our court of last resort. Intervene. Put Ricardo under medical containment until we know for sure what this 'new variant' is. Put him in an environment suit like your own if you have to, but don't agree to his banishment or execution!"

Ricardo, already annoyed at being bandied about in the third person, is stunned at the thought of living in an environment suit like the President's. The idea is frankly repugnant. Trillia must be coming up with some of this stuff on the fly. Seeing grandfather and granddaughter together here, Ricardo wonders how Cameron Spires ever fathered children. Probably it was an act more surgical than sexual.

Spires sighs loudly enough that they hear it clearly, even though the President is not in voice-amplified mode.

"The law is what it is, and I'm not above it. If I flout the rule of law by making exceptions, then who will respect the law—or *my* authority? How will it look if I intervene and your friend's new variant turns out to be contagious and infectious? We know the original pandemic prionoids have *changed*—and resistance is a spectrum, remember. Not just homozygous 'resistant' or heterozygous 'partially resistant' or homozygous nonresistant 'good as dead.' I myself may well have no resistance at all, you know."

"But—" Trillia begins. Her grandfather motions her to silence.

"I don't want to test that possibility, via your friend Ricardo or anyone else. Trillia, make no mistake: I have already signed the order under which Ricardo must face either exile or execution. Your friend here poses a danger to public health and safety."

Ricardo jumps up, no longer able to contain himself.

"Bullshit! 'Danger to public health and safety!' That's what they always used to say in the bad old days, right before their witch-hunts and exterminations for 'social hygiene'!"

Spires stands up from behind his desk.

"Man is a social animal. Ricardo Alvarez, you are a threat to our society, and we will protect ourselves—"

"Since when does spending your whole life in an isolation suit make *you* an expert on society? Last I checked, *human beings* were *conscious individuals*, not 'social animals.' This society is more a threat to me than I am to it!"

" 'Conscious individuals,' indeed! So you've been scanning the Zerzanists and Luddites, the disurbanizers and depopulators! Bunch of Pol Pot philosophers. *Their* followers were the ones who created and spread the pandemic—until they made the whole world their killing field!"

"Never proved! The vast majority of disurbanists condemned the pandemic—"

"We could have saved the world its great collapse, if we had taken the steps with them that our law will now take with you."

"Taken steps! I'll take some steps! I'll rip off your damn helmet and *breathe* on you!"

Before he can lay his hands on Spires, Ricardo is dropped by a bolt of electric charge. Coming around, he finds himself breathless, numb, and on the floor. Trillia cries as she rocks his upper body in her arms.

"You've killed him! You've killed him!"

"I've done nothing of the kind, my dear. He's very much alive—just hit with a little thunderbolt, is all. We do this by the rules. We have provided him with the same motorsailer and Merfolk escort that accompanied his mentor, Simon Lingham, into exile. When your friend comes around, get him out of here, then get him off this island. He's got twenty-four hours. Otherwise, my order will be executed, and so will he."

Spires sits down behind his desk again as Trillia helps Ricardo climb weakly to his feet. Leaning on her as they head for the door, Ricardo feels her stop and turn, cold and formal.

"Mr. President, does preserving the blessings of the past have to mean repeating all its errors?"

Her grandfather, working at his desk, pretends not to hear her. Trillia turns back to Ricardo. Together they make their way out.

By the time they are halfway to Ricardo's parents' place, he has recovered enough from the President's thunderbolt to walk without help. Trillia walks in silence beside him, caught up in her own thoughts. The pair move through the bustling, colorful streets, bright in the subtropical noontide. Ricardo realizes the world is full of people going about their business, oblivious to the painful journey he and Trillia have just embarked upon. The thought leaves him feeling hollow. Trillia squeezes his hand.

"What will you do now?"

Ricardo turns to her. Looking at her face, brushing back her hair, resting his hand on her cheek, he sees that the calm hope he noted in her eyes earlier is now replaced by sad confusion.

"What choice do I have? It's that old Romeo and Juliet thing: 'My life is here, but it's death for me to stay.' Only this time it's not just a scene in one of the President's favorite plays. It's real—and really time to leave everything I've known. Time to see that other world we've only heard about."

He shrugs and sticks his hands in his pockets. They walk on slowly. Trillia looks away, afraid he will see her cry, which he already has.

"Where do you plan to go?"

"I could go anywhere. I've been thinking about what I'd do if it came to this. Before Simon Lingham left, there were rumors he was working on some antidote or countermeasure to the prionoid shapeshift. I think I'll try to find him. He hasn't been gone *that* long. He can't have too big a lead on me."

"To the derelict spaceport in Florida, then, or to what used to be Atlanta?"

Despite himself, Ricardo smiles.

"Good memory. I haven't decided yet. Simon was planning to travel along the Intracoastal Waterway. I figure if I stick with that I can't go too far wrong."

As they turn the corner onto the street where Ricardo's family lives, Trillia looks up at him.

"What about your parents?"

"It'll hurt them, I know, but seeing me executed would hurt them more. They know what the Wersign policy means. My father is a simple, straightforward man—he'll recognize the need for my leaving. My mother's more complex, more emotional too, but she'll come around."

By the time he and Trillia climb the short flight of steps to his family's house, Ricardo's parents—a short bald man, round and brown, and a tall, bony woman, pale and graying—are already waiting on the porch. Ricardo tells them about the meeting with the President, and the decision the President has forced him to make. For the first time, Ricardo sees his father cry. Against all expectations, his mother, though jumpy and nervous, does not burst into tears as he expected. Together his parents show him into the bedroom. His travel gear is already laid out on the bed, ready for packing.

Getting everything packed keeps the four of them busy and distracted for the next several hours. When at last Ricardo stands at the door with Trillia, his parents revert to their more familiar roles. His father, grown steady again, comforts Ricardo's wailing and sobbing mother. She protests that she "just can't bear" to walk with them and see Ricardo off at the dock, so his father and mother kiss him and hug him goodbye.

Turning from them, Ricardo and Trillia make their way through slanting late-afternoon light down streets of lengthening shadows, toward the dock where the motorsailer waits. As they approach, the *Sea Robin*'s lights come on and its engines start. Three mermen spyhop, see him and Trillia, then disappear again into the dark water. Ricardo doesn't recognize them, but that's no real surprise. The only merperson he's close to personally is young Thaumas—a kindred spirit among the Merfolk, someone who, like himself, has always questioned the idea that his elders are never wrong. These three spyhoppers seem more like those elders than not.

"Your grandfather is leaving nothing to chance," he tells Trillia.

Ricardo steps up into the boat, shedding his pack. Trillia looks bewildered as she hands him the pack she's been carrying—her face betraying the confidence in her voice.

"I'm coming with you."

"I wish you could, Trill, but you can't. They won't see it as you fleeing the island and joining me in banishment. They'll say I kidnapped you. They'll just come after us and take you back. Maybe kill me for good measure, before I can even begin searching for Lingham and a possible cure."

"I can't just stay here and do nothing!"

"Then find things out for me. You've got access to all the Spires family records—use it. Find out as much about the abjurers as you can. Lingham said John Drinan is still at the old spaceport in central Florida, and Tomoko Fukuda is somewhere outside the ghost city of Atlanta. Find out where exactly, if you can. Your grandfather and New Bahama security must have something on the whereabouts of the rest of the abjurers. How many of them are still known to be alive, if any? Dig into as much of the history of the pandemic and its symptomatology as the computers will allow—"

"But what good will my knowing about it do *you*, if you're already gone?"

Ricardo reaches over from the boat to where Trillia stands at the edge of the dock. He takes her face in both his hands.

"Give it a month or so. Convince them you're getting over me. Maybe you will—who knows? If you still want to follow me, then in six weeks' time rendezvous with me at the mouth of the Savannah River, where it crosses what was once the Intracoastal Waterway and enters the Atlantic."

"I'll be there, if only to prove that I haven't 'gotten over' you. But what'll you do until then?"

"Try to find Drinan in Florida. Maybe Simon will still be with him. If not, then—if we manage to reunite near Savannah—we'll go inland together and look for Tomoko Fukuda."

She takes his head in her hands and gives him a long, ardent kiss— made awkward only by the need to avoid falling off the dock or out of the boat.

"Be careful. I'm afraid for you, trying to survive in that wilderness."

Ricardo doesn't even want to think about being captured or killed by Werfolk or barbarian Trufolk, himself—much less bring such dire possibilities up now, with Trillia.

"I'll look after myself. Don't worry."

They kiss and embrace passionately. He is sorely tempted to bring her on board with him now, so they might take a first and last pleasure in each other's bodies. Courting a "princess" as he has been, he has never made love to this young woman, but senses she too is willing, here and now. Out of the corner of his eye, however, he catches the watery eye of a merman glinting in sunset light, scrutinizing them from beneath the small waves lapping against the boat and dock. Ricardo pulls from the embrace and nods Trillia's gaze toward the lurking merman, who soon vanishes.

"Our parting is not as private as we might like."

Kissing and embracing again and again, they move beyond the prospect of physical pleasure to a deeper awareness of the physical absence that lies beyond this evening—the sadness and loneliness awaiting them both. By the time they finally relinquish each other, the stars have begun to come out, their numbers growing too many to count.

Together Ricardo and Trillia unmoor and free the sloop from its connections with the dock. They bid each other farewell—"Until next time!"—as Ricardo steers and waves. Looking back toward the dock, he tries to keep Trillia in sight as long as he can. The sight of her waving goodbye is swallowed up at last by night and distance.

Once out of the harbor, only the sea and the stars—bright and golden and innumerable—fill the world ahead of him. "Night's candles," as Shakespeare called them. And D. B. Albert's phrase, "The gods are putting on their porch lamps." Something homey and human in those descriptions. Ricardo wishes he could believe in them, but he can't. The gods before him are unknown gods. Their homes, in that glowing city above him, seem very far away. He listens, trying to hear the music of the spheres or the sounds of the gods' distant parties. Instead he hears only the endless falling of waves back onto the sea out of which they are forever arising, growing fainter as his home islands vanish astern.

17

Kekulé With a Möbius Twist
2033

TOMOKO DANCED TO THE SOUND OF UILEANN PIPES, CONCERTINA, bodhran, snare drum, guitar, and fiddle. By passing under the uplifted bridge of one couple's arms, the line-dance changed figure-eightwise into a snake eating its own tail, before changing further into a circle dance and ending again as a line.

Out of breath, Tomoko stepped away from the dance and toward the side of the big pavilion tent, leaving her two friends and Protean fellow workers Leeza and Anita still in line, waiting for the next dance to start. Hearing the rain drumming softly against the outside of the tent, Tomoko was amazed at the number of people dancing. The situation had been the same in all three tents she'd danced in all morning and afternoon, yet her amazement only grew as the day wore on.

She had attended folk festivals and Renaissance Faires for years, and this was her second time attending the Global Folkal Festival in North Bend, Washington. The difference today, however, was astonishing. Despite the fact that the weather was worse this year than last, the number of attendees had grown by at least ten times. People were lined up *waiting* to get into the dance pavilions, not milling round the food and crafts vendors, as they usually did at festivals like this.

What could have changed so much in a year? She watched in wonder, yet no clues presented themselves. She saw people of all ages—girls and mothers and fathers and boys and elders of both sexes—dancing without embarrassment, concerned only to learn the steps and moves of each dance and take them on as ardently and energetically as possible.

Shaking her head in happy disbelief, Tomoko walked out of the Celtic folk dance pavilion and into the light but steady rain. There was another difference today, too. Something not due to the weather. Looking south through the rainy midafternoon light, over the festival meadows and on toward pine-covered mountainsides, she tried to distinguish in the distance the top of Mount Rainier from the bottoms of the clouds. Nothing unusual about that. Nor was the difference due to changes in the extensiveness of her own dance vocabulary, for it, too, was as usual. Her mother had enrolled her in ballet classes when she was five years old. Tomoko had never much liked being *en pointe*, but fortunately her teacher, Ms. Zaki, also taught "character" and folk dances ranging from Nipponese to Serbian. Tomoko had learned them all and throughout her teens performed in all Ms. Zaki's recitals. As a result, Tomoko figured she could find her way around a dance floor pretty much anywhere in the world.

What was different about the dancing today was not so much that she was dancing differently, as that everybody *else* was. Gone was the self-conscious fear of looking stupid or ungraceful that kept most people in their seats or standing around on the sidelines. The usual tentativeness of those who had to work up the courage to walk out on the dance floor— that hesitancy was missing too. People seemed to have suddenly found so much joy in dance itself, they no longer worried much about how they looked doing it.

And they looked better and better *doing* it. Far faster than she would have expected. Had the "rhythmania" the mediaheads went on about also given people a better sense not only of rhythm but also of coordinated movement? Of dance?

Walking down a grassy lane of tents and booths set up by purveyors of foodstuffs, handicrafts, and psychic advice, Tomoko barely noticed how few customers were milling about, until she saw a scrap of paper blowing among the booths and tents. Picking it up, she saw it was a weathered flier announcing the Big Tent Revival Meetings held in these same fields just a few days earlier. She remembered seeing something about it on the news—huge crowds of the prayerful, swaying together.

Was that a type of rhythmania, too? She thought again of the long virtual mail she had received nearly a week ago. From that network manager or whatever he was down at UCLA Med, that Mark Fornash character.

And he *was* a character, too. She remembered meeting him in person— an energetic little man with curly gray-brown hair, wild gray eyes, and a stubbly short, almost white goatee. From his v-mail she concluded he was also a very intelligent albeit undisciplined theorist—an autodidact, putting forward ideas just this side of crackpottery. In his v-mail he had suggested that an epidemic was underway that allowed some kind of "archetype" or "shamanic complex" to enter into or take over consciousness.

Out of curiosity she put on her viewshades and called up his v-mail on her personal system. Here was the entire file, spoken and captioned both, which was why she remembered it as well as she did. Scanning through it, she saw that his message returned time and again to "consciousness," and "self," and "self-consciousness." She found Fornash describing consciousness as "a characteristic, self-perpetuating dynamical system of neurological behavior, not bounded by cause and effect, ultimately independent from its underlying neurological mechanisms." Further on, he contended the *self* was "the chaotic attractor in consciousness . . . the ongoing reflexive image of consciousness as a unique entity . . . the unique, fractal identifying pattern of the dynamical system of consciousness in the brain."

Whew! She paused the scan in her virtuality and tried to digest all that again. Most of it was at least intelligible enough, Tomoko supposed. Scanning on, however, she saw once more that, like many another well-intentioned crank, Fornash had to go and press the point, proclaiming that "Chaotic and fractal like the event horizon around the singularity at the heart of a black hole, consciousness is itself the event horizon between matter and spirit, wrapped around the singularity that lives at the heart of the mind."

"Spirit" and "heart of the mind"! Tomoko thought, pausing her scan again. What was all *that* supposed to mean? Stepping with some care along the slippery and slightly muddy grass of the lane, she thought it certainly didn't sound like the science *she* knew. Yet from such a mesh of mixed metaphors, Fornash concluded that this shamanic epidemic of his was (in the much-reported global rhythmanias) already beginning.

She stopped at a booth and ordered a veggie pasty from the massively mustachioed and stain-aproned man behind the counter. Only too happy to have a customer at last, the counterman placed the pasty before her— almost before she'd finished ordering it. Sitting on a stool at the counter, protected by an awning from the light rain, Tomoko munched her pasty and tried not to become too annoyed as she scanned more of Fornash's long, odd message in her viewshades.

Where was that part about his "prediction"? Here: "I propose that, in this shamanic epidemic already underway, a biological vector of unidentified type is already replacing the fourth D, 'drugging,' with its own neurochemical transformation. The effect of this vector is to intensify the previous three stages, permanently altering the consciousness of those who have 'caught' it."

Scanning on, Tomoko found Fornash's full prediction about the result of that alteration. According to him, the "overall course of this condition will follow a five-part shamanic pattern of drumming, dancing, dreaming, shapeshifting, and soul-flying." Global rhythmanias, Tomoko thought. To be followed by "dance fevers" so widespread as to put all previous episodes of tarantism in the shade. To be followed in turn by an outbreak of dreaming sickness the world over—then onslaughts of shapeshifting and soul-flying, whatever those might entail.

Only at the end of Fornash's message did it become clear why he had graced her day with such theories. He had contacted her in search of possible leads on what sorts of physical brain changes might trigger the "acausal, synchronistic quantum mental event" that might allow the "shamanic archetype" to flood into consciousness.

Not wanting to encourage the man in his delusions, she had politely ignored Fornash's v-mail the whole of the past week. Now, though, turning off her personal VR system and slipping the viewshades back into her pocket, she wasn't sure that would prove the best course of action.

Finishing her pasty, she thanked the man behind the counter and stood. While trying to convince herself that this was nothing new, that there had been dance crazes and fads before, she was at the same time reluctantly wondering if Fornash might be onto something. Continuing down the grassy lane of booths and tents, she thought again of the recent surge in the popularity of dancing, and the strangely unselfconscious way people just got up and danced in every dance pavilion she'd stopped in today.

Despite herself, she considered the possibilities. Something physical to trigger a "quantum mental event." The likeliest candidate, she thought, would probably involve one or more of the so-called "living fossil" receptor sites. Personally, she'd never liked that term as an explanation for one of the more problematic areas of neurophysiology, but the research community was stuck with it. Throughout the past several decades researchers had discovered in the brain several groups of neuronal receptor sites to which *nothing* that was naturally produced by the body would bind. Which was not to say certain substances wouldn't bind to them. It was just that the substances capable of binding with those receptors were all produced *outside* the body—and nearly all of them were strongly psychoactive.

Several theorists held that such receptors were remnants, leftovers from an earlier stage of human evolution when such substances had in fact been produced by the body itself. Others claimed the receptor sites were surviving traces from a time when the ingestion of psychoactive substances encountered in the environment played a prominent role in the original "bootstrapping" of consciousness. All agreed, however, that the remnant receptors were now essentially obsolete, vestigial, and useless.

Such explanations never quite satisfied Tomoko. If those receptor sites were useless, then why did the human gene pool continue to go to the trouble and expend the energy to keep such "useless" structures around? What survival advantage did they confer? If they provided no such advantage, then why hadn't they been eliminated long since by the process of evolution? Explaining living-fossil receptor sites was a mess considerably worse than the much earlier (and far more successful) attempt to explain the persistence of the vermiform appendix. Yet, even if the living-fossil receptor sites were somehow involved in these manias, that couldn't be the whole story—at least not for what Fornash was after. What would be the nature or character of the external thing necessary to activate or trigger such sites?

She stopped before a booth called OmphalOcentriC—the capital letters of whose very name were made up of snakes and dragons swallowing (in the case of the *O*'s) or chasing (in the case of the *C*) their own tails. The booth's proprietor, a long-haired, thickly bearded, fiery-eyed individual, both a glassblower and metalsmith, would have served admirably as a model for Bluebeard in an historical illustration. He was featured in the trideo interview floating in space near the sign, which caught Tomoko's attention.

"I became an artist because putting up a cross in my backyard and nailing myself to it every morning would annoy the neighbors."

Despite herself, Tomoko smiled at the craftsman's recorded words. She glanced over various wares, glad of the distraction. Most of the artist's work involved tail-swallowing figures done in metal or glass, each figure wrapped around the outside edge of a disk at whose center was a small depression or navel, sometimes painted in a contrasting color. The booth itself was hung and cluttered with all species of ouroboroi, most prominently snakes and dragons and various mythological worms. Other items were variations on the theme: Tao "yinyang" symbols, various knots and bends and hitches done in glass and metal, Klein bottles and Möbius strips and Escher-style optical confusions. Some Tomoko found grotesque, particularly the series being worked on at the moment by the booth's owner and operator.

Absently watching the glass sculptor bending and altering the shape of a molten spindle, Tomoko was struck by an unexpected and unsought vision. Before her eyes she saw detailed molecular models of her prionoids, saw her conformation-altering proteins themselves being altered and shifted, their lumpy-T shapes changed, abnormally conformed to endless lazy-eight loops and passed on by—what? Bacteria? Viruses? Until, altered, they spread their abnormal conformation in great cascades not of replication but *conversion*, long chains of rogue proteins resistant to destruction by heat, detergents, radiation—the very persistence and near-indestructibility that had led her to prions and prionoids in the first place, now gone terribly wrong!

She glanced up in horror at the proprietor of OmphalOcentriC, not really seeing him except to note his sniff of disdain. Turning away, she belatedly realized he'd misunderstood her look of horror—apparently thinking it a shocked response to his art—but Tomoko didn't have time to correct the man's misperceptions. Darting back toward the dance tent where she'd left Leeza and Anita, she could only think such a vision had granted her an anti-Kekulé moment—an "Uh-oh!" in contrast to the great chemist's "Aha!" at his dream of snakes swallowing their tails, which had led Kekulé to postulate, correctly, that the shape of the benzene molecule was a ring.

Walking into the dance tent, Tomoko realized her vision was one of shapeshifted prionoids shifting the nature of neurotransmitter production itself. If true, such twisted keys would prove far more potent for reopening the door into Fornash's "shamanic" realm than any drug ever could.

She spotted Anita and Leeza. Her friends—who were also, in the final analysis, her employees—were so reluctant to stop dancing that Tomoko practically had to drag them from the dance floor. Walking them to the edge of the meadow and punching in automated dispatch codes for a robocar, she pointedly ignored the complaints of her two young colleagues. She had much more important things on her mind—trial subjects to be relocated, tests to be run, actions to be taken.

The robocar pulled up and they climbed inside. Tomoko commanded the vehicle into manual operation and took control of the wheel. She glanced at her two friends in the backseat, both of whom looked annoyed. I have responsibilities they don't have, she thought. But how responsible am I? For what's happening to them? For . . . everything?

18

Spyhopping in Different Oceans
2066

SITTING BESIDE A NATATORIUM OPEN TO THE ATLANTIC, TRILLIA FLICKS HER VR viewshades off her eyes and up onto the top of her head. Through the transparent dome arching above the seaside pool, she sees a cloud-flecked but still sunny sky. To her immense frustration, she realizes that the injunctions Ricardo left her with, nearly a month ago, are in fact contradictory, even mutually exclusive.

How can she convince her grandfather and everyone else that she is over Ricardo, yet—at one and the same time—also search out everything she can find regarding the history and symptomatology of the pandemic, not to mention the history and whereabouts of the abjurers? Any discovery by her family that she is investigating the abjurers and the pandemic will call into question her supposed indifference to Ricardo's fate. *Not* risking the possibility of being discovered, however, might prove as damaging as real indifference.

She can only hope her grandfather is too preoccupied to notice she is playing both Juliet suddenly submissive to her family's will, *and* Hamlet going about his slow detective work. Day after day she has thrown herself into her historical studies of the islanders' physical and online archives—to occupy her mind against the waiting and loneliness, as much as anything else. It also seems to be the most acceptable option. As long as she isn't actually *asking* people for oral histories of the pandemic and the abjurers, she figures she can get away with a fair amount of research, even into rather offbeat topics.

Returning her gaze to the natatorium, she sees only young Merfolk learning and playing. There are times when she truly envies the merpeople and their seemingly carefree lives. She finds it relaxing to be near one of the teaching pools, too—probably for the same reason other people like having an aquarium with fish to watch, only her aquarium is a thumb of the ocean and her "fish" are mermaids and mermen.

She returns to her work, flicking the viewshades back down over her eyes, an unbreathed sigh catching in her throat. Wireless-linked to the local net and the islander-salvaged remains of the infosphere, she scans the electronic shards of that glittering world that once was, wondering if she'll ever uncover anything of use to Ricardo.

She didn't expect to find much on the abjurers. When they leave the islands to go into exile, all public records of their existence end. Even more annoying, however, is how much is still unknown about the pandemic. Endless speculations on the role of "biospheric burdening" in the creation and spread of the plague. Population density and megacity growth. Rapid travel and world monoculture. Global warming. Toxic chemicals. Ozone depletions and UV surges. Rainforest destruction and drained wetlands. Dump and sewage sites in cesspool oceans mixing up terminal cocktails of intermingling microbes. Weird weather washing plastics and pesticides, fertilizers and fuels, detergents and debris into the sea—until algal blooms haunted the planet, brown and red tides like mindless mobile genetic engineering labs, swapping antibiotic resistance factors, plasmids, transposons, virulence genes and God knows what else among viruses, bacteria, and algae.

All of that is important enough, she supposes, though none of it was important enough to have kept the speculators alive. So much of what *was* known is cloaked in arcane jargon and specialized terminology: *super-Roman decimation, index case, nosocomial, panzootics, zoonoses, genetic burden in regard to virulence vs. transmissibility.* Trillia finds less than helpful the theories claiming the catastrophe was caused by "non-Mendelian iatro-genes." More unhelpful still are those theories that toss causality out the window altogether, claiming the Great Plague arose from "the complex, nonlinear interaction of the dynamical system of human consciousness with dynamical epidemiological and ecological systems."

Dynamical turtles all the way down. Trillia shakes her head in disgust. Ricardo was *so* confident she would have access to "all Spires family records." Although it's true that as a member of the family she does have access to the family datasphere network, she has gained no access to any private presidential files on the pandemic, or on the abjurers' further travels—if such records even exist. All the materials concerning her grandfather's public presidential self fall under some kind of "national security"—far too encrypted for her to get at.

There must be a way to get beyond the official history! If, in that family network the rest of the islanders never see, there lurks a private level of her grandfather's data, she must find out where that information is embedded. But how? She has already been searching for such a "deeper level" for nearly a month and has made no progress at all.

Trillia's gaze drifts outward, beyond the gray-tapioca-meets-Brownian-motion of the screen saver jittering pseudorandomly on her 3D view-shades. Through the shades as through a hazy, smoking mirror, she sees two mermaids at the edge of the pool, staring at her. Freeze-framing them, she goes external and has the net confirm identification of the two. Just as she thought: Thetis and Psamathe, mer-girls with a Trufolk maturity-equivalence of age twelve or thirteen. She's known the two of them for years—and identified them correctly even through the dimness and distortion of the viewshades. Watching the two mer-girls, Trillia is struck by an idea. She activates the comm screen in the pool, where they now swim, and signals them via the screen.

"Thetis! Psamathe! I have some questions for you."

The mer-girls race to the screen and signal their attentiveness.

"When Nereus and the others returned from escorting Simon Ling-ham to the lands in the west, did they say anything about where they left Lingham? Or where he might be headed?"

The two mer-girls hastily confer with each other.

"We know the place they parted from tru-man Lingham," Thetis says.

"We can show you," says Psamathe, "but we can't tell you."

Great, Trillia thought. Old human place names and map images mean little to Merfolk. Still, such information might prove helpful some day. She sees the mer-girls rise to the surface for a breath and a spyhop-look at her.

"Can you *show* me where Lingham was headed?"

"Father Nereus did not say," Thetis replies.

"Sorry," says Psamathe.

Despite herself, Trillia smiles.

"Nothing to be sorry about. Thanks for your help. Anything else you remember Nereus or the others saying?"

Psamathe nods her head eagerly.

"Father Delphinus told Mother Doris that Lingham was *different* after a night on the land there."

"We heard him say it," Thetis agrees.

"Different? How different?"

"Changed," Psamathe says.

"Not body-changed like Werfolk," Thetis says, trying to explain, "but maybe changed like Werfolk in his head."

Trillia doesn't know what to make of that. She drops the idea of Lingham's mental metamorphosis for now. Another idea has come to her. These girl-creatures show unquestioning loyalty to their human creators in general—and to her grandfather in particular. Might her grandfather actually feel more comfortable and invulnerable around the Merfolk than around his fellow humans? Comfortable and invulnerable enough to let his guard down?

"When Greatfather Spires comes to visit you, does he ever repeat a string of numbers? Or letters? Or some combination of sounds?"

"Like this?" Thetis asks. She makes a long series of whistles and screeches. As the comm screen translates them, Trillia, on a hunch, records and reroutes the sequence to her VR access module. When the sequence finishes, her viewshades abruptly spiral down into a 3D vortex image like none she's ever seen before.

"No—you stopped too early," Psamathe says, correcting Thetis and adding her own sets of whistles and clicks. When the comm screen finishes translating and the shades complete their re-routing the vortex whooshes past Trillia. A rotating geodesic figure appears, a shape she recognizes as a buckyball, one of her grandfather's favorite forms. It quickly fills all virtual space before her. Trillia sees pictures and captions kaleidoscoping over the b-ball's surfaces as the multifaceted sphere rotates. Watching those surfaces, it dawns on Trillia that she is looking at an extremely ramified data construct—perhaps one complex enough to represent the totality of her grandfather's private records.

"I wasn't finished!" Thetis says. "I've watched him too. These are places he likes to go."

In the next instant Thetis and Psamathe join Trillia in sharespace around the rotating buckyball. The mer-girls dart Trillia into one surface after another, moving on when either of them grows bored or one feels the other is hogging too much screen time.

The mer-girls shift from one image-field to another too fast for Trillia to make completely coherent sense out of what she's experiencing, but she sees and hears more than enough. Discussions of prionoids and binotech. Ancient artifacts and mushroom extracts. A flying mountain over South America. A black hole sun over the American Southwest. A livesuited man like a manatee floating in a tank and directly wired into the infosphere. Alien signals from the heart of the galaxy. Machine intelligences already evolving in humanity's global networks. Peculiar suggestions that the pandemic of prionoid schizophrenia was somehow—"premeditated"? How could that be?

She wants to tell the young Merfolk to slow down so she can approach all this more systematically, but she doesn't—she can't. She finds herself paralyzed between historical fixation and guilty fascination at what she's seeing and hearing. She can only watch, helpless, as the innocent mer-girls dive into and out of still more confidential and protected areas of her grandfather's private records. She sees charts, graphs, lineage trees, still more obscure illustrations—evidence for a master project geared toward creating things labeled "Lapis" and "Triphibian," whatever those might be. Amid nearby fields and constellations of data Trillia sees her own name highlighted on a lineage chart, a "project breedline." Before the mer-girls can dive her virtuality into another data field, Trillia notes that her inheritance line, if that's what it is, stands widely separated from the line Ricardo's name appears on.

Does this chart have something to do with why her grandfather so vehemently opposed her seeing Ricardo? Her mind floods with paranoia, closely followed by disgust and dismay. Have the President and his associates been covertly "twisting fate"—under cover of protective regular health exams? Is what Ricardo suspected was done to *him* only the tip of an iceberg far deeper and colder?

Is it possible? Is her grandfather, President and founder of the culture she grew up in, manipulating the genetic and developmental patterns of all those born or made in the New Bahamian Polity? But why? Her head hurts, her mind surfeited with terrible things she thinks she sees and hears in these flashes and snippets—until at last she neither sees nor hears the information the mer-girls flash and flood through her virtual sensorium.

"Have you done this sort of thing before?" At her question, Trillia can tell it's *their* turn to feel guilty.

"Maybe once," Thetis says.

"Or twice," says Psamathe.

Trillia wonders if her grandfather might know of these security breaches but just doesn't care, given that they're "only" Merfolk.

"Yes. Or three times. Thetis, do you understand what you're seeing here?"

"Maybe—not really."

"Understanding is boring," asserts Psamathe. "Jumping from one to the other—that's what makes it fun!"

"Like spyhopping in different oceans!" Thetis says happily, infected with her friend's playfulness. Trillia thinks that if Merfolk could giggle, these two would probably be doing it now. She's thankful they can't.

"You're not going to tell, are you?" Psamathe asks.

Trillia finds herself caught once again by just how different and yet how similar Merfolk are to unaltered humanity.

"Tell? No, I won't tell. Not if you promise to meet me here in three days. And bring one of your sisters. Promise?"

"We promise," Thetis and Psamathe reply together, as solemnly as they can manage.

"Amphitrite will want to come," Thetis says.

"She likes adventures," Psamathe agrees.

Trillia's viewshades begin to chime and flash. A call from her mother. She gets the mer-girls to show her how to log out through their back door, then takes the call. Her mother flashes into virtual space before her, real time.

"Still studying? You haven't forgotten you're having dinner with us at Cafe Aromatica? Before the concert?"

Trillia tries not to roll her eyes—it confuses her VR system.

"I haven't forgotten. I'll meet you and Papa there in half an hour, then we'll hear *The Damnation of Faust* together, okay?"

Her mother looks a bit nonplused. They both know she would have preferred that Trillia come home and visit a bit first before the evening in public gets underway. Tonight, though, Trillia just can't handle any sort of at-home evening with the family. She's having enough trouble trying not to sound nervous and overwrought as it is.

"All right, dear, if you prefer it that way. Are you sure you're feeling all right? We don't have to make a big night of it, if you don't want to, you know. A quiet night at home would be just fine with your father and me."

"No, no. I'm fine. I'm looking forward to it."

They sign off from each other and Trillia exhales with relief—a bit too loudly. Her hands are shaking, though her voice is not. She wonders for a moment if she really saw everything she thought she saw in the mer-girls' hyperhopscotch tour of her grandfather's private records.

On her virtual space, she checks memory again for her grandfather's log-in. There it is: 3ma535n3p0. She wonders if it might be an anagram or covert spelling of something. Her grandfather's pass code—a very much longer alphanumeric string—looks to be at least pseudorandom and not meaningful as anything except a code key. Looking at the codes, she finds it hard to get over her amazement. Can she really be holding the keys that open the doors to the President's inner sanctum? Her good fortune—and her grandfather's arrogance in thinking himself so invulnerable to personal search—are, taken together, almost more than she *can* believe.

She wonders for a moment if this hasn't proven too easy—if this might not all be some sort of trap. But no. Before she hit on her odd brainstorm today, she spent weeks trying to approach the code-cracking job in a straightforward way and got nowhere. Who would have thought coming at the problem in a crazily lateral way—through a pair of finned and fluked mer-kids!—would provide the way in?

She shuts down her viewshades and the whole of her personal VR system. Standing and stretching beside the natatorium, she turns and walks up a ramp to a private street-level entrance. In the shadows, among the shops and market stalls, evening is beginning. Walking toward the cafe where she'll meet her parents, Trillia knows she doesn't know enough. Still, she is already much inclined to suspect foul play in the sudden way Ricardo was diagnosed as manifesting Wersign. No matter how guilty she might feel about doing so, she must revisit her grandfather's private infosphere archives, when the time allows.

If her suspicions as to her grandfather's plans for her and everyone else in the islands are in fact true—she shivers. Too revolting an idea for her ever to stay here, if she could prove such a thing. She has no intention of participating in some kind of eugenic experiment, against her will and without her informed consent.

What about everyone else, though? She thinks of her parents, whom she loves, despite the way they knuckle under to her paternal grandfather. Mom and Dad ought to be informed about it too. She already realizes, however, that they won't believe her if she just *tells* them. They are too caught up in believing what everyone else believes. About Ricardo and his supposed illness. About the plague. About the monsters off-island, which she is now more and more inclined to believe are vastly overblown tales intended to frighten and punish children.

Walking toward Cafe Aromatica, Trillia knows what she must do. Has known what she *will* do, from the moment she suggested the mer-girls meet her in three days at the natatorium. From the moment she promised Ricardo.

By night and boat she will flee toward the wilderness of North America, accompanied by the three Merfolk loyal to her.

Seeing her parents waving to her outside the cafe, her resolution falters. How can she leave them and everything else she's always known? Ricardo did it, yes—but he was under threat of execution. She's not.

All she'll have to help or harm her will be whatever truth she discovers.

She fears where that truth might lead, but she can't stop it from going there. She tells herself that what she was doing in her grandfather's records—what she will do in fleeing the islands—she's doing for everyone, not just herself. Walking into the restaurant to meet her parents, she almost believes it.

19

A Screaming Underground
2033

STANDING IN THE LOBBY OF THE YOUNGEST VIC THEATER, SIMON LINGham glanced around at his fellow audience members exiting the theater. He was in a mellow mood, still feeling the comic afterglow of having just seen a fine production of Wilde's *The Importance of Being Earnest*—and the alcoholic afterglow of having patronized the bar a couple of times too often during the interval between acts.

Nearby, a tall and lanky Asian teenager, with feathered hair and leather clothes, was joined by his equally young, thin, and similarly dressed (but much shorter) girlfriend. The teenaged boy had been pacing the lobby as he waited for his girlfriend to finish up in the lavatory—just as Simon, though not pacing, had also been waiting. For his ex-wife.

As he watched the young couple come together, Simon saw the boy's arm fall lightly across the girl's shoulder and the girl's hand hover over the boy's buttocks until it found a grip in his belt. The two looked so happy in each other's company they seemed to radiate pleasure in the form of a palpable aura.

"My," he heard Tomoko say as she came up beside him, "aren't we preoccupied!"

Simon smiled. During the course of the evening *she* had drunk nothing stronger than wine, and not much of that. Acutely aware of that, he replied with the verbal precision of someone fighting the noise-to-signal shift occasioned by a tad too much Scotch.

"You should talk! You fly all the way here from Seattle to speak with me personally. Then, first thing off the suborbiter, you suggest we see a play—one which you didn't fully concentrate on for more than ten minutes all evening."

"Guilty. One preoccupation at a time, please. Yours first."

They began walking over the wobbly paisley psychedelia of the carpet, toward the doors at the front of the lobby.

"Very well. See that young couple there? The ones dressed in urban black and brown? I was watching them and thinking what beautiful creatures human beings are. Thinking what a fundamentally beautiful thing human life is—despite all the ugly things we may do."

They left the theater. The night around them, though not quite yet spring, was nonetheless neither so cold nor so windy and rainy as other nights in recent memory. Tomoko turned to him.

"Beautiful lives, maybe—but short, too. None of us in the theater tonight will be alive in our original flesh in one hundred years—barring radical increases in life span, that is."

They walked down the night-lit street, headed toward the Stockwell underground station. Simon was inebriated enough to have to pick his way with some care, especially when they started down the steps into the tube station.

"True. And mostly true for the world as a whole. I suppose that's why I went into medicine, into epidemiology, to begin with. I don't like to see the beauty of human life struck down by disease—even if ephemerality is part of its beauty."

" 'Ephemerality'? You *are* in a meditative mood tonight."

Simon smiled. With his blood alcohol concentration, saying that word had been no easy task. They walked onto escalators descending into the bowels of the underground, the squeaking and chirping of their ancient belt-drives sounding to Simon like songs of artificial birds caged beneath his feet.

"Maybe it's just that I'm old enough to *think* about the beauty of human existence. That couple I saw earlier is still young enough to just *live* that beauty—thoughtlessly."

They reached the platform and waited for their train. A long gust of wind displaced from the tunnel announced the arrival of their train. Stepping from the platform they boarded a car that was almost empty, yet full of sound. A peasant-clad couple busked their way from car to car—a young man drumming on a tabla and a young woman dancing to the sound of her tambourine, weaving her instrument's slap and jangle into the polyrhythms created by her partner.

Simon saw Tomoko frown nervously at the young couple, though he couldn't quite understand why. They looked and sounded fine enough— not nearly as annoying as less talented buskers he'd heard over the years.

"I'd say that sums up my earlier preoccupation. How about yours?"

He caught Tomoko staring again at the couple drumming and dancing. They seemed intent on their performance, more to please themselves than from any hope of financial gain.

"You're still a regional coordinator with GEMS, right?"

Simon sat up straight in mock-salute.

"The Global Epidemiologic Monitoring System and its vast network of hospital observation stations, at your service."

Tomoko was undeterred by his flippancy.

"Are GEMS and WHO looking into these global rhythmanias and dance crazes?"

Simon absently ran a hand through his hair and stared down at his shoes.

"Strange you should mention that. Yes, we are, though I'm a bit embarrassed to tell you that."

"Embarrassed?"

Simon nodded slowly, glancing around the train car.

"Some higher-up's bright idea. On my way here from Geneva I had to stop at the Institut Pasteur—to discuss current directives on research into the 'phenomena' you mentioned. I'm surprised my French colleagues were able to keep straight faces."

"Do the French know something about the manias?"

"Of course not. The only thing all the rhythmaniacs and tarantists they've examined have in common is that they're antibody positive for this year's rounds of influenza and colds—like just about everyone else. Lucky they don't all have bronchitis or pneumonia, given the way they dance, drum, and dehydrate themselves to exhaustion, day after day."

"You don't think there might be a biological basis for these manias?"

Simon looked over his glasses in mild revulsion. Tomoko was treating this matter with far more seriousness than Simon felt it warranted.

"These 'outbreaks' of dancing and drumming are cultural epidemics, not biological ones. Not WHO's bailiwick. Heaven knows why we're wasting money on such things. It's as misguided as those parents you see in the news—the ones trying to force their doctors to prescribe antispasmodic and anticonvulsant drugs to 'cure' their kids of drumming and dancing! Next thing you know, the politicians will have us investigating the upswing in religious revivalism! Yet, tomorrow, I'm off to the Microbial Research facilities at Porton Down in Salisbury—on the same foolish drumming-and-dancing business."

The tube train pulled into Vauxhall and a raucous party of weekend revelers flooded into their car. The usual assortment of pub crawlers was this evening amply outnumbered by dancers and drummers dressed in dark urban faux furs and feathers and leathers. As the train pulled out of the station headed for Pimlico, Tomoko turned to him.

"Why foolish?"

"What harm have these 'outbreaks' really done? Besides preventing the trains from running on time once in a while? WHO's budget for the whole planet is less than Greater London's annual budget for street cleaning. We're insanely underfunded—always have been. There are *real* diseases out there, ones that are really killing people. We've got endemic occurrence levels of dengue-6 and dengue-7 in most of the major tropical and subtropical megacities. Supertuberculin outbreaks in New York, Moscow, and Beijing. Hemorrhagic red-blue fevers in Africa and South America. Typhus and cholera waiting to exploit wartime conditions in a dozen ongoing high-intensity local conflicts. Not to mention this year's influenza rounds—supertransmissible, though not supervirulent, thank heaven. *Those* are where our focus should be."

Tomoko nodded. Glancing around at the drumming and shimmying revelers in the train car, though, she clearly wasn't satisfied.

"Those diseases are fairly well understood. What concerns me are the new things, the unexpected things—precisely *because* epidemiological work is underfunded. Gaps in the disease control infrastructure mean something radically new could be overlooked, or its effects misidentified for months—"

"Tell me about it."

"—especially if it looks 'cultural' rather than 'biological.' You're already checking for possible new evolutions out of old strains?"

Simon made a dismissive wave of the hand, growing more sober as Tomoko's questions forced him to concentrate.

"We always look for those sorts of things. Several of the dengues do that—newer strains hijacking the victim's immune system through the same antibodies the individual created as a response to an earlier infection by a milder strain. We look for all of that—species-barrier jumpers, virus gumbo effects, you name it. Nothing new there."

More passengers boarded at Pimlico. Despite the fact that the train now made for a crowded dance floor, there was a lot of bumping and grinding going on among the partying passengers—not all of whom, Simon noticed, were young. Tomoko had to speak louder over the noise of the drumming and dancing revelers.

"What about prions or prion-like substances?"

"What about them?"

"Are the monitoring stations checking for conformation-altering proteins in the blood or cerebrospinal fluid of those they're examining?"

Simon was beginning to find this discussion irksome.

"Why? Should they be? You think this drumming and dancing stuff is like—what was it you called it? Fatal familial insomnia? Laughing sickness?"

Tomoko shook her head. Above the sound of the dancers and drummers, the train on its rails had begun to make a shrill, piercing sound that grew steadily louder. Tomoko had to speak more and more loudly over the high-pitched screaming of the train as it sped between Pimlico and Victoria Station.

"No. Not exactly. But one of the conformation-altering proteins my company developed may have had its own conformation altered. One of our prionoids seems to have been reshuffled, maybe bacterially or virally. We don't know exactly how—but we think we've identified the altered form in those you called rhythmaniacs and tarantists."

Simon stared at her. He knew microbes could swap genes, but he'd never heard of them swapping prions or altering prion structures. Not even the wildest retroviruses could backscan from finished protein to

RNA and DNA segment. The screeching of the train on its rails between Victoria and Pimlico was now so excruciatingly loud, he could not hope to speak over the noise. Moving to put his hands over his ears, Simon realized something.

The drumbeat was gone, replaced by the thrumming of unconscious, tetanic hands and fingers twitching on drumheads. The dancers' shimmying, bumping, and grinding had been replaced by convulsions and spasms, their faces slack-jawed, eyes remming or rolling up into their heads—all somehow *in time to* the painfully high-pitched shrieking of the train over the rails.

By the time the train got beyond whatever it was in that stretch of track that caused the screaming harmonics between train and rails, several of the dancers had passed out and collapsed. As the train pulled into Victoria Station the revelers who were still standing began helping up those who had fallen. Simon was stunned to see them smiling and shaking their heads as they exited, laughing and shouting "Whew!" and "Wow!" and "Bloody *fantastic*, that was!"—and "Just like last night!"

Good God! They knew it was coming. They were counting on it! They had purposely used something in that annoying sound to alter their states of consciousness!

Simon was suddenly afraid he was all too sober.

"Did you—?"

He stopped when he saw that, even as Tomoko nodded, there was something frightened in her look. The train pulled out again, headed onward to Green Park and Oxford Circus.

"Tell me everything you know about this escaped prionoid of yours. Just to be on the safe side."

20

Spacehenge
2066

ON THE ELEVENTH DAY RETRACING NORTHWARD HIS EARLIER TWELVE-DAY "misdirection" south, Ricardo finds the terrain ceases to be familiar. The plodding, rusting dredges have done their work uninterrupted here and the going is easy. At noon of the next day, north of the empty but surprisingly intact town of Melbourne, a long narrow tongue of land splits the watercourse, dividing Indian River and the intracoastal waterway proper from the Banana River.

Finally his old map makes complete sense. He curses himself again when he realizes how close this place is to his initial landfall, now nearly a month gone. Shaking his head, Ricardo paddles up the Banana, toward where he soon sees gantry towers looming like skeletalized buildings on the horizon to the north and east. He passes under the rust-stained and edge-crumbling causeway from Merritt Island, headed toward the much smaller bridge linking City Point to the Cape.

Getting out of his kayak and beaching it in the shadow of the bridge, he sets up his base camp at last. After fishing and cooking and eating, he bushwhacks his way up to the east end of the bridge in sunset light, then walks farther east, over the grass-blotched concrete and broken up asphalt of the highway. Amid a tangle of blown-down debris, he sees a large flat rectangle, still largely intact, though bent and paint-cracked along the midline. He lifts it up.

CAPE CANAVERAL AIR STATION, it says on its face. MAIN GATE.

Only now does he finally stop kicking himself. To his north and east lie Canaveral and Kennedy Spaceport. He's made it at last, and celebrates by shouting a series of whoops into the great silence.

He indulges his exultation only briefly. Tomorrow will be a long day. He heads back to his base camp to turn in for the night. Despite his usual exhaustion and greater than usual forethought, he finds he is too wrought-up to sleep until well into the night.

With sleep, the long night before the long day only becomes longer. Ricardo dreams that he wakes up and, in that waking within dream, relives again the long, misdirected trip he took south:

ARRIVING ON THE COAST THE DAY AFTER SETTING OUT. CONFIDENT— despite bad maps, his flawed sense of direction, the unhelpfulness of the mermen—that he is making landfall between the deserted cities of Palm Coast and Daytona Beach, within a few days' paddling of the Kennedy-Canaveral Spaceport. Opting for one of *Sea Robin*'s two collapsible sea kayaks. Carrying the collapsed kayak over sand to the Intracoastal Waterway, unfolding the small craft and heading boldly southward.

Encountering in his first full day of paddling the first of the sun-run robot dredges Simon mentioned. A rusting, weatherworn low barge, upright cylindrical sensor array poking up out of the field of its solar-power sheeting, robotic hybrid of octopus and elephant creeping along the waterway, siphon-arm tentacles sucking up and spewing out great volumes of sand and silt.

Passing the ruins of a city blasted by fire, hurricane, tornado, and storm surge—almost beyond recognition as a former place of human habitation—convinced it must be Daytona Beach. The going becoming more difficult below the ruins of the ravaged city. Sections of the waterway wide but shallow. Still-functioning robot dredges fewer and farther between. Two dead dredges, one with its solar-sheet power units ripped away, the other cannibalized almost to the water line.

Zigzagging his way through an obstacle course of sandbars, the water growing shallower still. The kayak bottoming out on the sandbars. Getting out of it and getting behind it, standing in the shallow water, shoving the gear-laden kayak across the bar and into the next stretch of water deep enough to paddle across, again and again. Setting up camp that night, footsore and bone-tired.

The canal becoming completely impassable at points. Islands of old dredge tailings, overgrown by riotous greenery. Pelicans and cormorants perching in remains of tumbledown shacks. No evidence of recent human habitation. Forced to portage again and again, unloading gear, collapsing and carrying the kayak, reloading the gear. Weather turning nasty cold, then spitting rain steadily for several hours. Camping that evening, the rain drumming over his tent flap.

Always fearing capture by Werfolk or savage Trufolk. His stores of dried food dwindling. Unhappy prospect of relying on local food sources. Thinking of the old pollutant poisons and microbial menaces, still lurking like landmines after a terrible war. Pfeisteria in fish. Lobsters losing their sense of direction due to strange microbial infections—and, once eaten, making gourmands lose their memories. Mosquitoes, all the other insects. Rats and other rodents. Three decades not nearly enough time to have purged the world of all its terrifying possibilities.

The weather clearing, growing warmer and more pleasant. Taking a day off from paddling. Resting, reconnoitering. Striding along the water-way's bank, compound bow in hand, arrow quiver and collapsed fishing tackle in a tube at his back, things less dire than he thought. Game plentiful and unfearing. The waterway again growing more open and passable. More of the old robotic dredgers still active, snailing along, spewing up sand, silt, and debris.

Fishing, with considerable success, but always scrutinizing his catch while scraping off the scales, removing the heads, slitting open the bellies, removing the entrails—and stoking the fire up hot. His ceramic water-filter and pump combo pull clean water. No such thing for filtering out the dangers in food—just eyeballing the catch to make sure it "looks okay," then cooking the hell out of it. No reasoning with microbes.

First inkling of misdirection, reaching a channel and inlet not on any of his maps. Unidentifiable inlet opening from waterway into Atlantic. Storm damage in the years since the pandemic? Ponce Inlet? Channel looks almost like a canal, a big one. Nothing like it anywhere near Ponce Inlet.

Puzzling fears forgotten amid leaping and splashing of joyful mer-man.

"Thaumas! Hey, buddy! How'd you find me?"

No translation screens. Understanding Thaumas's high whistly-clicky "speech" not an easy task, its frequency range as unusually high for him as abnormally low for Thaumas.

"Heard you had to leave. Something wasn't right, in the way of it. The way Fathers acted. Followed them and your boat to the coast. Stayed hid. Heard them talk about which way you headed. Swam beside the land. Found this way in, then waited for you. Thought you could use a water-helper. Herd fish for you to catch, like the old days."

"I appreciate it! Good to have you along. If the man I'm looking for hasn't gone inland, I'm going to be spending a lot of time on or near water. I can use your help."

The merman chasing fish day upon day, either driving them onshore for Ricardo to grab and toss up on the bank, or shoot with tethered arrows. Eating well, the weather fine, unexpectedly warmer. Sandbars, sunken boats, other obstacles still posing problems. Staying focused on the waterway—and paddling.

Should have reached Titusville by now.

Off to starboard, heron- and cormorant-dotted wildlands stretching away. To port, ruins of ostentatious mansions, green-scum-puddled swimming pools, weedy tennis courts and patios. Shredded mesh of screens hanging, indecipherable rusty or mossy flags of lost nations. Weather coming in through shattered windows, broken roofs of tile and shingle.

Imagining bones of the dead sinking into jumbled heaps inside palaces of decay. No bodies visible, no skeletons, no bones from all the billions of dead haunting the streets and buildings of an abandoned world. Not looking for such things. Not eager to explore. Avoiding all those places. The wild-dog packs of old report. The remains in their perfect silence reminding him of his own Wersigned mortality.

How many bodies not already rotted away? How many still intact—not torn apart and dragged away by packs of scavengers? How many scattered bones not broken down by wind and rain and sun? Grown over by grass, vines, weeds? Covered by dust in the hot sun, moss in the cool shade?

Passing broken-down docks crowded with huge dilapidated yachts, some piled up against each other, many listing oddly, already half-sunk. Vistas of ruin more and more grandiose—ivy-shrouded hypermalls, ruined causeways, buildings themselves more and more densely packed together on both sides of the waterway. To port and starboard luxurious homes and once-gleaming high-rises—now fallen on the hardest of times through fire and storm, rust and patina, vines and weeds. Waterway becoming a street in a ruined city of mazed canals, shattered docks and slips, decaying sinking yachts and harbor boats.

All wrong. Endless, dense, once-opulent ghost high-rises and mansions—and nothing like this where he's supposed to be. Collapsed buildings and broken boats blocking the waterway with a tumbledown mountain of debris. Well and truly lost, no signs to guide them, no one to ask for directions.

Breaking free of his paddle-vision at last. Looking for signs of just where they actually are. Scrambling about the wreckage, examining the exteriors of boat after boat piled against the mountain of debris, scattering geckos, other lizards and snakes from their sunning, lean mean sly shy feral cats leaping after them. Realizing that the preponderance of these boats name a single port as home.

Fort Lauderdale.

Good God. Fort Lauderdale! How in the world did he manage to screw up so badly?

Checking his maps, realizing what went wrong. First landing not between Palm Coast and Daytona Beach, north of Titusville and the Cape, but between Palm Bay and Vero Beach. Thaumas's unidentifiable inlet lying between Jensen Beach and Sewall's Point. Unidentifiable channel the remains of the St. Lucie Canal. The warmer weather, the greater number of palm trees and brushland and mangrove swamps—all from being closer to the Gulf Stream, curving nearer the southern third of the Florida coast. All the paddling southward now to be made up again—heading *north*.

"Thaumas, sometimes I think I *think* I'm just too damn good for my own damn good."

Wondering if all the effort of this journey can ever possibly be worth it. If Simon will still be with Drinan. And Drinan himself. What he remembers of Drinan's history lies far from Simon Lingham's lofty reason and science.

Nothing for it but to paddle back the way he came. Giving less attention to wreck and ruin on his way north, more to the plants and animals along the waterway. The scents of early flowers on the breeze in the cool evenings. Gulls and cormorants, pelicans, egrets, herons. Deer in the scrublands browsing the overgrown meadows, the shrubby succession plants on lost lawns of mansions and high-rise condos. Coyotes crossing tennis courts overgrown with low grass, behind curtains of vines draping high, rusting chainlink fences. Larger, more furtive presences. The long tawny shape of a puma leaping an incredible distance up and over an embankment. Alligators in the channels flowing into the waterway. Manatees among the sea-grass of the inlets. None of them worrying Thaumas, though.

Seeing the rare remains of post-pandemic campsites, and not knowing whether to feel hopeful or fearful but in the end feeling some of both. Sitting beside his own evening fires, swatting the occasional mosquitoes and flies away from his head, belly full of easy fish, finding less and less occasion to curse himself for his large initial misstep, despite the daily ache in his muscles—

RICARDO WAKES FROM THE DREAM IN WHICH HE DREAMED HE WOKE. HE lies in his tent, in the early morning light, thinking about the dream as it fades. Strange that his mind should have processed it all that way. Too much time spent alone, with no one to talk to but his merman friend.

Sitting in the tent, Ricardo remembers such misdirection happening once before—when he took Trillia on a boating excursion through some of the outer islands, and got disoriented. He stubbornly refused to admit he'd landed them on the wrong island.

"Trust me," he'd said. "I'm like those South Seas islanders who used to be able to navigate thousands of miles of open ocean in a canoe. When the sky clouded over and they couldn't navigate by the position of the sun or stars, those guys could flop their genitals over the edge of the canoe and tell, by the temperature and current swirling there, whether they were headed in the right direction or not."

Trillia shook her head and grimaced, pinching him, not so much in shock at the indelicate story as in simple annoyance.

"All I can say to that, Mr. Testicles-of-Direction, is I'm glad we've got a ship-to-shore radio."

Ricardo remembers it both fondly and uncomfortably. Later, when he refused to seek directions on the way home, Trillia called him a "passive-aggressive incompetent control freak"—one of her grandfather's pet phrases, he suspected—and stormed off to the other end of the boat. She cold-shouldered him the rest of the evening, dashing his hopes for a shot at intimacy, at least on that trip.

Maybe forever, now. The thought has occurred to him that perhaps it was because of their love that he has been plagued and exiled, but he still misses her deeply. Waking here alone, Ricardo yearns to see Trillia again, even more than he doubts that he will.

He tries to shake his melancholy by breaking camp. Under a flawless blue sky, he takes down his shelter and packs up his sleepsack. He gathers the last of his dried food supplies, meager as they are—saved for the occasion of hiking overland into the spaceport.

"Thaumas, look after my camp and kayak here, will you? I need to explore this island today. I may not be back until tomorrow."

Thaumas clickwhistles his okay and Ricardo sets off through the brush. Once past the bridge and on the road again, he notices that the asphalt quickly grows more broken up and overgrown until it is little more than a grassy track. Someone, however, has been keeping the track open amid the undergrowth, which he takes to be a good sign.

Following the track, he comes to something a weatherworn commemorative plaque labels Complex 5. On the launch pad of Complex 5, a machine called a Redstone Rocket Static Display has toppled over, smashed, and rusted—though not necessarily in that order. Hurricane damage, most likely. Locked and silent as a Pharaoh's tomb, the launch-command blockhouse for Complex 5 and Complex 6 stands stripped of its paint and slowly crumbling from salt air and years of storms. Vines cover one wall and the entrance is weed-choked. The ancient antenna atop its roof is bent and broken.

On the launch pad of Complex 6, the "Juno 1 Rocket Static Display" described by the historical plaque is also hurricane-toppled, lying in a crumpled, rusty heap upon the grass- and weed-splotched concrete of the pad.

As he walks farther along the cleared track, Ricardo recalls enough of the history of space flight to realize that these toppled rockets were already museum pieces when the old world ended—obsolete machines, long before the pandemic dashed humanity's dreams of migrations to other worlds. The sense that he is looking at what was already history *before* the end of history is confirmed when he comes across faded signs and plaques identifying the Air Force Space and Missile Museum.

The trail winds past more launch vehicles, rusting and faded but otherwise intact, canted over on their sides. Their patinaed plaques identify them as Thor and Atlas rockets, Mace and Matador Ground-Launched Cruise Missiles. These, however, were not toppled by hurricanes. They were purposely mounted on tow-trailers and viewed by climbing skid-plated stairs, now weakened by rust. This entire Canaveral complex, he recalls, fell into disrepair but was restored. Since the collapse it has fallen into deeper decay than ever, but who will restore it now?

Complex 26 Pad B is almost eerily well-preserved. Still embraced by the surrounding gantry structure, the static display rocket, a Redstone, has not toppled over—despite the heavy rusting and weather-wear on both gantry tower and rocket. The lower halves of both are also curtained and entangled in vines. Ricardo stares at vines and rocket for some time. It almost seems that what restrains the spacecraft from rising in flight is not the gravity but the *greenery* of the living Earth.

Some distance away, part of the track leads into Complex 26's command blockhouse, the door of which is slightly ajar. This blockhouse, though less damaged by proximity to the ocean, paradoxically feels more "underwater," inside. Its antiquated clocks, switch panels, and tape-drive machines are flooded by a greenish undersea light—daylight shining through the thick, multipaned glass viewing-windows at its front.

Following the track, Ricardo sees further variations on the same themes. Marsh and scrub encroach on what were once the lawns and service roads of Complex 17, pads A and B. Weeds and vines drape the lower sections of the gantry towers, while rust paints all of it. The concrete of the Complex 9 rocket stand, fire-blackened and storm-greened, settles into a long, slow, peace accord with invading creepers and weeds. The low bunkerlike shape of the Complex 9–10 blockhouse shows only thick walls, no windows—the launch pad viewed through rust-stained, angled mirrors visible atop the bunker.

The memorial plaque on the Complex 31 Missile Silo informs him that the silo was originally built for launching Minuteman missiles, but now beneath its massive concrete caps it holds debris from the *Challenger* space shuttle explosion. Nearby, the Complex 31 blockhouse is a sandbag-and-concrete structure shaped like a beehive crossed with an igloo. Heavily overgrown with weeds, the blockhouse is fronted by a heavy, locked vault door. Viewing periscopes jut from the structure's top.

Ricardo gradually begins to realize that this is more than a museum. It's also a graveyard, a memorial to that strange time called the Cold War, when human beings narrowly missed doing with a bang what the pandemic later accomplished with a scream and a whimper.

The Complex 21 hardsite, when he reaches it, is no longer quite so hard. Salt air and harsh weather have caused it to crumble extensively. Beyond its thick walls and rusting stairways, Ricardo sees huge blast-diverter pipes, and wonders at the power of the machines once launched from such places. Coming around a corner of the hardsite he thinks he sees, some distance away, a static rocket display not yet toppled by wind and storm. Then he realizes that the structure is in fact the Cape Canaveral lighthouse, already leaning toward the surf and much in need of new paint.

The track does not lead him to the lighthouse, but toward Complex 36. A railborne mobile service tower and fixed umbilical tower are both still standing there, surrounded by artifacts whose plaques describe them as "propellant tanks" and "hydrogen burn stacks." Other oxidized and lichened plaques describe various electrical, hydraulic, and pneumatic functions of the umbilical tower—but several of them are too eroded to read.

The track appears more heavily used around Complex 14, where the "memorial" nature of the areas he's been walking through is even clearer. Atop the heavy slab of Complex 14's Mercury monument is a freestanding metal icon. The slab's plaque identifies the sculpture as representing a number 7—for the original seven astronauts—inside the astronomical symbol for the planet Mercury. Under the monument slab lies the Project Mercury Time Capsule, to be opened in the year 2464.

The time capsule is on a motionless five-hundred-year time-travel journey, Ricardo muses. Its journey is only twenty percent complete, yet the monument and time capsule have already outlasted the civilization that built them. In another four hundred years, will there be a single human being left alive who will understand the early artifacts of space travel? Or even someone able to *read* the language of the monument's plaques, and open the capsule as scheduled? Ricardo would doubt both possibilities, but the fact that someone appears to be maintaining this monument (at least keeping back the creepers and weeds) makes him doubt his own doubting, for the moment.

The track winds onward to Complex 13 with its rusted gantry service structure and low mushroom-domed blockhouse. Nearby stand liquid oxygen storage and transfer facilities, amid mazes of pipes. Rust-stained concrete curbs rise up the ramp toward the gantry structure. Close at hand, Complex 19 is more of the same, more grass and bushes growing on crumbling launch pads, another blast diverter, a service tower gone horizontal—though whether by intent of the designers or calamity of weather Ricardo cannot say.

Complex 34 at first looks even less promising. He sees the now-familiar refractory brick blast-paving, atop thick concrete slab punctuated by grass and weeds. The scattered ruins of a few buildings border the massive concrete pedestal of a launch stand. As he walks toward the launch pedestal, however, Ricardo sees the track here is the best-maintained yet, though he can't fathom why.

Slowly Ricardo realizes this pedestal is in fact the most monumental of all. Not from its function or size or strength: Plaques inform him of its construction (concrete and steel) and its dimensions (27 feet tall by 42 feet long). At its top is a circular hole 26 feet in diameter and open to the sky—an "exhaust opening," rimmed by a torus ring of water nozzles designed to cool the rocket exhaust and the pedestal itself during rocket launch. Other plaques inform him that the pedestal was used for both Apollo 1 and the first successful Apollo launch, Apollo 7.

Ricardo recalls images of spacecraft rising on pillars of fire and smoke. Apollo. The moon landing. They put men on the moon. They sent probes throughout the solar system and into interstellar space. They built orbital habitats. How could they forget they were already living on the surface of a spinning habitat in orbit around the sun? Living in the thin, bright, breathable halo of a gravity-powered stone spaceship, with a huge electromagnet at its core? How could they let their human world grow so talk-sick it became toxic? If the pandemic hadn't hit, would the entire life-support system of the planet have gone down—not only for humans, but for *everything*—until the Earth became as lifeless as the moon?

The plaques on the legs of the pedestal do not answer such questions. They do make clear, however, that the pedestal's importance derives not from what it was made of or what it was used for, but from what happened here and the implications of that event. On one leg of the pedestal a plaque reads:

IN MEMORY

OF THOSE WHO MADE THE ULTIMATE SACRIFICE

SO OTHERS COULD REACH FOR THE STARS

AD ASTRA PER ASPERA

(A ROUGH ROAD LEADS TO THE STARS)

GOD SPEED TO THE CREW OF APOLLO I.

Nearby , another plaque gives Ricardo more of the history of the site:

LAUNCH COMPLEX 34

FRIDAY 27 JANUARY, 1967

1831 HOURS

DEDICATED TO THE LIVING MEMORY

OF THE CREW OF APOLLO 1:

USAF LT. COLONEL VIRGIL I. GRISSOM

USAF LT. COLONEL EDWARD H. WHITE, II

USN LT. COMMANDER ROGER B. CHAFFEE

They gave their lives in service to their country
in the ongoing exploration of humankind's final frontier
rememeber them not for how they died
but for the ideals for which they lived.

On another part of the pedestal he notices that the cryptic phrase he's seen throughout the day, in faded stencils and more durable stone-cuttings on large structures throughout the Cape—ABANDON IN PLACE—has here been permanently altered, cut into the stone as ABANDON IN PEACE.

Looking up through the great circular hole in the pedestal's top, Richard sees that the sun is farther to the west and the day is later than he thought. He will have to be starting back to his camp soon.

"At the right time on the right moonlit night," says a voice behind him, "the view through that circle is spectacular."

Ricardo turns about, startled. An older man, with an enormous yet puppyish buff-colored dog at his side, steps out from the shadow of one pedestal leg. The man's long gray beard hangs from a face heavily tattooed with purple whorls and dotted red lines. He's dressed in a jumpsuit with identification patches at the shoulders and chest.

"I think of this place as Spacehenge, myself," says the old man, looking up through the great hole in the top of the pedestal, toward the cloud-flecked blue sky beyond. "A stone temple linking life down here to the moon and stars out there. To the whole universe."

The man turns his gaze from the hole into the sky to stare with piercing dark eyes at Ricardo. Not knowing what else to do, Ricardo nods. The old man thrusts out his hand. Ricardo shakes it.

"John Drinan. This young horse of a dog has the fancy name of Ozymandias the Fifth. He's the great-great grandpup of a pure-bred mastiff, though he isn't so pure of breed himself."

Ricardo pumps Drinan's hand with grateful enthusiasm.

"Just the man I've been looking for! I'm Ricardo Alvarez. Is Dr. Lingham still here, sir?"

"Lingham? Simon Lingham? Now that's a name I haven't heard in quite a while. No, son. He's not here. I haven't seen him since I left Spires' islands, more than twenty-five years ago."

"He hasn't been here? He said he was headed here when he went into exile."

Drinan slowly breaks from the handshake. Now it's his turn to be shocked.

"Exile? Simon Lingham in exile? Of his own free will? Spires must be lording it awful high and mighty, to drive Simon away. Come along, Alvarez. Tell me about it while we walk from the past into the future."

At first Ricardo thinks the older man is speaking poetically, but he soon sees that he is speaking the literal truth. As they walk and Ricardo tries to explain Lingham's situation, his own, and the general state of affairs in the

New Bahamian Polity, he and Drinan and Oz the Fifth arrive at the grounds of Kennedy Spaceport proper. Ricardo can only nod as Drinan tries to explain what they see around them.

"Here the older style rockets were replaced by tetherships. By rail-gun-launched payload boosters, winged single-stage-to-orbit space-craft—all sorts of systems, some successful, some less so. Unfortunately, it didn't much matter in the end whether the space agencies managed to transform themselves into spacesuit-and-tie profit-makers or not. Every-thing launch-ready was destroyed. Riots and last-ditch escape attempts during the Plague Year took out the majority of the fleet. Years of storm and neglect before we set up shop here got most of what was left. But not all—not all."

Through westering light, Drinan guides Ricardo past the maze of broken-windowed spaceport terminals. The buildings are fire-damaged at a few points, too, but otherwise appear to be structurally intact. They come to an astoundingly huge structure, rust-stained and faded, which Drinan calls the Vehicle Assembly Building.

Approaching the open narrow edge of an almost unbelievably tall door, Ricardo sees the shadows of figures. They haul or drive carts of what look like junk and debris into the interior of the cavernous building. He is a bit unsettled by it, since the comings and goings of the dozen or so people he sees before him is more organized human activity than he's seen anywhere since he left the islands. As they walk toward the tremendously tall door, Ricardo gestures at the activity around them.

"What's all that about?"

"Just snagging more solar units. Cannibalizing computers. Scavenging for maneuvering thrusters. Anything we can get."

As they enter the building, Ricardo feels almost agoraphobic, after being on his own and alone for weeks.

"But why?"

"For a space program, of course. A stripped-down one, built from scav-enged parts, but a space program nonetheless."

Drinan smiles his gap-toothed smile as the two of them move through the gigantic yet cluttered workshop space of the Assembly Building. Ricardo tries to recall what he's heard over the years about this abjurer's mental stability, or lack thereof. Was John Drinan the one who was some kind of crazy street-person even *before* the outbreak? Was he the one who claimed he was not from this universe at all, but from a closely parallel one? Ricardo had hoped he was confusing Drinan with someone crazier, but now his worst fears about the man's mental state seem to have been realized. Drinan, with the help of a handful of equally demented Tru-folk—and maybe Werfolk too?—is ransacking the spaceport for salvage.

"There she is! Sol-Flier 1. Our Phoenix for rising from the ashes!"

Before them, flooded in more artificial light than Ricardo has seen in his entire lifetime, is something that is more abstract megasculpture than spaceship: a pair of funnels, or cones, placed big end to big end, ringed by a flange, or collar. The whole contraption stands upright in a holed pedestal not so very unlike what Drinan called Spacehenge. The thing on the pedestal, however, bears little resemblance to the rockets Ricardo saw clasped by gantry towers earlier.

"We had a heck of a time finding this ship," Drinan says, showing evi-dent pride as he walks Ricardo around it. "Searched for fourteen years before we finally located it. The Space Agency was shipping it across the country just as the plague was hitting its worst stages. We scared up full transport documents, bills of lading, you name it. Everything pointed to its disappearance somewhere in the state of Florida. The folks transport-ing it were smart. Took us forever to figure it out. They hid it in a stor-age facility full of old circus and carnival equipment! Anyone who found it but didn't know what it was would assume it was an amusement park ride!"

Trying to humor Drinan, Ricardo lets that sink in. He wonders if these people are crazy enough to be trying to launch an amusement park space-ship into orbit. He doesn't put it past them.

"How does it work?"

Drinan turns toward where a woman oversees a wrecking crew break-ing up and stripping solar-power units out of big panels.

"Best to have someone with the background explain that. Hey, Malika! Got a minute? We've got a visitor from the Bahamas wants to know how the ship works."

The crew boss approaches them. Drinan introduces the tall, regal-looking black woman—less heavily tattooed than Drinan himself and dressed in a red-and-gold caftan—as Malika Hardesty. Drinan bends down and pats the head of his big dog as the woman explains the space-ship's operation to Ricardo.

"It's called a lightcraft, and not just because it doesn't weigh much. The entire bottom side of it is an optic surface, a circular base mirror that curves inward. The parabolic shape means any light beam directed at it will be focused toward the annulus—that's the ring-shaped structure along the central collar's trailing edge, there."

"But where's the engine? Where's the fuel?"

"We leave all that heavy stuff down here. Propellant, energy source, engines—we won't carry any of that up the gravity well if we don't have to. And we *don't* have to. Its energy source—solar-pumped pulse lasers, in this case—we leave behind on the ground."

"How do they move the thing if they're on the ground?"

"Big lasers directed onto the bottom side of the craft focus tightly enough at that annulus edge to strip electrons from atoms of the sur-rounding air—a process known as Inverse Bremsstrahlung absorption. The stripped-electron plasma has a temperature of 30,000 degrees Kelvin, five times as hot as the sun's surface. *That* creates a pressure wave of several thousand atmospheres, for thrust."

Despite himself, Ricardo thinks it almost sounds as if it might work. The woman seems straightforward and levelheaded—not a loony at all, the situation notwithstanding.

"What about when you run out of 'surrounding air'?"

"We need only minimal propellant reaction-mass for operation outside the atmosphere. For that, we've been scavenging detonation wave engines. Scramjets. Magneto-hydrodynamic fanjets. Rotary pulsejets. Electrostatic thrusters. Whatever we can get to work. What we're doing now—besides always increasing the power base for our propulsion lasers—is bundling together and testing those other systems for their compatibility with beamed power. Once we've got enough laser power, enough tracking capability, and the right maneuvering-thruster package, we'll be ready to fly."

"Fly where? To an orbital habitat? The moon?"

John Drinan looks up from his dog.

"Eventually, yes, though not at first. Remember, we've only got one lightcraft—and we don't have the technical capabilities to build another. We don't have the industrial base to build even chemical rockets. Most of the chemically based propellant systems were blown up during the Plague Year."

Malika nods sharply.

"Or have since degraded past the point of usability. Chemical propulsion systems have a nasty tendency toward blowing up on their own, too. The lightcraft approach is higher tech but lower complexity, in a number of ways. It relies on quantum rather than chemical effects; its component parts are more stable. The Collapse, and the time that's elapsed since it happened, have had less of an effect on the solar-pumped lasers and computer gear needed for lightcraft operation than they've had on chemically propelled spacecraft."

"That may all be true, but that still doesn't explain where you intend to fly the thing."

He sees a quick glance pass between Drinan and Hardesty. Drinan looks away, into some indeterminate space.

"I'm in the wrong universe. I've known it for thirty-three years. A third of a century. I've been trying to explain it to people here almost since the moment I arrived. I don't know what's driven me all these years to prove it, but final proof is almost at hand."

Ricardo feels his newfound confidence in the sanity of these people and their activities slipping away with each word.

"I . . . I don't understand."

"Same planet, different universe. In those days I was an independent space pilot. I was traveling with the great-great grandsire of this Oz—my first dog named Ozymandias. I had just finished debugging robot miners scheduled for work among the asteroids. We were on our way in for some rest and relaxation, when the Light hit us."

"The 'Light'?"

"Something to do with a ring of orbiting 'information refractors' being used by my cousin Jiro. I don't fully understand it, but I *can* tell you this: It wasn't just what comes out of a lamp. Or a laser."

"What kind of light was it, then?"

"Not sure. Malika and I have trying to figure it out for years. Whatever it was, it must have disrupted the boundaries between two universes right next to each other. My ship, the *Helios*, fell through the hole, the rift-tunnel the Light opened from my home universe into this one. That plunge disabled my ship. Bad. Oz and I were lucky to survive. We arrived here only by accident—crash-landed our escape pod in the desert on 'your' Earth, in this version of Earth, not too long before the pandemic hit."

Ricardo thinks he hears some demented metaphor for birth-memory in the old man's story.

" 'Holes' between universes? 'Rift-tunnels'?"

Drinan gives a small smile.

"Right. Not a light at the end of the tunnel, but a tunnel at the end of the Light."

Malika frowns.

"You have no idea how long I've been trying to break him of thinking of this mission in terms of 'parallel universes' and 'holes' between them. Don't start with universes. Don't even start with worlds. Start with *words*."

Ricardo's expression must convey his confusion, for the woman tries to explain further.

"In the system of all possible words, every word is made out of all the traces of all the words it is not. In the system of all possible *worlds*, every world is made out of all the traces of all the *worlds* it is not. In the system of all possible universes, every universe is made out of all the traces of all the universes it is not. In fact, for every universe of the plenum, the part is greater than the sum of its 'holes'—the traces of all the parts it is *not*, the absences from which its presence is constituted."

Ricardo shakes the hair out of his eyes.

"Heady stuff."

John Drinan laughs, then addresses Malika in an odd tone.

"Is Nothing sacred?"

"It sure is."

"I don't get it."

" 'Is nothing sacred?' was intended to be a joke, the first time I said it to Malika. Years ago. Trying to keep up with *her* led me to tell her about the realm I passed through, when the tunnel, or vortex, or whatever it was the Light opened up, shot me from my home universe—"

"Call it Universe A," Malika interjects.

"—to this one."

"Call it Universe A Prime."

"What I remembered was that it was like I passed inside a ring of light, where I could see all times at one place, where I could see all spaces at one time. Only, through all of that, it wasn't exactly 'me' that was doing the seeing. I couldn't tell whether my ship was moving and space-time was standing still, or vice versa, but as 'I' watched I saw how each decision in any mind in a given universe caused a nearly parallel universe to branch off. The result was not so much branched like a tree as webbed, like a cross between a plasma globe and a net—only every node of the net was another globe of nodes and nets."

Malika nods.

"I was struck by the image. The plenum view that comes from it leads to the idea that 'nothing'—the nothing out of which everything comes—really *is* sacred. The plenum theory *works*, too. One photon acting like more than one in the classic two-slit experiment is proof of quantum interaction between nearby universes."

"Or look at the curves and spirals of cloud chamber traces," Drinan suggests.

Ricardo has no idea what that refers to, but they both seem to understand it. Malika tries to explain.

"In particle physics, you know which test-bed the elephant slept in by the broken bedsprings it left behind. In a plenum context, that means we can build an interferometer to detect the signature radiation emitted where nearby universes make contact. If we can get close enough to the place John remembers, that interferometer will pin down the exact location of the contact point between our universe and the one John came in from."

Ricardo can only stare, dumbfounded. His head is swimming—in waters far over his head.

"That's why, now, a third of a century since I last saw my home universe, we're trying to scavenge, beg, borrow, or steal enough technology and technical know-how to put together a functional spacecraft."

"If we can return to space," Malika adds, "we'll find the way into that rift-tunnel, if it's still there."

With a grimace, Ricardo stares at both the oldsters who've been talking at him.

"But how do you know this hole, or rift, or portal between universes, or whatever it is—how do you know it'll be open when you get there?"

A quick glance passes between the ex-spacer and his would-be ground controller. Malika stares at the floor, then at Ricardo.

"We don't. That's the tough part, admittedly. But first we have to find the right door to knock on."

"My cousin Jiro made that door open somehow," Drinan says. "We know it can be done. There's got to be a way to reactivate the 'portal' as you call it."

Ricardo shakes his head.

"Why? Why go to all the trouble?"

"So I can return to my home universe before I die."

"How can you be so self-centered? All this effort from all these people—just so you can go home again? Aren't there about a million *more important* things that need to be done first?"

Drinan looks at the ground and smiles wanly. Malika, however, looks as if she wants to knock some instant sense into Ricardo.

"Not just for him, you boob! He may be our best shot for contacting a nearby universe. Universes of the plenum are not only 'parallel'; they're *alternate*. The road taken here—including the pandemic—may not have been taken there. If we can contact the universe he came from, they may know why it happened here, and how we can cure it for good!"

Standing in the shadow of their spacecraft, Ricardo suddenly feels like an idiot. If it's true he's infected with a new strain of the prionoid—and if Drinan and Hardesty and their crew can pull off what they're planning to do—he might be among the first to personally benefit from what they've planned. Anything he says now will sound hollow and empty even in his own ears.

"Sorry."

Drinan smiles and claps him on the shoulder.

"I've been called crazy before. That's why they drafted me into the clinical trials of their prionoid neuromodulator in the first place."

"You were in the Protean/Spires program? You were treated with the original form of the prionoid?"

"Afraid so. I was infected with the pandemic strains and I survived, even though I don't possess any sort of genetic immunity. Among all the other participants in the clinical trials who didn't have a genetic immunity, none gained immunity from having been treated with the original form of the prionoid."

"So they went through the plague stages?"

Drinan nods.

"My immunity, whatever its source, couldn't be transferred to anyone else. That didn't keep Spires from trying to prove I was the index case, though. Patient Zero, Patient One, whatever it was called. Simon Lingham was big on that, too. Which makes it all the stranger when you say Simon has gone into exile. You sure he was looking for me?"

"That's right."

"Yet he hasn't shown up. Any idea where he might have been headed?"

"North. Along the old Intracoastal Waterway. He said he wouldn't be going further north than the empty city of New York."

Drinan nods and glances toward Hardesty. She seems both shocked by—and also somehow *expecting*—the look, though Ricardo can't say why. Drinan turns back to him.

"You've piqued my curiosity, son. Stay here with us a few days. I might just decide to accompany you on that trip north."

"What about your work here?" Ricardo asks.

Drinan glances up at the bottom funnel of the spaceship, then at Malika Hardesty, who turns on her heel and stalks back to the work crew she was overseeing, without explaining.

"I'm afraid Malika's proven more prophetic than she'd like. The lightcraft won't be ready to go for several months at least. They won't need me to pilot her before then. I've wanted to see New York again for a long time—even if it's no longer the city it once was."

Ricardo follows John Drinan's glance upward, toward the parabolic base of the lightcraft. All he sees in its funhouse-mirror bottom and ringed edge are their own images, distorted and drawn away from them, before returning.

21

Corroboree in Ephemeral City
2033

WHEN MARK FORNASH SAW THE LIGHTS AND EXPLOSIONS ON THE TWILIT desert, he shook his head in awe and wonder and not a little fear. Pulling off the road that linked Cadiz to Highway 62, Mark and the other members of his drum circle steered their lo-fly cars and hovertrucks onto the cracked flats of Danby Dry Lake. A helicopter, patrolling the edge of the dry lake, thrummed past overhead. Sixteen-year-old Janeen, banging a hand-drum, jumped out of Mark's vehicle almost before he stopped.

"There it is! Uproot City. Population two hundred thousand—at least!"

Several of the drummers around Mark began hammering out a wild polyrhythm. Mark belatedly joined in, striking his shaman's drum. They walked across the flats, a ragtag marching detachment from Los Angeles led for the moment by Bikram, their Balinese Kendang player.

"Look at this sign! Encrusted with neogalactic space-tribe alien freak stickers!"

Mark, approaching the sign, saw that it also (almost incidentally) informed them that they were approaching the latest incarnation of Mobile Permanent Autonomous Zone UPROOT CITY. Beneath the paradoxical name were the words "A City On The Move." Below *that*, others had graffitied, "We'll Move On—But We Won't Go Away!" and "Uproot All Cities!" and "NO FUNTS!"

"What's a FUNT?" Janeen asked, frowning. Bikram laughed.

"A Fat Ugly No Talent, maybe?"

"I think it has something to do with cameras and recordings," Mark said, trying to remember where he'd heard the term or name before. He called to Greg Elliot, a dark-skinned man in his twenties with wildly beaded beard and hair who had been among the first to join the drum circle. "How many places like this did you say there were?"

Greg, dressed in little more than a penis sheath and sandals, didn't miss a beat as he continued banging on a large cowbell.

"Hundreds of big VTCs in North America. And more of them everyday. Worldwide, there have to be at least tens of thousands of MPAZs of various sizes. They're not all as big as MPAZ Uproot City, but it's not the biggest, either. Not by a long shot."

Mark nodded. Whatever shift in consciousness humanity was undergoing, it was bringing new and unexpected things with it—new jargon, not least of all. As they walked across the flats, he racked his brains for a moment before he remembered that VTC stood for Voluntary Transurban Community.

Approaching the outskirts of the city of tents and vehicles and mobile homes, Mark banged his drum with the rest. Not so long ago, he used to wear his antlered headpiece, his fringed vest, his buckskin leggings and his moccasins only on Halloween. Back then, he'd felt his urban-shaman twist made him different from everyone else—especially since he couldn't wear such garb to work without facing a major hassle with the higher-ups.

Now his costume didn't make him feel so special or unusual anymore. He could dress in it every day, if he liked. His bosses, like bosses everywhere, would let him wear what he wanted, so long as he still showed up for work and did his job. Finding people still interested in "holding down jobs" was getting harder and harder everywhere—even among the bosses themselves.

Every day is Doomsday. Every night is Halloween. He'd thought that disparagingly of John Drinan, when they first met. That statement was literally true, here and now. He wished John and Malika could see Uproot City, but Tomoko Fukuda had called John back into the program for "follow-up tests," and Malika had accompanied him.

At least Mark's note and query to the Protean founder had accomplished that much. Her v-mail informed him that she was "investigating whether artificial prionoids tested by Protean might have a role in the current rhythmanias and tarantisms." She wrote that she had also informed "a friend well-placed with the World Health Organization" concerning Mark's theory on the outbreak.

Further action didn't seem to be forthcoming, however. WHO and CDC had been around—what? Eighty years? Institut Pasteur even longer, probably. More than enough time for good dense bureaucratic thickets to have sprung up and choked out innovative responses in their respective fields of expertise. The desk jockeys and pencil pushers at WHO and GEMS and CDC and Institut Pasteur had done so little to sound the alarm that recently Mark had taken it upon himself, sending his proposed chronology of the shamanic epidemic to everyone he could think of—from local newspapers and doctors to hospitals and government agencies. Their polite but distant responses, however, let him know he was being written off as a kook. Mark turned and shouted to the smiling Greg, over the symphonic cacophony of Uproot City.

"Freak has gone mainstream in the biggest way."

"So let it!"

"We're not in charge or in control of things anymore. Especially when it comes to the drum circle."

"Don't be bugged! Hey, when everyone's a drum major, the people lead and the leaders have to follow, right? Let it go!"

They drummed and whirled their way into the inside-out city. Mark heard brass percussion and whirring plastic bullroarers and homemade didjeridoos, wind-snapped flags and banners and tent sides—all counterpointing the complex polyrhythm woven from a thousand different drum circles. Over that beatline rose a strange orchestration of sitars, gunshots, songs, and laughter. Sirens and dirt bikes and hollow crashing demolition derbies. Buzzbomb-powered go-carts, exploding fireworks, self-consuming artifacts collapsing in flames. Bad poetry and robot war-fests and seismically amplified violins—all embedded in the oceanic roar of a human crowd 200,000 strong. Near him Bikram shouted, whirling like a dervish.

"Whew-hoo! Instant mud orgy solar wind mobile Martian portapotty tribal theatre shoestring technology culture of the frequency-uncontrolled!"

That barely began to describe it, Mark thought. He had understood and embraced the shamanic-complex changes from the beginning, almost as if his long-ago mind trip had given him a premonition of the shapeshift of things to come. Now, however, the changes were enough to make even a shaman-in-waiting a little nervous. For all its wild beauty, Mark found the shift from advanced urban lifeway to what Bikram called "the archaeofuturosapien cultural pattern" disorienting. Especially when that shift was occurring on the scale he was seeing here.

Mark and his fellow drummers moved through a hallucination-triggering townscape, lit more by fire and fireworks than by the infrequent stored-solar lightposts. Above the tents and vehicles around them rose skeletal buildings, hastily erected scaffold structures strewn with sputtering torches, twinkling holiday lights, or blazes of neon. Figures—nude, seminude, masked, face-painted, snake-draped, body-painted, pierced, and tattooed—pranced wildly around/over/through fires, lights, projected images. They danced contortedly, rolled on the ground, barked like dogs, tore at their hair, sobbed chanted screamed in unknown tongues and distorted voices, swayed, convulsed, twitched, trembled, to musics heard and unheard.

The youngest seemed the most hysteric, the most taken by the "spirit." Others, in their "possession," struck Mark as more self-possessed. Some of the more experienced trancers, like priests and priestesses training new initiates, showed the young those techniques that would help them take control of their ecstasy. Others—drum trancers, stilt-walkers, fire-breathers, fire-eaters, fire-in-the-belly dancers—moved all around, oblivious to all control.

Smaller versions of gatherings like this had taken place before the world's population began to shamanize, Mark knew, but one huge difference separated past "zones of free radical self-expression" from what surrounded him now: The prohibition against "Funts" was being heeded. No one in this impromptu freakartplay city was taking photographs, or videotaping, or holorecording—except, perhaps, for the people in the helicopter patrolling the perimeter of the dry lake. Whoever they were, media or military, they were keeping a healthy distance from the playful local gunshot noise.

Unlike the observers in the helicopter, the people around Mark were totally involved in the immediate experience—not in the making of the moments to be recorded or replayed. Smash the surveillance machines, Mark thought, recalling the anarcholudd motto. Abandon the cities. Live your own myth. Is this how it begins?

"I see the wavy Left," shouted a man naked save for a cardinal's miter, crozier, and mirror mask, "for whom the individual is merely a delusion, a node of little importance in the all-important network of social relationships! I see the particulate Right, for whom the individual is atomically alone, the ghostly network of social relationships only made real in the all-important individual node! Those are the only versions of reality they allow us! Deny them both! If we are to survive, all cities, states, and corporations must die! This is Cape Carneval! We are Saturn-aliens! Burning Rainbow astronauts launching a new world!"

Something about this guy's rant sounded familiar. He couldn't pin down exactly what it was, but Mark thought he'd seen or heard the ranter before. He wished John or Malika were here to see this. John, with his ex-spacer and "parallel world" past, would have appreciated "Cape Carneval" and "astronauts launching a new world."

Listening to the naked cardinal, Mark lost his drum circle friends. They disappeared into the chaotic heartbeat of this place, into that rhythm pushing outward to comprehend all the inside-out city's myriad forms of self-expression, but also pulling inward, trying to make all this varied craziness cohere into a single living community.

A diaphanously dressed crone barked at the passersby. Around her, men and women slowly danced and writhed—everyday folk turned fakirs, flagellants, and freaks, pushing rods and nails and spikes into and through their flesh.

"Are you hungry enough to eat a bullet for your art? Your science? To live the truth that kills? I didn't think so!"

Something hypnotic about the spectacle held Mark's gaze, so much so that his drumming lapsed. Was all this sacred, or profane? Was what was happening around him transcendent, or a sideshow, or some sort of sideshow transcendence?

"The important thing," said a young woman dressed and Glo-sticked and sparkle-painted as a wood nymph, "is less to be heard for voices crying in the wilderness than to be heard for the wilderness crying in our voices—and soon, or soon no wilderness will be left in which to cry out."

The woman whirled away, but not before handing him a flier with "Rethink Redesign Replace. Re-educate Redistribute Revalue. Transvaluation of all values!" hand-lettered and calligraphed upon the flimsy sheet, above a "Food Chain Chart" with a starred location at the bottom, captioned "Wish You Were Here."

Mark passed a bony guitar-strumming cowboy, but only caught a snatch of melody as he walked by. He came to the nearest periphery of the portable city, where a small crowd watched as a crew placed the last of what looked like lightbulbs in holes in the ground and buried them. A master of ceremonies said something about "planting bulbs in the cold soil of November in the hope they will sprout green rays and yellow stars in March." On cue, green-rayed fireworks burst from the ground and soared into the air, to burst into yellow stars above *oohs* and *aahs* and applause. Nearby, a woman in a dress half red and half white spun like a top while chanting "Hope is Desire in a white dress. Desire is Hope in a red dress."

Strange. He'd expected the shamanic complex to only be about drumming, dancing, dreaming, shapeshifting and soul-flying—not wild bursts of generalized creativity. Church attendance, too, was also way, way up—especially the speaking-in-tongues charismatic variety. He hadn't expected that at all. How many around him had already "caught" whatever it was that made the shamanic complex happen to them? How many were just actors and poseurs and hangers-on, freed to radically express themselves in the space opened up by those who *really* had the "bug"?

As the smoke of spent fireworks settled around him, Mark thought how out of place he felt—here, among the ecstatic, where he should have felt so much at home. Why had he, so far, been denied the shamanic raptures he so craved—the ecstasies which seemed to come so easily to so many now? How many here were like himself, their consciousness not really altered? Or, if altered, then by no more than a "contact high" with all this alteration they found around them?

Was this wild creativity part of the whole shamanic show? The dreaming coming into the world, before the world went into the dreaming? Mark had seen carnivals and Mardi Gras, Halloweens and performance "scenes" aplenty, but none of them were more than embryonic precursors to this. The thousands of animal-headed and god-masked dancers and drummers and performers here—were they precursors too, somehow foreshadowing the shapeshifting stage he'd predicted?

Looking at the burning and exploding festival city in front of him, however, Mark wondered if something, present here in playful show, was already barreling down on them—real and earnest—from out of the future. Cities always had a strong element of the *spectacle* to them, but this MPAZ was the city distilled to pure spectacle. If spectacles were always about *forgetting*, to some degree, then what was Uproot City helping them forget? Was it a city for the forgetting of cities, their uprooting from human love and memory? But why? For centuries the world had been increasingly headed in the direction of becoming all one vast global city—

Glancing up at the sky, he saw an enormous full moon just clearing the desert hills to the east. The moon became a pale Petri dish, its craters microbial colonies. As he watched, the spreading microbes reduced that same Petri-dish moon to clean-boned skull. Shaking his head, he looked away quickly.

Rorschach foreshock, he thought, Bikram's flippant phrase rising unbidden into his thoughts. *Apocalypse is the spectacle in which history is forgotten ...* Fighting down the chill that swept over him, he plunged back into the roaring, fiery maelstrom of the temporary city.

"Baby is Narcissus for two!" chanted a man and woman dressed as skeletons and operating an enormous bloated puppet baby.

"Putting it off to the next generation will be too late!" said a contingent of men dressed as lumberjacks, but all with antlers on their heads.

"Tolerate the incommensurable!" shouted a man with round spectacles, devilishly curled mustaches and pointed beard, dressed in the traditional lab coat of the scientist.

Mark smiled awkwardly as he made his way around the mad scientist. Dodging a man-sized robotic centipede, he realized he'd stumbled into an encampment of Tildenists and their biobots. Overhead, wing-lit robotic peregrine falcons stooped and darted with the speed of feathered cruise missiles. A mirror-feathered, micromachined hummingbird flitted from place to place, quick and distracted. Mark nodded to the controllers and moved on.

Leaving the biobot area, he saw fly-by-wire dancers, dressed in business attire, miming with perfect precision an aquaballet of synchronized swimming in holographically projected "water." As Mark watched, the holojected sea the flying dancers "swam" in became more and more wave-ridden, turbulent, tempest-tossed. The swimmers, however, persisted in their perfect synchronization until all were "drowned."

He stared at the scene as it went dark and then began again. In a tempest, Mark thought, synchronized swimming becomes synchronized drowning. Was that where society and civilization were headed now—synchronized drowning? Lemmings who'd finally found their way to the beach? He walked on, too deep in thought to bother drumming. The loss of his drumbeat would hardly be noticed amid all the thousands sounding here. He tried not to pay attention to the manifold madness going on around him, but it broke in on his reverie again and again.

Here, a group of what looked like professors with guitars played raucous paeans to memories of their wild youth. There, out of a dream-doorway in a pillow, ancient Chinese taotie monster-faces danced forward. South Asian dakinis in bikinis danced on what appeared to be corpses, then danced around someone garbed as a Buddha, in meditative pose, the index finger of one hand extended to touch the earth.

Mark caught snatches of poetry and invocations. A woman, dressed like a nun or priestess, sang "Show us the shadows we all hide—Illuminated, from the inside." A man—his face covered in a reindeer mask and crown of horns, his hands and feet covered in hooves and "nailed" to a cross—still managed to shout at a parade of men and women in slippered biolab cleansuits, emblazoned with outsized BIOHAZARD captions and icons, who danced the twisted mirror of DNA unzipping in mitosis around a slowly walking nude woman with a bright red apple in her hand.

"Not just words made flesh!" said the woman with the apple. "Not just pages out of the jigsaw dictionary of sex! Hack your own code and become God!"

Among the spectators a male voice shouted, "Love ain't nothing but organic computing misspelled!" The man fled, laughing, but Mark heard the nervousness in his laughter. That was the deeper problem here: the boundary between performer and audience, between what was simulated and what was real, was seriously blurred. He couldn't tell where one ended and the other began. Simulation overwhelmed meaning.

Was that an old shamanic problem—or a novel age-of-code issue? In archaic tales shamans whose souls were killed in spirit fights also died in physical reality. In futuristic tales combatants who died in virtual reality also died in physical reality. *Archaeofuturosapien*, he thought. Bikram's word for the human world in which the near future increasingly resembled the distant past. Whatever the name, it signified *un*consciousness was on the march again. All the millenia of human consciousness, about to be rounded with a sleep once more—sinking back into the dreamtime out of which all those millenia had arisen, so long before.

"Watch out for the heavenly doors, please!" a pair of herald angels intoned in front of two heavy, glowing slabs that opened and shut quickly behind them. Through the doors Mark saw various holy men, priests and preachers, rabbis and roshis, mullahs and monastics. Each wore a bright, beatifically smiling sacred mask, partially covering a face twisted up in a dark scowl of bigotry, intolerance, and hatred. A short, bespectacled, blond woman skippingly chased after them, shouting "Bad God! No sacrifice!" She spun Mark around as she whirled past him. The dizzy world slowed down to present him with figures painted to resemble skeletons masked with death's-heads—grim reapers, all carrying mirrors, clocks, hourglasses. Nearby, a skeleton soliloquized to his skull in the mirror:

"Burst smilingly, my heart. Ah, but what is a smile but the primate feargrin twice removed? And who do the bones greet with that everlasting rictus, but Death? Deathless time is timeless death!"

Once the death band passed him by, Mark found himself back at another of Uproot City's fractal edges. Despite all the different ages and backgrounds of people here, masks and mirrors, gods and time fascinated them all. Part of the shamanic complex too? Nearly all shamanic traditions involved disguises of one sort or another. A number of them had traditions of speculomancy—mirrors as powerful shamanizing tools.

"Before the Big Bang, Word of God, and Word of Honor," said a hyperamplified voice out of the city behind him, "Kids! Don't Try This At Home!"

A white flash bright as a dozen simultaneous lightning strikes caught Mark's eye. He turned around just in time to hear the booming *whump!* from the fireball and feel the blast wave of a tremendous explosion mushrooming hundreds of feet in the air above the center of the dry lake. For a moment he thought Uproot City was under attack by tactical nuke or fuel-air bomb. The boom echoed and re-echoed, leaving in its wake the screaming of hundreds of vehicle alarms. A great human roar of awe rose from the mobile city, followed by thunderous applause.

Mark turned his back on it, shaking his head and smiling. These people would probably consider a twenty megaton airburst a really grand firework—until the blast, burn, and radiation effects took them out. Ah, well—no spectacle without death.

Between him and the surrounding desert now stood only a scattering of people, portable toilets, and a cluster of half a dozen Red Cross Medical Aid Station tents. In the lull after the bomb and the applause and the car alarms, things were a good deal quieter, if only for the moment.

He didn't remember when it left, but the perimeter-patrolling helicopter was gone. In a way, he was sorry it had departed. Its presence had indicated at least some concern on the authorities' part regarding what was going on here. Why wasn't there *more* concern, though? Was the generalized outburst of creativity he'd seen here also masking the deeper effects of the drumming and dancing plagues? Hiding the reality of the whole shamanic complex condition—the numbers of whose "victims" must by now be reaching pandemic proportions worldwide?

How many of these people around him returned to their jobs or at least their lives in cities and towns—and how many were permanent residents of this transient city? If he checked recent sales of hunting gear and mobile homes, would he find those numbers had already skyrocketed? Where was the money coming from to run this city and feed its population—much less thousands of other lightfoot communities worldwide?

He'd heard rumors and rumblings of a massive but mostly silent shifting of funds already underway—out of personal accounts, through the cashing-in of stocks, the selling off of nonmobile assets like homes and other real estate. Recent wild volatilities on the world exchanges, along with hints of alternate economies springing up like mushrooms after rain. No one in the public sphere was connecting any of those effects in the overall techonomy to the drumming and dance plagues, however—except a few "conspiracy therapists" in odd nooks and crannies of the infosphere, other Web-heads like himself. With all the drumming and dancing going on, why were so few of the powerful looking and listening with any understanding? Or were they caught up in it, too?

The drum circles slowly began searching out their rhythms again, but the desert night was for a moment quiet enough for Mark to hear individual conversations, strange as they were. He walked on, trying to focus on what he was hearing.

"People in cities are already close to the edge of their narrowly circumscribed psychological boundaries," said a young man with an intricate cosmogram tattooed across his back.

"Like nomads aren't?" asked an older woman incredulously. "They're always on the lookout for their next meal! A hand-to-mouth existence!"

Approaching the quiet medical tents, Mark drifted out of that conversation and into another.

"Knowing which changes to embrace and which changes to resist," said a woman, "is crucial to the survival of any organism—or organization."

Yes, Mark thought, that's it! That's it exactly.

He stood before the entrance to the nearest of the med tents now. The black woman who had spoken—a doctor or nurse-practitioner, from her garb—disappeared into the tent. Her male colleague, seated on a camp-stool outside, continued to stare at the Circus-city now returning to its frenetic, pulsing, burning, exploding pace.

Mark walked past the man, into the large pavilion tent. Of the dozen beds in the tent, perhaps half were filled with sleeping patients. He had walked nearly halfway down a middle aisle, between rows of beds on either side, when the black woman noticed him.

"May I help you?"

Mark introduced himself—along with UCLA Harbor General as his affiliation. Not a lie, though something of a sin of omission, since he neglected to mention he was a systems analyst there, not a doctor. The woman introduced herself as Dr. Salima Ezzell of Doctors Without Borders.

"I overheard what you said about knowing which changes to embrace and which to resist. I was wondering if you could tell me what you've been treating here."

"Mostly it's been the usual bruises and broken bones you'd expect in a gathering of this size in the desert. No major heat strokes yet—too early in the season. A couple of cases of food poisoning. Far fewer drug overdoses than I'd have thought, which is odd. I'm still trying to figure out why my organization sent me here. Local and regional health care systems could be handling these patients, if they hadn't chosen to ignore the MPAZs and their voluntary refugees."

Mark nodded, trying to look professional.

"The people in these beds are the drug overdose cases?"

"No proof of that. At first I thought they were just sleeping—exhausted from all this dancing and drumming. It's more than that, though. Friends or neighbors here brought them in when no one could wake them up. Most of them have only been here a day or two, but they've all been sleeping for at least seventy-two hours."

"Some kind of sleeping sickness?"

Dr. Ezzell smiled, almost laughed.

"Not trypanosomiasis, that's certain. I had their blood samples checked for that, just in case, but I knew there'd be nothing there."

"Oh?"

"Until a week ago I was in the elephant-grass country of southern Sudan. The trypanosomes that cause African sleeping sickness are carried by the tsetse fly. Not a lot of tsetse flies in the California desert, would you say?"

"So you've never seen anything like it before?"

"I have, actually. Look here. See the eyes?"

Mark looked more closely, and soon saw it. In one patient after another, he saw that the eyeballs were jittering madly back and forth beneath the eyelids.

"Rapid eye movement."

"Exactly. That's the curious thing. I've timed their sleep stages. These people are spending far too much time in REM sleep. They're dreaming nearly full-time."

Ezzell stared down at the sleeping/remming patient before them. Lights, bells, and whistles began to go off in Mark's brain.

"You said you've seen it before. Where?"

"In the slums outside Khartoum. Just before I caught my flight out, I was detoured there. Precisely *because* I had been working in the tsetse-fly-infested south. Local clinicians in Khartoum were afraid they might have a sleeping sickness outbreak on their hands. But it wasn't trypanosomiasis—it was this. Three cases of it. No trypanosomes, but REM stages of extreme length—"

"But what is 'this'?"

"I wish I could tell you. I've only been able to find one thing in the medical literature that it bears any resemblance to—and that's more by way of contrast than anything else."

"What's that?"

"D178N-M129 fatal familial insomnia. If you took FFI's effects on the thalamus and inverted them, you'd come up with a fairly good approximation of this. Frankly, though, this 'somnia' condition in these patients must only bear a superficial relationship to fatal familial *in*somnia."

The drumming and fireworks sounded more loudly again from outside the tent. Mark raised his voice a bit over the noise.

"Why *only* superficial?"

"FFI is caused by an inherited mutation at the same protein site, residue 129, where Creutzfeldt-Jakob disease originates. The CJD mutation is coupled to valine at 129, though, while FFI involves methionine. Both of those are inherited prion conditions, in any case."

More lights, bells, and whistles filled Mark's head—and not just from the wild city nearby.

"Have you tested these patients for the presence of shapeshifting proteins, like those?"

"I don't see why. The odds are very much against the possibility that these six people here, all from different families and backgrounds, would show up with the same, *inherited* prion-like disease at the same time. We have to tend to these people *practically*, first—not chase wild geese. I don't even know yet whether or not they'll come out of this dreaming condition."

Mark reached into his shirt pocket and took out a hand-held computer. Poking its screen with a stylus, he printed out a Talking Book card with contact numbers and addresses for Tomoko Fukuda at Spires Biotechnologies' Protean subsidiary. He handed Ezzell the smartcard.

"They'll come out of it, all right. Use this to contact Dr. Fukuda. Tell her about your patients here. See if she won't make a little donation to Doctors Without Borders so you can run those tests for offbeat proteins."

"Why should she?"

"Her company has created a line of artificial prionoids, one or another of which may just be 'transmissible.' Let her know what you're seeing here. She might even want to run those tests herself for you—free of charge. Her friends at WHO might be interested in this, too. Tell her Mark Fornash sent you. Tell her I said, 'The Dreaming Phase has begun. When are you going to tell people what's going on?' Got that?"

"Got it. Maybe my organization had a reason for sending me here after all."

"They might already know more about this than they're letting on. Got to know which changes to embrace, and which to resist, right?"

Clutching the smartcard, Dr. Ezzell smiled but looked preoccupied as they shook hands and said their goodbyes. Mark took a last look at the patients dreaming in their beds, then hurried from the medical tent. Maybe there was still a role for him, even if the Fates had chosen to deny him the strange ecstasy now sweeping the world. He ought to try to find the people in his drum circle he'd given a ride out here. If he didn't come across them within the next hour, they'd just have to find a ride home with someone else—if they were planning on going home again at all.

Banging his drum, Mark set off for a final walk through the heart of the ephemeral city.

22

An Outlander's Journey Inland
2066

TRILLIA HATES BEING EARLY—AND SHE IS. WEEKS EARLY.

No choice about it, really. With the help of Thetis, Psamathe, and Amphitrite, on what turned out to be her last day on the island, Trillia accessed and began downloading to dataneedle storage as much relevant material as she could—fearful she would not have leisure to peruse everything the mermaids had earlier helped her discover in her grandfather's private datasphere.

She wasn't downloading long before her activities were discovered. Whether the discovery was made by the President himself or by his security people didn't matter. Her fears were confirmed. She found herself and the mermaids promptly whitenoise-purged from the system they had just begun raiding.

Her hand had been forced, but she was ready. So ready she surprised herself. She promptly dressed in sturdy boots and dusty black-and-green outergear, rugged but breathable stuff of pre-pandemic manufacture scavenged from the mainland years back. She had already put together the same assortment of gear she saw Ricardo take into exile—plus a map pad far more effective than the laminated paper foldups he'd taken.

She commanded the three mermaids to meet her where the *Sea Robin* was docked. That boat had carried both Ricardo and Simon Lingham into banishment. Since her retinoscanned identity as a Spires allowed her to activate the boat's systems, Trillia felt it only appropriate that she should "borrow" the sloop-rigged motorsailer to carry her into self-imposed exile—and that the boat should remain in exile as long as she did.

With the more-or-less helpful assistance of her mermaid companions, she fled the New Bahamas by night through a sea of low swells. The next day she came in sight of land once more. From the map pad synched up via microradio to her headplug, Trillia learned that she and *Sea Robin* stood offshore at a point between Cumberland Island and Jekyll Island, in that part of the continent formerly known as Georgia.

For the three days since then, she has been cruising northward along the old inland waterway. In the machineless world of the mainland her first encounter with one of the robotic dredges is startling. Soon, however, the sight of the slow elephantine robots doing their jobs becomes familiar, even comforting.

Off to starboard lies the broken necklace of coastal islands and open ocean. Away to the port side are marshes and a mosaic of forests and savannah. Near at hand, the ruins of Jekyll Island resorts stand or lean or fall—dilapidated, overgrown with wild grape, hung with Spanish moss. Very much the way the towns of her home islands would look, Trillia thinks, if they were left out in the wind and weather, untended and uncared for through a third of a century.

With the mermaids sporting about her bow like sailing-ship figureheads come to life, *Sea Robin* makes its way through twisting labyrinths walled in tall green marsh-grass. At her boat's passage, snowy-white egrets startle. Mullets leap, crabs scuttle away, sunning turtles plop into the water—even the occasional loglike mass of an alligator slips beneath the surface. In reedy thickets and grassy marshes she sees rice birds and red-winged blackbirds and a few others she can name—but far more she cannot. Where the island forests of palmetto and sea pine come closer to the waterway, she sees deer, wild turkey, squirrel, and rabbit. Once her packed provisions run out, she will be forced to hunt and fish—but she will have no excuse for starving.

Odd. She didn't really expect to see so much animal life.

She thinks of her grandfather. During her childhood in the islands, he often told her of the six Great Extinctions which life on Earth had endured during its four billion-year history. The first five mass extinctions had been caused by natural catastrophes: meteors from space, sudden shifts in global climate, that sort of thing. The sixth Great Extinction, however, was the result of human activity over the last ten or twelve thousand years—and most sharply during the last three hundred years—before the pandemic.

The mass extinction that humans wrought upon their fellow species was less abrupt than those earlier decimations resulting from natural causes, but no less catastrophic. Human activities had wiped out ninety percent of the world's species—before the pandemic went a long way toward balancing that score, by wiping out considerably more than ninety percent of *Homo sapiens.*

Trillia remembers hearing several of the faux-youthful oldsters back in the islands claim that in the worst days—the last days of the old world and the first days of the new—the plague survivors had scavenged all the old civilization's foodstuffs they could find. What saved most of the survivors as those supplies ran out, the oldsters claimed, was the loose system of preservation parks and diversity reserves some foresighted people began setting up even before the big boom in human population. When the old world ended, the plants and animals that survived the excesses of City-world began to spread out again, whenever and wherever they could, from the fragmented forests and fields of the old greenspaces and biopreserves.

The reserves were mainly last-ditch biomuseums, Noah's-ark parks for preserving biodiversity against the onslaught of human population, agriculture, and development. They were intended as "insurance colonies" for the endangered species they housed, yet they unexpectedly turned out to be insurance for the humans who created the reserves, too. She wonders what happened to the most remote insurance colony of all—the Orbital Biodiversity Preserve once such a big part of the first full-scale space habitat.

Yet here are all these creatures around her now, already with so many ways of living, only slightly more than three decades after humanity toppled from its high cities, like Humpty Dumpty. *Humanity sat on a wall,* Trillia thinks. *Humanity had a great fall. All Grandpa's Merfolk and all Grandpa's men couldn't put humanity together again.*

Is the rest of the planet restoring itself to some sort of post-human balance? So fast? No doubt things ecologically are still crazy and in flux, but can new species evolve in so short a time to fill so many niches?

The only creatures she hasn't seen are human beings—but that too changes. As early morning light shoots across the waterway near the south end of Sapelo Island, she sees smoke, smells fish cooking, hears people calling in a familiar yet unfamiliar dialect. Perhaps it is what her map pad's guide screens call Gullah, from the culture known as Geechee. But her guide screens say that language and culture were nearly extinct before the pandemic. How strange if it should have survived, when so much else hasn't.

Beside Sapelo Sound, at the north end of the island, she is startled to see two dark-skinned children riding horses in the shallow surf. At seeing her boat moving up the channel, they halt their horses. They stare fixedly at her as *Sea Robin* passes them.

After gazing at them for an awkward eternity, Trillia ventures a wave. Immediately the children—a boy and a girl—set their horses to swift flight, over the pale beach and into the somber forest of pines, palmettos, and live oaks covering the island—into dark shades veiled with Spanish moss and wild grape.

The sigh that floods out of her with their disappearance reminds Trillia of how lonely she feels. The sight of the two children vanishing makes her think of all she left behind in the islands. All the world she knew. Her parents. The kin, too, of her mermaids: companions whom her hasty escape—or thoughtless escapade?—also puts at risk.

Her grandfather, and the rage he must feel at having his boat-of-exile stolen by his granddaughter, using the family key codes. Are search parties from the islands already making their way to these low country shores? Already scouring the coastal plains, looking for her? (Almost unconsciously she looks up, remembering the small private force of stealth aircraft and helicopters the President once commanded. They were destroyed years ago, however—during a Wer raid.) Has her grandfather instead convinced everyone including himself that, given her mermaid escort, Trillia is in no danger? Or worse, might he know *she* is the one who was caught in the act of downloading his private files—and be glad to be rid of her?

These questions are thorns in her mind on which Trillia twists again and again as she travels north through a world of marsh grass and sea grass, beaches and dunes, wild horses and horseshoe crabs, sea pines and sea grape and palmettos. Only rarely does she see the rust-stained, weathered, broken-down and burnt-out structures which once housed human lives, buildings stuccoed in that mix of oyster shells, sand, and burnt-shell lime her map pad calls "tabby." Wisteria vines run rampant over lost houses, tendrils covering the eaves and climbing through the trees, blue grape-cluster clouds heavy with first bloom.

Rarely seen, that is, until the evening of her fourth full day on the inland waterway. Not far south of a place her map pad calls Thunderbolt, she reaches the outskirts of the abandoned city of Savannah. The first empty city of any size Trillia has encountered, her map pad insists on calling it "Historic Savannah" and its old homes "stately." Apparently it was already centuries old before the pandemic—and is now collapsing fast to make up for lost time.

In the westering light of evening, its populace are red-winged blackbirds rising and falling through marsh reeds. Gulls and cormorants glide down empty streets, noisy feathered ghosts. As they make their flights to shelter for the night, the birds miss colliding with *Sea Robin*'s bow only at the last possible instant.

Hawks soar and terns flit through sunset light. Great herons wing their slow and solitary ways toward unseen roosts, long necks folded back upon themselves, long legs dangling behind. So many birds, she thinks. Are *they* what became of the ghosts of this city? Have those centuries of Savannah's ghostly residents, no longer finding living mortals to haunt, now chosen to manifest themselves as birds? Sailing onward, she shivers against the chill of evening.

Looking at the map pad and the labyrinth of islands—Elba, Oatland, Whitemarsh, Wilmington—surrounding her, Trillia realizes that Ricardo, with his trademark aptitude for misdirection, has gotten it wrong. "Rendezvous with me at the mouth of the Savannah River," he said, "where it crosses what was once the Intracoastal Waterway and enters the Atlantic." That's great, but where the Savannah River crosses the Intracoastal Waterway is not necessarily the same place where it enters the Atlantic. The riverfront of the city of Savannah itself is some distance upriver from the ocean. The Savannah River can be said to flow into the sea not just at *one* place, but at several.

Despite the company the mermaids might afford her, were she to seek them out, Trillia cannot shake an unpleasant sense of solitude, of desolation in an unpeopled world. Exhausted and frustrated, she decides that for tonight at least, the rendezvous point "where the Savannah River crosses the Intracoastal Waterway" is just east of Oatland Island. It may well not be the same place where, weeks from now, she hopes to see Ricardo once more, but she has time to relocate if need be. Too much time.

Trillia anchors *Sea Robin* east of the abandoned city. Bedding down in the ship's cabin, she finds she cannot sleep. To her list of thorny questions, new ones add themselves, tormenting her throughout much of the night. Now that she has, more or less, reached Savannah and the rendezvous point, should she just sit tight and wait for Ricardo to eventually arrive? Or is that a stupid waste of time? Ricardo might begin suffering, even dying, of his Wersign at any time, if the islander medics are right in their diagnosis. Should she head south in hopes of running into him—and thereby shorten the length of time until they are together again? Or, in doing that, might she risk missing him altogether? She is nearly to the point of tears with exhaustion, anxiety, and depression before sleep at last floats her clear of the dark tide of her troubles.

Morning finds her somewhat better rested but still groggy. Her mermaids leap and tumble with a small pod of itinerant dolphins. Trillia decides to give herself a break and cruise just a short distance today. Upriver—maybe just as far as "Historic Savannah's" riverfront.

Stepping down the mast—a major task for a lone person, but a necessary one if she has to pass under any low bridges—she starts toward the city. She sets her map pad and computer out in the morning sun to bask their fill of photons, pumping up the electron reservoirs of their batteries. In an emergency, both could be run off her own body's bioenergy, via backflow microradioed from her headplug, but the only time she's ever done *that*, it gave her a splitting headache.

The haste of her departure and the distraction of her subsequent travels have prevented her from determining how much and how many of the files she actually *got* from her grandfather's datasphere before the system booted her out. Cruising slowly upriver toward Savannah, she supposes now is as good a time as any to find out. At least searching the files will let her put off deciding whether she should stay near the rendezvous point or travel someplace else.

She dons her virtuality shades. The results of her infotheft are disappointing. The downloaded stuff is all fragmented. She finds nothing of the "project breedline" she thought she saw in her first reconnoitering run through the datasphere with Thetis and Psamathe. Running a global FIND on the word "Triphibian," Trillia brings up only a jumble of phrases and snatches, mainly old stuff from her grandfather's memoirs, logged in the first decade or so after the pandemic: ". . . born like Trufolk . . . essentially immortal like the manufactured Merflok . . . possessing the mental powers and capabilities of the Werfolk, but under conscious control. . . ."

That's all very well, but *what* or *who* is supposed to have or *do* or *be* that—and how is it supposed to come about? The memoir fragments offer few clues. Was her grandfather just engaging in idle speculation? When the mer-girls first flashed this material past her, was her earlier impression of a "secret master-plan for manipulating the population of the islands in some sinister experiment" just paranoia? That's such an outmoded, pre-pandemic habit of mind that Trillia feels foolish. Was there no need to run? She hopes she hasn't allowed some ill-thought-out, half-cocked, crackpot scenario to drive her into exile.

Her feeling of foolishness dissipates a bit, however, when she begins searching through the material that earlier led her to suspect the pandemic was in some manner *premeditated*. There's more material in this area, all pre-pandemic. It raises possibilities both tantalizing and frightening.

Doing a global FIND on "prionoid" brings her a record of a virtual teleconference between her grandfather and two much older-looking men, a Dr. Vang and a Dr. Stephan "Stepka" Dorogov.

VANG: . . . yeast, a fungus, the prion-like molecules Sup35p and Ure2p have prion-forming domains that seem to contain octapeptide repeats, similar to those found in mammalian prion protein. That's why I've contacted Stepka here, whose research includes the production of natural and artificial peptides.

DOROGOV (nodding): Yes. All the way back to Vector and Bonfire programs, under the Biopreparat directorate. Regulatory peptides with central nervous system effects were our primary focus. Myelin toxin. Genes spliced into *Vaccinia* for beta-endorphin production, with possible biowarfare applications.

SPIRES: Good, good. Most neurotransmitters are not proteins, however.

DOROGOV: Ah, but there are *peptide* neurotransmitters. Somatostatin, Substance P, many more.

SPIRES: Would it be possible to design an artificial prion—let's call it a prionoid—which might be able to alter enzymes in, say, the serotonin synthesis pathway? And by such alteration produce a "novel" substance?

DOROGOV: You *could* create a "prionoid" that would alter a given enzyme. Hmm. We are talking serotonin synthesis. So let's say 5-HT-N-acetylase. That could alter the reactive/binding site so that, instead of acetylate, it could methylate—forming, let's say, dimethyltryptamine. DMT is a powerful psychotropic substance. You could have something equivalent to *in vivo* synthesis of LSD, practically. If you wanted, you could skip prions or "prionoids" altogether.

VANG: Oh? How's that?

DOROGOV: A viral vector—using homologous recombination to replace the endogenous enzyme with one that has been, um, engineered.

VANG: Let's just stay with our hypothetical prionoid for the time being—for protein folding reasons.

SPIRES: Can you think of an ubiquitous microbe that might serve to vector our hypothetical prionoid into humans? We'd want to be able to limit its scope, of course—

VANG: What we're really looking for is a sort of two-step "infection process." Microbe vectors prionoid into humans; highly transmissible but not particularly virulent microbe is dealt with by the immune system, but in the process of destroying the vectoring microbe, the prionoid is released into the human system.

SPIRES: Any blood-brain barrier problems with such a scenario?

DOROGOV: Ubiquitous, you say? . . . adenovirus, cytomegalovirus, herpes virus, all could work. Intracellular bacteria like mycoplasma. You would probably want something relatively innocuous, too, as a vectoring vehicle. Immune cells *do* traffic across the blood-brain barrier, although when they do it's usually not a good sign. That's how HIV got into the brain, via macrophages. Certain sites of entry into the brain are not so hard to get into, though. The idea of the vector being destroyed, releasing said prionoid into the bloodstream, which enters the brain—that's too complex. I would aim for a direct brain infection, or macrophage invasion to get it into the brain. Maybe encephalitis would do. Even immune cells responding to influenza could do it. Ubiquitous yet innocuous, though. And limitable. Hmm. I'll have to think more on that. . . .

After viewing the fragmentary record again, Trillia takes off her screenshades and sits, pondering. Even though the record contains no mention of any sort of global or universal release, she is still suspicious. Were these men planning what she *thinks* they were planning in this meeting? But why? What political or social advantage could anyone gain in wiping out most of Earth's human population?

Even Ricardo, in his most vitriolic ranting against Cameron Spires, would not have accused her grandfather of such insane plotting. No. She cannot believe these men were talking about creating the pandemic. But if not that, then what? It sounded so similar! What were they trying to do with their prionoids and their vectors? Did something they were working with go wrong, bringing on the pandemic as a result?

Questions ringing in her mind, Trillia pilots *Sea Robin* past enormous half-sunken freighters and rusting hulks. Once, they crossed oceans in a commerce of vast productive capacity—which now the world may not see again for a thousand or even ten thousand years. If ever. Why bring all that to an end? Was that really what the men in the conference record were discussing? What were they trying to do—and why? Were they even *aware* they were putting all humanity at risk by what they were doing?

Coming into the old city and riverfront proper now, Trillia suddenly feels very tired of spending all her time on the boat. What has she been afraid of? Werfolk? Barbarian Trufolk? Large hostile animals? Such fears seem outlandish in the bright light of midmorning. Of course, such fears *should* feel outlandish, she thinks. She's an *outlander*, after all. This world is strange to her.

She also has cabin fever, though, and needs to spend some time on solid ground. She moors the *Sea Robin* beside a river landing and takes up her map pad. Hesitating a moment, she decides to take her hunting bow too—along with a quiver filled with impressively tanged arrowheads mounted on clear-lacquered shafts fletched with blue feathers.

Wondering what she is afraid of, she takes the gear anyway, nocking an arrow loosely to the bowstring and leaving it there, like a gun with the safety off. For the first time since leaving the islands, Trillia steps off the boat, glancing back at the bow as she does. The mer-girls are staring after her with a bland sort of curiosity.

"I'll be back soon. I need some time off the boat. I think I'll look around."

From the weed-grown esplanade of the Riverfront Plaza she makes her way into the deserted streets of Savannah, under ancient oaks garlanded with thick hangings of Spanish moss. The city's parklike squares have run to weeds, understory brush, and sapling trees. Everywhere vines swallow up buildings. Ivy, wild grape, and loud blue wisteria overperch walls, cover windows, rise into trees. Window boxes, run riot, dangle tendrils into the weeds, dust, and debris of broken streets.

Dirt and grime streak walls and statues in patterns at once predictable and unpredictable. Dead fountains stand over pools gone to scum and sediment. Paint—scratched and cracked and chipped in innumerable ways—flakes away to gray weathered wood beneath. Rust leaks like fine dried blood from gutters and pipes, clots slowly on the teeth of wrought-iron fences, gates, balcony railings. Brickwork bleaches, mellows, fades in sun and rain. Copper monuments go green with patina, then pit and corrode. Stone weathers, erodes, cracks. Slimed by probing tongues of damp air, statues are resculpted, losing their faces and fine features to thin dirty crusts of salt, to organic defacement by bright lichen and dark moss.

Walking through the abandoned city, however, Trillia sees how much remains. Dolphin waterspouts and griffoned cornices. Row houses built in styles her map pad describes as Georgian and Regency. Colonnaded entrances, porticos, and porte-cochères of the Greek Revival style. Fairy-castle ornateness of Victorian and Queen Anne townhouses. Through shattered windows and broken doors, she looks in on what rain, sun, grit, and dust do to black marble floors, grand, sweeping staircases, skylit rotundas.

Trillia opens a gate in wrought-iron fencework and walks into the courtyard it seals off from the street. She startles at seeing piles of bones, bleached and eroded and jumbled, beneath a rusted awning along the far brick wall. Some of the remains are dressed in tattered flags of faded clothing. Skulls have toppled and come to rest in no particular order among the other remains. All are recognizably human. The tall wrought-iron fence must have kept dogs and other scavengers from dragging the corpses away from where they fell, Trillia thinks. The awning must have protected them a bit, too.

No scent of death here now. Just the dry tang of bone dust in the sun. It reminds her of when she was a little girl, planting flower bulbs on the island with her mother. Tossing a handful of bone meal into each hole before mixing it with a double portion of soil, setting the bulb in place, then filling in the hole above the bulb with more dirt. A more elaborate burial, and preparation for resurrection, than any of these poor people received.

The last days of the pandemic left their mark here. Trillia sees abundant evidence of death, street debris, fire and broken glass. Even words, painted in quick cursive on walls, doors, and pillars around the corpses. Strange words, like "haig" and "plat-eye." She stares at the last, trying to make sense of it.

"Know what that word means, child?" asks a raspy, accented voice. Trillia whirls around, heart pounding, bow at the ready.

"Where are you? Step out and show yourself."

An old woman's cackling laugh answers her, echoing in the courtyard, making it impossible for Trillia to pinpoint where the sound is coming from.

"You'll have to excuse me for not *acceding* to your *request*. I'm where I should be: where I can see you, but you can't see me. I hope you'll understand. The world is not as civil and genteel as it once was, you know."

"Who are you?"

"A watchful ghost, maybe. Maybe a haig—and these are my haints. Maybe even a plat-eye, an old-timey shapeshifter, with one big glowing eye out in front of my head! Lots of people saw 'em around here in the bad old days—when there were still people to see 'em. I been watching and seeing you, so you better watch yourself, Bahama girl!"

Trillia is so startled by the woman's knowledge of her origins, she almost drops her guard. The woman laughs her broad laugh again.

" 'How'd she know that?' That's what you're thinking, right now! I read your mind in your open-book face! I watched you coming up the river, honey. Don't get many guests here—and none of mine come cruising up old Savannah in a scrubbed and painted motor-sailboat! Where else *would* you be from, hmm?"

Keeping her bow and nocked arrow raised, backing and circling, Trillia moves toward the street, trying to extricate herself from the enclosed space of the courtyard.

"That's right. Get along with you now. Back to your boat. Keep going, just like that. Ghosts don't like guests. We don't like traveling over water, either. Stay close to your boat, child. Not every ghost you meet is friendly like me."

Trillia backs warily through the fencing, hooking the gate with her foot to slam it shut. Only when she has retreated some distance along the weedy street does her heartbeat begin to slow, and then only for an instant. Something—a rat the size of a lap dog? an opossum?—bolts from a debris-filled alley nearby with noise and clatter, sending a wave of roaches flowing into the street beside Trillia. She breaks and runs, back toward where she came from, back toward the *Sea Robin* and her Merfolk escort.

Running, hot under the noonday sun, Trillia thinks she hears laughter at her back—but only once, and not for long. Glancing back over her shoulder, she almost runs over an alligator, beside a courtyard fountain a short distance from the river. The hissing reptile alarms her enough that she retreats and detours around it, catching her breath, trying to calm her thoughts.

By the time she returns to the boat, her mind is more composed and under control. Seeing her pocket-sized solar computer with her virtuality shades beside it, Trillia thinks again of that conference she watched in shadespace, earlier. The more she remembers about the early days of post-pandemic history and the beginnings of the New Bahamian Polity, the more she thinks that (aside from her grandfather) the abjurer named Tomoko Fukuda might be the best person to answer her questions about the pandemic. Fukuda's last reported location was near Atlanta, at a Centers for Disease Control and Prevention facility. Didn't Simon Lingham say he was going to stop and visit her there, on his way north? Maybe he's still with her.

On her map pad, she calls up an image of what was once Georgia and stares at it. Why not stay aboard the *Sea Robin*, accompanied by Thetis and Psamathe and Amphitrite, and follow the Savannah River north and west as far as, say, Augusta? From there she can follow something called

Interstate 20 west, to Atlanta and the CDC research campus near Covington, Georgia. According to the map pad's datalinks, that was the last major bioresearch facility built by the CDC before the pandemic. Roughly half the local CDC employees moved there, from the old Clifton Road campus, less than a year before the end. If Tomoko Fukuda is still anywhere in this part of the world, it's probably there.

Unmooring from the city of Savannah, Trillia steers the *Sea Robin* between cityside and Hutchinson Island, then past the smaller islands of Onslow and Isla. *Sea Robin* is of fairly shallow draft, the season is spring and the water is running deep, but still she wonders. The river hasn't been maintained by the same robotic dredges that work the Inland Waterway. Will its channel grow too shallow? Will she have to leave her boat behind, before reaching Augusta? The map pad shows the sizable Clarks Hill Lake and dam complex, north of Augusta. That should still be stabilizing waterflow, but who can say how the dam is working, with no human oversight for more than thirty years?

Not much she can do about it, in any case. Escorted by Thetis, Psamathe, and Amphitrite, she feels strangely protected by their presence, at least while she is on the river. Perhaps the unseen "hag" in the abandoned courtyard was right about ghosts not liking to pass over water.

What about attack or pursuit by Werfolk, though? Or barbaric Trufolk? Or even her grandfather's security forces? If that last fear comes to pass, if she is captured by people from home, will she resist—or will she return home with them, reluctant but secretly relieved?

Despite such troubling thoughts, she cannot help but relax as the boat drones upriver, through cypress-tupelo swampland, past forests of bottomland hardwoods, patches of savannah and grassland in the distance. She sees wading birds, some of which she can now identify without further help from her map pad's linked guides. Snowy egrets and great blue herons standing on cypress knees, spearing minnows and pan fish. Storks feeding or perching in the moss-hung trees. Watching them feed, Trillia thinks of her own dwindling food reserves. She too will very soon have to depend on what the river provides.

Late in the afternoon the sky clouds over and rain begins to fall. She moors in a bend of the river, not far from what, according to her map pad, was once the town of Clyo. She hoped to put more distance between her and the ghosts of Savannah, but this will have to do. The day's events, added to her troubled sleep of last night, have left her exhausted. She drifts off to the sound of rain on *Sea Robin*'s planking and sleeps the whole night through, waking only once, groggy, thinking she hears the sound of drums or thunder. Moments later, a hailstorm commences—scary in itself, but short-lived.

The next morning dawns bright and new-scrubbed. At breakfast she finishes the last of her food supplies. Lunch or dinner will have to be wild-caught—and hand-cleaned, she thinks, with some distaste. The bright spring morning, however, drives such unpleasant thoughts from her mind as she stands behind *Sea Robin*'s wheel. Daylight brings to life around her the denizens of this subtropical jungle river. Birdsong moves in waves through the tress. To yesterday's wading birds are added waterfowl— ducks, geese, swans, coots—skittering away from *Sea Robin*'s approach but rarely lifting into full flight.

During the day she sees water snakes gliding through the shadows near the banks. Softshell and slider turtles disappear beneath the surface or continue sunning themselves, ignoring her presence altogether. She sees more alligators here too, and worries for a moment about her mer-girls. They are not at all concerned, however.

Trillia neglects to stop for lunch, but the mer-girls don't let that stop them. She sees one or the other of them taking time to eat, ranging ahead and falling behind by turns—Amphitrite peeling open claw-flailing cray-fish, Thetis cracking open freshwater clams, Psamathe chewing on some sort of sunfish.

Merfolk really are amazing, Trillia thinks. How do they shift so easily from living in the ocean all their lives to swimming up this freshwater river? She must remember to ask them about that.

By the time she stops for the evening, she is overwhelmed by the abun-dance of the local wildlife. She sets up camp onshore, in what was once a riverside and roadside park, just north of the rusting bridge where Route 301 crosses the Savannah. Consulting her map pad, she can't quite figure out the reasons for that. It's as if she's stumbled into the heart of one of those "genetic reserves" or "insurance colonies." The material in her map pad hints that the area known as the Savannah River Site might once have served such a sanctuary function—yet the map pad also describes it first and foremost as a production facility for nuclear material during the twentieth century.

A biodiversity preserve cheek by jowl with a nuclear weapons plant? One to help save the world, one to help destroy it? More proof things were already crazy long before the pandemic hit.

The mermaids help her catch fish that night, doing so much of the work themselves that it's almost too easy. After gritting her way through the bloody, slimy task of cleaning and filleting the fish, she finds that the results, once fried over her campfire, are not at all bad. That night she falls asleep to loud choruses of frogs calling for their mates in the spring night.

In the morning she wakes to bird cries and clouds but no rain. Striking her tent and unmooring from the river's western bank, she sees bald eagles and wood storks. Other creatures she matches to her map pad's illustrations of "freshwater clams," "gopher frogs," "tiger salamanders," and much else—all surprisingly dense and varied, and obvious to the rusted-away and broken-down fences of the Savannah River Site.

Not that it's a particularly peaceable kingdom. At times it seems every creature Trillia sees is stalking, catching, or eating something else—the whole world red in tooth and claw. Yet it's more complex than that. All the killing and eating has its place, but it's only a piece of the larger story unfolding around her.

Preoccupied with learning the landscape and navigating the river, she enjoys the shady day. The river is growing a good deal more silted up and sandbarred here than it was down below, but Trillia remains confident she'll make Augusta before the day is too old. Once there—even if she weren't planning to follow Highway 20 toward Atlanta—she'd still have to abandon *Sea Robin* and the river, at least according to the map. Not far above where Interstate 20 crosses over the Savannah, a series of permanent obstacles begins: Augusta City Lock and Dam, Stevens Creek Dam, then Clarks Hill Dam and the big lake beyond.

The attack comes while she is contemplating this plan. Amid youthful whoops and laughter, arrows wing their way across the water, striking *Sea Robin* about the prow. Amphitrite spyhops a peek.

"*Get down!*" Trillia shouts at the mermaid, who obliges, submerging a slim second before more arrows strike the prow near her.

Arrow nocked and drawn, Trillia steers with her left elbow and scans the right bank of the river—the South Carolina bank. The arrows come from there, but in the thick woodland she can't see the archers. She looses a precious arrow that only elicits youthful male laughter in response. She might as well be trying to kill the woodlands and swamps with bowshots.

Her archery does have one result, though. The mocking laughter is accompanied by no more arrows. Neither is the silence that follows. The archers on the right bank, however few or many there may have been, vanish into the landscape as completely as if they'd never existed. The only proof of their reality is *Sea Robin*'s prow, quilled with half a dozen stuck or dangling arrows.

Trillia continues upriver, more slowly, another arrow still nocked to her bow and both held at the ready. Steering with her elbow grows cumbersome, however. Eventually she relaxes her pull on the bowstring. Steering with her left hand, she continues to keep a close eye on the river's right bank—and a right-handed hold on bow and arrow at the bow's handgrip. She wishes belatedly that she had managed to beg, borrow, or steal a gun before fleeing the islands.

As noon passes into afternoon without further incident, she wonders about the attack. If the hidden archers had wanted to hit *her*, Trillia reasons, their arrows would have struck or fallen closer to her. Were they shooting at the mermaids, then? No, that didn't seem right either. They were trying to hit the bow of *Sea Robin*, but she can't fathom why.

In late afternoon Trillia passes the weedy riverwalk, broad grassy streets, vine-decked buildings, and impromptu "hanging garden" parking structures at the center of what was once Augusta. Moments later she rounds a bend in the river. Between two sandbars, in a long canoe floating at the center of the river channel, four people wait, dressed in hide leggings and scavenged pre-pandemic shirts and jackets.

On the bar at the right stand patched tents and tethered horses. Nothing stands on the sandbar to the left, but that's no help to Trillia. The boat in the middle of the channel effectively bars her way. The water on either side is too shallow for passage. Assessing the situation, she eases down the engine speed to slow *Sea Robin*. She could have the mermaids attack the canoe, if necessary. Or she could run *Sea Robin* over the top of the craft blocking her way, if she has to. Either maneuver would be risky in the extreme.

The dark-skinned man standing in the stern of the canoe, leans on a pole with one hand and waves with the other. He appears to be unarmed.

"Yo ho! *Sea Robin*!"

A ruddy woman with cornsilk-colored hair—his wife?—stands and waves slowly at the bow of the canoe. She too appears to be unarmed.

"Our apologies for what our boys did to your boat!"

Between the adults are two youths, lighter in color than the man but darker than the woman, looking downcast as they paddle to keep the canoe in place in the river. Trillia wonders if this is some sort of trick. Deciding to hear them out, she slows *Sea Robin*'s engines further, so that the boat remains more or less stationary in the river current. The man whacks the nearer of the two boys smartly on top of the head with his hand.

"We'll have them repair the damage for you, if you'd like. It's the least they can do."

As a sign that it's up to her, they signal the boys to bring the canoe around, parallel to the current and into shallower water. The woman gestures to the tents on the right.

"While they're fixing your boat, we'd be honored if you'd join us for supper at our camp."

The parents' words—and the boys' chastened looks—are enough to convince Trillia.

"All right. The damage isn't that bad, but I'll gladly join you for a meal."

She runs *Sea Robin* into the shallows by the right sandbar, safe against the current. She shuts down the engine, and the wheel automatically locks. After lowering a ladder to the shallow water Trillia climbs down and splashes ashore, keenly aware that—if things go wrong and these people decide to kill her in hopes of taking the boat—at least they won't have the codes to operate *Sea Robin*.

The man, who shakes Trillia's hand as she steps onto the sandbar, has long, dreadlocked hair and rim-taped glasses. He introduces himself as Raheem Wilson. Trillia does not give her last name, leery of any resonances the name Spires might have for these people.

The woman with the fine spiraling tattoos around her neck greets Trillia and introduces herself as April Grayson. Their two boys are Phenix and Shawnee. She says she has a daughter too, Hephzibah, who is gathering wood for the fire. Raheem sets the two lanky boys to digging out *Sea Robin*'s quills and patching the arrow-holes with pitch. Glad to have another woman to talk to, April walks Trillia toward the evening cookfire in its circle of tents.

"Sorry the boys did that," April says. "Their manners are not as good as they could be. We hunt and fish between here and the sea. Some seasonal cropping, too. It's a gypsy sort of life, but a good one for the children—the boys especially, or so you'd think. We don't see many people, though. Phenix, the fourteen-year-old—he's good at getting himself and his younger brother into trouble. He needs a rite of passage so he'll stop acting like a boy in a man's body."

Raheem joins them around the cookfire, shaking his head.

"He needs a 'rite of passage' across his backside, you ask me. I don't know what it is with these kids sometimes. Maybe it's living after the end of the world, or being a Savannah River postnuclear mutant makes him like that. Maybe it's 'bad blood.' "

"Or maybe it's just being a teenager," April says. "Don't you remember what you were like at that age?"

"I don't like to. I was exactly his age when the old world ended." He sighs and looks away a moment. "I'll take him on the big trek to Atlanta this summer. Travel through the wild lands, show him what used to be. Let him sing and dance around a Wer campfire or two. Scavenge usables from a broke-down skyscraper, or what's left in the ruins of a shopping mall. That'll give him his 'rite of passage'—and fast."

The youngest child, Hephzibah, looks to be four or five years old. She walks up among them with an armload of wood and drops it on the sand beside the fire before darting behind her mother, who thanks her for bringing in the firewood. April strokes the girl's tawny curls and tries to introduce her to Trillia, but Hephzibah is having none of it.

"She's shy. Seeing anybody besides her brothers and parents is rare for her. Especially a stranger in unusual clothes, out of a big boat."

Trillia nods. Lurking behind her mother, Hephzibah seems torn between fascination and fear at the presence of the strange woman in their camp. The little girl helps her mother and father prepare an evening meal of what looks like fish, clams, and duck, along with greens Trillia doesn't recognize. They flatten wet doughballs of cornflour onto a metal sheet and cook them into biscuit or flatbread.

"Atlanta is where I'm headed," Trillia says, trying to pick up the conversation again where it left off.

"Oh?" Raheem asks, a quick glance passing between him and his wife. "What takes you there? Not your boat—leastwise not much further!"

Trillia smiles and nods, getting the joke, but she chooses her words carefully when she answers.

"I'm looking for a woman who's from where I'm from. She left years ago. I think a man who left more recently may be with her."

"This woman," April says, tending to the frying fish, "does she have a name?"

"Tomoko Fukuda."

"You mean Dr. Fukuda?" April asks, a look of something like relief flitting over her face. "She's good people."

"You know her?"

"Nothing very amazing about it," Raheem says, poking at the oysters in their steaming pan on the grill above the fire. "Every year or so, she and her people come out this way, to what used to be the State Medical College in Augusta. Looking for supplies to haul back with her. Even if she didn't, it still wouldn't be amazing. Probably aren't many more people living in the whole of ol' Georgia now than used to live in a small town in the old days. We all move around a good bit, too. Everybody pretty much knows everybody else."

"Really? What would you say the population is, now? For what used to be Georgia, I mean."

Raheem frowns. April laughs.

"Sounds just like something Dr. Fukuda would say! You're Bahamian, no doubt about it!"

"Is it that obvious?" Trillia asks, vaguely put out. She tells them about her encounter with the hidden woman in Savannah, who also guessed as much. Now it's Raheem's turn to laugh.

"Ol' Missy Crabcakes—has to be! Still talking about hags and plat-eyes. She's a bit sprung in the head, but harmless enough. Probably the best crabber in all the low country, too."

Trillia doesn't know what to make of such a description.

"But why does asking about the population sound like Dr. Fukuda? Or tell you I'm from the Bahamas?"

Another glance passes between the couple—the "Now, dear" kind she's seen pass between her own mother and father.

"Because that's all in the past," Raheem says. "I've talked with Doc Fukuda. What difference does it make whether the survival rate after the plague was one in a hundred, or one in five hundred, or one in a thousand? Say there were five hundred million people living in North America when the plague hit—"

"It was probably more than that," April puts in.

"Whatever. Five hundred million's a good round number. So if one in five hundred survived, you've got a million people spread out over all of North America. If one in a thousand survived, that's half a million people in the whole continent. Doesn't make that much difference, see? At least compared to the old days."

Trillia rather thinks it does, but as she's a guest, she doesn't argue the point. Raheem checks the oysters.

"Personally, I don't care whether it was the will of God or the mistake of science or some kind of biotron bomb that wiped out most everybody. Fact is, they're gone. Trying to figure out who or what or how or why isn't gonna change a damn thing. It gets to me when I see educated people like Doc Fukuda spending so much of her time trying to change the past—"

"How can they find a cure for the plague unless they know how it happened in the first place?" April asks. Trillia can tell this is old territory for her hosts, but she wishes one or the other of them would explain "biotron bomb." She's never heard the term before. Raheem removes the oysters from the fire.

"It's not even the same plague anymore. If it was, you wouldn't be alive, April my dear. We need to be practical. Those of us who are still left should be working on salvaging as much as we can from the old world, so that maybe we can use it again, someday."

April removes the fish from the fire and cuts it up.

"There's plenty left over from the old world. They made things for *billions* of people. We've got more than we need of their old junk."

"Where I'm from," Trillia ventures, "we've tried to keep things working like they used to work. But we still have problems with the plague. My friend Ricardo was exiled because they say he's got some 'new variant' Wersign in his blood."

Shaking his head and turning to April, Raheem takes the duck off the spit where it has been turning and roasting.

"See? Wasn't I right? Entire islands filled with some of the best brains left on the planet, and what do they spend their time doing? Living in the plaguey past—that's what I mean."

April sniffs.

"They've got the best of that old 'technology' you're so hot about, but it hasn't done them a whole lot of good, has it?"

"Only because they won't face the new reality!"

"New reality?" Trillia asks, meekly.

"Where you're from, April and I wouldn't even be allowed to marry, much less have children."

"Why?" Trillia says, coming to the defense of her homeland. "Because you're black and she's white? That's not much of a problem."

April and Raheem smile awkwardly. Raheem takes April's hand and gives it a squeeze.

"No, not that. Everybody has pretty much figured out that color or country or creed don't mean a helluva lot when there are so few people left on Earth. Love is where you find it."

"Even if it takes you fifteen years," April says, squeezing Raheem's hand back.

"Then why?"

"I'm Wer. A shapeshifter."

"As a family, we don't quite fit into anybody's tribe," Raheem says. "So we make up one of our own. Folks leave us alone and we leave them alone."

"I'm lucky," April says. "Doc Fukuda says I've got a 'long-period polymorph' of the plague. I was already almost ten when the plague hit. I might well live another ten years yet."

Trillia doesn't know what to say to that. She is beginning to suspect that the tidy division of all humanity into three parts—Trufolk, Werfolk, Merfolk—might be too simple.

April announces that the food is ready. Phenix and Shawnee join them amid the small circle of tents. Raheem turns to the boys.

"You finish fixing what you did to this woman's boat?"

Phenix stares intently at the place in the sand he's digging at with the big toe of his right foot.

"Yessir."

"Good. We'll eat now. I'll check your work after we finish supper."

The meal is delicious, despite or perhaps because of its simplicity. Over dinner little Hephzibah urges her mother to tell her again about life when April was little. Hephzibah seems particularly enchanted by the idea of a machine for holding a pocket of housebroken winter, the "refrigerators" old-time people kept in their homes. Trillia, watching the look of fascination on the little girl's face, realizes how far gone the old world is for these children. Refrigerators might as well have housed butchered paleolithic mammoths inside a mythical cold Land of Plenty.

As Trillia helps April and little Hephzibah clean up the dinner's remains in the river, Raheem goes with the boys to examine their work on the *Sea Robin*'s bow.

"You're headed toward Atlanta, you said?" April asks as they finish up the work, side by side. "By way of old Twenty?"

"That's right."

"Why don't you let us look after your boat until you return, then? You can't take it with you down that road."

They get up from their finished chores at the shoreline and return to the campfire. April and Hephzibah toss more wood on the fire, which is soon crackling and sparking against the cool spring evening. As they sit down around the fire, Trillia stares at April. Watching her weave twigs into a basket fish-trap, to repair it, Trillia finds she trusts this woman—notwithstanding everything she's been led all her life to believe about Werfolk.

"I appreciate the offer. I suppose the mermaids could guard it well enough, but it *would* be nice to have someone on land to look after it, too."

"Tell me about your mermaids! I've heard about them. I thought they were just some old fairy story come to life again after the Collapse—even when Doc Fukuda's people swore they'd seen them. I caught a glimpse of things like skinny manatees when you came ashore. They're real, then?"

"Quite real, but I don't think they'd appreciate your comparing them to 'skinny manatees.' "

April laughs.

"And—human?"

"I suppose they are. They don't think like us, though. Not like shapeshifters or standard humans, I mean."

"That's not much of a surprise. Living like fish or dolphins all the time, you could hardly expect them to."

"It's more than that. We created them, but I don't think we really *understand* them yet."

"They were an experiment, then? I don't know if I approve of experimenting with human beings."

"If they *are* really human. Depends how you define 'human,' I suppose. A werwoman captured in a raid on the islands—Lupe, she called herself— she said the Merfolk were human beings who had been permanently shapeshifted."

April tilts her head, chin in toward chest, taken aback.

"Wersign taken to the extreme, you mean? I never thought of it that way."

Raheem enters the circle of tents with the now somewhat less downcast-looking boys.

"What's that you were thinking of?" he asks.

"I was thinking we could look after Trillia's boat here while she heads toward Atlanta. And that maybe you and Phenix should accompany her, since the country and its ways are foreign to her. Heppie and Shaw and I should be fine here while you're gone."

Trillia marvels at how April came up with that—without missing a beat. Raheem looks at his wife with narrowed eyes. Trillia suspects this is also April's way of getting him to stop postponing whatever rite of passage it is he's supposed to be working out for the older boy, Phenix. Raheem's brow eventually relaxes out of its furrows.

"Sounds like an idea. I'll give it some thought."

For a time they all stare at the flickering fire. The day has been long and trying. Yet also rewarding—at least for Trillia, at least so far. April puts the children to bed, one by one.

"You mentioned a 'biotron bomb,' earlier," Trillia says to Raheem. "I've never heard of that before."

"I don't know if it ever actually existed. I heard about it from an old guy who used to drive a truck into the Savannah River plant, before everything collapsed. The biological equivalent of a doomsday neutron bomb, he called it. Something that would wipe out humanity but leave the rest of the world still standing—including most of the cities."

Trillia startles. The virtual record of the conference she viewed, seemingly ages ago, is suddenly fresh in her memory.

"Who would want to do that?"

" 'Space aliens,' according to this old guy. Killing off the human roaches before they moved in."

Raheem stares deep into the fire. Trillia pokes at it with a stick.

"You don't give it much credence, I gather?"

"If some sort of space-alien roach bomb caused the plague, then the space invaders are awful damned slow about moving in. All this 'looking backward to the apocalypse' Doc Fukuda and you island people do—it's all like that. A waste of time."

"Why's that?"

"That world is over—so get over it. This is the new way of the world. All those people are gone, yeah, but life goes on. Trying to figure out why all those people are gone, instead of going on with being alive—what a waste! I've heard too many theories about the End to care anymore."

Trillia thinks how different Raheem's response is from the older islanders' survivor guilt.

"Like what? Besides space aliens, I mean?"

"Like what this itinerant preacher told me. That everybody we thought had died really hadn't—they'd been 'Raptured.' All of us still alive are the ones the Rapture left behind. The Preterite, he called us. God has taken His own, the Devil has taken his, and we're left to fend for ourselves."

"Without gods or devils?"

"Or space aliens, either."

"Just chance, then—an accident. No one really responsible for it. That's pretty much what I was taught where I grew up. Something the binotechs were working on that happened to get loose."

"I've heard that one too," Raheem says. "But what were they working on? And why? I wonder if anything is ever really just an 'accident'—just 'fate.' In the last days, there was a lot of talk of conspiracies. Things like Tetragrammaton and Medusa Blue."

"Tetragrammaton? Medusa Blue? What are those?"

Raheem laughs.

"Oh, no you don't, kiddo! No more theories about the past. See how tempting that stuff is? Everybody trying to find somebody to blame? You *almost* got me, there. Remember, I was only fourteen when it hit. You want to know about all that, you talk to Doc Fukuda. She was in the thick of it."

"I intend to," Trillia says, stifling a yawn.

"Then you better get some sleep," April adds, from where she now stands behind them. "You too, honey—if you're planning on guiding her along the way, that is."

Raheem stands and stretches—and swats April lightly on the butt.

"I might just do that—despite your *wanting* me to do it."

April gives him a look less cross than it purports to be, before turning to Trillia.

"You can sleep in the girls' tent with me and Heppie, if you'd like. We've got room."

Trillia debates with herself a moment—before deciding she's too tired to hassle with going back to the boat, fetching her tent, and setting it up.

"Thanks. Your offer is really too kind, but I'll accept it anyway."

April and Raheem smile at her.

"All right, then. If you want to join me and Phenix tomorrow, then bid farewell to your fishy friends in the morning, and we'll head on to Atlanta."

Raheem bids the women good-night and heads toward his own tent, close by the one his sons are supposed to be sleeping in—although the occasional giggling and shushing coming from that direction makes Trillia wonder. Inside the third tent, April moves a sleepy Heppie closer to her mother's side of the tent. Trillia herself has no sooner been furnished with an old sleeping bag and mat than she is sound asleep.

The next morning she wakens to overcast skies. After breakfast she talks to the mermaids and tries to explain her plans to them. She promises them she'll only be gone a short while and convinces them to stay in the vicinity of the *Sea Robin*. Returning to the campsite, she is startled to see Phenix leading three large animals onto the sandbar.

"Horses! We're riding horses?"

Raheem pats a large bay mare on her broad neck and saddles her.

"Looks that way, doesn't it? April was against our keeping them at first—too much trouble moving them along the banks when we move downriver."

"It's been a challenge," April says, saddling a chestnut gelding. "Believe me. They're a big nuisance most of the time, but every once in while they come in handy."

"Just wish they were a bit less work, sometimes," Raheem says, helping Phenix saddle the third horse, a sorrel mare.

"If wishes were horses—" April says.

"—beggars would drive Porsches," Raheem says, nodding, then glancing at Trillia. "Something my daddy used to say. You ever ridden?"

"Once. When I was a little girl. We don't have many large animals in the islands."

"I'll give you the basic operating instructions, then," April says. She helps Trillia mount the sorrel mare, then shows her how to make the mare move left or right, speed up or slow down or come to a complete halt. "Raheem and Phenix will teach you the finer points along the way," she says, finishing the lesson.

Trillia debates with herself on whether or not to bring her map pad, small solar computer, and screenshades. Popping a dataneedle into the back of her skull might startle her companions, but access to virtuality could prove helpful, too. She can always have the dataneedle play directly off the computer, instead of the running it virtual out of her head onto the shades. That might make Raheem and Phenix more comfortable. Pad, comp, and shades combined won't weigh that much. They're all small enough to be wearable—the first two slipped into stretch gloves and the last riding on the bridge of her nose. Might as well bring them.

Once they've loaded all their travel gear, Raheem steps up into the stirrups of the big bay mare and Phenix legs-over onto the chestnut. Waving farewell to April and Shawnee and Heppie, Trillia and her guides ride into the swamps, forest, and savannah on what was once the South Carolina side of the river. Raheem explains that the grasslands are younger than the forests—"product of heating up the planet," as he puts it. Before long they ride over an embankment, toward a gaunt-ribbed and time-worn but still impressive bridge where Interstate Highway 20 crosses first the Savannah River, then the green-slimed Augusta Canal.

Grass, weeds, and kudzu have crept across it, and sections of it have buckled, eroded, and cracked, yet Highway 20 remains in passable shape. Trillia has often viewed historical records of such roads and the streams of vehicles that flowed back and forth over them, but this is the first time she has actually traveled one of the great "rivers of stone" of the pre-Collapse world. Even in disrepair, the stone river of Highway 20 is impressive.

On the road just west of Augusta, they pick their way through a thick jam-up of abandoned vehicles. At times they have no choice but to leave the roadbed entirely and detour around flat-tired, rusting (and sometimes burnt-out and overturned) kudzu-draped hulks. They make their way through the jumbled vehicles with little commotion, other than scattering mice from stuffing-blown upholstery and rotting interiorwork, rabbits from behind broken windshields and streaked windows, the occasional snake or lizard from its haunt in fender and door panel.

Once past the worst of these instant junkyards, they make good time over the increasingly empty highway. Trillia notices that some of the abandoned vehicles appear to have been moved since the Collapse. She also sees tracks that almost match the great treaded tires on the abandoned vehicles, but not quite—tracks that seem more recent than the fall of the old civilization. When Trillia points out the tracks to him, Raheem frowns.

"Off-road raiders. A real problem the first five, ten years after the Collapse. Had their own little turf wars, for a while there—mostly about caches of fresh fuel and replacement parts, as I recall. Not your smarter survivalist types. Gave them a wide berth. Too much booze and bullets, not enough brains in the lot of 'em. They didn't much like solars or hybrids for their vehicles—no matter how scarce or expensive their fossil fuels got. Lucky for the rest of us."

Trillia guides her horse over a particularly pronounced pair of ruts.

"What happened to them?"

"Oh, some of them are still around. Nursing those old off-road monsters of theirs. Lots of abandoned logging roads to get lost on, especially around the Oconee. Their kind of terrain. When they're not scraping together parts and fuel, I suppose they're pretty much doing like the rest of us. Hunting. Fishing. Growing small crops on food plots. Last time I saw one of those off-road dinosaurs, the owner was using it to do the spring plowing."

"You said something about too many bullets, but you and Phenix each have a gun in your gear. . . ."

Raheem smiles crookedly.

"I wondered when you'd notice. Mine's a twelve gauge. The boy's carrying a thirty-ought."

"For hunting?"

Phenix snickers and mutters, "Humans, maybe," before Raheem explains.

"Not usually. Bows, spears, snares, even slingshots are plenty good enough for hunting. Shells and bullets are too dear for deer—and more precious everyday."

"You'd think there'd be more ammunition left—"

"Oh, Americans had plenty of guns. Don't get me wrong. A *helluva* lot of small-arms ammo got used up in the last days, though. A lot of the big stuff, too. You'll see that in Atlanta, all the bigger cities. Vines and weeds cover up a lot of the small-arms damage in the smaller towns. The military usually didn't bring the heavy-duty stuff into Mayberry. Guns are a last resort for us, now—protection against whatever won't listen to reason."

Trillia nods, though she has no idea where Mayberry might be. They travel in silence for a time. The land here—generally flat with some rolling hills, especially along the larger watercourses—is different from the terrain she piloted *Sea Robin* through, between Savannah and Augusta.

"That's because we're in the Piedmont country now," Raheem tells her. "You're above the Fall Line."

Trillia doesn't know what the Fall Line is. Among the hardwood ridges and the stands of conifers their road passes through, she *does* see plenty of fallen logs and old rotting tree stumps. As the day continues, she finds it more and more difficult to concentrate on what Raheem is telling Phenix, pointing out to his son the holly trees and sweetgum and elderberry bushes, the maples, red cedars, mosses—and *all* their uses. Through her growing malaise Trillia is surprised to see that Raheem has the boy keep a notebook on such things—not unlike the one Raheem himself carries.

The famed nature-knowledge of the hunter-gatherer, Trillia thinks hazily. But April and Raheem's clan are not just hunter-gatherers. They are small-scale farmers and herders, too. Equivalent to what? Neolithic? But then there's the smattering of higher remnant technologies, as well. What does that make them? Retrolithic? Postapocalithic?

Her head begins to ache, but not from speculation. She grows more and more woozy. It's not just motion sickness from being on horseback. All the details of the landscape, with its creatures and herbs and trees, its dilapidated and creeper-draped lost towns, just off the Interstate—they all start to blend together in her mind as the clouds, threatening all day, at last start to drizzle.

Before the rain starts in earnest they break from their broad highway "trail" and set up camp. Trillia is relieved at the change. The end of the trail day finds her riding half-asleep, almost passed out in the saddle. Putting up her tent seems a Herculean labor. She doesn't know why she should be so tired. She doesn't have much of an appetite either, but she forces herself to eat the supper of dried venison and hard biscuit Phenix and Raheem give her.

In the middle of the night, on her hands and knees in pouring rain, heaving up her stomach's contents along with what feels like her stomach lining and segments of intestines too—all of it acid-puréed before bilious ejection—she is certain she should *not* have eaten that evening meal. Her torment continues throughout the rest of the night, from both ends of her digestive tract, until by daybreak she is as weak as a starved kitten and as miserable as she can ever remember being.

She groans herself awake. If these are the joys of the Postapocalithic close-to-nature way of life, then they can keep all of it. But they're not "them" anymore. She has become one of them. Not least because the plague and collapse exiled the surviving remnant of humanity from its own history as surely as Trillia exiled herself from the islands. Making her experience and all humanity's the same, that way. Is that a delusion of grandeur, or a delusion of persecution? Maybe she'll have Raheem jot that thought down for her in his notebook—if she lives long enough to tell him about it.

"Sounds like you got a bug in your guts," Phenix says matter-of-factly, when the boy and his father look in on her.

"Good reason to take a break from the trail," Raheem adds, nodding.

Trillia does not appreciate her mortal illness being reduced to a "gut bug." Yet, despite everything, she will play her part bravely. She tries, weakly and not very coherently, to protest the delay. To tell them she has to meet Dr. Fukuda. Then get back to Savannah in time to meet with Ricardo. That she may have to travel still farther after that. Maybe as far as New York City.

Even through her thick mental fog she can tell Raheem and Phenix aren't about to break camp and move on. They nurse her through the day. She sleeps through most of it—at least when she is not explosively ejecting or excreting from primary orifices. Raheem makes her a not particularly tasty broth of herbs. He insists she drink it. Weakened and malaised to the point of delirium, she laments to Nurse Raheem.

"I thought dangerous animals or savage human beings would do me in—not that I'd be laid low by a germ."

"Wouldn't be the first time," Raheem grunts, trying to get her to drink more of his medicinal soup. "When I was a kid I read this book about how microbes wipe out invaders from Mars and save the human race. We're Martians too, though—as far as the microbes are concerned. The plague proved that."

Trillia nods, not quite understanding what he's getting at. Raheem's story only makes her wonder if some nasty vector might even now be infecting her with some new variant of the old plague.

Almost as fast as it came upon her, however, the worst of the sickness passes. Maybe Raheem's medicinal broth helps, though she can't say how. By the next morning, she is able to stand up and walk and keep her thoughts about her—all at the same time. She still has no real appetite, but Raheem and Phenix will allow her nothing except the broth for breakfast anyway.

"Sorry. Sorry I was such a baby."

To her relief, they laugh and dismiss out of hand any need for such apologies.

In a long bright day on the road, Trillia marks many things. More abandoned towns sink into brushy, vine-clutched wilderness. Where the vegetation hasn't conquered so thoroughly, wind makes the empty cities and towns ghosts in loud shrouds—banging, booming, and rattling anything that's loose. Windless is worse, though: an entombing silence. The road itself eventually crosses a long stretch of bridge above a lake. Amid forested ridges, the lake snakes away to both the northern and southern horizons—a lake that, Raheem claims, "you can tell is man-made just from the shape of it."

Many things, but few people. Once she sees smoke in the distance, which might or might not be of human origin. Soon thereafter she hears what sounds like distant song on the spring breeze. Her companions, however, say nothing about such rare signs, so she does not mention them.

That evening, when they stop by a small river to set up camp and put the horses to graze, she is tired but alert. She eats some of the biscuity flatbread, and keeps it down—a relief. She sits beside the fire with Raheem and Phenix, watching the sun set and the stars fill the sky. Raheem tells stories about the days before the plague—about the magical tools and powers of the old ways. About the cars and trains and aircraft he traveled in. The constellations of city lights seen from the air, stretched out upon the land like another heaven of stars, fallen to Earth.

Phenix—trying to maintain the apparent disinterest of a teenager who has heard such stories dozens of times—pretends not to be listening. His pretense gets harder to pull off when Raheem tells of his own upbringing in Columbus, Georgia—just across the Chattahoochee River from the town of Phenix City, Alabama, for which his eldest son is named. Trillia has heard survivor tales among the islanders many times, but Raheem's are different, more immediate somehow. Maybe it's just that the contrast, between the world that was and the world that is, is stronger here, under a night sky in a dark land where scattered Wer and Tru survivors go about their inscrutable business, among ruins of towns and farms disappearing into forests and grasslands.

Raheem at last stands up to stretch and look at the sky. Phenix and Trillia do the same. The stars are thick and golden overhead.

"Hello, God!"

Raheem says it like a joke, but they know he means it. Trillia feels it, too. Maybe that's why we've always put God or gods in the heavens, she thinks. We'll never have complete understanding of all this we're standing under—and we've always known that. Maybe it's good to know there are some things we'll never know.

Raheem urges them to bed with the promise and the threat of an early rising followed by arrival in Tomoko Fukuda's vicinity well before noon. Trillia, however, crouching down beside the river to wash her face before bed, finds herself still puzzling about understanding the heavens. The motion of the river itself under the stars catches her attention. The river is dark, but it shines by reflecting the light. In its water, eddies whorl up, bright and spinning like small spiral galaxies. Each vortex whirls along in the river's current for a while, then disappears back into the stream as Trillia watches.

That's how we live and die, she thinks. But the river keeps flowing, the light keeps shining. Walking back to her tent, she wonders if the geniuses of the old times knew how much they were losing when they traded all the constellations of stars for lights on boulevards.

Raheem makes good his threat of early rising. As they ride, Trillia tells her companions about how, when she was first coming down with her illness, she tried to figure out what technological level Raheem and April's family fell into—Neo-Neolithic? Retrolithic?

"Mom says we live in The World After Toilet Paper," Phenix says impishly, then imitates his mother's voice—" 'Toothbrushes and toilet paper are all that separate us from the animals!' "

Raheem frowns a moment, then nods.

"April insists we scavenge those items whenever and wherever possible."

Trillia laughs. "I'm happy she does—especially as sick as *I* was."

The three of them reach the sprawling campus of the last great complex of the Centers for Disease Control and Prevention, near the former town of Covington in the former state of Georgia, before the sun is well up. As they make their way into the campus, Trillia sees that roughly a quarter of the complex suffered heavy fire damage in the past. Tempted to consult her computer about it, she asks Raheem instead.

"Some people attacked it near the end."

"I was always told this place was closer to solving the riddle of the madness plague than anywhere else on Earth. Why would anyone want to attack it?"

"As near as I can remember, they attacked it as a *source* of the plague. Because the scientists here knew more about the pandemic than anyone else."

"Knowledge is dangerous," Trillia says, shaking her head.

"Especially when the ignorant grow envious."

Trillia follows Raheem and Phenix into a broad sector of CDC Covington that is not only intact but also maintained. They pass a barefooted, tattooed, hide-clad, bone- and shell-ornamented group—Werfolk or barbarized Trufolk, Trillia can't say which—of perhaps twenty people. All are singing work songs as they plant seedlings in the newly turned soil of what was once a stretch of campus lawn. The food plotters eye the strangers warily, but say nothing. The largest group of human beings she's seen since coming to the mainland, these trustees do not strike Trillia as particularly well-disposed toward strangers. They break neither the rhythm of their song nor their work as the travelers on horseback ride past.

In a courtyard farther on, in front of a building that reminds Trillia of a box made out of crystal, Raheem hails a small elderly man.

"Rolph! Rolph Martinez! That you?"

The man, tending a grape vine trellised on the side of the crystal building, stares up from under a broad sun hat, brushing an enormous white mustache away from his lips. The riders come to a stop a short distance from the man. He has piercing blue eyes embedded in the dark, weathered face of someone who has spent a lot of time outdoors.

"Raheem."

"Doc Fukuda around?"

"Not here. The zoo."

"What's she doing there?"

"Labs. Facilities. Supplies."

"Gotcha. You say hello to your people for me, okay?"

Martinez glances at Trillia, then at Phenix, before speaking to Raheem. "You be careful in Ghostlanta."

"Will do. We're off to the zoo."

"Know how to get there?"

"Still in Grant Park, last time I checked."

"Hasn't moved. Doc's at the Frozen Zoo Dome, like as not."

Raheem nods and waves. The old man goes back to tending his vines as the riders turn away. Raheem, Phenix, and Trillia ride back out of the CDC campus, through abandoned Covington, back onto the broken concrete of Interstate 20. They travel at a steady trot until, near Conyers, they hit a nightmare junkyard of abandoned vehicles far larger than the one near Augusta.

The derelict vehicles are dusty and decayed. Nearly all are dented and battered. Those on what was the grass median are draped with creepers. Not a few—especially hovercars and ground-effect trucks—have overturned before coming to their final rest. Some are burned down to their wheel rims. Raheem identifies a particularly spectacular wreck as the entangled remains of two lo-fly cars.

They pick their way through and detour around the helter-skelter landscape of smashed vehicles. Not all the drivers or passengers escaped their cars, here. Behind peeling steering wheels, dead control sticks, crack-crazed and shattered windshields, the bleached heaps of rag-draped bones sit in blown-out seats, their only mourners the nesting birds and mice, the spiders, snakes, and other creatures that call this charnel lot home.

Not far beyond the worst of the vehicle graveyard, the three riders reach the first of the scorched suburbs of Atlanta. Thirty years of wind, rain, rust, vines, and weeds have still not erased the devastation. It goes on and on, worse in some places, less complete in others, but terrible everywhere. At points, the destruction spills onto the blackened and bomb-cratered Interstate as well.

Within view of downtown, Raheem stops and points out those buildings he can still identify from the shattered towers and burnt-out husks of the Atlanta skyline. Among the nearer structures, walls of upper floors have collapsed and sagged into tangled webs of twisted rebar, still clutching chunks of gray concrete like the heavy corpses of cocooned moths in abandoned spiderwork.

"This poor city. Ripped apart by fire and battle twice in less than two hundred years."

He spurs his horse forward and waits for Phenix and Trillia to catch up.

Trillia is content to listen for a while—especially since Phenix is full of questions for his father.

"What was all the fighting about around here?"

"About the madness, and who was to blame for it. You have to remember the history. What was once the United States of America had been replaced by the Christian States of America, about fifteen years before the plague, I guess it was. Before I was born, anyway. Then, during the churchstate wars, the preacher-politicians were overthrown. Most of what had been the Christian States went back to being plain old United States again—not all, but most. Just about then, the plague hit. It chose a really bad time to show up."

"Why's that?" Phenix asks.

"The preachers said the madness plague was God's vengeance against the people for having overthrown the Christian States. The plague got the Christco people all fired up too, so they were ready to go."

"I thought the plague just made people drum and dance and dream. At least until you shapeshifted and died."

"Not that simple. That was the basic pattern, but first it made you more what you already were. Think of the way your head works as being like a really complex system of locks and canals."

"Like the ones around Augusta?"

"Right, only a lot more complicated. What the plague did to people's heads was kind of like what heavy rainstorms do to canals or rivers. More and more water coming in, faster and faster. How your brain already worked, even how you thought and what ideas you'd been raised with—those were the canals, the locks, the pipes, the waterworks directing the flow. The water flowed in, more and faster, but it could only flow through the plumbing that was already there—through who you already were."

"Until the channels flooded and the pipes broke," Trillia puts in. Raheem nods. The boy Phenix stares at her. Trillia regrets her words, remembering April and her Wer affliction—even if it is a long-period form. She thinks of Ricardo too, and wonders. She rides in silence for a time, until the intensity of the devastation south of Decatur makes her blurt out a response to it.

"I can't believe anything short of nuclear weapons could have done this kind of damage!"

"Nope," Raheem says. "No nukes here, but just about everything else. Homemade fertilizer truck bombs, napalm, fuel-air explosions. As if it wasn't bad enough having the military and civilians going at it, the Purple Cloud Commandos had to show up, too, afterward."

"Who were they?" Phenix asks.

"Fire freaks. Set cities on fire everywhere, just to watch 'em burn down. Don't know why more cities weren't nuked, really. That would've been the ultimate in fun and games for the Purple Cloud types."

"Maybe the safeguards the militaries put in against the *old* madness worked against the new," Trillia ventures.

"Maybe. Or maybe we haven't heard the last of that stuff, either. I met a guy from down around Kings Bay, years ago, said ghost submarines with skeleton crews were still cruising around the world's oceans. Waiting for the command to launch their missiles and finish the job the pandemic started."

"That's crazy," Phenix says quietly as they skirt a large blast crater. The boy's father shrugs, opens his hands slightly.

"Crazy things happen. First time I came through Atlanta, it was still smoldering. Most everybody was already dead or gone or both. The few survivors I saw were way shocked out. Guess I was too. I remember seeing one guy walking around in this burned-over zone, most of his clothing blasted off his body. Carrying a television set like it was everything he'd ever loved in the world. Trying to find an outlet to plug it into, in a city that probably hadn't had electricity for half a year. And *he* was better off than most, in a lot of ways."

Down an eroded off-ramp they leave the Interstate and turn into an overgrown street called Boulevard. Raheem points out where the Turner Field Massacre took place—one hundred thousand shapeshifters put to death, in the scorched bowl-shaped building visible on the horizon, not far away.

"One blast. Everyone inside was incinerated instantly. Bomb went off about two hundred feet above second base."

Yet even here, so close to the scene of that atrocity, Grant Park still stands, overgrown but otherwise remarkably undamaged. The same is even more true of Zoo Atlanta.

"This is it. None too early, either. Don't want to be wandering around the streets of Ghostlanta after dark, if we can help it. Still a few Werfolk around who haven't forgotten the ball field massacre."

They move through the park, following the faded and broken but still discernible trail of signs pointing in the direction of the Frozen Zoo Dome. Trillia wonders what happened to the animals. Did they escape—to die of starvation in this foreign country? Did they succumb to strange diseases? Were they eaten by starving humans? Trillia tries to recall what she's scanned in the histories, but none of those options sound right.

The Frozen Zoo Dome's roof, though faded, still bears a distinct resemblance to Earth's northern hemisphere as seen from space. Through the Dome's bank of open doors, Trillia hears the thrum of a generator, providing power to the lights she sees shining inside. On either side of the bank of doors stand two young men, barefoot and tattooed and shell-ornamented, like the people working the food plot at CDC Covington. These two, however, are also dressed in scavenged work clothes and carry machetes with brightly painted hilts. Their preternatural alertness at the riders' approach calms just perceptibly as Raheem dismounts from his horse. Phenix and Trillia follow his lead.

On foot Raheem approaches the young men, moving slowly toward the rubber-tired cart stacked with equipment off to the right side of the guards.

"The boy and I are friends of Doc Fukuda's. This woman we brought with us is someone who has come from the New Bahamas to see her—"

At that moment Tomoko Fukuda herself, dressed in a worn lab coat, walks out of the building, toward the parked cart. She carries a round piece of equipment Trillia recognizes as a centrifuge. Emptying her arms of that gear, Fukuda welcomes Raheem and Phenix warmly. Further explanations to the guards become unnecessary.

As the scientist greets Raheem and Phenix, Trillia notes that Fukuda's hair is streaked with gray—an effect the woman accentuates by wearing the grayest strands woven together in tiny snakelike braids. Overall, the doctor looks to be about Raheem's age, although that can't be right. Raheem was only fourteen when the plague and the Collapse hit. Fukuda had to be at least twenty years older. Trillia puzzles over this a moment, then remembers Fukuda's years on the island—under longevity treatment.

"And you are?" Tomoko Fukuda asks, addressing her.

"Trillia," she says, shaking the doctor's hand. "Trillia Spires."

"Cameron's granddaughter? You were only a toddler when I left the islands! Come, I'll show you around. You must catch me up on everything!"

Before disappearing inside the building with Trillia, Tomoko suggests that her guards water and feed the horses. Raheem and Phenix go with the guards and horses, promising to rejoin Tomoko and Trillia after the animals have been looked to.

Tomoko takes Trillia on a quick tour of the Dome and its several belowground floors, pointing out the old Laboratory Suites, Medical Research Suite, Administration, and Facility Support spaces. She describes the Frozen Zoo's former role as a "genome resource bank" cryopreserving scarce genetic material. She shows Trillia what were once the plant-cloning and tissue culture facilities. Farther on she points out the Dome's labs for animal in-vitro fertilization, artificial insemination, sperm and embryo cryopreservation, even embryo transfer.

"Not as up-to-date as what you have in the island, I'm sure, but in its day this was state of the art. This was an SSP zoo. The plague left this place mostly intact—except for what was lost when the Collapse killed the power grid."

"SSP?"

"Species Survival Plan," Tomoko says as they walk up a spiral ramp. "*That* came in more than fifty years before the pandemic. The American Zoo and Aquarium Association was behind it. The point was to make zoos better at managing their endangered species populations—for health, genetic diversity, demographic stability. If a species could be reintroduced to its original range, its population would then have a better shot at becoming self-sustaining."

"I've heard of that. Zoo Arks. Conservation insurance colonies."

Tomoko nods as they come to the top of the ramp.

"Those were the popular names for it, yes. Very important work. Especially for ghost species—the ones already extinct in the wild, existing only in captive breeding programs or frozen germ plasm. Eventually the SSP coordinated with ISIS. Another acronym—sorry! There were a lot of agencies called Isis in those days. The International Species Inventory System is the one I mean."

Trillia glances past Dr. Fukuda, toward the dome above them. The building strikes her more and more as a weird temple from a doomed and lost civilization.

"But what happened to the animals that were in this zoo?"

"The same thing that happened to most zoo animals. During the last days they were repatriated. The flood tide of human population made the arks necessary in the first place, but once that human tide really began draining away there was no need for the arks anymore. The choice was either to reintroduce the animals to their original habitats, or risk losing them completely when the civilization that supported the zoos collapsed. We took them home and set them free."

"And it worked?"

Tomoko leans back against a railing, thinking about it.

"The human population crashed faster than damaged habitats could recover and regenerate. The effects of habitat destruction lingered on, even after the human population was gone. We lost a lot of individual animals, and probably too many species as well. If you look around the world now, though, I'll bet we saved far more than we lost."

"We?"

"Action For Animals. Thousands of people helped in the beginning, when the human population was just beginning to crash hard. I'm proud to say I myself had more than a little to do with getting the animals back where they belonged. Your grandfather too—he put up a lot of the money for shipping and reintroduction. You've never heard?"

"People talk about how he evacuated particular survivors to the islands, mostly."

Tomoko glances at the bright marble floor beneath their feet, then looks up and smiles quickly.

"But here I am, doing all the talking! Tell me, what brings you here? What takes you away from New Bahamas?"

Walking slowly out of the Dome, past the returned guards, and into the lengthening afternoon light, Trillia tells Tomoko about recent island history. As briefly as she can manage, she tells the doctor about the Wer raid, the death of Simon Lingham's son, and Lingham's abjuration—which stuns the older woman. Tomoko listens to the story of Ricardo's protest career, his Wersign diagnosis, his flight into exile in search of his mentor and other abjurers. She seems very interested in Trillia's hoped-for rendezvous with Ricardo.

"No," Tomoko says at last. "I'm afraid I haven't seen either your friend Ricardo, or Simon."

Immensely frustrated, Trillia shakes her head and plops down on a crumbling concrete bench in dappled shade nearby.

"Sometimes I just don't get you old-time survivors."

"Oh? What about us don't you get?"

"Look at Raheem. He thinks Bahamians are trapped in the past, yet *he* knows more of the history than most of us in the islands. He brings up weird things like Tetragramma Blue or whatever it is, then tells me I'll have to ask you about it. Before Simon comes to the mainland, he says he'll visit you, but then he doesn't. You were married to him once, right? You'd think you exiles here would keep in better touch with each other, through a network or something, but you don't. You're the ones who came up with 'species survival plans' for a bunch of *animals* before the pandemic, but not only *don't* you come up with one for humanity—you even *plan* how to self-destruct!"

Dr. Fukuda seems about to answer, until Trillia's last statement catches her off guard, makes her suddenly wary.

"What do you mean, 'plan how to self-destruct'?"

By way of answer, Trillia activates her wearable cybergear and plays for Tomoko the record of the virtual conference between her grandfather, Vang, and Dorogov. A surprising range of emotions passes over the doctor's face as she watches the record: puzzled recognition, then horror, then—relief?

"How did you get this?" Fukuda asks when the record has finished.

"Hacked it our of my grandfather's records. Lucky me."

"You are lucky. Lucky to be alive. As are we all. I always blamed my work with prionoids for much of what happened. Now you've shown me something that says maybe the blame spreads further than I thought."

"Assigning blame," Trillia says, still feeling peevish.

"It's as much about knowledge as about blame or responsibility. You

asked me about a species survival plan for humans, Trillia. The governments and corporations never came up with a public one for humanity
because we did not see ourselves as threatened or endangered."

"You mean *nobody* saw anything like the plague coming?"

Tomoko Fukuda gazes off into the middle distance.

"After the Cold War didn't end in nuclear winter, we didn't think
of ourselves as an endangered species anymore. Except in the most
improbable scenarios—say, alien invasion or immense natural disaster.
No one could realistically plan for those. A few people *were* worried that
some self-replicating mechanical or biological creation might get out of
hand and wipe us out, but it was the Age of Code. More and more of the
world's techonomies were based on nanotech and biotech. Market imper-
atives drove research further and further into self-replicating and self-
modifying 'smart' technologies. Voice an objection, and you were just an
'alarmist' or a 'Luddite.' "

The doctor shakes her head and sighs.

"Survival is not only about preservation. It's about change. About
adapting, changing yourself in response to changes in your environment.
About evolving. Some people *were* thinking about that. Before the pandemic, there were theorists who claimed we had never been contacted by
extraterrestrials because intelligence, consciousness itself, was an evolutionary dead end throughout the universe: Species intelligent enough to
create civilizations also invariably reached a level of technological prowess
where they destroyed themselves, or their environment, or both."

"Is that what happened to us?"

"No. I refuse to believe that *real* intelligence and *real* consciousness are
a dead end. Stupidity, shortsightedness, and greed are still the best candi-
dates for our exterminators. Consciousness evolved to help us find our
way *out* of cul-de-sacs. *Human* species survival plans, though covert, were
real consciousness in action, in some ways."

"Then why did it all fail?"

"I don't know," Tomoko replies. "Maybe over the years the planners
lost their way. Their plans supposedly evolved out of the days of the Cold
War, after all. From scenarios drafted by the intelligence agencies, the
KGBs and CIAs and such. The survival plans outlived the agencies that
had created them. One of those 'fossil' survival plans had already evolved

into a program, a consortium of sort, called Tetragrammaton. One of its projects was called Medusa Blue."

"Raheem said you'd know about this stuff. But why?"

"I had my reasons for learning about it, during the last days. That man in your record here—Dr. Vang—was rumored to be a big part of Tetragrammaton. I never saw proof of any link between your grandfather and Vang, though, until that prionoid discussion you just showed me. Makes perfect sense, in a way. Vang's work was as much about breaking down barriers between minds and machines as your grandfather's was about breaking down barriers between species."

Her grandfather? The man who acts as if Werfolk and unaltered humans are two different species—when obviously they're not? Cameron Spires, a breaker of species barriers? Then again, he *did* create the Merfolk. . . .

"Wait a minute," Trillia says, her head spinning as she tries to remember something she heard a preacher say in one of the historical records. "Are you saying the plan for *saving* humanity might have been responsible for *destroying* it?"

"Is that any stranger than what we've always been led to believe? That a technology *I* created, intended to 'cure' certain forms of insanity, instead created a superpathogen that inflicted certain and near-universal 'madness' on humanity as a whole—devastating our species far more profoundly than any previous plague in history or prehistory? Do you have any idea what kind of burden that's been for me to live with?"

Trillia, hearing the personal anguish and ardor in the older woman's voice, doesn't know quite how to respond. In Fukuda's voice she hears survivor-guilt raised to the nth power.

"But the idea that something intended to *save* could destroy—"

"The technologies we thought would be our parachute instead became our noose. No one knows exactly how it happened—even now—but I still think it would be a good thing to find out. I don't know why Simon didn't stop to see me, either. We abjurers are a solitary lot, I admit. We don't 'network' much. Why Simon didn't put in an appearance, though—that might be a good thing to find out, too. Where did you say he was headed?"

"No farther north than New York."

"That makes sense. New York City was the seat of your grandfather's power, before the pandemic. His private oracles, the artificial intelligences that helped oversee his corporate empire—they were all there, anyway."

Fukuda stands up suddenly, as if having come to a sharp decision.

"I'd like to join you on your little journey, Trillia, if you'll have me. I could be of some help, I think."

"I don't doubt that," Trillia says, coming more slowly to her feet. "What's in it for you, though?"

"I'd like some questions answered. I left the Bahamas because of those questions, Trillia. Because there was something *false* in the history your grandfather put forward—and everyone believed so readily, as if it was a magic spell putting everyone's cares to sleep. We might find the answers I've been looking for, along the way. Then, maybe, we might just break that spell and wake everyone up."

In the slanting light of the westering sun, the two women see Raheem and Phenix waving.

"Took you this long to look after those horses?" Dr. Fukuda calls to them.

"Naw," Phenix says. "We went to see that big painting, 'The Battle of Atlanta.' In the whatchamacallit."

"Cyclorama," his father says. "Saw the Confederate locomotive 'Texas' too. Good for the boy to get a sense of what slavery and the first Civil War were about, given my background—and his."

Trillia and Tomoko nod.

"We need to leave first thing in the morning," Trillia says. "I'm supposed to rendezvous with Ricardo at Savannah in a few days."

"Then we'd better get moving now," Raheem says, "if we're going to get back to CDC Covington before full dark."

"We may not have to," Dr. Fukuda says to Raheem.

"Why's that?"

"I'm going to be joining your friend on her trip. The quickest route from here to Savannah doesn't run by CDC Covington—it's old 75 to Macon, then old 16 from Macon to Savannah, not the 20 past Covington."

"But what about my boat? April and my Merfolk are still looking after it near Augusta."

"No big deal," Raheem says, thinking. "If you have to get to Savannah fast, Phenix and I can pilot your boat downstream from Augusta—if we can get it started, and your fishy friends let us at it. I still don't like the idea of camping out somewhere in Ghostlanta tonight, though."

"I've stayed overnight in the Dome before," Dr. Fukuda says, toying absently with one of her gray braids. "We've got generator-power for lights, and we can put guards around the front doors in shifts. We should be fine. If you could take the gear I've collected here with you to CDC Covington on your way back to Augusta, that would help too."

"I'll give you the ignition codes for *Sea Robin*," Trillia says, "but you'll have to convince the mermaids of your good will on your own, since I won't be there with you."

"I think I can manage that," Raheem says. The adults are agreed, but Trillia sees Phenix is not happy with the idea. The boy's overcast looks call Dr. Fukuda's and Raheem's attention to him too.

"Don't you be bugged because we have to cut our trip short," Raheem says, looking at his son. "If I can convince your mother, you might get yourself a *real* 'rite of passage'—all the way up the coast!"

That bucks up the boy's spirits, and promptly.

Trillia smiles as they head for the Dome. On the way, Dr. Fukuda tries to convey what it's been like to be both a scientist and tribal elder overseeing the mostly Werfolk research staff she's put together over the past fifteen years. Tomoko seems tremendously relieved, as if her life is no longer twisted up by the idea that the pandemic is *her* fault—with no ultimate responsibility ceded to bacteria or binotech buyouts or anything else. They may not have the full history yet, but Tomoko seems a much happier person already.

Drifting into sleep that night, Trillia thinks of her rendezvous with Ricardo, then following Lingham and the trail to a possible cure. She feels less alone now, part of a community in embryo—even if it is a community of questers and loners, half-breeds and misfits. In these lands she has never known, in a world of new alliances growing and crystallizing all around her, Trillia feels more at home than she ever thought possible.

23

Dancing Inside
2033

IN THE WARD OF THOSE SOMNIACS WHO HAD PASSED FROM DANCE INTO dream, Sister Vena sighed. Despite all the medtech ambience of electrodes, EEGs, and real-time brain scans of her pathologically sleepy patients, Vena wondered if she was still really doing science anymore.

I spend my days tracing their dream states and recording what they remember in their rare waking phases, she thought. I've become more an interpreter of dreams, an oneiromancer, than a scientist. Especially here, in this room, in the night hospital, surrounded by sleepers sighing in their dreams.

Through a pair of viewshades, Sister Vena revisited the virtual notebook she had been keeping for her weekly reports to Mother Mary in Calcutta. Her reports posed difficult questions for those who believed the sudden increase in stigmata cases represented a "new age of miracles." Vena's problematic questions, however, had apparently been swallowed up in Mother Mary's (and Mother Church's) general euphoria at the recent upswing in conversions and vocations. Sister Vena soldiered on, but being ignored made the young nun feel old.

The dancers were in some ways easier to deal with, she thought. Not physically, maybe—coping with their frenetic movements was exhausting for all the doctors and nurses—but intellectually, at least. No problem at all finding a mother lode and a load for Mother on the history of dance. The same, alas, could not be said of this new dreaming phase, which so many of the dancers had now entered.

Researching through the infosphere, Sister Vena found much more on dance's long history of spiritual connection, and the entries in her virtual notebook reflected that. Chaitanya, the fifteenth-century founder of the Bengali sect of Vaishnavites, preached *bhakti*, passionate devotion to Krishna in which music, singing, and especially dancing were seen as instrumental in bringing human adoration into accord with divine love.

The celestial nymphs or Apsaras, favorite dancers in the court of the god Indra, were in the *Rig-Veda* associated with soma, the celestial drink that incited Indra to create the universe.

Many ancient rituals involved dances through mazes and labyrinths. The Talmud described dancing as the principal function of the angels. Dancing and singing angels had long been prominently featured in Christian iconography, too. In Christian art, the story of Theseus and the Minotaur was a prefiguration of Christ's harrowing of Hell, with Theseus as a type of Christ, the Minotaur a type of Satan, and the passage through the labyrinth a type of descent into the underworld.

In religious traditions throughout the world, Sister Vena noted, labyrinth or maze or spiral dances were believed to mime the journeys of the dead, the winding path of the dance representing the soul's wanderings. She had found images chock-a-block with spirals from the 5,200-year-old Neolithic Irish passage grave at Newgrange in the Brugh na Boyne. Tracing the patterns in her virtuality, Vena was surprised by the double-headedness of the spirals: Following the lines with her finger from outside to inside, she found at the center of one spiral the head of another spiral, coiled in the opposite direction to take her out of the maze again. From her infosphere researches, too, she knew that many scientists and mathematicians also considered spirals to be particularly important shapes—representations of the relationship of circle to center, schematic images of the evolution of the universe from uniformity to multiplicity.

On a psychoanalytic dream-interpretation site modeled after an immense palace of many rooms, Vena found that, in dreams, spirals tending inward were believed to represent movement toward unconsciousness, while spirals tending outward were believed to represent movement toward consciousness. Spirals could also be mandalas representing "the identification of individual being with Supreme Being."

She sat back in her chair, trying to make her notes bridge the gap from dancing to dreaming. In its spiraling outward from an initial dot, was the universe itself tending toward ever greater levels of consciousness? Or, given its chiral or "handed" asymmetry, was it moving instead toward unconsciousness and the great sleep of final entropy? Why should dancing lead to gods and supreme beings and conscious universes? Or, for that matter, to dreaming, as it had done in these sleepers all around her?

And why dancing the gods through *animals*? That animals *were* involved was something she could not deny. Her patients, in their rare waking phases, testified again and again that, in their dreams, they talked to animals, or *became* animals, or became half-human, half-animal creatures both more godlike and less human than ordinary waking mortals.

So far, however, what Sister Vena had been able to dig up on such questions in the infosphere didn't hang together very well. Here in India thirteenth-century Apsaras on temple friezes doing a hasta moudra hand dance—only their arms didn't end in hands but in long-necked peacocks. Dances of the Varanas, the gods' animal attributes—particularly Vishnu's incarnations as bird-man Garuda, fish-man Matsya, tortoise-man Kurma, boar-man Varaha, lion-man Narasimha—all dancing. Even the Buddha's association with deer. Outside India, animal-masked dancers of many tribal religions claimed the god was revealed behind the mask of the animal: Dance the animal, and the animal's divinity will respond, restoring the dancer to harmony with nature.

Yet, eye-flipping through her virtual notebook, Vena was confronted by more questions than answers. What was she to make of the fact that humans had supposedly learned how to dance from the animals? Or of dance as a ritual metamorphosis, a mask to both facilitate and conceal divine transformation? Or that orgiastic Bacchic dances, like dreams, freed the dancers from bodily limitation? Or that witch cults worshipped gods in animal guise? Or that the old religions were full of horned gods and prophets—antlered Cernunnos, horned Moses, and Dionysus? Or the horned and dancing Devil?

Taking off the viewshades, Sister Vena rubbed her temples, half-expecting to find horns sprouting there. Instead she found only a headache pulsing like a wayward second heart. She tried to quiet her mind, but *that* only made her think of how many mystical traditions practiced meditation as a sort of "dancing inside." Buddhist and Hindu *mantra* and *pranayama* systems, Hesychast "prayer of Jesus," Islamic *zikr* practice— just a few of many that made use of psychotechnic practices that were essentially *dance* reduced to posture, or breathing, or rhythmic repetition of sacred formulae.

Rhythm made her think again of the long-lived drumming craze. Long before the current rhythmania, however, many sects believed sound was the fundamental substance of the cosmos—and that rhythm was movement of that fundamental stuff, its transposition into space and time. The aim of ritual chanting and ritual drumming was, she thought, the same: by Om or by drum to reach the "sound behind creation." To attain to a state beyond the illusion and dissolution of forms. To contact the Nothingness which is All.

Wheeling out from behind her desk and standing up, Vena wished she could dwell in such a state of bliss. All of that struck her as too paradoxical, however. She was not contemplative by nature. Prayer, like research, was quiet action, but still action. Far too much still needed doing in the world—research work and devout prayer both, not least of all in this ward, in this hospital, with all the problems its dreamers presented to both Church and science.

Sister Vena walked among the sleepers on their beds and pallets now, thinking of the bizarre assertions the dreamers held to with such fervor in their rare awakenings. Not enough that they claimed to talk to, or even become, animals or half-animal god-mounts in their dreams—some *insisted* they were able to talk to animals *while awake*. Most problematic of all, though, were the dreamers' spontaneous stigmata.

Sister Vena gazed down at the sleeping, hospital-gowned form of Padma Narayan. The light in the ward was subdued, but still bright enough that she could see Padma's eyes jittering behind her eyelids in dream state sleep. *Dancing inside*, Sister Vena thought suddenly. Is that what the dreamers are doing, too?

Looking at the slender young woman with her long hair loose and parted in the middle, Sister Vena noted Padma's unique stigmatic constellation: not only the traditional crucifixion wounds in wrists, feet, and side, but also a small bleeding cross inside a perfect circle, of about the same size in about the same place as the puttee dot a traditional Hindu woman would wear in the middle of her forehead.

That was part of what didn't fit. Most of the patients she saw around her, like Padma, were not particularly devout or saintly. Still stranger, however, was the fact that Padma's stigmata were multiculturally determined, combining elements from both Christian and Hindu frameworks. Padma, as an Indian girl who had been raised Roman Catholic—not unlike Vena herself—was at least unconsciously familiar with both of those cultural contexts, even if she was nondevout in multiple religious traditions.

Those same frames of reference, Vena realized, now co-existed more and more uneasily in herself. Yet she showed no stigmata, multicultural or otherwise. Just as she also had not been caught up in either the drumming or dancing manias—as apparently all these dreamers had.

The dreamers' spontaneous hemorrhagings, healings, and claims of extra-species communication just did not match the traditional doctrinal models of stigmata and animal communication. As she moved onto the next dreaming patient, young Gopal, Sister Vena saw no potential Saint Francis of Assisi. Like Padma, Gopal also exhibited the crucifixion wounds in wrists and feet and side. The most heterodox of his stigmata, however, was to be found on his chest. Where one might have expected to find an image of the sacred heart of Jesus, this young man instead displayed a *shrivatsa*, the star-cross of the Jains. The *shrivatsa*'s three-dimensionality was particularly fascinating. No mere blood tattoo, the Jain star-cross over Gopal's heart was a series of elevated contours raised above the surface of his chest.

Perhaps not as striking as the flesh that formed itself into nail-like protrusions in Saint Francis's case, or the wounds of an invisible spear preserved in the heart of Saint Theresa of Avila, but Sister Vena still thought it impressive. Especially in a young man so very ordinary and contemporary in every other respect.

Nor did her dreamers' odd somatic and parapsychological experiences match the scientific models of "psychogenic purpura," "conversion hysteria," or "conversion disorder," in which psychological conflict was supposedly converted into bodily disturbance. Aside from their drumming and dancing episodes, Sister Vena's dreamers were not the ecstatics the Church expected them to be. Neither were they the "hysterics" or "pious frauds" science proclaimed all stigmatics *must* be.

In her infosphere research into the phenomenon, Vena had come across one prominent group of secular stigmatics—UFO abductees. None of her dreamers claimed extraterrestrial contacts, however, and only one, Chittihara, claimed heavenly connections. Even in her case, the divine "connection" was long after the fact. None of these dreamers had any history of self-abuse or self-wounding followed by either deceit or amnesia about such self-harm. The Sisters and other hospital staff kept the stigmatics under almost constant observation and would have noticed any episodes of self-wounding. No one had seen anything of the kind. Vena's stigmatics invariably claimed to have first noted their condition upon waking from a dream-filled rest—and in every case the bleeding episodes recurred during sleep.

Whatever plausibility Sister Vena might have found in the traditional doctrinal models or scientific explanations, they ultimately failed for her. She saw nothing hysterical or conflicted in the dreaming of her sleepers—nor anything especially beatific, either. Yet the "bodily disturbances" of these dreaming patients were growing more marked with each passing day. Searching through the infosphere and conferring with those few of her colleagues who were willing to discuss the matter in depth, Vena had succeeded in eliminating all explanations save one: Autosuggestion, to the point of self-hypnosis and beyond.

Did the mind have so much power over the body? If her dreamers' unconscious self-hypnosis could lead their bodies to bleed in culturally determined ways—to raise even *shrivatsa* stars on their chests!—how far might that mental power go? She thought of her patients' dreams of becoming half-human, half-animal mounts of the gods, and shivered.

Mother Mary had initially assigned her to observe the Protean/Spires one-shot injection trials. Were they involved in all this? Or was their synchronicity just coincidence? Were the prionoid trials and the epidemic spread of drumming and dancing and dreaming related? Somehow she couldn't believe there was no connection. Participants in the program had been the first to become drummers, then dancers, and now dreamers. But how?

Returning to her desk, Sister Vena put on her viewshades and reentered virtuality once more. She stayed awake through the night researching—the lone true *in*somniac in the ward of the dreamers. Her research proved both puzzling *and* gratifying. In this ward she had seen with her own eyes decisive evidence of the power of cultural influences on the way the new stigmatics were manifesting their wounds—yet no one in the entire infosphere had put forward such proof, as far as she could determine.

Not long before the first hints of morning appeared through the windows to the east, she must have dozed off. One minute she was viewing text and the next she found herself staring into her viewshades at something resembling a wire-frame chalice—in fact an image of an Einstein-Rosen Bridge, also known as a wormhole.

Vena had found the three-dimensional wormhole graphic a couple of weeks back, during her researches into spiral and vortex motifs in dance. Finding the somehow archetypal image endlessly fascinating, Vena made it a screensaver in her virtuality. Sensing no appropriate activity from her after she fell asleep, her virtuality system had put itself into sleep mode too. The shifting image of the wormhole was the only outward sign of the machine's dreams.

Before her virtuality, reawakening, too, could disappear it from her viewshades, Sister Vena froze the image upright. Looking at it, she pushed the "chalice" idea from her mind and tried to think about it in more scientific terms. The wormhole resembled two vortices, one the mirror image of the other, which had merged together, narrow end to narrow end, at what should have been the plane of the mirror but was instead a throat, a hole through space-time.

Her speculation soon grew less idle. In the course of her night's researches and reviewing, Vena had come across the postings and main site of one Mark Fornash. His virtual site, intended to resemble one of the great prehistoric art caves of France, housed rather odd speculations about a "shamanic complex" as an explanation for the drumming and dancing manias. Vena was thinking of something else in his pseudo-art-cave site now, however. She returned to it, moving through the cave and its hyperlinked prehistoric art until she came to an area she had seen before, a side chamber in Fornash's cavernous virtual space. Zooming in on a text chiseled into one wall, she found again what her eyes had earlier passed over without giving much attention to it.

This time she lingered on it long enough that Fornash's quasi-autonomous site noted her interest. A dancing half-man half-elk creature popped up in a corner of the virtuality and said aloud what she was reading: "Chaotic and fractal, like the event horizon around the singularity at the heart of a black hole, consciousness is itself the event horizon wrapped around the singularity—of the Incomplete, the Uncertain, the Unknown—that lives at the heart of the mind."

Not just a black hole, Sister Vena thought. A wormhole. A conduit—shaped like a chalice, like a *grail* . . .

She snagged the image of a 20,000-year-old spiral from the wall of a cave and juxtaposed it with a 5,200-year-old two-headed spiral from Newgrange. Then she juxtaposed the two of those with a double-headed axe, or *labris*, from a Cretan labyrinth. Then she juxtaposed the three of those with a late medieval painting of the Holy Grail flanked by angels. Then she juxtaposed those four with a photo of a spiral galaxy rotating around its core black hole. Then she juxtaposed all five with her favorite image of the wormhole.

Just a metaphor, Sister Vena thought, looking at the juxtaposed images. *But a persistent one, nonetheless. They are all metaphors for what consciousness is about. Connecting spirit to matter and matter to spirit. One end of the two-headed vortex spiraling ever more tightly upward and inward from matter to life to instinct to awareness, the other spiraling ever more tightly downward and inward from spirit to soul to psyche to self, until the two merge at the shared narrow throat of the I. Yet "up" or "down," "inward" or "outward" are all relative to which side of the singularity the observer is looking from. Consciousness is a shortcut for getting from matter to spirit—which have nevertheless always been connected the long way round.*

Just an analogy made between the mind and the universe. Yet for someone like herself—who had trouble seeing the contemplative's "Face that is no face that lies behind all faces," trouble hearing the "soundless sound"—thinking of the wormhole this way was a big help. It was as good a picture of the Absolute Paradox, of the link between herself and the divine, as she was likely to find. She said a small prayer of thanks for it.

Studying Fornash's prehistoric art cave site more thoroughly, Sister Vena moved about it, the little antlered-man agent tagging along with her. In a main chamber of the art cave she saw a "wall carving" dating to a few months back, which outlined Fornash's predictions regarding the course of his shamanic epidemic. She read the predictions carefully.

Vena did not fully accept the shamanic spin Fornash put on the course of this epidemic, but she could not deny the accuracy of his predictions. If the date of that wall carving was right, then he had foreseen the dreaming phase before it had occurred in anyone anywhere, as nearly as she could tell. The shift from dancing to dreaming exactly matched what she had seen. His predictions of the next stage, too—shapeshifting—matched the dark foreboding she herself had felt, wondering just how far beyond the current wave of stigmata this power of mind over body might extend. If Fornash was on to something, then he might be a good person with whom to establish contact.

Gazing off into the simulated space of Fornash's virtual art cave, Sister Vena considered her options. Mother Mary never expressly forebade her from making her notes available to the public. Her superior, though, probably would not appreciate Vena's putting out both the idea and the evidence that the new stigmatic "miracles" were heterodox and culturally determined in the extreme. Speculating publicly too that recent major benefactors to the Missionaries of Charity—namely Protean and Spires—might be somehow involved in the release of a plague organism or mechanism—*that* wouldn't much endear her to Mother Mary either.

But this was too important a matter for her to be constrained by the niceties of Order hierarchy or the subtleties of Church Office politics. She assembled her notes and evidence in support of both the culturally determined nature of the stigmata *and* the possible involvement of the Protean/Spires prionoid in the worldwide outbreaks of rhythmania and tarantism. She drafted a cover attachment that sketched quickly the nontraditional nature of the stigmatic miracles and then sent the whole bundle to both Catholic and skeptic publications. She sent an additional flurry of notes and queries to medical and technical publications, in regard to both the new stigmata and the involvement of something like the Protean/Spires prionoid in what seemed to be a global plague.

Better to beg forgiveness than to ask permission, Sister Vena thought. Either the silence will be deafening, or I'll catch an earful of trouble.

To doubly ensure the likelihood of the latter, Vena posted all her material to Fornash via his art cave site. As she was leaving Fornash's virtuality, the antlered elk-man agent morphed into Mickey Mouse, in his robe and wizard's-cap costume from *The Sorcerer's Apprentice*.

"Takes more to be a wizard than just wearing a funny hat, ha ha!"

Vena shook her head and smiled wearily at Mickey. After bingeing on virtuality, she was having difficulty returning to the physically real. Taking off her viewshades, she considered what the cartoon mouse had said. Was she, like the sorcerer's apprentice, messing about with powers she could not hope to control?

Even if that were true, it was too late now. With ghostly touch she had reached out through infosphere and night and darkness in search of other minds like her own. Others in a strange disembodied community, on a strange disembodied quest. Her ghostly touch had gone out to them, and now it could not be recalled. . . .

"Sister! Sister, wake up."

Startled, Vena looked around to see a black woman in the white sari and blue stripes of the Missionaries of Charity. Groggy, Vena recognized her as Sister George.

"What are you doing, still here? Your shift was up hours ago—go home!"

Nodding and thanking Sister George, Vena got up. She walked through the hospital, her mind blank but for the churning image of a wormhole graphic. Stepping out the doors of the main entrance, she walked down the broad stairs, toward the bicycle rack where her own bicycle stood. The homeless man who panhandled in the nearby park lay behind the rack, so still she wondered if he were dead, or only dreaming. She determined it was the latter, then looked across the street, toward the free-speech zone in the park across from the hospital. Besides the usual crowds chanting in the vocal percussion "languages" of India, besides the drummers interminably banging and dancers interminably whirling there, a Christian endtimer argued via bullhorn with followers of the teacher who had recently been proclaimed the last and future Buddha, Maitreya. Others, among the Maitreyists—themselves microphoned and amplified—were in turn arguing with a small cluster of Hindus, who asserted that Kalki, the last and future incarnation of Vishnu, had appeared in the form of a guru preaching among the Tamils in the far south.

Mounting the bike, Sister Vena looked into the hazy morning light and felt the warm breeze stirring. The city settled itself on the seat of the new day, argued with itself about whether it wanted to be called Bombay or Mumbai, then rode away with her.

24

Uncertainty and Incompleteness
2066

RICARDO STANDS AT THE HELM OF THE SOLAR MOTOR-LAUNCH *STAR Thrower*, John Drinan's smallish boat with jury-rigged sails. John and John's dog Oz Five have been traveling northward from the Cape with him, but John is snoring in the cabin at the moment and Oz is sleeping in the patchy sun on deck. The merman Thaumas has left his accustomed place in the bow wake—gone on one of his food-gathering forays, Ricardo thinks. For the moment, he is alone.

He's glad the trip from Canaveral has been as free of incident as it has turned out to be. It seems only yesterday they shared a farewell dinner with Malika. Almost to the moment they climbed on board *Star Thrower*, she was explaining to him how the universe was a "single quantum system" and the plenum was "not a thing of branching universes, but an infinite ensemble of universes, evolving in parallel, displaying greater diversity as time goes on."

Ricardo smiles, remembering. He didn't quite understand it, no matter how many times Malika went over the "natural selection of 'favored' universes," or how "the fundamental lattice structure of space-time on a scale of 10^{-43} reconciles Einstein and Euclid, giving us back our monkey bars of Euclidean-Cartesian gridspace when we need them." Monkey bars? Gridspace?

She'd gone over it with him more than once. He could remember much of it in a parroting way, but he certainly didn't catch all the nuances of how "the plenum is essentially infinite and complete, but radically inconsistent, while any single universe within it is essentially finite and consistent, but radically incomplete." What that has to do with the "merely physical multiverse" being like Turing's universal computer—"running an infinite number of programs, but each program containing only a finite number of symbols"—he never has figured that one out.

Despite the way her explanations flew over his head, it was still fun to see Malika's enthusiasm for explaining such wild concepts. Yet, when Ricardo remembers it now, he thinks it was a little sad, too. John told him that when Malika was younger, she'd planned a career as a scientist and college professor. The plague put an end to all that. Bereft of that future she'd planned before The Year Everything Went Wrong, Malika seems incomplete. Maybe that's true of all the survivors, Ricardo muses. They had their lives kicked out from under them. They've been in a slow-motion free fall ever since, around a world that no longer exists.

Traveling up the waterway from the Cape toward Savannah, the crew of *Star Thrower* has seen few traces of recent human activity and even fewer people. Only one group, near the old fortress at St. Augustine, paid them enough attention to remain in the open as they approached. From their masks, tattoos, and scavenged clothing adorned with wildly flashing ornaments, Ricardo took them to be Werfolk. When John hailed them, however, those watchers too remained aloof.

Something about their tribal identifiers reminded Ricardo of the wolf-woman Lupe. Convinced these might well be the tribe to whom Simon Lingham was traveling at his landfall, Ricardo pressed John to make contact. They steered the boat close in, toward the base of the fortress looming over the waterway.

"We're looking for a woman named Lupe," John Drinan called to the three men standing loose guard on shore. "She came from the Bahamas with a man dressed like this one. You seen them?"

The three men, leaning at ease on long spears, conferred together a moment, casting many a sidelong glance toward John and Ricardo aboard *Star Thrower*.

"They're not here," said one of the trio, a man with long, matted locks. "Why you want them?"

"The man from the Bahamas was my friend, a long time ago. He was this man's teacher. Do you know where they were headed?"

Another brief conference ensued; then the man with the matted locks pointed northward, up the waterway—silently but emphatically. Ricardo nodded and John thanked him.

A wonderful scent fills Ricardo's nostrils, breaking his reverie. As *Star Thrower* approaches the city of Savannah, he sees a thick gray python of vine wrapped around columns and pillars, ending in a mountainous mass of flowers stretching itself over and between two buildings and climbing high into a tall tree between them, before flowing over a wall to the water's edge. The great wave of vine, though somewhat sparse of leaves, is thickly covered with dangling, grapelike clusters of purple and blue and white flowers. A low drone sounds from the mountainous floral wave.

"I thought I smelled purple," John says, emerging from the boat's cabin, yawning and rubbing his eyes. "That's one big happy wisteria. My grandmother used to call that smell 'the scent of memories yet to come.' Quite a poet, she was."

John, stretching, whacks Ricardo on the back. Ricardo remains glum, despite the beautiful day they're sailing through.

"Looks like nothing but memories in this town, now."

"Come on, kiddo! Lighten up! What's got you down on a spring afternoon like this?"

"Wondering if this trip north is futile."

"Why would you think that? It was your idea to talk to those tribesmen at St. Augustine—and a good thing, too. You saw the direction their headman pointed."

The merman Thaumas, popping up in a quick spyhop from the wake, has now rejoined them. Ricardo nods his head, although not satisfied. He stares out over the water.

"I saw. But how do we know he understood what we were getting at? Even if he *did* understand us, how do we know he was telling us the truth?"

John shakes his head.

"Got to accept a little uncertainty in the world. Otherwise, there'd be no need for trust."

"But for all *we* know, Simon Lingham is already long dead."

John gestures at the city off to port, going to rust, brush, and ruin.

"You can't know it all beforehand. It's like trying to understand how all *this* happened. Going up against all that with mother wit alone is like trying to harpoon a whale with a toothpick."

Ricardo follows the older man's gaze toward the city, on to the whole lost continent beyond. A bullfrog, a big one by the sound of him, calls mockingly from swampy ground near shore. John smiles.

"Hear that frog laughing at us? He knows. Before the Plague Year we thought we had the unknown on the run. Only problem was the more you push into the unknown, the more it pushes back into you."

Ricardo moves the wheel in his hands as he tries to explain.

"I was thinking earlier that a lot of people who survived from the old time act like they've lost something they can't get back."

John nods, chagrined but not bitter.

"We lost ten thousand years in less than a year and a half! I've done a lot of traveling, looking for materials for our project down at the Cape. Those of us who survived had a hole blown through the middle of everything we thought we knew. We all deal with that hole in different ways."

Ricardo steers *Star Thrower* more toward the center of the waterway as they pass into the swamps between Whitemarsh Island and Thunderbolt.

"Are the abjurers better at it than the other people on the mainland? Or worse?"

"We go as right and as wrong as any of the other survivors. Doesn't matter whether they were genius scientists or engineers before the Collapse or not. This is more personal."

John pauses, then starts ticking off examples on his fingers of what happened to the other abjurers, at least those he remembers.

"In what was Louisiana, Muwakkil has set up a minor fiefdom. In what used to be Tennessee, Novikov is living as a hermit. In old Texas, Audouze keeps Werfolk slaves. Englert is slave to a Werfolk mistress in what was once Alabama. There are advantages and disadvantages to the knowledge we brought with us from the islands. Ten thousand years are gone, but their ghosts live on."

Ricardo drums his fingers absently on the console, until John glances at him and he stops. Ricardo realizes he has been doing more and more of that lately. He can't help himself. He hopes it's just a nervous tic he's developed from being cooped up aboard ship. John goes on, distracting him from his worries.

"All of the abjurers I've met, we're like witnesses to an accident. Every one of us has a different take on what exactly the pandemic was, what exactly the collapse did. That's the big unknown, the big mystery each of us is trying to make sense of. Sometimes I think we're as valuable for what we *don't* know as for what we do."

"What do you mean?"

"Not to 'mean' anything. Just to be—alive and here, on the water on this beautiful afternoon. Not knowing what the day will bring is not necessarily a bad thing. If you already know everything, you stop paying attention. Hear all those bumblebees in the wisteria? Did you pay attention to that? Did you know they were bumblebees? Not knowing everything is what keeps it all interesting."

John goes astern then, to talk to his dog. Thinking about what he said, Ricardo finds it a little annoying. He remembers his long detour on the trip to Canaveral. *Not* knowing has gotten him into trouble enough already. He told Trillia to meet him where the Savannah River crosses what the old maps labeled the Intracoastal Waterway. The scale on the old maps wasn't so good, though—and because he didn't know that, he's going to have to run *Star Thrower* between Oatland, Elba, and Tybee Islands until he finds some sign that Trillia has made it to the rendezvous—if she has.

"Hey, Ricardo," John calls from the stern. "Pull inshore up here, will you? Oz needs to do his business and my legs could use a stretch."

Ricardo pulls in toward Oatland Island. John and Oz Five go splashing happily overboard and head toward the beach. Ricardo waits on board, impatient. He wants to *know* that Trillia is waiting for him somewhere near here. He doesn't want to be kept in suspense, between hoping she'll be there and fearing she won't.

The wait for John and his dog grows excruciating. One minute Ricardo's heart is pounding at the prospect of seeing Trillia again, and the next he's upbraiding himself for acting like a lovesick schoolboy. He castigates himself for being so enamored of a young woman who has never fully given herself to him. Then he remembers how vulnerable and intimate they have already been with each other, in other ways—and how those memories should make him act more responsibly toward her. One minute he blames Trillia for his Wersign troubles and his exile; the next, it's not the result of his love for Trillia at all, but the work of her grandfather and the deep corruption of Spires' rule that have ruined his life.

John and Oz return at last. They are barely aboard before Ricardo is heading seaward down the divided flow of the Savannah.

When *Sea Robin* appears, anchored off the seaward end of Elba Island, the familiar boat's presence catches Ricardo by surprise, despite all his expectations. By the time he has turned *Star Thrower* toward *Sea Robin*'s anchorage, Thaumas has already raced ahead, joining three mermaids leaping in great joyful, splashing trajectories of recognition and reunion. Bringing John's boat alongside *Sea Robin*, Ricardo sees a group of eight or nine people waving to them and calling from the shore. John calls back to someone he recognizes. Oz Five barks in confused excitement.

Ricardo sees the people on shore push an inflatable dinghy into the water, paddled by a teenage boy and two young men. The latter two are Wer, judging by all the permanent adornments of their tattoos—and all the temporary ones of their feathers, flowers, crystals, and beads. Trillia sits in the little boat, along with an older woman. Ricardo hears Trillia calling his name then, and hears and sees no one and nothing else. He doesn't remember dropping *Star Thrower*'s anchor, but he has done so by the time the inflatable pulls alongside.

Ricardo and John clamber down into the inflatable while Oz takes the direct route, flopping into the water and dog-paddling ashore. John embraces Tomoko Fukuda, and the two oldsters launch into talk of how long it has been and what they've been working on and is Malika still helping him. Ricardo quickly loses track of their conversation, lost himself between looking deep into Trillia's eyes, and kissing her, and returning her kisses—all with more public passion than would have been considered seemly in their home islands.

Once the dinghy is ashore, Trillia and Ricardo, arms around each other's waists, climb out of the boat and walk up the beach toward where a small group awaits them. Trillia introduces them as Raheem Wilson and April Grayson and their children, a young boy named Shawnee and a small girl with the big name of Hephzibah. One of the oarsmen who rowed them ashore, the somewhat awkward teenage boy Phenix, is also part of their family. The boy will be joining them on their trip north, if they are still planning to undertake it.

Ricardo shakes hands and says hello all around. Trillia explains what a great help these people have been to her, lending her a horse and guiding her on the trip from Augusta to Atlanta, where she met Tomoko. Together the two women rode down Highways 75 and 16—both roads crumbling, overgrown, and utterly abandoned except for rusted and faded wreckage. Trillia, Tomoko, and Tomoko's two guards arrived two days before April and Raheem managed to bring *Sea Robin*—*three* days before Ricardo and John arrived, today.

Overwhelmed by this whirlwind of introductions and "catching up" on what Trillia has been doing, Ricardo barely has time to catch his breath before all of them sit down around Raheem's campfire. The rest press Ricardo to tell of his own travels. He begins with some reluctance, since he must first tell of "misplacing" the Cape at his landfall—and his long misdirected tour south, all the way to the ruins of Fort Lauderdale. Embarassed, he tries not to go into too much detail on that. He quickly moves on to the part about getting his bearings straight and heading north again. He tells them how he came at last to the Cape complex, and there met John and Malika and the rest of their crew, still at work on the return to space they've been trying to bring about for so many years.

Of the rest of his trip—from the Cape to Savannah with John and Oz—Ricardo has little to say. He does describe their encounter with the three men in front of the old Castillo near St. Augustine—especially their headman's wordless indication that Simon Lingham (and perhaps his werwoman companion Lupe too?) have headed north up the inland waterway. Everyone agrees the sign from the three Wer guards at the Castillo was a good omen, even if not a particularly detailed one.

"Enough storifying for now," Raheem says at last. "The afternoon's growing old. We still need to get together something for the evening meal, or the pickings will be plain and slim."

Despite the proposed moratorium on "storifying" while they all try to scare up some food, Raheem and April and Tomoko are still interested in hearing more about John's efforts at the Cape. When Trillia and Ricardo last see them, those four are walking toward the north side of Elba Island, with Shawnee and Hephzibah in tow. Phenix and Tomoko's two Wer guards, Caster and Paintee, plunge into the island's scrub palms and pines—and soon disappear.

Walking hand in hand, the young couple approach the water's edge and manage, after some effort, to catch the attention of their Mer companions. In the shallows on the south side of the island, Ricardo and Trillia set to work gathering in fish. The merman and three mermaids act as sea shepherds, driving their finned flocks toward and onto shore, where the young couple wait to snatch them up with fast hands, laughing.

In his pocket Ricardo carries a cord with a slim metal stake on one end and a metal ring on the other—a stringer which, with Merfolk help, he and Trillia soon crowd with fish. In a finger of the inlet, tethered to shore through mouths and gill covers opening and closing with captive life, the fish swim weakly along a crooked line. Ricardo squats down beside Trillia where they both wash their hands in the cool water, rubbing off sand and fish slime.

"That went fast enough."

"We're getting pretty expert at it, by now."

He turns toward the mermaids and merman, who wait expectantly. He thanks and dismisses them, sending them back to camp, then turns to Trillia.

"Think we filled our quota before the others?"

"Probably. We had an unfair andvantage, though."

Trillia stands up, shaking water from her hands. She stretches and runs her hands through her hair, which is longer and more sun-bleached than Ricardo remembers. Her skin too has a higher color—darker yet rosier. Her flesh looks tighter on her bones, more compact and muscular. She catches him gazing at her and gives him a veiled look.

"Any suggestions on how we should spend the time until the others catch up?" she asks, too innocently.

Ricardo gets to his feet, glancing up and down the shore and away into the brush as he does so. Seeing no one about, he moves toward her. They come together in a fervent embrace, kissing long and deeply. His voice is soft but husky when he speaks.

"I think we both might have some ideas."

Dancing in the mirrored halls of each other's eyes, they walk the short space inland to where the shallows of the inlet give way to sand and the sand gives way to grass. They take off their shoes and socks, then sit upon the grass, embracing, kissing, caressing each other.

"I've missed you—"

"—so much."

Leaning back side by side on the grass, they kiss, lips and cheeks and ears and neck. Their hands move with wills of their own. They begin taking off their own and each other's clothes. Soon they are nude, eyes drinking deeply of what they see, each all the world to the other, beneath the cloud-dotted canopy of bright sky, upon the green grass, quiet water stretching away beyond their feet. From the inlet a wind blows over them, gentle but cool, stirring their hair, making the hairs on their arms and necks erect, making their nipples taut and hard. Trillia runs her hands over Ricardo's shirtless shoulders and chest, then her right hand down the curve of his left side to his hip and buttocks.

"You look so good. Like a dream."

"You look better than my dreams."

Ricardo cups her breasts in his hands, kissing them, tonguing her nipples. She does the same to his, then reaches down and around to where he stands singularly erect, for all their lying horizontally on the ground together. With tremulous ardor they guide themselves over and into each other. What surrounds, surrenders to what penetrates—only so what penetrates can also surrender to what surrounds. Top becomes bottom becomes side, all their young strength and young sweetness rolling together, their bodies different continents of the same globe, coming together and moving apart, mutually seduced but not subducted, their love releasing its energies at last in waves—measurable, if not on the other side of the world, then at least on that other side of the self, which is the beloved.

Having come apart together, they gaze at each other, separated by a distance superficial as that between Africa and South America which, though no longer physically connected at the surface, are still rooted in their depths.

The cool of the evening settles more sharply upon them now. Ricardo and Trillia quickly dress. Putting on their socks and shoes again too, they stand in the westering light, arms around each other's waists. Voices call them from a distance. Ricardo takes up the stringer and its abundance of fish. He and Trillia head back along the beach, hand in hand, toward the gathering at the seaward end of the island.

Tomoko and John take their catch from them as they approach the camp, offering to clean it. The two old abjurers also can't resist dropping innuendoes around the young couple.

"What took you so long?"

"Is this all the fish you caught?"

"What do you mean?" Trillia asks, flustered.

"Probably more than the rest of you caught, put together," Ricardo says, embarrassed. The two old abjurers nod sagely and wave them on toward camp. There, Raheem and April are overseeing the butchering and cooking, with help from their children and Tomoko's Wer guards.

The meal is a blockade-runner's banquet of fish, shellfish, turtle, and marsh hen, served up with spring greens and sponge mushrooms. Ricardo eats to fullness—and then some. The adults are already adrift in postprandial lassitude from the big meal when Raheem breaks out the dusty old bottles of bourbon and scavenged Scotch. April produces a dozen equally precious but much cleaner glass tumblers brought down with them aboard *Sea Robin*. While the adults talk over their drinks, Heppie drifts off to sleep. Shawnee fights the nodding fight to keep from following her there.

Caster and Paintee aren't about to let the rest off that easy, however. After a drink or two, Caster begins drumming on the shell of the turtle whose flesh they have just eaten. Paintee produces a pair of small, shaped bones which he plays alternately as clappers or scrapers, as the mood strikes him. Ricardo joins the others, clapping to the rhythm the two young Wer have set up.

Glances and nods pass between April and Raheem, who disappear in the direction of the travel gear they have taken out of *Sea Robin*. When they return, April makes a big show of presenting to Trillia a phallic-looking flute. Raheem makes an ever bigger production of giving Ricardo a slit-drum carved to resemble a woman's body between navel and knees—with a prominent pelvic triangle carved and painted above the slit. For some reason Tomoko and John find this profoundly amusing.

Ricardo and Trillia try to ignore the older abjurers' winks and pointed fingers while they try to play these unfamiliar instruments as best they can. Every misplaced fingering on the flute and dropped beat on the slit drum, however, occasions more raucous laughter from the elders.

Raheem and April disappear and return again to the campfire, April carrying a bodhran frame-drum for herself and a pair of shaker rattles for Phenix, while Raheem carries a chalice-shaped doumbek. Soon everyone has worked themselves into the beat, playing instruments or clapping—even the Merfolk swimming nearby, plashing the water with their flukes.

Handing over their turtle shell and bone clapper-scrapers to John and Tomoko, Caster and Paintee launch into a wild, leaping dance about the fire, a choreography skillfully mimicking the movements of dozens of birds and animals they've seen in their recent travels. From the water comes the sudden spectacle of the Merfolk leaping, too, finned foursome arcing through the air as one, or hurtling in permutations and combinations drawn from out of their number—somersaulting, backflipping, corkscrewing, tailwalking, all the dances of leaping and diving.

The last thing Ricardo remembers seeing is the Werfolk and Merfolk trying to outdo each other in wild acrobatics under a newly risen full moon. His eyes half-closed and rolling up into his head, he straddles the slit drum, weaving the complex pulse of the universe into and out of his drumming—until the drum is a horse, its rhythm the pounding of swift hooves, a strong horse, carrying him upward, into the sky, past the moon, outward among the stars.

Raheem shouts loudly in his ear, shaking his shoulder. Ricardo, disoriented, smells the alcohol on the man's breath. Raheem's speech is a bit disjointed, too.

"Hey! You can stop drumming now. Everybody's gone to bed, or going there soon."

"Hmm—?"

"You been drumming a long time. April and the kids are all gone to bed. Even Castee and Painter, or whatever their names are—they threw in the towel, too. Give it up, for now. See you in the morning."

Raheem plods off. Ricardo stands up slowly, his hands sore where they aren't numb. In his mouth is a taste like copper gone bad. He glances toward the far side of the fire. Trillia, Tomoko, and John eye him with concern.

"You do know you're rhythmanic, right?" John says at last, stroking the head of his sleeping dog and looking up at the sky. "Lunar periodicity makes it flare up."

"What? What do you mean?"

"Rhythmania," Tomoko says. "The initial phase. The first externalized 'Wersign.' "

"I don't know what you're talking about."

"Yes you do," Trillia says, a catch in her voice. "You were diagnosed with a new variant of the pandemic."

"When, exactly?" Tomoko asks him. Ricardo shrugs. As the fire fades, they are all becoming just voices in the darkness.

"December."

"A fast mover," John says, nodding. Tomoko's tone becomes very much that of the medical professional again.

"On the way to the rendezvous here, did you experience any episodes of compulsive drumming? Hands and fingers tapping or drumming? Five, ten minutes at a stretch?"

Ricardo says nothing. What can he say? If he denies it, John will just contradict him.

"This is bewildering. Your new variant is progressing as fast as the original pandemic—if not faster. Have you experienced any unusual colds or flu during the last six months? Any unusual respiratory discharges?"

"Nothing like that," Ricardo says, hoping against hope that this might somehow mitigate against the diagnosis the island docs handed him.

"Strange. The original prionoid pandemic always vectored in through microbial infection."

"Not infection," Ricardo says, anger flaring in his voice. "Injection. Damn Cameron Spires to hell!"

An unreadable, quick glance passes between Tomoko and John, before Tomoko turns back to Ricardo.

"You think it's iatrogenic?"

"If by that you mean did the medical people give it to me, then yes."

"An accident?" John asks.

"Not likely," Ricardo says, falling into a disgusted silence.

"Ricardo thought my grandfather might have set all this up," Trillia says quietly, standing up on the other side of the fire. John and Tomoko do likewise. "Or at least the diagnosis, anyway."

"Why?" Tomoko asks.

"To get a troublemaker out of his hair and off his islands," Ricardo says, tossing a small stone into the dying campfire.

"I can't believe that," John says. "Not even of ol' Spires."

"I think I could—almost," Tomoko says, a significant look passing from her to Trillia.

"Why risk unleashing a potent new form of the pandemic into the world just to get rid of a lone troublemaker? Nobody's crazy enough to do that."

"Unless, of course," Tomoko says, "this new variant has been tweaked to make it noncontagious."

"Wasn't the original prionoid supposed to be noncontagious, too?" John asks pointedly. Before Tomoko can respond, however, Trillia steps forward and clutches Ricardo above his left elbow.

"If he's not contagious, that's all well and good for the rest of us, but what about Ricardo? What's his prognosis?"

Another of those enigmatic glances flashes between the two old abjurers.

"No one knows the full etiology of the original pandemic, even now," Tomoko says slowly, "but you know the basic symptomatology of the original. We can't say anything certain about this 'new variant,' if that's what it is. You should both be aware, however, of the gravity of Ricardo's illness."

"Which means?" Ricardo asks. Tomoko looks absently into the embers of the fire, then stares hard at him.

"You may well die of your symptoms—or 'transcend,' as the Werfolk would have it—in less than a year's time. Perhaps significantly less."

"Isn't there something we can do?" Trillia asks.

"Probably the best place to have Ricardo looked after," John puts in, "is on the islands you come from."

"Not an option," Ricardo says. "I'm under an automatic death sentence if I return. A year may not be long, but it's better than nothing. I'll take my chances here."

"What about the other abjurers?" Trillia asks. "Do you know where they are? Could any of them help?"

"You're headed north looking for Simon Lingham, right?" Tomoko says. "There *are* some people along the way who might be able to help. I don't know if they're still alive—they left the islands early on."

"Who?"

"Mark Fornash, for one," John says. "Last I heard, he was holed up in what used to be the Research Triangle, in North Carolina."

"Sister Vena Srinagar, too," Tomoko says, nodding. "Those two were probably the islands' best, when it comes to the symptomatology of the pandemic—the shamanic complex and all that. Sister Vena is in the empty city of Baltimore."

"Simon mentioned both of them before he left! Let's go find them!"

"Trillia," Tomoko says, gently but firmly, "don't get your hopes up too much. Sister Vena and Mark Fornash turned abjurer early on."

"So?"

"So they abandoned your grandfather and his longevity bribery," John says, "a long time back. They weren't the youngest people in the islands—Fornash especially. If they're still living, they're not young anymore."

"But it's still worth the effort, don't you think? Especially since we're headed in that direction anyway?"

"It's worth a shot," John says with a shrug. Tomoko nods and turns to Ricardo.

"If Ricardo feels up to the trip—"

He looks around him at the faces lit now more by the westering moon than by the fire's last embers.

"I do. It's my best hope, at the moment."

They retire to their tents then. Ricardo and Trillia hold each other in silence, her head pillowed on the right side of his chest. Trillia's breathing soon becomes slow and steady with sleep. Ricardo remains awake, listening, pondering.

Now, he thinks, just when I realize this woman really is the woman I've always been looking for—on the same day, it's confirmed I'm going to die of incurable plague.

He shakes his head, thinking the sun of love should not be eclipsed so soon by the moon of death. The latter has *no right* to follow so close upon the former. A lifelong dream should not have to jostle for bed space with a lifelong nightmare—on the same night!

Ricardo feels himself falling upward as he begins to drift off to sleep. He jerks awake, thinking, *To transcend, as the Werfolk would have it.* That's what Tomoko said. He knows the old Werfolk claims for that, too. He's heard the stories. The Great Shift. The terrible beauty born from all the dying of the Last Days. The horizontal vertigo of slipping into that last sleep falling them all upward in final rapturous soul flight. Innumerable ascensions and assumptions into heaven. Black-robed souls rising out of the dying cities like flocks of beatified starlings. Could such antigravity apotheoses be real? Could any conceivable transcendence possibly have been worth the pain, suffering, and death of billions of people? Or was it all just vultures misperceived, as they wheeled and rode in the smoke-columned skies above the burning towns?

When Ricardo wakes the next morning, camp is already being broken up and preparations made for the journey north. Over breakfast, he learns that Paintee will be returning to Atlanta with Tomoko's horse, along with the ones on which he and Caster rode south. Caster, however, will accompany them on the journey as Tomoko's bodyguard.

Loading gear into the *Sea Robin* and *Star Thrower*, Ricardo sees the rest of young Phenix's family bidding a tearful farewell. Of that family, only the older boy will be joining them. His father seems a bit bleary-eyed as he tells the travelers that his son is "well-skilled in hunting, fishing, trailblazing, and all woodcraft" and that the boy "will be a big help to you on the way." Ricardo suspects that the prospect of parting with his son was what led Raheem to drink more than he was accustomed to, last night.

To the small group they leave behind, Ricardo, Trillia, and Phenix wave from the *Sea Robin*. John, Tomoko, and Caster do the same from the deck of the *Star Thrower*. Amphitrite, Thaumas, Thetis, and Psamathe splash flukes and Oz barks, until the boats are out of sight of the people on the shore. Ricardo wonders if he will ever see this place or these people again. At the thought of it, he holds Trillia more tightly about her waist, beside him.

25

Corroboration
2033

CAPTAIN KRUGER ARCHED HIS EYEBROWS AT LIEUTENANT LOSABA AS SHE came into his bright, sparely furnished office. A hard-eyed, florid-faced man with a full head of meticulously groomed graying blond hair, Kruger gestured to her to take a seat, then adjusted one white shirt cuff beneath the sleeve of his dark blue suit jacket. Leira Losaba was all too aware of her standard police-issue attire as she sat down. Kruger glanced through a stack of printout flimsies. Absently stroking his bristle of silvery blond mustache, he looked at her expectantly.

"What am I supposed to make of this report?"

"I know parts of it sound implausible, sir—"

"To say the least! Let's set it aside for the moment, shall we? Now, if you would, please tell me in your own words about the course of this investigation."

Leira didn't know where to start, but from Kruger's lingering gaze she knew she'd better start somewhere, and soon.

"I was assigned to coordinate our efforts relating to the Parktown killings."

"To work on a series of related murders."

"Yes, sir, that's right. And no, sir—it isn't."

"*Which* part isn't *what*?"

"Yes, I was assigned to a serial murder investigation. And no, that's not what it has turned out to be."

"Last time I watched the news," Kruger said with none-too-subtle irony, "the Parktown murders were 'a run of nearly identical and thoroughly gruesome killings.' Thirteen of them so far. Correct?"

Gruesome—yes, they were undeniably that, Leira thought, remembering her trips to the morgue, her time spent with the forensic pathologists.

"Only partially correct, sir. Initially I suspected a serial murderer, too."

Kruger drummed his desk lightly with his fingers, until he became aware of it and stopped.

"Well? What changed your understanding?"

"The murders may have seemed 'nearly' identical, but there were enough differences between them that we began to look into the possibility of more than one killer. We soon had a list of suspects."

"Copycat killers, then?"

"In a manner of speaking, yes. As the investigation unfolded, however, I realized we were seeing 'copies' of a 'cat' like none I ever suspected."

"Stop there," Kruger said, raising a hand. "Let's not jump into wild speculations yet, shall we? Tell me more about the murders themselves, if you would. Although each of them is quite *beastly* in its savagery, each presents ample evidence of having been committed by a human being—not an animal."

"That's not quite what I say in my report—"

"I know what's in your report, Lieutenant, but I want to hear it from you. With specifics."

Leira Losaba took a deep breath, glanced at the notes on her glove-back computer, and nodded.

"The forensic people I met with referred to different examples as either 'piecemeal' or 'wholemeal' dismemberment. Significant damage to the viscera of most of the victims. Evidence of ripping, chewing, and gnawing of internal organs. Puncture wounds and bite marks on the skin. Tearing and rending of skin and flesh by something one pathologist described as 'more than fingernail, yet not quite claw.' *Several* incidents of tooth marks on brow and eye socket. One of the forensic technicians—an anthropologist by training—identified those marks about the orbit of the eye as 'remarkably similar to the puncture wounds leopards make on the skulls of baboons, when they grip and drag prey of that size?"

Kruger's glance strayed over his desk to the flimsies again. When he spoke, it was almost dismissively—as if he didn't really want to hear the answer he knew his question would bring.

"Anything else you found peculiar about these killings?"

"The murders peak at times of the full moon."

"And from this, you have determined that these murders were perpetrated not by some more ordinary lunatic but—if I may quote from your report—by 'human suspects temporarily transformed into were-creatures bearing traits of both human and animal provenance.' Is that correct?"

She knew how absurd it sounded, yet she had no choice but to admit it was still the best explanation for what she'd seen.

"Yes, sir. That's correct."

"And you stand by that interpretation of the evidence?"

"Yes, sir, I do."

"Would you allow me to propose an alternative theory? Just for the sake of argument?"

"I'd be happy if you would."

"All right, then," Kruger said, standing up from his chair and appearing to wander idly about his office. "Let's look at your suspects. Tell me about them. Do they share any traits? Ethnicity? Cultural background? Gender?"

"The suspects are an ethnically and culturally diverse group of individuals," Lieutenant Losaba said, feeling herself on more solid ground here despite Kruger's bad-cop pacing to and fro. "They are male and female in roughly equal numbers—in marked contrast to the established profile of serial or mass murderers, who tend to be overwhelmingly male."

"Are any of the suspects in contact or communication with each other? Do they share any similarities in terms of their history and background?"

"Those already in custody are all currently under lockdown psychiatric care. None of them claim any awareness of the murders committed by the others, nor knowledge of any of the specifics of those, beyond what they might have gleaned from media reports—which have been kept purposely vague."

"Yet the murders have been almost identical, you say—despite the thin detail in the media. Doesn't that suggest to you at least the possibility of collusion, or even conspiracy among these people? At some time in the past—*before* they were captured and placed under psychiatric supervision?"

She glanced at him, wondering why he was interrogating her this way. Yes, her story was strange, but his questioning seemed to have an almost personal edge to it. Given her situation—a mixed race police officer being interrogated by a white superior officer—she found it hard to keep the specter of racism out of her thoughts.

"Polygraph examinations suggest the suspects are telling the truth when they claim no prior knowledge of the circumstances of the previous, similar murders."

"But we all know how problematic such tests are as evidence of guilt or innocence. Any similarities in background among them?"

"All those already in custody, or otherwise under surveillance, share a history of rhythmania and uncontrollable dance urges."

"Like more and more of the general population," Kruger said, discounting the connection with a shrug.

"All have recently awakened from a coma-like, prolonged sleeping or dreaming episode. Many were housed in the University Hospital, Eton-Rock Ridge facility."

"And the circumstances of this 'awakening'?"

"Most claim to have awakened either at the scene of the murder or soon thereafter. The majority claim no memory of the event. The few who remember something like a murder initially suppose they dreamed it, until shown otherwise."

"And we should believe—what? That this is some kind of—well, what *would* you call it? Somnambulism? Dream amnesia?"

"Those terms would be consistent with what the suspects have described, yes, sir. The stories of the suspects themselves are remarkably consistent with each other, as well."

" 'Remarkably consistent'—hmm," Kruger said, coming around in front of Losaba. "Do the suspects admit to any prior knowledge of each other? Any personal acquaintance of familiarity?"

"They do—as my report makes clear. The overwhelming majority of our suspects worked, until fairly recently, in the Early Man excavations at Sterkfontein."

"What kind of work?" Kruger asked from behind her.

"In one manner or another, all were connected with a research project investigating whether an extinct Big Cat called *Dinofelis* was an obligate predator upon protohominids and early hominids—our ancestors."

"That's not what I'm asking," Kruger said, standing beside her left shoulder. "What were their occupations—their jobs?"

"Oh. Sorry. I misunderstood your question. They worked for the project at many different levels. Day laborer. Volunteer. Summer intern. Graduate student. Anthropologist. Paleozoologist. Archaeologist. Most of the latter were from the University of the Witwatersrand. Two of the suspects are full professors, in fact."

Kruger came around in front of her and leaned his backside against his desk.

"I heard about this research project in the news some time ago. They concluded that this extinct Big Cat fed more or less exclusively on our 'ancestors,' as you called them?"

"That's right."

Kruger paced behind her again, drumming on the back of her chair as he went.

"So their research ends and they all go their separate ways. Many of them don't communicate with each other again. That does not, however, rule out the possibility that people on this project could have formulated some plan of action among themselves—*before* their dig broke up."

"No," Lieutenant Losaba said, growing weary. She'd been over these possibilities in her own mind too many times already. "I suppose it doesn't."

"Don't underestimate the ordinary human capacity for perversity or downright evil, Lieutenant. If we're not looking at one or a very few culprits, then you should consider some of the alternatives."

"Such as?"

"Such as the possibility that perhaps the only thing 'supernatural' or 'extraordinary' about these events is that they may be the acts of a cult engaged in ritual murder."

Lieutenant Losaba shook her head.

"I've already considered and rejected that possibility. These people are rational and scientific. Many of them have no particular interest in religion whatsoever. That they might be part of a ritual murder cult just doesn't fit the profile."

Captain Kruger leaned forward, close to her face.

"But transforming themselves while sleeping into some kind of saber-toothed tiger and *somnambulistically* ripping people limb from limb—that *does* fit the profile?"

The lieutenant sat back more deeply in her chair.

"I did not say they became dinofelids. In my report I suggest a creature half-human and half-dinofelid—or at least how these people, as a result of their work, imagine *Dinofelis* to have looked and behaved."

"Ah, 'imagine.' Then you admit these 'dream amnesiac somnambulists' of yours may have only *imagined* they became powerful were-cats. Only *imagined* they prowled the streets of Johannesburg in search of human prey. Might they all simply be suffering some type of collective delusion—as a result of a shared trauma encountered at Sterkfontein?"

"I thought of those possibilities, too," Losaba said, warily and wearily. "No one recalls anything particularly traumatic about the dig. Only those members of the dig who have gone through the drumming, dancing, and dreaming episodes have any connection to the murders. No one from the dig who has not gone through those manias has any connection to the Parktown deaths, so far as we can ascertain. Yet those few who have *not* drummed or danced or dreamed recall no trauma, either."

"Collective psychosis, then? As a result of exposure to some agent encountered at their dig?"

Lieutenant Losaba shook her head emphatically.

"We checked those, too. Millions of people have visited the underground rooms and rock formations of the Sterkfontein Caves. The only thing remotely supernatural about the caves is that the large underground lake there is reputed to have special healing powers. As far as exposure to an unidentified chemical or biological agent present at the caves is concerned, there's no precedent for that. No one has ever before exhibited such murderous 'symptoms' as a result of a trip to the Sterkfontein Caves."

"So all those involved with the dig," Kruger said, leaning back against his desk again, "all of those who have been through the drumming and dancing and dreaming manias, that is—they have all turned into, or will turn into, this 'were-cat'?"

"Not all. One of the anthropologists who worked on the dig a year and a half ago, and has since been working on San rock paintings in the Drakensberg—he went through the drumming, dancing, and dreaming, but he hasn't turned into a were-cat."

"Really?" Kruger said, standing upright suddenly.

"He claims he turns into a were-*eland*."

"*What?*"

Leira Losaba leaned forward in her chair, gesturing with her hands as she explained what was still new to her, the product of her own recent research.

"A half-human, half-eland. The San medicine man or shaman, while in trance, was supposed to link the world of the spirits to the world of everyday people. Trance-dancing is how the San responded to environmental stresses and pressures. The San shaman, through dance and trance, healed the sick, talked with the spirit world, gathered information about people and things distant in space and time. What the shaman saw in trance was communicated to his people through the medium of rock paintings and engravings. Many of those illustrations feature creatures that walk upright and move like human beings, but who also have horns and hooves and other animal attributes."

"Someone dressed in an animal skin?"

"No—the San themselves insisted those were not illustrations of men in animal disguises. They were representations of the transformations healers underwent while in trance state. Medicine men inclined toward good deeds supposedly adopted the forms of antelope—most often the eland. Medicine men bent on harming others supposedly metamorphosed into large predators."

Kruger walked slowly back behind his desk.

"So your were-eland anthropologist took the form he did because he had good intentions? And the rest of the dig workers became were-cats because they were inclined toward doing evil?"

"It's not quite that simple. I think they worked with what was on their minds. If they didn't know about were-elands, they wouldn't be able to assume that form."

"What makes you suppose that?"

"In the infosphere, I came across something by a nun in India who has been investigating stigmatic patterns among long-dreaming patients. Many of these dreamers bleed at odd times and from odd places—I've seen it in the hospital wards myself. This Sister says the stigmata of her patients are 'culturally constrained.' "

"Which means?" Kruger asked, sitting down.

"The example she gives involves the way stigmata patterns have changed over the past eight hundred years. For centuries, stigmatics' wounds appeared in the palms of their hands—the same way artists of those times portrayed Christ crucified on the cross, with nails driven through the palms of his hands. Eventually, physical evidence accumulated that crucifixion through the palms of the hands wouldn't hold the upper body to the cross—and that the nails were in fact driven through the wrists. Artistic depictions began to reflect the new understanding, showing Jesus nailed through the wrists, not the palms of his hands. Then stigmatics began showing stigmata on their wrists, too, instead of their palms."

"Life imitates art," Kruger said quietly.

"More than that. What the stigmatics believed in their minds to be true *became* true in their bodies."

Kruger drummed his desktop absently, then deliberately stopped himself, shaking his head slowly.

"I can't accept that. Stigmata are enigmatic enough, but they are nothing compared to the wholesale physical transformation you're telling me these murder suspects go through. It's just too incredible. Maybe they *believe* they become were-cats or half-eland, but it can't be physically happening."

"I thought the same thing," the lieutenant said, leaning further forward. "I refused to believe the direction in which this investigation was going—until I saw what happened, with my own eyes."

Kruger glanced at the printout flimsies of Losaba's report once more. "The shooting?"

"Yes, sir. The pattern we'd found connected the murders to those on the dig who had gone through the drumming and dancing manias. That led us to place several of the Sterkfontein workers under surveillance, particularly those still in the dreaming phase."

Kruger stroked his mustache, then looked up from the report.

"These veterans of the Big Cat project—they were on the floor of the hospital that works with the sleep cases?"

"Yes, sir. The patients were under light restraints at most."

"Why were you on hand when this particular event supposedly happened?" Kruger asked, eyes narrowing in their focus on Losaba.

"It was the night of the full moon," she said with a shrug. "The murders had previously clustered around the time of the full moon. I felt ridiculous being there just because of the phase of the moon—too much like an old horror movie!—but I stayed, on the off chance that something might happen."

"And it did," Kruger said, putting the report flimsies aside, straightening their edges as he did so.

"Yes, sir," Losaba said in a monotone, trying to suppress the stark emotions evoked by her memories of that night. "One of the sleeping Sterkfontein workers, Phillip Voyi, came to the attention of Officer Mbokwue. Voyi had begun writhing and spasming violently. Mbokwue left Voyi's room and came out into the hospital corridor, calling for help from nurses and other officers. When we entered Voyi's room, he was convulsing and metamorphosing, right in front of us. By the time we began to pile onto him, he had already become a man-beast with tawny fur, vertical-slit golden eyes, and prominent fangs. He was growling, snarling, ripping through his restraints."

Reliving it made Leira's heart beat faster, her breath come shorter. Kruger nodded slowly and drummed his fingers on the printout of the lieutenant's report. Losaba used the brief pause to bring herself more fully under control.

"Voyi escaped from his room and onto the hospital floor?"

"Yes, sir. He bit and clawed his way through three police officers and four burly male nurses. He went through us like we were made of paper. None of the standard take-down maneuvers or holds were effective against Voyi. Officer Mbokwue, when he was being treated for lacerations later, told me it was like trying to wrestle a creature with the strength of a gorilla and the agility of a tiger."

Kruger glanced up again from the report.

"How did it happen you were the one that fatally shot Voyi?"

"I had come from farther down the corridor than the other officers, so I was at the back of the group of people trying to subdue Voyi. As Voyi broke from his bed and his hospital room, I was knocked to the floor by one of the other officer's bodies. I was closest to the door, so I was first in pursuit. When I came out of the room, Voyi was loping away in a crouching run. He headed straight toward a nurse who began screaming at the far end of the hall. I pursued Voyi and ordered him to halt. When he did not do so and continued toward the nurse, I fired a warning shot. He spun around and came at me. When he again refused to stop, I fired at him as he leapt toward me. One shot took him in the shoulder, another in the chest."

Kruger leaned forward in his chair.

"And the second shot was fatal?"

Lieutenant Losaba nodded.

"Hit him high on the abdominal aorta. A great deal of blood. Covered a whole section of the floor."

"What about his transformation?"

"It didn't last. The nurse who was screaming—she was a medical infomatics tech, actually—she was the only other witness to see Voyi shift *back*. She said it was like watching a machine return to default mode. The only proof of his change that remained was the increased size of his canine teeth and the unusual thickness of body hair, but the teeth and hair fell out not long after time of death."

"Those are the samples Forensics examined?"

"Yes, sir."

Kruger exhaled slowly.

"You do know how this looks, don't you?"

Losaba nodded.

"Use of unnecessary and deadly force against an unarmed man."

Kruger looked at her in a bland, inscrutable fashion.

"It would be easy to write your story off. To say you really didn't see what you thought you saw. That your report is the product of an officer suffering from nervous exhaustion as a result of working too long on a series of horrific murders. An officer overwhelmed by guilt, seeking some sort of rationalization for having shot an unarmed man, even if he was mad as a hatter. Tell me: Why shouldn't I discount your story in exactly that way and put you on leave?"

Losaba sat quiet a moment, pondering her options.

"Because I have corroboration."

"Go on."

"I was disturbed by the incident. Maybe more than I would have liked to admit. I returned to the investigation on a different level, searching the international police networks and databanks. Interpol. NCIC."

"This isn't in your report," Kruger said. For some reason he was less surprised by the revelation than Losaba expected.

"No, sir. I was doing this on a second-shift basis—my own time. I intended to put it in as an addendum if it turned out to be of value."

"What did you find?"

"My experience was neither so isolated nor so bizarre as I first thought. Very few of the other incidents have been as bloody as the murders we have been investigating, but the reported *urban* instances of strange creatures, particularly were-creatures, has skyrocketed in the last two months. Vampires in the Balkans—particularly in Hungary. Legends of 'the long sleep' of the Magyar shaman, or *taltos*, are still prevalent there. Were-wolves in that region, too, as well as in London, Paris, New Orleans. Were-bears and Minotaurs in the financial districts of New York and Chicago. Were-jaguars from Mexico to Argentina. A host of shapeshifters in Japan, China, and India. Even were-sheep—worshippers from the 'flock' at an Assembly of God church in Atlanta, Georgia. The list goes on and on."

Kruger nodded and stood up.

"You've obviously been spending quite a bit of time in the infosphere. You've let some of this information out through that medium, too—in the form of queries and speculations connecting our incidents here with other, similar episodes throughout the world. That may have compromised our investigation here, you know. Isn't that true?"

Leira Losaba was startled.

"It was not my intent to compromise our work, sir."

"I don't believe it has—luckily for you," Kruger said striding around in front of his desk. "You see, Lieutenant, I believe you. There is other corroborating evidence."

"The hair and teeth?" Leira Losaba asked hopefully.

"Yes," Kruger said. "Forensics found some very peculiar things in those samples. Representatives from the World Health Organization and Spires Biotech are looking at those materials now."

"WHO?" Lt. Losaba asked, her head spinning. "Spires? How did they become involved?"

Kruger allowed himself a small smile.

"Your research in the infosphere has not gone unnoticed. The Special

Interest sections where you posted your queries and speculations are at best only semiprivate. I only learned of your second-shift work last evening. From Dr. Kunishige of WHO and Ms. Crane of Spires Biotech. You'll be meeting with them in a few moments. Judging by the way they've been v-mailing and phoning medical institutes all over the planet, I'd say they're representing more than just themselves and their particular organizations. Apparently you're the first to connect these shapeshifting incidents to each other. By also connecting shapeshifting to all these drumming, dancing, and dreaming episodes, you seem to have linked it to what they believe is a developing worldwide pandemic. Congratulations."

Kruger shook her hand, bringing Leira Losaba to her feet.

"Good police work, Lieutenant. Perhaps far more than just that. We may all end up owing you quite a debt."

"But sir, why did you interrogate me like this, if you already believed my report?"

Kruger's odd smile grew—yet seemed at the same time also shadowed by a deeper concern, even worry.

"We don't want our profession or ourselves to look foolish. I wanted to see whether you would stick with your crazy story, under persistent questioning, without knowledge of other corroborating evidence. I also wanted to see if you were worth our hopes."

" 'Hopes,' sir?"

"Lieutenant, we've already lost more officers and more work hours to these manias than you know," Kruger said, his expression growing grim as he walked her toward the door of his office, then into the hall. "In my own family, my younger daughter has been sleeping unusually much, of late. Her older sister is dancing all the time now, just as her younger sister was, until recently. My wife has uncontrollable bouts of glossolalia and spirit-trembling. It's happening everywhere. I sometimes find it all I can manage just to keep down the impulse to drum with my hands, or tap with my feet, or avoid getting hypnotized by the simplest rhythms. I don't know where all this is headed, but I don't like it—especially if it's some kind of pandemic, the way these scientists suggest. A lot of families will be deeply affected by this 'shapeshifting'—my own among them. Maybe you can help us understand what's going on, what we can expect. Good luck."

Captain Kruger shook Losaba's hand again, then introduced her to tall, thin Dr. Kunishige and short, blond Ms. Crane, waiting for her in the staff room. Just that quickly, the world opened out before Lieutenant Leira Losaba. The broader responsibilities of that world would soon settle more heavily on her shoulders.

26

When Darkness Shines and Silence Calls
2066

AT THE HELM OF *STAR THROWER* JUST NORTH OF OLD TOPSAIL BEACH, Trillia thinks of their ship-hopping. The seven land-dwellers—herself, Ricardo, John, Tomoko, Caster, Phenix, and the big dog Oz—have not stayed solely aboard either *Sea Robin* or *Star Thrower*, but have shifted from one boat to the other in various groupings. They have not shifted about as often or as easily as the four Merfolk, perhaps, but frequently enough that no one has grown familiar with either craft to the point of carelessness—or bored with each other's company.

John, Ricardo, Phenix, and Oz cruise alongside in *Sea Robin*, Thaumas and Amphitrite at their bow. In *Star Thrower*, Tomoko is asleep down below. Caster—shirtless on this warm day and eye-candy attractive, in his leanly muscular, indigenous sort of way—is scouting from up in the bow. Trillia has no one to talk to, so she might as well eavesdrop. On board *Sea Robin*, John is trying to explain how his friend Malika's idea of the "plenum" differs from the "Everett DeWitt Deutsch" (or is it "Everett-DeWitt-Deutsch"?) idea of the "multiverse."

"The multiverse covers only the infinitude of *physically real* universes," John says, "but the plenum is much bigger, since it covers *all* possible universes. Not only the physically possible ones that exist in space and time, but also the *logically* possible ones that exist nonspatiotemporally."

When Ricardo speaks up, he sounds confused to Trillia's ear. Although he is not dancing or drumming much today, he is in some ways dreaming.

"How can that be? If I remember correctly what Malika told me, you can build a universal computer whose VR capability covers every *physically* possible environment—but you can't build one that includes every *logically* possible environment."

"That's where the idea of the multiverse went wrong. The multiversalists believed multiversal mind, or plenum consciousness, was reducible to a universal computer and its computations. Plenum mind, though, is a virtual reality generator whose repertoire includes *all* possible universes, logical *and* physical."

"The metaphysical as well as the physical, then?" Ricardo suggests.

"Not if by 'metaphysical' you mean 'unreal.' In the plenum, all that is possible is *real*. Your own mind can generate scenarios that are logically but not physically possible. Malika says that's proof of self-similarity between your own consciousness and the consciousness of the plenum as a whole."

Trillia shakes her head. As the *Sea Robin* pulls ahead, John is still going on, explaining how the plenum involves "higher dimensionality," and "spiritual," "entelechial," "noumenal" existence. Despite all the tutoring in pre-pandemic physics John Drinan seems willing to give anyone, Trillia has learned very little of such stuff. She is not very interested in all that. Why talk about parallel universes, she wonders, when we know so little about this one we're already in—especially since the pandemic and the collapse?

Which is not to say she has not learned much—about much more practical matters—on this journey so far. Traveling out of April and into May, through what was once South Carolina into North Carolina on canal and open sea, Trillia has grown adept at running rigging and sail. She knows how the wind from astern or abeam will affect the ride and roll of a boat, through short fetch or long over open water. She can estimate wind speed in knots and figure its effect on the steepness of the waves. She knows that the grinding, snapping, popping sound in the boats at night is the hull-amplified noise of shrimp snapping their claws and fish feeding on barnacles and other hull growth—and the reason why the travelers prefer to set up quieter camp ashore as often as they can. All *that* is more practical and valuable knowledge than any "parallel universe" blather.

She knows she still has much to learn. They have not had only clear days or smooth sailing by any means. She wishes it could always be salmon-pink sunsets, passionate lovemaking with Ricardo through the cool nights, orange-gleaming sunrises, the salt scent of sea breezes playing through her hair, the boat rocking like a gentle cradle beneath her feet, the sound of the plashing waves a lullaby the ocean sings to her—but it hasn't been.

They've had their share of rain and thunderstorm, wind and sudden chill out of the northeast. Days when most of the crew members of both boats were spread-eagled on deck, holding tight to anything bolted down while the boats themselves pitched and rolled, sending everything flying that wasn't securely stowed beforehand. *These* have taught her and all her companions new things about themselves and each other—especially about their endurance, and their ability to think clearly under pressure.

Twice they have had to steer their craft far up inlets and into backwater creeks, tying up to stout cypresses in order to ride out gale winds in something approaching safety. On the waterway, they have often had to push aside overgrowth of tree and bush and vine to pass through with *Sea Robin*'s mast still upright. At other times they have had no choice but to step her mast down completely—to make their way through places where the wildland canopy has on either side grown into a green tunnel over the water.

Still worse are the places in the waterway itself where the dredges have stopped their work, or where their silt-and-sand disposal islands have grown so large they prevent passage as well. Some of the locks too, once meant to aid passage along their route, now block it—forcing them to backtrack and make unavoidable runs over the open ocean.

The obstacles to moving up the waterway have at times been so frustrating as to make all of them want to abandon the inland route altogether for a faster run off the coast. Sailing between Cape Island and Winyah Bay in thirty-five knot winds, however, reminded them that neither *Sea Robin* nor *Star Thrower* are up to the stronger stuff the open sea can throw at them. Battered and torn and drenched, they slipped into Winyah Bay and back into the inland waterway near the ruins of Georgetown, grateful for the more sedate travel of the inland way.

Trillia consoles herself, too, with the thought that they are taking Simon Lingham at his word. If they are to encounter him anywhere before New York, it will likely be along the waterway. Other advantages of the inland way are undeniable, too. The abandoned towns and cities along the waterway sometimes seem a monotonous riot of rust and stain and vine and weed, but there is great beauty there too, even in neglect and decay.

In the decadent frontier they've been sailing through, the ruins of cities are like echoes of a frozen music slowly melting away. Trillia has seen the misplaced Mediterranean world of Harbour Town on Hilton Head—and at Sea Pines the canted spars of sunken yachts, like a neglected field of crosses for all those buried at sea. She has caught her breath at the profusion of azaleas and dogwoods blooming in the lost gardens of Charleston—gardens even now seemingly better tended than the ruins of the grand old city itself. Burned and broken by the strife of the last days, then by the storms and hurricanes that have lashed this coast since, Charleston is a weathered gray ghost of its former self, opulence gone far into decay, the skeleton of a grand old city softening into oblivion.

As the daylight lengthens, however, the scars of the old towns become less visible. The new green on everything from marsh grass to scrub oaks is a fat eraser, each day rubbing out more of what human beings once wrote on the landscape here. Not just "rubbing out," Trillia thinks, but even more "covering up"—as if the landscape were a palimpsest where the greenery writes over what human beings once made, and then is itself partially rubbed away each autumn, the imperfectly erased human past becoming once again a bit more visible in the harsh light of each winter's return.

For all the beauty of this world after civilization—and it is beautiful—it is lonely too, and strange. Few and far between are those times when they have seen any evidence of recent human presence: the distant smoke or nearer ashes of a cookfire, or even a shell midden from someone's meal. Around them, cypress lift their knees from dark waters. Oaks and maples rise from inpenetrable thickets warred over by creeper and kudzu. Labyrinthine creeks and rivers lose themselves in the endless green of marshland. The turtle that basks in the sun on a half-sunk log is eaten at evening by log turned alligator. On long lonely beaches, pale and windswept beside high tides under a full moon, Trillia has seen horseshoe crabs mating by the tens of thousands—scuttling scorpioid tanks far older than the dinosaurs, lumbering out of the surf and leaving jewel-hordes of eggs like green pearls behind them. She has seen where storm and surge have gnawed away old piers and houses and trees, until they become only buried giants' finger bones still reaching for the heaven they could not hold on to.

As she looks around her now at the power of what wears away the past, at the oblivion of rust and crack and root and leaf, at the forest that will never know her name or share her thoughts, a green melancholy pierces Trillia. It seems to her everything comes into the world only to be pushed out of it again. And never in a straight line—always in a roiling, curving, chaotic fashion that tolerates no straight order for long. Without human consciousness in the mix, what was the world again but a mindless children's game of scissors-paper-rock played on the grand scale of animal-vegetable-mineral? Rock breaks scissors, scissors cut paper, paper covers rock; mineral breaks animal, animal cuts vegetable, vegetable covers mineral. Round and round.

Tomoko, awake and on deck, sidles up to her in the afternoon light.

"You look pensive. Something on your mind?"

Trillia sighs as she steers them through yet another in a long succession of dredged paths and land cuts, behind sand spits and duned banks topped with grass and scrub off to starboard. She looks into the wall of verdure off to port, where greenery, with the slow hunger of roots and leaves, swallows up the broken-ribbed remains of what were once summer cottages. Trillia wonders whether Tomoko has been keeping an eye on her—and wonders even more why she should feel both annoyed and grateful at the thought of it.

"I was thinking that I'm glad to be traveling in the company of other people."

"Oh? Thanks, I suppose. What made you think that?"

"Spring. All this life around us, swallowing up what human beings once made. And all this death, too. The leaves eating the sunlight, the alligator eating the turtle . . ."

"Life lives on death," Tomoko says. "The old Buddhist conundrum. Look at us. On this trip alone we've feasted on—what? Lobster. Blue crab. Silver mullet and speckled trout and bluefish. Shrimp, clams, oysters. Ducks and wildfowl. Deer and boar."

Trillia steers the boat into a deeper section of the dredged channel, thinking of those meals—and all the skinning and cleaning and cutting up that preceded the cooking of them. Although she should enjoy such bounty, her stomach has been fluttery of late. She often feels queasy or has no appetite—even for foods she enjoyed at home. Nothing as serious as that "bug" in her "guts" she had on the way to Atlanta, but unpleasant nonetheless.

"Caster and Phenix and the Merfolk—they make all that hunting and gathering seem almost too easy."

"In some ways it is," Tomoko says. "How do the Werfolk put it? 'Nature is willing to give, so long as we only take what we need'? You notice how quickly we've adapted to being on the move—just getting up each day and traveling on? Deep down, I think our evolution has wired us for being nomadic. Before agriculture and cities rooted people in place, we were rootless travelers. We followed the migrations of what we hunted—the herds and the birds and the fish. We remembered what fruited where, and when. Since the pandemic, the numbers of the plants and animals we eat have come back faster than our own numbers have."

Trillia nods, staring into the thick undergrowth off to port.

"Few devouring humans left, but lots of plants and animals left to devour."

Tomoko gives her a sidelong glance.

"I gather it's not what we're eating that's eating you. It's what's eating us, in the end."

"What do you mean?"

Even to her own ears Trillia sounds more suspicious than she should. She wonders why she's gotten so moody of late. Then again, waking up as she has—nauseous and paralyzed by self-doubt every morning for three days running—would not help anyone's disposition. Tomoko only looks innocently out over the water, into the distance of memory.

"Hungry dogs. Blind worms. Meat maggots. Our great death was their great feast. They stripped the flesh of all the billions who died in the pandemic. At least those who weren't burned or properly buried, anyway. That was most of them, in the end. Far too many dead for the living to account for, much less look after."

Trillia nods. Still feeling a melancholy all out of place in the sunlight of the bright day, she thinks how all the flesh and bones of the corpses were just an appetizer for entropy, before it tucked into the big main meal of stone and steel.

"The cities that were left behind, too. A banquet for the winds, the rains, the waves."

Tomoko watches Trillia carefully as she steers the channel dotted with dredged-up islands of silt, the older ones clothing their nakedness with cloaks of trees and birds.

"They're just eating the monuments we made to ourselves," the older woman says. "Turnabout is fair play. If we'd had the chance, we would have eaten the whole world and shat out *nothing but* monuments to ourselves. Maybe our fall was fortunate, in some ways."

Trillia says nothing, though she does wonder at hearing such language from a woman so dignified and restrained as Tomoko. She wonders too how the loss of so many billions could possibly be a "fortunate" fall.

"You'll have to forgive me," Tomoko says, looking down. "Living through the endtimes affected all of us who survived. Those of us who abjured probably worst of all."

Trillia tries to look only at the space of the waterway ahead of her.

"How's that?"

"Even on an island of exiles, we couldn't get along. Exiled ourselves from the island of exiles. You've met some of us now—what do *you* think?"

Trillia looks straight ahead when she answers.

"You're loners. Even when you build these little communities around yourselves, you're always apart from them, somehow. Like you're always too busy searching for something to get to know other people. I can't think of any abjurers I've heard about ever having families, either—except for Simon."

Tomoko looks up at her and nods, but the older woman's face is unreadable. Immediately Trillia regrets her words. Why did she bring up the family stuff? Misplaced fear on her part—over missing another period? She tells herself she shouldn't regret so much the absence of a biological process she's never found pleasant—one that made her grumble that "God is male, and He must hate women." Missing *those* is hardly the end of the world. She shouldn't let it work on her this way.

"Which of course set us apart from everyone in your father's domains,"

Tomoko says, unfazed. " 'Be fruitful and multiply to the nth degree' was the everyday commandment there. Since human population levels had already crashed, there was no ethical or ecological reason not to. Yet we refused. Shirked our duty. Some in the islands said it was 'intimacy failure.' "

Trillia nods, but then remembers her more recent days as a Bahamian.

"They're still arguing about that. Only now, it's about all the *un*agers getting divorced and having new families in series."

Tomoko gives a small laugh.

"I wondered what would happen to marriage and family once we could stop the aging process. 'Until death do us part' is a long time, when you don't age. You don't need a caretaker spouse, and you might live several hundred years!"

Ahead, Trillia sees the *Sea Robin* moored off to port, on the far side of the mouth of what her map pad calls the New River. She reduces *Star Thrower*'s speed as they cross New River Inlet. Her map pad tells her that where *Sea Robin* is moored was once part of Camp Lejeune Marine Corps Base.

"Why did you turn abjurer?" she asks Tomoko.

"I told you the main reason, back in Atlanta. His version of history didn't mesh with mine. I didn't think Cameron was allowing us to put enough effort into really figuring out the full nature of the pandemic so we could cure it. That was all dead past, to him. I don't think he really cared if it was cured, as long as we were safe from it in the islands. Your grandfather was focused on the future. Longevity treatments for the islanders. Perfecting the Merfolk as a home guard. I was suspicious, too— at the way everything had worked out, the way all of us in the islands just *happened* to survive, while everyone else didn't. The way Cameron had everything set up. It was all just too damn *convenient*."

Trillia looks at the older woman a moment, before they pull up alongside the *Sea Robin*. Phenix is the only one waiting for them, floating in a battered inflatable dinghy.

"I don't know if I'll ever understand you people from the old time," Trillia says. "You almost had it all, then you lost everything."

Tomoko gives her a piercing look.

"We lost everything *because* we wanted it all."

Now Trillia feels like apologizing again. If her moodiness, her queasiness, her bad mornings, her missed periods—if they mean what she fears they might, she certainly doesn't want to alienate the only other woman in this traveling company. Although Tomoko has never had children of her own, she *was* trained as a doctor, after all.

Seeing that *Sea Robin* has dropped anchor, they do likewise. Caster calls from the bow to Phenix as he brings the dinghy alongside.

"Why've you stopped? We've got light for another couple hours."

"Something's wrong with Ricardo. John took him ashore. I'm supposed to bring you to them."

Trillia's heart is beating fast enough for her to feel it race. Her head is full of questions she can't bring herself to speak. She climbs into the dinghy with Tomoko close behind, carrying a small medical kit. Caster follows in a Kayak. They paddle around a headland, toward where a broken maze of metal objects like three-dimensional iron asterisks rust and crumble in the surf. Weaving through the broken field of hull-rippers, they make their way ashore. Trillia and Tomoko follow Phenix over a small grass-topped dune to the wind-sheltered side of a long-abandoned concrete coastal fortification.

They find John crouched over a supine Ricardo. Ricardo's head is pillowed on a ball of wrapped-up shirts, but the gentleness of that is belied by his bloody nose and the leather belt between his teeth, pulled tight behind his head. Caster joins them as they crouch on either side of the prostrate young man. Spasms rack Ricardo's body intermittently.

"His Wersign flared up," John says. "I had him tethered so he wouldn't dance himself off the boat, but he was just sitting there when this happened."

"When what happened?" Tomoko says, prying open Ricardo's left eye with her right thumb and forefinger, revealing the upward-rolled, jittering eyeball. She injects Ricardo with muscle relaxants and anticonvulsants.

"When he started spazzing out like this. His eyes started flashing in his head and he began talking about how this place is full of ghosts. Crazy stuff."

"Not so crazy," Caster says, banging a slow soft beat on a small handdrum. "I feel it too. That's why I didn't want to stop here."

John gives a shrugging nod, then turns to Tomoko and Trillia again.

"When the convulsing really got bad, he started foaming at the mouth. I put my belt between his teeth, so he wouldn't swallow his tongue."

Tomoko nods. Gradually, under the effect of the injections or the drumming or both, the spasms begin to subside. Trillia watches as Tomoko examines Ricardo, lifting his head, paying particular attention to thin red eruptions, like a mixture of blood and sweat, on his forehead and about his hairline.

"Crown-of-thorns stigmata," Tomoko notes quietly, then turns to check his wrists. The same thin, bloody effusion is there too, on both sides of both wrists. Trillia helps her strip off Ricardo's shoes and socks and finds the canonical wounds repeated there—not only the thin bleeding, but holes, too, as if the flesh has reconfigured itself around invisible nails.

Caster keeps drumming, ever more softly. Trillia and Tomoko wipe the serous effusions away from the stigmatic wounds. At length Ricardo's spasms drop to an occasional twitch. His eyes stop their jittering. Trillia loosens the belt from around Ricardo's head, removes it, and gives it back to John. At last Ricardo falls into a deathlike sleep.

"The spirit grabs him hard," Caster says, awed. "Harder than anybody I ever saw."

"Look at these wounds," Tomoko says to Trillia. "See how quickly they're healing? No scarring, either. Self-repair like that still says nanomedicine, binotech, to me."

Trillia vaguely recalls something she saw in her first, all too brief peek into her grandfather's files.

"There's a link between that and the pandemic?"

Tomoko stands up and stretches, able to relax at last, now that Ricardo seems to be out of immediate danger.

"A lot of us thought so. We never could figure out how the prionoids and nanomeds were connected, though. Your grandfather put a stop to that research. Said it was 'potentially dangerous to the efficacy of the longevity treatment.' That was just a half-baked rationalization for shutting down our work, as far as I could tell."

"When Simon Lingham left, there were rumors that something he was working on might cure the pandemic but also weaken the effectiveness of the longevity treatment, too."

Tomoko gives her a surprised look.

"Maybe there was more to that rationalization than we suspected, then."

They make camp for the night. In twilight Caster and Phenix bring *Sea Robin* and *Star Thrower* closer to their camp, into the shadow of the old coastal defenses, though not so close as to entangle them in the field of boat-killing obstacles between the tide lines. While John, Tomoko, and Trillia set up their tents and unroll their sleepsaks inside, Caster and Phenix disappear into the forests further ashore, in search of food and firewood.

The evening meal is nearly cooked before Trillia notices Ricardo rousing himself from sleep. She and Caster bring him food, which he eats greedily. His voice is hoarse, but he's able to talk. He complains of a coppery taste in his mouth, but it doesn't seem to dampen his appetite any. Eventually, leaning on Trillia and walking a bit unsteadily, he joins the rest of them around the fire.

"What did you mean before," Caster asks him, "when you told them you felt ghosts around here?"

"I saw them. They weren't really ghosts when I saw them, but I guess they are now. They were soldiers, part of the Urban Warfare Training School. They had rifles and machine guns and computers. Helicopters and armored personnel carriers. Jump jets and MOPP guns and Light Amphibious Reconnaissance Vehicles."

Trillia startles. She supposes he could have looked up some of these Camp Lejeune "memories" on her map pad, but not all of them—and she knows he has *not* done so.

"How do you know all that?"

"I saw it, like I said. Like a memory, only I was right there. I was one of them. Weird."

John writes and erases symbols in the sand with a stick, Oz watching him intently.

"A lot of the military people who came out of Urban Warfare Training ended up trying to keep order in the cities. Killed a lot of people, on all sides, before dying or being killed themselves. You must have postcogged them."

"Postcogged?"

The fiercely tattooed older man looks up, as if about to speak, but says nothing.

"Postcognition," Tomoko says, leaning back, looking into the stars and shaking her head. "Seeing into a past you never personally knew. Knowing that past without interacting with it. The opposite of precognition. Mark Fornash was intrigued by all of that."

"All what?" Trillia asks.

"That 'paranormal powers' nonsense. That's probably why he headed toward Duke and the Research Triangle after he left the New Bahamas. Before the pandemic, there was a parapsychological research center there. Mark was always hot to go there and check out their machines for enhancing 'psi' phenomena."

John nods, apparently remembering it, too.

"Mark thought the paranormal stuff, especially out-of-body experience, was all of a piece with the shamanic tradition of 'soul-flying.'"

"Soul-flying? Ricardo shouldn't be experiencing that sort of thing already. He hasn't shapeshifted! He hasn't even really gone into the dreaming phase yet!"

Tomoko takes Trillia's hand and squeezes it, trying to reassure her.

"We know that. But you have to remember that Mark Fornash's 'shamanic complex' outline was more *de*scriptive than *pre*scriptive. Not everyone followed every stage exactly the way Mark predicted. In some cases the 'stages' fed back into each other, or a particular stage might contain the others in embryo."

"Then some people expressed these 'paranormal powers' in earlier stages? When they still had more time left?"

"They claimed they did, yes," Tomoko says, nodding and squeezing Trillia's hand again. "Mark's idea of a 'shamanic complex' allowed for general *prediction*, but it didn't provide a general *explanation* of what was going on."

"We're probably headed for the right person, though," John says. "If he's still alive, Mark Fornash knows more about the subtle powers of the prionoid-altered mind than anyone else."

Ricardo raises his head and looks around at his friends in the firelight.

"These subtle powers—would they account for why I keep getting this feeling that we're being followed?"

"Followed?" Tomoko asks, arching an eyebrow. "By whom?"

"I don't know. Shadowed by Werfolk and Merfolk, maybe."

John tosses aside the stick with which he was scribbling in the sand. Oz lumbers after it, in no particular hurry.

"That 'power' sounds more like *paranoia* than paranormal. We've already got Caster here, and Thetis and Psamathe, Thaumas and Amphitrite around the boats—and Phenix, well, God only knows what to make of *him*."

Phenix laughs when the tattooed elder slugs him on the shoulder. They all relax a bit—Ricardo not least of all.

"We'll have the Merfolk stay alert for any of their own kind," Trillia says.

"I don't think there are too many Werfolk around," Caster says to Ricardo, "though my senses might not be as sharp as yours about that."

After helping the others clean up the remains from dinner, John, Caster, and Phenix scout inland a distance, just to make sure no mob of Werfolk is waiting to descend upon them. Trillia, Ricardo, and Tomoko walk to the shore to alert the Merfolk there that Ricardo suspects their little company is being shadowed by Merfolk in hiding. The mermaids and merman seem puzzled. They are certain they would have detected any of their own kind anywhere in the vicinity, but they promise to keep on the lookout in any case.

"I didn't mean to slander anyone with what I said before," Ricardo says to the two women as they walk slowly back toward camp with him. "After all the obstacles we've had to face and overcome, and all the ways Caster, Phenix, and the Merfolk have helped, I don't want to sound—what? Racist? Speciesist?"

Tomoko nods.

"That's the question, isn't it? What categories do we put everyone into? Before the pandemic, there were biologists who claimed the notion of human 'races' was scientifically untenable. That humans didn't really have races so much as 'geographical variants.' But then what to do with the Merfolk and Werfolk?"

Trillia glances at Ricardo.

"In the islands when we were growing up, the Werfolk were viewed as a different race at the very least."

"And we were told the Merfolk are pretty nearly a different species," Ricardo says. "I don't know if I believe any of that anymore. Not after spending so much time with them lately."

Returning to the embers and small flames of the dying fire, they sit down around it. Ricardo pokes at the fire with a stick and throws a couple more pieces of wood in as it flares.

"At the end, right before he left, Simon claimed the common humanity we share is more important than our obvious differences."

Tomoko cocks an eyebrow at Ricardo.

"Simon said that? Sounds like he finally began to really think about his own epidemiologic stats."

"How's that?" Trillia asks, staring into the fire.

"I always thought the number of human beings crashed harder than he would accept. From what I've seen, I'd say about eight million survivors worldwide is where we really are—not Simon's sixty to eighty million."

"What's that got to do with 'common humanity'?" Trillia asks, tired from the long and traumatic day.

"When you see those sorts of extinction-threatening numbers, you realize it's stupid to put more exclusionary clauses in the description of what it means to be 'human.' "

Ricardo nods.

"I've thought about those numbers too. Especially in regard to my own survival chances."

"And?" Tomoko says, looking at Ricardo in the flickering firelight.

"Why the huge discrepancy in initial death rates? Why should those rates have risen to ninety-nine percent and more among high-tech urban populations, while at the same time death rates among hinterland hunter-gatherers were sometimes less than fifty percent?"

Tomoko stares into the fire.

"Secondary effects were a factor. We came up with the usual lot. May-hem. Anarchy. Criminal opportunism by thugs and gangs. Infrastructure collapse—in transportation and power, water and sanitation, medical and other systems. The higher the tech dependency and population density of a given area, the more thoroughly that area's population was deci-mated. The lower the tech dependency and population density of a given area, the greater the likelihood of survivors. Unfortunately, most of the people living on Earth at the time resided in high-tech, high density cities."

Eventually the pieces of wood Ricardo tossed in catch fire, making more light than heat. He jabs lightly at the fire with a long thin stick. In response, a small firework of sparks lifts into the air and drifts on the light wind, before vanishing. Trillia shrugs more deeply into her clothes.

"That's the part I never understood. High levels of technology, especially medical technology, should have meant *better* survivorship chances."

"Just the opposite," Tomoko says, with a hapless gesture. "Population density and tech dependency were both *inversely proportional* to pandemic survivorship. Mark Fornash claimed the differing survival rates also had something to do with hunter-gatherers knowing better how to 'handle' the shamanic complex—that survival chances were cultural, as well as biological. He was never able to prove it, though."

At that moment Caster, Phenix, John, and Oz walk back into camp.

"We scouted quite a ways into old Lejeune, sir," John says, mock-saluting Ricardo. "No bogeymen waiting to leap out at us from the woods. We'd better get some shuteye, if we want to make it through Bogue Sound tomorrow."

Ricardo shrugs and mutters an apology. Phenix and Caster put out the fire and build their preferred shelter of boughs and bark, while the rest retire to their tents. Inside his and Trillia's tent, Ricardo soon falls asleep and starts to snore. Trillia lies in her sleepsak, weary but wide-awake, listening to the dark symphony of insect sounds, nightbird calls, and frog song—along with the occasional cries of creatures she can't identify.

It's not that she's afraid to sleep. It's that she dreads waking again, nauseous, doubting herself and fearing her body. So far she has kept her situation hidden from Ricardo, but how long can that last? She promised herself this morning that today she would tell him about her skipped periods and her morning sickness. How was she to know the day would bring with it a sudden aggravation in Ricardo's condition? They both have enough to worry about already, without the additional possibility that she might be pregnant with his child.

When she finally sleeps, Trillia dreams a great disconnected mess about the First Days of the New Bahamas. She and Ricardo are in the dream, too, somehow, mocked by the oldsters of the islands—even by the abjurers. All of them condemn the young couple for their love and its consequences.

She wakes to a warm, sultry morning. She doesn't feel nearly as queasy today. After his episode the previous day, Ricardo too is doing better—so much better that they make sudden and fierce love, in denial of unspoken fears. As the realities of the day displace the dark fantasies of the night, Trillia suspects today will be unseasonably warm—even before that becomes the theme of breakfast conversation around the rebuilt campfire. Over the calling of morning birds on the hunt, John and Tomoko sagely discuss "global warming spikes," "greenhouse hangover" from "two and a half centuries of pre-pandemic industrialization"—and the "fortunate fall in sunspot-cycle activity" that's supposedly saving all of them much suffering and disaster.

After breaking the fast and breaking down camp, Trillia joins Ricardo and Phenix aboard *Star Thrower*. They weigh anchor and head the short distance back down the New River—John, Tomoko, and Caster following in *Sea Robin*. Near the New River Inlet Trillia is thankful for the stiff breeze that cools the hot and humid day. Before they make much progress north and east, however, the waterway grows abruptly more shallow. The dredges have not been at work here. *Sea Robin* and *Star Thrower* begin bottom-dragging their rudders and keels.

Ahead of them, for as far as they can see, stand shallow tidal flats dotted with sand spits and sandy islands. Frustrated, they shove off from the shallows and make their way back to the New River Inlet. They move into the open waters and unnerving chop of Onslow Bay, headed northeast. Near Brown's Inlet and Bear Inlet both, they find the same sandy and silted-up shallows—more evidence the dredging work has long since ground to a halt in this stretch of the waterway. Only after reaching Bogue Inlet and Cape Carteret do they find dredged channel and replenished barrier islands again.

Bogue Sound is broad and shallow, dotted with so many wooded and bird-covered dredge disposal islands and sand spits, it could pass for a maze of aviaries. Redwing blackbirds, herons white and blue, cormorants, hawks, gulls—all abound. Keeping to the main channel of the waterway is tricky, Trillia finds, since it diverges into multiple channels and reconverges so often and so unexpectedly that they hit dead ends in the labyrinth of islands again and again.

After a long, hot, frustrating day of backtracking and sidetracking, Trillia is sunburnt and out of sorts. She and her companions are happy to make landfall near the tumbledown town of Morehead City. Unlike Charleston's opulence in decay, Morehead is decay without the opulence, a city being swallowed by the resurgent forest and grassland greenery of what was once the Croatan National Forest.

Setting up camp and catching and eating dinner are motions they all go through without much conscious interest. What little conversation takes place is terse and direct. All of them turn in early, glad the day's heat is abating with the sunset, even if the humidity is not—yet.

Trillia wakes to a startled yelp from Oz. She, and Ricardo beside her, are being dragged out of the tent into moonlit darkness. Flipping her roughly onto her belly, her captors in an instant truss up her hands in what feel like leather bands behind her back. A moment later she and Ricardo are raised to a standing position and prodded forward.

As the sky lightens with the first hint of morning, Trillia sees that none of her friends have escaped. She and Ricardo are soon joined by John and Tomoko—and a muzzled Oz. Moments later, Phenix and Caster, both bloodied from valiant but futile resistance, are dragged into line with the other captives.

Their captors, Trillia sees, are a mixed squad of muscular young people, a dozen or more men and women dressed in skins and scavenged prepandemic clothes, armed with rifles and spears and bows, some with Werfolk tribal tattoos, some Trufolk. The raiders ransack the camp, grabbing up clothes and shoes and boots.

Her own and her fellow captives' requests for information—"Who are you?" and "What do you want?"—are met with quick glances but no words. Everyone is forced to walk barefoot through the overgrown streets and ruined buildings of Morehead City, their "Where are you taking us?" met with stony silence.

Not an uncomprehending silence—the kidnappers know what Trillia and her friends are saying. They just don't bother to respond as they force-march the barefoot captives through the dead town's debris.

"Your paranoia turns out to be true," Trillia mutters to Ricardo.

"Looks like it," Ricardo says, before one of their guards prods him along with the butt of a spear. "I just have to work on my timing."

Their taciturn captors lead them to a small meadow outside town, where perhaps a dozen horses are grazing. Trillia wonders if this is where she and her friends will be killed. Shot, or left porcupined with arrows and spears jutting from their bodies? Her captors roughly blindfold her with a rolled-up piece of blue cloth and heft her onto a horse's back. They position her in the saddle and stirrups. Trillia imagines the noose being slipped over her head at any moment.

The noose never comes, however. They balance and bind her into the saddle. Soon, they lead her and her horse at a jogging pace along what sounds like alternately crack-strewn and grassed-over roadbed. Trillia hears the sound of other horses being led the same way.

Wriggling her eyebrows, jaws, scalp, and ears—yet trying to remain unnoticed while doing so—she manages to loosen and reposition the blindfold so that if she tilts her head just right, she can make out a good bit of the country they are moving through. Weird kudzu topiary, patchy meadows, hardwoods of resurgent wilderness—*that* doesn't tell her much. Sometime after midmorning, though, she catches a clear glimpse of a sign beside the road. Faded and rust-stained, the sign informs her that the crumbling and slowly disappearing roadbed they are moving over is Interstate 70.

Sometime before noon, leaving a long, sunbaked stretch of roadbed, they enter the remains of a field turning to forest. Helped and dragged off her horse, her blindfold temporarily removed, Trillia sees a cluster of small weed- and vine-clutched buildings. Two young women hustle her into the shelter of one of the buildings, through a door marked WOMEN. One of her captors—a dark-haired, dark-complected woman dressed in a long afghan—stands guard, long gun at the ready. The other, a freckled blonde dressed in workshirt and pants and wearing a necklace of deer teeth, removes the bonds around Trillia's wrists and directs her to a toilet stall.

"You have five minutes," the blond tells her—which is as much as Trillia has heard any one of this band say all day.

She checks the stall and toilet for spiders, snakes, mice, or insects, but finds none. She figures they scattered when the women came inside and the light came on. Yes, light. Settling gratefully onto the toilet seat after the jouncing morning ride on horseback, she voids bladder and bowels while reading a dusty plaque on the inside of the stall door. The plaque informs her that this "full-service roadside rest area" is served by "solar-powered composting toilets," for her "health and convenience" and "protection" of the "local environment" as well.

Despite the hardship of her situation, Trillia still finds time to be amazed. The culture that built this roadside rest area is gone, but the toilets still work. The less dependent a system was on human maintenance, the longer it has continued to function. The solar power units have not been stolen or overgrown by weeds and trees. She wonders where the bin of clean compost is, and where the used compost is automatically shuttled to. . . .

Before she has time to ponder further, her guard bangs on the door and she has to vacate the stall. On the way out she sees Tomoko for a brief instant before being led away. Outside, she is given a wide, thin sheet of pemmican to chew on for sustenance. The thin chewy fare tastes better— or she is hungrier—than she expected.

She sees Ricardo, John, Caster, and Phenix only at some distance before she and Tomoko are bound and blindfolded once more, then mounted and anchored upon their horses again. Her blindfold is tighter this time, and she can't loosen it enough to see as much as she was able to before.

They are slowly gaining elevation, she thinks. Moving over hills and valleys. Given her blindfold and the rolling gait of the big mare she is seated on, she can't be sure. The heat and humidity seem less oppressive than they were the previous day. Still, by the time the kidnappers break from the trail to make camp for the evening, her blindfold is soaked with enough sweat that it trickles annoyingly into her eyes from time to time.

Freed of their bonds and blindfolds, in shifts of two the captives are allowed to eat an evening meal of pemmican and dried fruit. They are camped in a mixed forest of pines and hardwoods with fat young green leaves—even a dogwood shifting from bloom to green in the understory of the forest.

Looking at the rolling country around them in the sunset light, Trillia thinks they must have covered a lot of ground since Morehead City. Her muscles are sore—and she was on horseback the entire way. When she thinks of how far they have come, and that her silent captors were running alongside the horses the whole distance, she feels a grudging respect for them.

"Respect" does not make sleep that night any easier. She and her friends are trussed up again after dinner, hands bound tightly behind backs, then forced feet first into sleeping bags to find what rest they can—untented, all of them together, under the watchful eyes of a pair of guards who make clear their displeasure at seeing their captives make any attempt to speak among themselves. A strong rope links all the captives in a loose circle around the trunk of an enormous oak tree, straight and stout as a pillar supporting the sky, its broad canopy cradling the moon and stars in its branches above them. In the distance, Trillia hears an owl screech.

Searching for a position in which her aching body can be less uncomfortable while bound this way, Trillia spends the night turning from belly to back and side to side like a fowl roasting on a fitful rotisserie. Only after she has completely given up on the idea of ever being comfortable again does she catch a few hours of dead sleep.

In the morning she wakes nauseous, then vomits. Tomoko eyes her, carefully and sympathetically, but says nothing. Without a word passing between them, Trillia realizes the older woman knows that what Trillia only *fears* may be true, is, in fact, the reality.

After a long morning of riding blindfolded and bound over crumbling Interstate, they stop in early afternoon. Unblindfolded, in the center of a square in the center of yet another ghost city, Trillia sees only more of all the usual. Rust-stained façades. Patinaed roofs and statues. Cracking and flaking concrete. Faded and eroded brick and stonework. Gray weathered wood. Draperies of thicket and vine. Two toppled trees rotting in the weedy streets. Debris fallen and swept by wind into corners and niches and mounds—impromptu seedbeds for more resurgent greenery.

Yet—here, farther inland, more removed and protected from the ravages of wind and sea, spared the death-throes of fire and fury she saw in Atlanta—this city is the most intact Trillia has encountered. Their guards may believe they have hidden their route from the captives, but Trillia is observant enough to deduce that the "square" they are in is a park adjacent to the grounds of the Governor's Mansion, and the nearest road is Peace Street.

After rest and food their captors return them to bonds and blindfolds and more time in the saddle. They remain under such restraint for less than two hours before they stop and dismount. Their bonds and blindfolds removed, the prisoners are marched along a broken stone path, past a long pond or small lake and through the grounds of what must once have been acres and acres of gardens—now fallen to neglect but still hinting at former spring glories. The captives are led up a wooded hillside, on whose top Trillia earlier saw distant buildings, when her eyes were first freed of the blindfold.

At the top of the hill, Trillia and the others find themselves surrounded by a Gothic fairyland. Walking from a cracked stone path onto what was once a tree-lined lawn—now gone halfway to forest from the original trees' seedlings—they see around them stone buildings with parapets and pointed arches, turrets and towers, gargoyles and great antique doors.

"It's like being back at Cambridge," Tomoko says in wonder, before catching herself. Their guards seem less anxious about their captives' conversations now. "Or maybe Oxford. At least it would be, if they kept up the lawns and cut back all the vines and saplings."

"These can't be medieval," Trillia says, turning as her gaze slowly takes in their surroundings. "None of this can go back that far. What is this place?"

"The West Campus."

The short man who has spoken walks toward them, ancient and grizzled and lame, dressed in high moccasins and a knee-length robe pied and patched from black and white hides, decorated all over with mazes and spirals and knotwork. The old man leans on a tall staff topped with an ornate head. As he comes into their midst, their captors move aside deferentially before him. The man gestures with the ceremonial staff as he speaks.

"Welcome to the kudzu-covered halls of Duke University. The building with the collapsed roof there is the Perkins Library. Fire damage. That one is the Allen Building. And the cathedral-like structure there—with the big tower broken at the top?—that's Duke Chapel."

John Drinan steps forward and peers at the short man with the wild gray-white hair and rheumy bright eyes.

"Good God! Mark Fornash—is that you?"

The white-haired little man smiles crookedly. He wipes at his eyes, then leans forward from the waist and shakes hands with Drinan.

"Who else would you know around here, Johnny? I can hardly recognize *you*, with all those bad tattoos. Now Tomoko here—she hasn't changed a bit."

Tomoko and Fornash embrace a moment, but then Tomoko stiffens and pulls away. Her voice rises in incredulity and indignation.

"You're the one who had us kidnaped? Had us ridden over hill and dale, bound and blindfolded?"

Fornash lifts his hands and staff in a propitiating gesture.

"All will be explained. Maybe some will even be forgiven. You're really the first visiting dignitaries we've ever had."

"If you treat them all the way we've been treated," Ricardo says, "you're not likely to get many of them in the future."

"I know, I know. My most sincere apologies. If you'll come with me I'll try to clear things up. If we only had more time I'd gladly give you a tour, show you all the archwork and the niches, the great chapel organs, the stained glass. It's not the Rose Window in Chartres Cathedral, but it's not bad. Most of *our* work, though, is in the Rhine Research Center, on Buchanan—"

He turns to walk away. Trillia and her friends are slow to follow.

"And if we don't want to go with you?" Caster asks in a sullen tone.

"Then you're free to leave," Mark Fornash replies, sounding a bit annoyed. "Yes, I do mean it. Look, I'm truly sorry for any rough handling you might have received at the hands of my people here. That's my fault. I sent out five parties looking for travelers. We didn't know just where we'd find you. Remote psi-viewing isn't exactly a global positioning system, you know. We knew you were coming, and that time would be tight. We didn't know who our dragnet might pull in, so we had to be careful—especially about revealing our location. I told my young friends here to capture and bring back any groups of travelers they encountered in the correct general vicinity. I told them to act first and let me ask the questions later."

Exhausted from a nearly sleepless night and two days spent bound, blindfolded, and balanced in a saddle against her will, Trillia is in no mood to be gentled down.

"You mean take prisoners first."

Fornash strokes his white goatee with his free hand. Trillia can't help thinking of him as some kind of ancient wizard.

"Yes, I suppose that's what it turned out to be in practice. Fortunately yours is the first group we brought in, so we can end our search. Sorry you were bound and blindfolded, but it was imperative that we all meet—and soon."

"Why?" Ricardo asks, following the old man as he slowly walks away. Trillia and her fellow prisoners-turned-guests—including John's dog Oz—follow too, if more reluctantly.

"Because we're moving toward a cusp-point in our post-Collapse world. Maybe the biggest thing that's happened since the pandemic. Some weird thirty-three-year periodicity to it which I can't figure out. You're all part of it, though. Follow me. I'll show you."

They walk down a long quadrangle, where renascent forest and pseudo-Tudor buildings wage a slow battle for control of the field. Feeling like a child of Hamlin following this strange Pied Piper, Trillia (despite her disgruntlement) can't help listening to Fornash as he explains how he ended up here.

"—where it all began, really. That's why, after leaving the island, I made my way to North Carolina, to the abandoned research laboratories and libraries here at Duke. This is where J. B. Rhine began his work in parapsychology, more than a century before the pandemic. The first major research into paranormal phenomena, the parapsychological powers of the human mind. ESP, telepathy, clairvoyance. Clairsentience, precognition, postcognition. Psychokinesis, micro-PK, out-of-body and near-death experiences—the whole gamut of psi phenomena."

"Pseudoscience," Tomoko mutters. Fornash laughs.

"I heard that! You say to*may*to, I say to*mah*to. You say pseudo, I say subtle. The pivotal question is, Can you *study* experiences and events which suggest consciousness subtly influences the physical world? Rhine thought so. So did a lot of other people, later on."

"Such as?" Trillia asks. Around them, festoons like long green wounds flow down exteriors of those buildings where plants have gained a foothold in high cracks and crannies. Overall, however, the local castles of higher learning appear to be holding their own against the creeping onslaught of vine and branch. Fornash strides along, setting a good pace with the help of his ceremonial staff.

"Such as all the big national intelligence agencies during the Cold War and after. They all had what they called 'mental espionage units.' All the alphabet soup agencies worked on psi-spy stuff, especially remote-viewing. The Army had a bunch of remote-viewing types working out of Fort Mead, for instance."

Slowly the travelers and their guide pass out of the confines of the neo-Gothic West Campus.

"The only 'remote-viewing' I ever came across," John says, "was periscopes, telescopes, and cameras in bunkers down at the Cape. Sounds like you're talking about 'human periscopes.' "

Through the trees and vines, Trillia sees buildings of simultaneously more modern yet less grand architectural styles. They make for less impressive ruins than the West Campus's turrets and towers and spires—a difference which, Trillia suspects, will only grow more pronounced with time. Fornash leads them along a ramp, past a stained and grimy example of century-old concrete brutalism. He makes good time for a lamed man with a walking staff.

"That's not a bad way to think about it," he tells John. "Only, instead of it being a human periscope that pops *up* from the ocean below to look at what's above, a remote viewer is a human periscope that pops *down* into the quantum ocean from our macro-level up here, in order to look around."

"You lost me," Ricardo says, shaking his head.

"If you've been hanging around with John—and Malika, too?—you should know something about the quantum ocean. Maybe they call it quantum 'foam' or quantum 'vacuum.' I like 'ocean' the best, since we're describing the universal sea of energy out of which all matter arises and to which it all ultimately returns."

"Fine, then—ocean. What about it?"

Fornash marches them along a partially grassed-over street, around the occasional dead and rusted automobile-turned-planter, then leads them across the street and onto a path. Trillia feels like a student on a class field trip, with Fornash in the role of professor.

"If you analyze the waves of even the ordinary ocean of water, you'll find that they're information-rich. As long as a wave pattern persists, it can tell you about the passage of ships, wind direction, shoreline effects, lots of things. Boats, for instance, don't just make waves as they pass through the water—they're also rocked by the waves they themselves pass through, which include the wakes of other vessels. The ocean interconnects the motion of all vessels on its surface."

"And this has something to do with parapsychology?" Tomoko asks skeptically.

"Just as the ocean of water interconnects the motion of all the vessels on its surface, so too the quantum ocean interconnects the motion of events that occur in space and time. The quantum ocean functions as a holographic field, encoding the particulars of the motion of events and transmitting those particulars to 'inform' the motion of other events."

Fornash and his audience take the once-asphalted but now largely grassed-over pathway along a wooded hillside.

"None of that transcends space and time the way psi phenomena are supposed to," Tomoko says as they crest the hill.

"Oh, yes it does. The information in the quantum ocean is holographic— distributed and simultaneously available at multiple locations. Propagation of the holographic wave patterns is essentially instantaneous because they are *scalar* waves: longitudinally propagating waves of information rather than force. Fluctuations below the energy threshhold of particle-pair creation."

The group proceeds down the hill, toward a forest of old hardwoods interspersed with myriad upstart succession plants.

"Then even if they *could* propagate independently of the speed of light," Tomoko counters, "these waves would have too little energy to have any real effect."

Fornash brings them to a stop beneath the splendid canopy of a tall, highly branched oak tree.

"Don't be so sure about that. Look at the branches above us and think of the whole canopy as a 'green brain.' Think of the branches as dendrites. In the brain there are an awful lot of branching dendrites—far more than the leaves of this tree. Those dendrites release ions, and each of those ions is a tiny electric field vector. There are ten billion neurons in the brain, each with an average of twenty thousand connections. Action potentials within the neural nets are *significantly* affected by the scalar topology of the quantum ocean—much the way the gentlest of breezes from the ocean of air affects the leaves of this tree. Our cerebral hemispheres act as specialized scalar interferometers, responding to the presence of scalar waves, much the way the leaves of this tree respond to that gentle breeze."

" 'Interferometers'?" Tomoko asks, doubt oozing from her words. "How can that be possible?"

"Holographic functions in the brain require coherent nonlinear interactions between neuronal networks and individual neurons. Alter the initial conditions of the nets and those alterations can, in turn, be amplified by the chaotic attractors that govern cerebral processes. A shift in scalar topology which shifts the action potential of the *smallest* neuronal cluster can create a butterfly effect that triggers—in a *huge* collection of neurons—an abrupt simultaneous shift toward one or another chaotic attractor. Boom! The avalanche of attractor-shift *amplifies* those quantum-ocean fluctuations, enough to produce observable effects on the brain's info-processing. Quantum-ocean fluctuations interact with the ultrasensitive chaotic state of the brain, which turns those tiny fluctuations into a cascade of *significant behavioral inputs.*"

"Butterflies and cascades and avalanches of effects," Tomoko says, shaking her head. "I don't believe it."

Fornash shrugs and walks on, Trillia and the others following.

"Denial is a deep river," he says, glancing back over his shoulder and smiling slyly, "but no river is so deep the ocean does not accept it. People didn't *believe* there were statistically more avalanches during the full moon either, but there are."

"Really?" Trillia asks. She wonders if that odd fact might have some connection to the long association of violence and madness with the full moon—and with the lunar periodicity of the pandemic's Wersign symptoms, too. Fornash nods.

"The presence of the Moon stabilizes the Earth's axial tilt—and also makes life more likely on this planet by doing so. The energy from that stabilization has to go *somewhere*. Where it goes, paradoxically, is into greater chaos dispersed throughout the subsystems of the Earth-Moon system. That 'chaotic stabilization' influences not only avalanches but also life. Coral reefs, the largest structures made by life on this planet, spawn in time to the phases of the moon, for instance—"

"Horseshoe crabs, too," Trillia says, remembering. Fornash gives a quick nod.

"I could give you hundreds of examples—and I will, if you're not careful. It's all been proven. So has the link from quantum flux to brain chaos to behavior—so I am *not* confusing the classical and the quantum, since this bridges the two."

Before them, Trillia sees a white clapboard building in a neo-Colonial style at the back of a lawn dotted with tall, spreading trees. A sign, weathered but maintained, informs her that they are approaching the Rhine Research Center. Fornash leads them up the walk toward the building's front door.

"And you're the one who proved it?" Ricardo asks.

"I wish I could say I was, but it wasn't me. The Tetragrammaton people discovered it, through their Project Medusa Blue."

Trillia is trying to figure out what is so strange about this building when she suddenly realizes it's probably the only one she's seen since coming to the mainland that has been painted within recent memory.

"Dr. Fukuda told me a little about Tetragrammaton," Trillia says. It grew out of the survival plans of what you called 'alphabet soup agencies,' right?"

"That's right," Fornash says, opening the door and glancing back over his shoulder as his guests come into the foyer with him.

"I don't know what this Medusa Blue was about, though."

"That's because Tomoko doesn't want to talk about it," Fornash says, smiling wickedly at the doctor as he leads them upstairs. "More poetry of paranoia. Too weird. I used to think so, too. Precisely because it deals with all the 'subtle' stuff Tomoko still thinks is 'pseudo.' "

At the top of the flight of stairs they turn right down a hallway. Fornash walks them into a long room filled with a lozenge-shaped conference table and chairs on a rug of intricate pattern. He takes a chair and gestures for the others to sit down.

"Medusa Blue was a project aimed at enhancing psi-effects, with the goal of seamless mind/machine linkage, even computer-aided apotheosis—anything from thought recognition to the translation of human consciousness into a machine matrix."

"What was the point of that?"

"To generate the levels of quantum information density needed to create a controllable singularity—a transdimensional gateway for faster-than-light travel to anywhere in the space-time continuum."

Ricardo suddenly brightens, as if he's made a connection.

"Like what John and Malika have been working on, then?"

"Only slightly," John says, shaking his head as he pats Oz seated on the floor beside him. "It sounds like what Mark's talking about is movement *within* the single space-time continuum of this universe, not *between* different universes of the plenum."

This parallel universe stuff makes Trillia's head hurt. Seeing Phenix's eyes begin to roll up too, she realizes she's not the only one. Even Ricardo absently drums the table. Trillia can't figure out whether he's manifesting Wersign again or just bored.

"You mentioned *enhanced*," Trillia says. "Enhanced how?"

Tomoko looks hard at the table and frowns, as if recalling a distasteful memory somehow petrified in the grain of the table's wood.

"One way," she says, "was through chemicals that were antagonists to 5-hydroxytryptamine—better known as 5-HT, or serotonin. It's primarily an inhibitory neurotransmitter that functions as a sort of governor on brain activity. If you put into the central nervous system a strong enough antagonist to that inhibition, though—a supertryptamine, say—the result is enhanced neural sensitivity throughout the entire brain."

Fornash nods.

"The kind of spontaneous neural activity characteristic of chaotic systems," he says. "The kind of chaos that's hypersensitive to quantum effects—what Medusa and Tetragrammaton were after."

Tomoko's frown deepens as she looks up from the table and around the room.

"Such 'enhancement' came at a terrible cost," she says. "Medusa Blue operatives paid ob-gyns to pump their patients with supposedly 'uterotonic' biochemicals—mainly KL 235, ketamine lysergate, or 'gate,' along with a few other supertryptamines they'd extracted from an obscure

South American fungus. All in hopes that their babies might develop 'unusual talents.' Psi talents. Instead, a lot of the mothers became long-period schizophrenics and the kids either went crazy, or their abilities never developed, or both. It didn't work, anyway, and that was that."

Fornash stares with narrowed eyes at his old friend.

"Not quite. Some of the supertryp kids' latent talents *did* shift over to 'active.' A number of chaotic hypersensitives were created—people attuned to the scalar topology of the quantum ocean. A whole range of latent talents—'dream leakers' and 'dream shifters,' direct mind-to-mind 'shield telepaths,' the empath-boosters codenamed 'starbursts.' None of it was really unexpected, but it didn't end there. Maybe the cost has been more terrible than we imagined, too."

Tomoko looks sharply at him.

"What do you mean?"

"Tetragrammaton and Medusa Blue didn't close up shop that easily. These things don't die. They mutate."

"But the plague—" John begins.

"Exactly, though not the way you're thinking," Mark Fornash interrupts. "There are aspects of 'soul-flying' that feel one heck of a lot like clairvoyance. Or remote-viewing. Or out-of-body experiences. There's a link between the pandemic, the shamanic, and the psychic. So the real question is not 'Did the madness plague kill Tetragrammaton?' but rather 'Did Tetragrammaton give birth to the madness plague?' "

"*What?*" Trillia and Ricardo ask simultaneously.

Fornash nods self-assuredly.

"First they tried the machine-only approach. When that didn't work, they tried drugs and machine intelligences. But maybe they didn't stop there. I've been thinking a lot about your old story, John. In the nearby universe you say you came from, your cousin Jiro was responsible for that Light thing that knocked you into our universe, right?"

John barely gets in a nod before Fornash is off and running.

"I used to think self-awareness is to ecstatic awareness 'as the moon is to the ocean,' but maybe it's more like what Malika used to talk about. Maybe it's more 'as this universe is to the system of all possible universes.' Maybe your cousin went to the next stage. Maybe he figured out that what was needed was something quantum-level. Subtle. Lasting."

Tomoko grimaces, almost as if she knows where Fornash might be going—and doesn't want to go there.

"Such as *maybe* what?"

"Such as maybe biotech meets nanotech—what Cameron Spires called *binotech*. Maybe, after the attempt with drugs and machine intelligences failed here, Tetragrammaton tried some subtler approach *in this universe*. But, instead of the transcendent Light John's cousin Jiro experienced when *his* bio met nano, when prionoids met nanomachines *here*, we got the near-universal death of the pandemic."

For a moment all Fornash's captives-turned-guests can only stare at him.

"I'm more certain my cousin died than that he 'transcended,' " John says.

"But you thought you saw him, alive in *some* way, months after he died. See? Death or transcendence—which is it? That's the same question the pandemic raises for all of us, all the time."

"A nanomechanical complement to the prionoids was never proved," Tomoko says with a sigh. "Believe me, I wish we'd proved it was 'prionoids plus something else,' but we never did."

"*We* have!"

Trillia can hear the hope rising when Tomoko responds.

"What? You've isolated something?"

"No, no. The binotech proof's indirect—the distinct similarity between paranormal states and scalar communication between nanodevices—but it's solid. The pandemic prionoid is a *conjugated* protein, and a nanomechanism is part of what it's conjugated *with*."

Tomoko's earlier hope sours into sarcasm.

"Your 'psi phenomena equal pandemic shamanism' theory?"

"We have something much better than that. We salvaged some scalar-effect amplifiers from Fort Mead. When you hook anybody Wer up to them, they shapeshift and soul-fly all over the place. Hook unaltered humans up to them and the most they get out of it is a lightshow and a headache. The amplifiers prove that a nanotech complement is involved—in the shapeshift and soul-flying stages, at the very least."

"Before I was exiled," Ricardo says tentatively, "doctors in the New Bahamas told me I have a 'new variant' of the pandemic. I've 'postcogged' too, according to John. These scalar-effect amplifiers of yours—could you hook me up to them?"

"I don't see why not. My people here always try to make it into some kind of a sacrament. I'd prefer to make a party of it. We'll compromise and call it an experiment."

"Then let's do it," Ricardo says. "As soon as possible."

"Tonight will be time enough. First you all need to be wined and dined! Old wines from before the pandemic, and newer vintages we've been putting up—"

Fornash steps out of the room for a moment. A siren sounds, so abruptly it makes Trillia and all her friends jump. Oz is alternately whimpering and howling when Fornash returns.

"Excuse my dinner bell—sorry, boy."

He leads them out of the conference room and downstairs, then onto and into the stretch of maintained greensward behind the house, regaling his guests all the while with the story of how he first got interested in "the weird stuff." Trillia gathers that long before the pandemic, while working as a net manager for a think-tank corporation, Fornash snuck a peek at some security files he wasn't supposed to be able to access.

As they are joined by others of the mixed tribe Fornash serves as elder and shaman, Trillia thinks of her own bite of forbidden fruit, the "peek" she "snuck" into her grandfather's private records. Forbidden knowledge—as old as Eden and as new as virtuality passwords. And, ever since the first bite of that fruit, everyone always hoping knowledge would restore what was lost in Eden.

Fornash introduces the visitors to his tribe, including some of the visitors' former guards, now much more friendly and talkative. Trillia, Ricardo, and John help Fornash and some of his people with all the preparations for the feast, while Tomoko, Caster, and Phenix help others of the tribe set up the screened pavilion tent that will serve as venue. Fornash busies himself working and making introductions. Pouring himself a glass of wine, he argues with John Drinan over who convinced whom to accept Cameron Spires' forceful invitation to his island research facility.

"John, you *know* I never wanted to find a 'cure.' I had no interest in an inoculation or antidote to the the pandemic. I joined up with Spires during the last days because I wanted to *understand* the thing, not eliminate it.

I wanted to modify it enough so the transcendence it offered would become a matter of *choice*, not 'evil fate' or 'divine providence.' "

John shakes hands with another of Fornash's little tribe as Fornash introduces him.

"That's not how I remember it," John responds to Fornash. "You were as disturbed and frightened as anyone else by what it was doing to the world back then."

"True, true. But even in the darkest days I never rejected the potential for transcendence the shamanic complex presented. The plague let God out of the box we'd made inside our heads. I always *embraced* that."

"But *my* Wersign doesn't exactly match your 'shamanic complex,' " Ricardo says.

"How so? Describe it to me."

Ricardo does so, including the "feedback" and "each stage holds all the others in embryo" explanations Tomoko and John gave him. Fornash nods in growing agreement and interest, particularly regarding the Camp Lejeune ghosts, until Ricardo asks him about the nature of the "transcendence" the final shift holds—if it's not simply death.

"I'm afraid I can't tell you much about that last step," Fornash says, deeply thoughtful. "I can only tell you what I believe. I've passed through all the stages of the shamanic complex. Aerial-voyaged and soul-flown *without dying* more times than I thought possible. That's what we do here—learn to control it as much as we can. But the only people who really know what that last stage is about are those who have gone there for good."

Swirling the wine in his glass, John calls Oz over to him, then turns to Fornash.

"Sister Vena had plenty of theories on that, back in the old days. Her spin on the whole transcendence-religion thing."

"What do you mean?" Trillia asks.

"She said my coming from an alternate universe was part of it. That there were other universes which had 'transcended into the spiritual realm.' "

Mark Fornash smiles and looks away, shaking his head.

"Vena was always more *lovably* crazy than I was. All I know is, every time we precog it, you Bahamian exiles and some connection to John's home universe turn out to be the big cusp, the fulcrum on which the future balances. The rest is silence."

Fornash takes his leave of them then, explaining that he has to gather together the gear for their after-dinner festivities. Trillia makes her way toward the dining pavilion, walking with two of her profusely apologetic former captors—the freckled blond woman, Karen, and the long-haired black woman, LeDee, who led her to the toilet during her captive ride. Both are now dressed in the loose, flowing black robes so many of Fornash's people seem to favor. Trillia glances from one woman to the other as they walk.

"What did he mean when he said, 'every time we precog it'? Do you do a lot of that around here?"

"A fair amount," LeDee says, smiling. "We've got a lot of moon children among us."

"She means trained psi-people," Karen explains with a laugh. "There's more strong psi now than at any other time in human history. Almost everyone who's gone any distance into Wersign has some of it. Fornash's powers are really strong, though. In some ways *he* drew us here, as much as his message."

"His message?"

"The idea that anyone can navigate the passage from the bestial to the divine," Karen says, nodding, "if only you have the courage to do it."

"Following the high hard way, though," Le Dee says, "means you have to take on the shapes of animals before you can take on the shapes of gods. Zoomorphic first, theomorphic later."

The implications of such a "faith" perplex Trillia—even more so the idea that someone from the New Bahamas propounded it.

"I don't understand. He lived in the islands for years."

LeDee nods.

"He came to Wersign late, and he came to it slow. Maybe that's why he's got such good control. Why he's been able to soul-fly and come back alive again, so many times."

"His blessing and his curse," Karen says.

"How so?"

"He's old," LeDee says. "He wants to know what the final step is all about. But he can't finish it. He keeps coming back to himself."

Trillia shakes her head.

"I always thought the whole *point* of a journey is to come back to yourself."

"For us, maybe," Karen says. "Not for him. Not anymore. Especially since Sister Vena died."

"She and Mark were—I guess 'soulmates' is the best term for it," LeDee says.

To hear of death parting lovers saddens Trillia, but she still can't imagine not wanting to "come back." That would mean death—or madness. Neither one of those options appeals to her.

Trillia and her former captors walk toward where a blue-and-white pavilion tent is transforming a large area of lawn into an improvised dining hall. Outside the pavilion tent, Trillia sees a circle of children, playing and singing:

> *Close your eyes, pretend you're dead—*
> *Watch stars come out inside your head—*
> *Hush little baby, we must be fed!*

The children mime eating the one who's "it." Trillia stops with a jolt.

"Know what that's about?" Le Dee asks, watching her.

"I've heard stories," Trillia says awkwardly. "A nursery rhyme with a past. Like 'Ring around the Rosey' and the Black Plague, hundreds of years ago. I sang the 'Gobble Song' myself when I was little."

"It's called that," Karen says, "because, in the last days, parents began abandoning potential Wer babies in those parts of cities controlled by Wer streetkids, hoping the streetkids would raise the abandoned babies. They used the babies in soup instead, as a protein source."

"Understandable, at some level," Le Dee says. "Food to keep them going, in a world where they were regularly tracked and killed by Trufolk hunting parties—most often led by off-duty law-enforcement types."

"More than enough atrocities on every side," Trillia says, shaking her head sadly.

"And hardly a conversation topic to improve one's appetite for dinner," Karen says, walking on toward the tent entrance. "Let's go in."

Trillia helps the people hauling tables around, inside. They put the head table on a small grassy knoll at the far end of the big tent, as a sort of impromptu dais. The dais forms the base of a U, while the U's arms are two parallel rows of tables facing each other across the open-ended space. During the meal the travelers will sit at the head table with Fornash. His tribe will sit at the tables that face each other across the open area.

Once it is laid out before them in the great tent, the meal is a wonderful thing. The elegance of snowy table linen, crystal goblets, fine china, and gleaming silver on tables set upon the grass. All of it opens for Trillia a tiny window backward in time: out of the neglected, abandoned, and decayed ruins of mainland civilization, into the glory and opulence that were once an everyday part of life for at least the wealthier members of that civilization. She savors deeply each course of the meal—the salads made with ephemeral wild mushrooms and cinnamony fern fronds, the wild-caught meat, fowl, and fish, the wines and beers old and new, the desserts of early berries and other fruits.

"I'm amazed at how rapidly a new type of culture has grown up among you and your band of friends here," Tomoko says to Fornash over dessert. "Much more developed than what I've been able to achieve down south."

Fornash shrugs. The yellow torchlight that bathes the interior of the tent mellows the aged lines of his face.

"Culture abhors a vacuum. We've worked with that fact. The rituals and traditions we've developed are how we fill that vacuum, while at the same time putting our Wer capabilities to solid cultural use."

"How's that?" Ricardo asks.

"Ah, that's a little harder to explain. Basically, it's a way of learning that exploits the psi abilities of Werfolk. What you'll experience once you're hooked up to the psi circlets, the quantum scalar-effects amplifiers, will be—how can I put it? You could think of it as part personal myth-making, part telepathic sending and remote-viewing, part salvaged psi-enhancement media machines. But it's more than that. An 'instinctual ritual' of remembrance, in which you learn again what you've always already known. The drummers, dancers, deep trancers—they'll all be working you toward that learning *with* them."

"Learning without language?" Tomoko says with a look of warning. "Sounds like a group hallucination."

Fornash laughs.

"Simon Lingham couldn't have put it better himself. I wish he'd stopped here on his way north, so I could have confronted him with what we've accomplished here. That Lupe woman you mentioned, too—something familiar about her. What did you say her full name was?"

"Guadalupe Sanchez," Ricardo says. Trillia looks at him, surprised by the sharpness of his memory. "At least, that's what I think Simon said her name was."

"A lot of Werfolk have worked with us here over the years. Trying for better conscious control of psi-powers and shapeshifting. She might be one of them. Maybe she's already confronted Simon with some of our work. Simon would have a tough time wrapping his head around *that*, let me tell you."

"Why?" Trillia asks.

"He always used to say 'Language and consciousness are absolutely co-extensive.' I always believed consciousness was bigger than language, myself. Everything I've experienced since I went Wer confirms that. Human beings had nonsymbolic precursor thought—call it 'ecstatic awareness'—before we had symbolic thought—'self-awareness,' if you like. Psi phenomena are rooted in ecstatic awareness. But if you want to know *there*, you have to *go* there."

Ricardo looks around at the others.

"I don't know about the rest of you, but I'm willing to give it a try right now."

Fornash rises to his feet. He taps his glass with a spoon for attention from the rest of his tribe.

"People, one of our new guests wishes to join us in our holy partying!"

From the two long parallel rows of tables, there are cheers and applause.

"Tonight we welcome a new initiate!" Fornash says, to more cheers and applause.

"Make that two," Caster says, standing.

"Three," Phenix says. The cheers and applause grow raucous.

Although Caster and Phenix haven't been saying much, they must have been listening carefully, Trillia thinks.

"You say all this will do to us 'unaltereds' is make us see lights?" she asks.

"And give you a headache too, alas," Fornash says, smiling and playing to the crowd.

"What have I got to lose."

Trillia stands up beside Ricardo and clasps his hand. They exchange glances briefly, hers letting him know that she is doing this for him—and that she's not fond of feeling pressured to do so, which in fact she *does* feel. Everyone looks expectantly at Tomoko and John. Tomoko casts a concerned parental glance at the young people in their party.

"No thanks. Somebody has to look after you high-fliers."

"I have to take care of my dog," John deadpans.

To good-natured laughter the meal breaks up and everyone adjourns to another section of the broad lawn, outside the tent. Members of Fornash's tribe disappear briefly. When they reappear, they carry drums and noisemakers. Several are dressed in dancing attire that hangs lightly upon them—despite being extravagantly feathered, flowered, studded with crystals, and beaded. Together with the guests, Fornash's people form a rough circle around a firepit, some of them already stoking up a blaze. The evening has grown cool, since sundown. Both the fire's smoke and the coolness of the evening should keep down the numbers of bugs and mosquitoes, Trillia hopes.

Several of Fornash's people—mainly black-robed "initiates"—make their way around the circle, helping their tribal elder distribute the psi circlets. Fornash himself positions one of the silvery circlets on Ricardo's brow. Ricardo looks tense.

"How are these things supposed to work?"

"If you were just looking at an EEG, all it would show is an increased interfacing of deep Theta and Delta wave states. Neurotransmitter readings and PET scans show more detail, but not much. The circlets amplify quantum scalar effects so those effects can synch up better with brain chaos—particularly if that chaos is already pumped up by the presence of neurotransmitter-altering prionoids."

"This prionoid-neurotransmitter connection—" John asks, "is that what Malika used to call a 'trigger'?"

"Right. 'Allows for the creation of a mental state *meaningfully related* to physical changes in the brain, without exactly being caused by those changes—remember?' "

"So how does the trigger work?" Ricardo asks. "And what does the 'gun' do when it fires?"

"In pumping up neural gain and brain chaos, the trigger reformats the state space attractor in your head—enough that its energy does one of two things, as nearly as I can figure it. Either the gun's 'firing' quantum-mechanically 'opens out' the individual's ontogenetic and mythologic surround from the holographic field where that information is stored, or—and this is the more likely option when you consider what these psi circlets do—the energy of that shifted-around state space attractor becomes detectible by the nanomechanical complements of the prionoid the pandemic loaded up into us."

"Complements which you *believe* were loaded up," Tomoko says, correcting him. "Occam's razor, Mark—don't multiply entities more than is absolutely necessary."

Fornash places one of the circlets on Trillia's brow. The only sensation it gives her is one of cool dead metal.

"Yes, yes," he says dismissively to Tomoko. "Our definitions of 'absolutely necessary' don't agree. My 'entities' are multiplied by exactly as much as is necessary to fit a very complex set of facts. Anyway, as I was saying, the manifestations beyond drumming, dancing, and dreaming—the stigmata, the quick healing of stigmatic wounds, full-blown shapeshifting, quantum level soul-flying—all those occur as a result of communication between the quantum ocean and what the prionoid-nanomech conjugate does to the mind/body system."

"Which is what, exactly?" Ricardo asks the tribal elder.

"Chaotically hypersensitizes the brain. Makes flesh and bone more 'plastic.' Material out of the 'surround' or 'unconscious' *reinstantiates*—not only informationally, but also physically. These psi circlets make that communication more efficient but not, unfortunately, as conscious or controlled as we'd like."

"If it's all unconscious," John asks as Fornash checks the circlets one last time, "then why did people manifest Wersign differently in different cultures?"

Straightening up, Fornash is joined by two more of his helpers.

"Vena's 'cultural constraints.' The idea that there's a 'cultural unconscious' as well as a 'personal unconscious' is at least as old as Freud's distinction between id and superego. An Australian aborigine becomes a were-kangaroo, a Paleolithic European becomes a were-elk, an Olmec becomes a were-jaguar—*because of* his or her cultural unconscious and surround."

Fornash's helpers inform him that everyone is now circleted and ready to go.

"Let's switch 'em on, then."

Fornash walks away from Trillia's and Ricardo's part of the circle, toward the central fire. A tall blond woman bends down and puts a circlet on Fornash's own head and kisses him lightly on the brow. A young man hands the elder a black leather box about half the size of an attaché case. Fornash taps at it briefly.

"All right. Close your eyes, now—all of you. When I activate the circlets you'll feel a tingling, prickling sensation. After it abates, I'll improvise a poem. Once that's done, there will be no more words—just drumming, dancing, and trancing to whatever places the spirit moves us."

Thinking of the *Close your eyes* line in the children's morbid Gobble Song, Trillia feels foolish sitting on the cool grass with her eyes shut. The prickling and tingling of the circlet on her brow so startles her, she almost opens her eyes. The tingling and prickling abate. She begins to see swirling stained-glass colors as Fornash intones in a deep and level voice:

> *What I see when my eyelids are closed*
> *Shining in darkness as deep as the heart*
> *Is a grander cathedral's window of rose*
> *Cradle of all high spiritual art.*
> *There's a beauty to it, a beauty to it all*
> *When darkness shines and silence calls.*

The poem is a slight, spare thing—yet Trillia finds that it perfectly describes what she is seeing. The light behind her eyes becomes superabundant, in colors more numerous, more finely hued, toned, and shaded than she has ever seen.

Now she hears drumming and dancing begin around her. Its rhythms modulate the light, breaking it into rolling, rippling grids, bars and parallel lines, pulsing arcs and flashes and zigzags, explosive starbursts. When for an instant she opens her eyes, those luminous patterns—enlarging and contracting, pulsing and blending—project onto the earth and sky, pink and yellow when she glances up, lavender and green when she looks down.

As she watches strange phosphorescent birds in the air, neon snakes in the grass, the sense of her vision ending at any sort of edge or periphery begins to erode. She closes her eyes, fighting off a feeling of vertigo. The swirl of color expands beyond left and right, beyond up and down. Her visual field wraps around to full-circle and then full-sphere, ensphering her. She is the point dark with excess of bright standing at the center of that sphere. She is the circumference of that sphere, too, watching the light stream toward her as particle, and wave, and something much more.

Then it's not the light that is streaming toward her but she who is streaming into the light. Drawn into it, called into it, down a tunnel lined with geometric patterns and the glowing, rippling latticework she saw earlier, a tunnel that gradually begins to turn—rotating into a vortex. She opens her eyes to see the full moon followed by the traces and visual echoes of many moons, all following the first one spinning down the vortex with her, all headed toward the bright point at the end of the tunnel. She closes her eyes once more and waits to pass into the center of that brightness.

When she opens her eyes again she sees a landscape too nightmarish to be real and too real to be nightmare. All around her, Fornash's people are shapeshifting, becoming zoomorphic humans and anthropomorphic animals, were-birds and were-animals, mantis- and grasshopper-headed and-torsoed composite creatures—not least of all shaman Fornash himself, now become a laughing, snarling wolfman before her eyes.

Is she dreaming? Hallucinating? Glancing at Ricardo, she sees with horror that he is rapidly, almost convulsively, shapeshifting beside her—not into a single composite of beast and man, but a man-thing, overswept now by waves of chitin and scales and feathers and hair, whose arms and legs and hands and feet become pincered, finned, lobed, webbed, salamander-fingered, dragon- and bird-taloned, clawed and nailed, whose eyes jittering in his eye sockets grow fish-round, then slitted, then human again.

Trillia shakes her head, as unable to believe what she sees as she is to scream at seeing it. She moves toward him, her movements, all her responses, infinitely slowed, vastly laborious. Several of Fornash's people see Ricardo's convulsive shifting, too. They gather around him, dancing and trancing, trying to settle him down as much as they can. Ricardo's shifting is far more rapid and intense than any they have ever known—a throwback to the days of the Great Shift itself, and more.

With startling agility for a man so aged, Fornash strides forward, palms up and open, bleeding from stigmatic wounds. Fornash's people help the convulsing Ricardo to his feet, easing open his clenched clawed taloned fists to reveal the palms—bleeding, too. Fornash clasps Ricardo hand to hand, palm to palm, wound to wound, holding him tightly, refusing to let go, no matter what Ricardo metamorphoses into.

In moments, as if old Fornash has drawn a poison out of the younger man, Ricardo's convulsive shifting slows, stops. He collapses to the ground, breathing in the slow rhythms of deep sleep. Trillia barely has time to notice it before she and those around her are overcome by a sudden, overwhelming fatigue.

Passing out, she plunges fully into Fornash's vision. Sharing in his consciousness, she leaves his body with him and flies above the landscape at unbelievable speed. Beneath them and before their eyes pass all the world, its climes and creatures and enormous ruins, its lonely scattered bands of surviving humans. Again and again, faster and faster, the trancers travel with Fornash, until it as if they are partaking of the thoughts and perceptions of a brain operating at infinite speed. At that unattainable limit, everything freezes: a mind at the top of its trajectory, where space and time mean nothing.

Then, with him, they are all falling back down infinity's rainbow, back through the many universes of the plenum this single universe has touched. Trillia sees all the rusts and vines and weeds of abandonment stripped away. She looks again at the crowded and complexified world of pre-pandemic civilization, its glowing towers, monoliths, ziggurats, and monuments to itself, the roar of its airways and seaways and highways, the buzz and whir of all its communications—and then sees in turn all that world *unbuilding itself,* not in the decay and dilapidation of collapse and ruin but in the running backward of all the original making and constructing, backward and backward, unbuilding and unbuilding, shrinking and contracting, the fabric of shelter shifting from concrete and plastic, to brick and stone, to wood and wattle, to hide and cave. Machines of quantum and code disappearing into machines of combustion and steel, into machines of iron and steam, into animal muscle rolling wheels and pulling plows and grinding grain, into human muscle wielding metal and clay, wood and stone, antler and bone. Tamed animals and grains escaping again into their wild ancestral forms, humans chasing after them, until those who chase cease to be human—

—until at last the traveling mind she and all of them share returns via a strange Möbius loop into Fornash's body upon the ground. From out of his head and heart and every plexus of his life's energy a brilliant flash erupts, surging upward, soaring into the sky, past the moon to the bright sky-river of stars, whorling the stars themselves into spiral and vortex until his light disappears into that whorling shining tunnel.

Trillia wakes to others awakening—comes to, to others coming to. Beside her, Ricardo still sleeps. Already the visions begin to fade, dreams at morning, their strangeness vying with their vividness in her mind, raising argument and counterargument about their reality. What did she see—and how did she see it, when *she* has shown no Wersign?

Near her, she sees Fornash's people lifting the old man to a sitting position. Fornash is smiling, but whether the expression on his face is the look of bliss achieved, or of poison-bottle warning, Trillia cannot yet say.

27

Fearful Synergy
2033

TO THE FIFTY TETRAGRAMMATON OPERATIVES—A GALLERY OF MOBILE faces floating in virtual space before him, sharing his conference call— Cameron Spires pumped the images directly.

Media and military helicopters hovered in place about a smoke-towered city center, whirring carrion flies hanging motionless over a bloated concrete corpse. Masses of police and National Guardsmen in urban smart-camouflage performed riot control—tangle-webbing and truncheons and tear-gas, rubber and plastic and wooden bullets all coming into serious play. Sometimes the event-recorders lingered on the law enforcers enforcing their law on crowds of people achingly ordinary: clean-cut looks, well-groomed hair, socially acceptable attire, familiar emblems of traditional religious groups. The media lingered far longer, however, on those enforcing order (if not law) on the archetypically masked and head-dressed and costumed, the feathered and flowered and beaded, the drummers and the thrummers, dancers and trancers, shakers and quakers, wailers and flailers, shamans and witches—all the nude, tattooed, and didjeridooed wildfolk with no respect for traffic, laws, or schedules.

"As you know if you've been following the reports in the media," Spires told his fellow conferees, "these could be images from any number of cities. There are so many in similar condition, why bother to name a locale? Just another city under martial law. The police here might be trying to protect technical installations from the machine smashers. Or trying to protect self-titled Werfolk from those religious zealots who would burn them as witches and demonically possessed. Or, conversely, trying to protect the traditional religious from angry Werfolk. Whatever the case, the citizens here are lucky: The forces of law and order in this city are not yet using live ammunition and napalm. Other citizens, in other cities, have not been so lucky. Nor have the points debated there been so lofty or philosophical."

On his virtuality shades, Spires glanced around at the fifty faces hanging in the infosphere before him. Some of them were familiar to him. The ancient yet somehow ageless Ka Vang, with his thin gray hair and spectacles. Lilly-Park's Egan Ortap, with his blond short-cropped hair, Vandyke beard and faux eyeglasses—the latter apparently intended to make him look either more mature or more intelligent than he actually was. Balance Tien-Jones, coming in delay-corrected from the orbital habitat. Michael Dalke's iconic Digital Persona, cartoon manatee standing in for the man in his float tank in Cincinnati.

Most of the other faces, icons, and DPs did not look familiar to Cameron, but he was not much bothered by that. He knew the most important faces in this crowd, and all of them knew who he was.

"A plague or pandemic of 'prionoid schizophrenia,' " Spires continued. "That's what the news shows are calling it. As a direct result of that attribution, there have been several attacks on my company facilities, particularly on my Protean Pharmaceuticals subsidiary—headquartered not far from the city you're looking at now."

"Is that why you called this meeting?" asked Egan Ortap. "Why not just let the governments and law enforcement handle it?"

It was all Cameron could do to keep from sneering. Yes, Egan, you'd like that, he thought. A competing pharmaceuticals firm being torn to pieces, while you stand innocently by. What could please you more?

"The world's governments, corporations, and international organizations," Cameron said heavily, "have been blindsided by the manner, rapidity, and totality of what we're up against here. I've sent massive private security in to my facilities. That's helping, but it's damnably expensive and can't, on its own, contain the public anger rising against my businesses. I am not going to keep taking the spear, personally or corporately, for projects we are *all* involved in."

A murmuring buzz spread among the conferees as they consulted with each other. Spires waited.

"What would you have us do?" Dr. Vang said at last, speaking for all of them.

"Many of you have strong connections to the adfotainment media. Use them. Help us put out the word that we didn't release this stuff. In a very real sense we didn't, at least not in its present form. Get behind us in placing the blame on the anarcholuddites. We need to get people to sign onto the idea that the lo-tekkers and disurbanists released this plague *themselves*, as part of an attempt to point up the horrors of technologists 'playing God'—and thereby push people toward their cause. Imply that the lo-tekkers' strategy has terribly backfired. Repeat that story loud and long enough in enough media and it will draw the ire and fire away from my companies."

The buzz of the conferees sounded more positive—until Egan Ortap interrupted again, shaking his head.

"I can't accept such a proposal. This is a publicity black eye for Spires Biotech only. Why should the rest of us concern ourselves with it at all? It doesn't involve us."

Spires laughed.

"Egan, I know you're not *that* naive. We're quite a bit beyond stories about heavy drumming in Central Park creating a 'public nuisance.' We are *all* affected by this, or soon will be. We *are* involved, and you know it. Judging by the number of digital personas I'm seeing before me, many of you have been hit by this plague yourselves. For now, it's true, most people are lying low, staying home to avoid the madness in the streets. The problem is, it's not just in the streets—it's in the overwhelming majority of homes too."

"What of that?" Michael Dalke asked in his computer-generated voice. "Drumming, dancing, dreaming—so what? No one has yet died of this 'plague,' at least not directly."

"The key word is 'yet'—and that too is debatable. The rhythmania and dance manias showed up worldwide and the public powers misinterpreted them as peculiarly widespread fads or hysterias—disruptive, but no deep danger. Outbreaks of the dreaming phase have appeared in most cities worldwide, now. That's caused panics in developing countries with weak social control and medical infrastructure. Even for our benighted 'world leaders,' that's a worrisome development. Let's *don't* follow their example of complacency. The idea that these outbreaks are still 'containable' grows more absurd every passing minute."

"But they *are*," Egan Ortap said. "Whatever this plague or pandemic is, I can't believe it constitutes a genuine threat to global civilization."

The plane is going down, Cameron thought, shaking his head, *but no one notices so long as the food is still fine in First Class and everyone keeps their windowshades down for the in-flight entertainment.*

"I'm sure we'd all like to believe that," he said, "but *I* can't. Not anymore. For the last two days, at my research library here in New York City, we've hosted a hastily convened conference on all of this—a conference which wraps up tomorrow. What follows comes out of that conference, as well as from some of my associates' earlier infosphere winnowings."

Into virtual space Cameron Spires projected Mark Fornash's predictions of a shamanic complex and its five-stage symptomatology. Then he displayed Tomoko Fukuda's biochemical descriptions of the action of rogue prionoids in the brain. Cameron followed that with news footage of drumming and dancing mobs in parks, streets, deserts, and forests, then Simon Lingham's epidemiological projections for WHO. By the time Cameron called into their shared virtuality Sister Vena Srinagar's speculations on the role of dreaming in the development of stigmata among hospitalized sleepers, he knew he had their full attention. He flashed up an abstract of Lieutenant Leira Losaba's reported experience with shapeshifters in South Africa.

"Only now," he said, freezing the presentation, "when initial outbreaks of spontaneous metamorphoses have started to appear—only now have those in public power begun to implement travel restrictions, quarantines, and crash programs to combat 'prionoid schizophrenia.' All much too late. Crowd dynamics are intensifying. The diffuse crowds of fads, manias, and crazes have shifted to expressive crowds manifesting all the psychophysical fervor of religious revivalists or swooning concert fans, only in a much more powerful and prolonged fashion. These in turn are now becoming acting crowds—rioters, posses, lynch mobs. Our *best-case* scenarios call for all the mad old animosities—religious, political, racial, tribal—to return with a vengeance in the coming months, before spiraling wildly out of control."

"On what do you base such scenarios?" Dr. Vang asked.

"We're already seeing more cross-border incursions, anarchic gang wars, pointless regional conflicts. It's much easier to demonize your enemies as inhuman creatures who commit unspeakable acts—if, as a result of moon-linked shapeshifting, they have in fact *become* those creatures and *done* such things."

"Shapeshifting?" Egan Ortap said suddenly, in a scornful voice. "That hasn't been proved. It's not scientifically plausible. Ranks right up there with the Loch Ness monster, Bigfoot, and the Abominable Snowman. The recorded images have to be hoax material—there's no other explanation. Those eyewitnesses who are honest and well-meaning must be the dupes of hoaxers and pranksters."

Cameron Spires nodded.

"Certainly there's room for argument, so I'll show you one, between two of the authorities on what's going on. One is Mark Fornash, who predicted the overall 'shamanic' pattern of the disease. The other is Simon Lingham of WHO, who has put forward the best epidemiological models to date. Neither of them knew they were being recorded when this discussion took place, so we can assume it wasn't 'staged' or 'faked' in any way."

Into their shared virtual space Camerons Spires flashed an image of Mark Fornash standing with Simon Lingham in the Spires Research

Library, gesturing at an illustration of a dancing figure in what was apparently a book of photos and sketches of ancient cave art.

LINGHAM: Saying the artists at Les Trois Freres couldn't have dreamed up such a hybrid image as the one you showed me—that it has to be a literal and "realistic" depiction of an actual event—is like saying only ancient astronauts could have built the pyramids or Stonehenge, because ancient humans *must* have been incapable of such feats! That's a damn strange way of dehumanizing the human beings of earlier times. Something very like the *opposite* of ancestor worship.

FORNASH: If you won't believe it in the past, then how about in the present? The genetic engineers always say they're just doing what evolution does—only a lot faster. Even when they're doing things evolution *never* did, stuff that breaks down the boundaries between species. What if they stumbled on a trigger that erases species boundaries and makes *individual* shapeshifting happen "a lot faster"?

LINGHAM *(dismissively):* What if, what if! More scientific implausibility.

FORNASH: Then what about the weirdly contorted facial and skeletal musculature seen in these latest Plague victims? What about their unusual hair-growth?

LINGHAM *(dismissively again):* The products of the later stages of a disease.

FORNASH: Not the reemergence of an ability latent in all human beings? That's what these 'Werfolk' say it is. They say every creature is made out of the traces of all the creatures it is not. That's another way of saying the traces of the entire evolutionary history of any organism are still somehow present in the living organism—waiting to be set in motion by the appropriate trigger. Maybe the prionoids are the trigger, and finding those traces is what the brain hyped on prionoids *does*.

LINGHAM *(walking back to his research carrel, fornash accompanying him):* The whole of the mythos of these so-called Werfolk is just sad self-delusion and disease-related hallucination.

FORNASH *(smiling):* Okay, then. Go ahead. Take the easy way out. I can't say I blame you.

LINGHAM *(with a tired sigh):* Scientific rigor is not the "easy way out." To my mind, the best explanation for the pandemic is neither cultural nor supernatural but simply natural—albeit with a little scientific and technological help to get it started. *(Speaking slowly and deliberately, almost as if explaining to a child for the twentieth time.)* Artificial prionoids, developed as treatments for mental illness, have unexpectedly been modified by bacteria and swapped into a ubiquitous airborne vector. In their modified form the prionoids alter the shape of enzymes involved in the synthesis of neurotransmitters—

FORNASH *(laughing):* Oh, *puh-leeze!* This crazy plague has never been just about "neuromodulator prions" and "bacterial vectors." It's really about how the brain/prionoid synergy taps into those traces of evolutionary history in the human organism. How the new shapeshifting and soon-to-be soul-flying "thing" interacts with the individual psyche and the old cultural complexes—

LINGHAM *(angrily):* You and your "cultural complexes"! The only true "shapeshifting" involved here is the way a prionoid morphs enzymes into further copies of itself. The only real "soul-flying" here may well be the out-of-body experience of death—all too soon, for all too many people. If the time frame for your "stages" and my epidemiological predictions are both correct, and if this thing *does* prove fatal, then 10,000 years of human civilization are doomed to crash in as little as *ten months* from the infection of Patient Zero. Have you considered that? Isn't that "complex" enough to explain what's happening to the world? Isn't that enough?

Cameron Spires stopped the recording and let the silence open a moment around all of them, before he spoke once more.

"I'm afraid that explanation *won't* prove to be enough. Dr. Lingham and Mr. Fornash couldn't know that they were under surveillance. They also don't yet know how truly complex is the thing they're trying to deal with. Because they don't know Tetragrammaton or Medusa Blue the way we do."

A buzzing murmur shot through the small virtual crowd once more. When it died down, Vang seemed to speak for all of them again.

"What are you getting at?"

"Supertryptamines. Living-fossil receptor sites. Crystal memory and La Brea communications binotech. For the co-extensive mind/machine interface. For the quantum infodensity singularity."

The virtual silence around Spires became very real again. He waited.

"Go on," Dr. Vang said. Spires flashed supporting text and graphics into their shared virtual space.

"Consider this scenario. Suppose Dr. Tomoko Fukuda developed a mammalian cell-line system to pump out artificial prionoids for neuro-modulation of a number of brain disorders. Suppose that my companies, working for Tetragrammaton, used the same technology to make an artificial prionoid that alters the tryptophan metabolic pathway—in such a way as to synthesize supertryptamines that interact with living-fossil receptor sites. Suppose that, also at the behest of Tetragrammaton, we purposely inserted a genetic production sequence into a cell line, in order to manufacture that artificial prionoid for a limited Medusa Blue investigation into particular psi-phenomena."

"That's a helluva lot of supposing," Dalke's computer-generated voice said into their shared virtual space. Cameron Spires raised his hand for quiet and continued to hit them with graphics and text to support his scenario.

"Suppose further, however, that a virus of much greater transmissibility swapped that prionoid-making gene into itself. Let's call it 'inadvertent weaponization.' Suppose that highly transmissible virus and others like it infected humans in immense numbers. In each case, the virus dies, but in doing so it has already delivered an artificial prionoid payload, via macrophages or whatever, into the brain. That payload alters conformation of tryptophan metabolic enzymes to produce KL 235-type supertryptamines. Levels of the supertryptamine build, binding with fossil receptor sites, initiating the 'growing quantum mental event' and 'realization of the shamanic complex' Mr. Fornash has described."

Silence again opened up around Cameron while those in the virtual crowd pondered what he was proposing. When Egan Ortap spoke, he actually seemed to be evaluating Cameron's points objectively, for once.

"Such a scenario might produce the purely psychological effects of the drumming/dancing manias and the dreaming sickness, but it still wouldn't explain the reported physiological effects of these 'stigmata' and 'shape-shifts.' "

"Not entirely. But what if the genes that code for the artificial prionoid also code binotechnically for the construction of one or another of those *Tetragrammaton-sponsored* nanomechanisms I mentioned earlier, as a complement—and the supertryptamine-sensitized brain is hyped enough to direct that binomech's activity?"

The silence that opened up in the virtual world this time was a busy one. Cameron could almost see the intelligent agents swarming through the infosphere, running probability checks on what he had suggested. Balance Tien-Jones, coming in from farthest away, broke the silence first—despite the time delay.

"The blueprint for building this organic nanomechanism, this binomech—it got into billions of human beings the same way the prionoid did?"

"That's what I'd like to *know*," Cameron Spires said, slowly scanning the whole of the virtual crowd before him.

Brushing a wisp of his thin gray-white hair back from his forehead, Dr. Vang leaned forward into virtual space.

"If you're implying that someone other than yourself did that, then you need to look more closely in your mirror."

Now it was Spires' turn to be surprised.

"What do you mean?"

Vang gave a small laugh.

"Really, Cameron. If you thought you could blackmail us into assisting you—by threatening us with the revealing of Tetragrammaton's 'role' in this pandemic—you should have considered your own role more deeply."

"I have already truthfully presented that role! What I object to is seeing that role presented as larger than it actually is—with the negative consequences to my businesses that I have already mentioned."

Vang gave his tittering laugh again.

"Do I have to spell it out for you?"

"Spell away."

Cameron was all too aware of the audience hanging on every word of this exchange. In virtual space before him, Vang was staring down at something out of view. *He's accessing his intelligent agents in the infosphere,* Cameron thought. *Probably has one of those biocybernetic habitats running scenarios on it as well.* Noting Michael Dalke's strangely quiescent digital persona, Cameron considered the possibility that Dalke, too, was helping Vang at this instant. The old man was calling in a lot of his info-processing chips.

"You've been working on longevity treatments, isn't that right?"

"That's public knowledge."

"Ah, but it's not public knowledge that you've 'adapted'—or should I say 'stolen'?—those Tetragrammaton-sponsored *communications* nanomechanisms, now is it? Altered them, for your *medical-repair* binotechnology. My associates inform me that your 'adaptation' has done quite well for you. Nanorganic immortality is within reach. Congratulations. But have you considered the possibility that your little medical-repairers might also still retain some vestige of their original roles as quantum communication devices?"

Cameron's head began to spin. Could it be possible? Might the plague be a bad binotech synergy of prionoid and nanotech and microbe? A global madness brought on by microbes doing what we should have *expected* they'd do? By prionoids doing what they were *reconfigured* to do? By altered nanotech doing what it too was latently still *programmed* to do?

"I—I hadn't considered that."

Vang was looking offstage again—obviously consulting his intelligent agents in the infosphere once more.

"I'm sure you'll have time to find out. I recommend that we accept your proposal to have the media place responsibility for this plague on the shoulders of the anarcholuddites and disurbanists. In exchange for such action, however, I have a counterproposal for you."

"I'm listening. My lawyers will be too. Go ahead."

"Then, out of your own funds, very publicly set up a research institute to investigate this pandemic. Put it on an island somewhere. Pursue all avenues toward a cure."

Cameron paused, pondering the proposal.

"That will give the matter a positive spin in the media, as well. I'll see to it."

"Good. I'm sure there must be at least some small percentage of the worldwide human population whose neurochemistry does not respond to the conformation-altering properties of the prionoid. Due to genetically based polymorphisms, or what have you. There must also be a few, too, who were exposed to the vector, yet who never took up the prionoid into their nervous systems or brains—for whatever reasons. You and your institute might want to pursue those possibilities."

"We will."

Vang smiled benevolently.

"Then we're all agreed, I believe. Any risk which eliminates its intended benefit is not a risk worth taking. We have much work to do, if we are to stave off the disaster Dr. Lingham fears. Let's get to it."

Cameron Spires watched as the real-time faces, icons, and personas vanished from the gallery hanging in his virtuality, one by one, like stars disappearing with the return of the sun at morning.

At the cost of no small humiliation, he had learned something in his confrontation with this Tetragrammaton crowd. Yes, he would create his island institute, as Vang had commanded. But he would make it his own creature, not theirs. If things went the way the worst-case scenarios were predicting, it might prove to be insurance not only for him but for all humanity—or at least for that part of the human race he had any interest in saving.

The conferees at his research library, for instance. Those he had invited to the conference had helped him see and understand what was coming. He owed them at least the possibility of sanctuary. Before the conference ended and they scattered to the four winds, he would see to it that each and every one of them would be given a panic button to push— a transceiver with a geolocator. Should things go utterly crazy and civilization fall apart, they would only need to push that panic button. No matter where in the world the situation at last forced their hands, he'd have them airlifted out to his safe zone. That should make them all appropriately beholden to him, too.

Such a plan would allow him to keep an eye on them as well. Oh, he would pursue all routes to a cure, certainly. Some routes Cameron might not allow his researchers to take to their ends, however. He privately reserved the right not to pursue to conclusion any avenues that might defeat the immortalizing function of his longevity binotech. Not a thousand Vangs, nor a million of his risk-benefit analyses, nor a billion innocent deaths would persuade Cameron to deprive himself of *that* option.

He replaced the vanished Tetragrammaton faces with newsfeeds of violence and destruction from cities around the world: the usual churn and burn, state terror and the terrified state, same as always, only more so, and more of the same, all of the time.

28

Catechism
2066

RICARDO AWAKENS WITH A SERIES OF COUGHS, BLEARY-EYED IN A DRIPping, drizzling world under a gray sky, that bad copper taste in his mouth again. He's lying in something like a cross between a hammock and a stretcher. No sooner does he become aware of its skidding, bumping motion, than that motion comes to a stop.

"Thank God you're awake!" Trillia says, looking down at Ricardo in the travois.

"Where are we?" Ricardo asks, seeing others in their small horseback caravan gathering around him as well. John Drinan gestures toward the horizon from atop a chestnut horse with a black mane.

"Trying to get off the old highway into those trees before this storm gets any worse. Just let us get to those trees, and we'll bring you up to speed."

Ricardo sees Trillia nod, hears her walk away. In a moment her horse and the travois he's lying in are both moving again. Soon they are off the buckled and broken stone of the roadbed, crossing stands of weed and grass, to arrive among the dark roots of old trees.

Trillia and Phenix help him up from the travois, but he is still too weak and disoriented to walk. They prop him up against the base of a tree. The wind blows harder. Above him, the tree's branches rock and creak. The leaves show their undersides to the wind—pale and trembling, as if from fright.

"What happened? How long have I been out?"

"His mouth seems to be working fine," Tomoko says to Trillia as she and John dismount from their horses. "He's full of questions, at any rate."

They crouch down near him, under the tree's sheltering canopy. Ricardo feels muddled and foggy. Trillia tries to wipe the rainwater off his hair and face with a towel that's already damp.

"You've been out for four days. Somewhere between coma and sleep. You gave us a terrible scare."

"Have we been on the road the whole time?"

Trillia shakes her head no as she checks her map pad.

"Three days. Traveling north and east from Durham along old Interstate 85. Right now we're near the ruins of Dinwiddie, Virginia."

"Headed toward the James River and Newport News," Phenix adds. "So we can get back on the inland waterway and go to Baltimore."

"Why there?"

Over the rumble of not-so-distant thunder John Drinan tries to remind Ricardo of details he should already know.

"That's where Sister Vena's people are. Tomoko and I thought that would be best, given the sort of sleep you've been in. Sister Vena was an expert on the dreaming phase."

Tomoko looks beyond the trees into the downpour.

"Unfortunately, she's been dead for some time. Her people are still around, though. Her nuns live in the Baltimore cathedral. Fornash's tribespeople know their whereabouts."

Images flood into Ricardo's mind.

"Fornash! How is the old guy doing?"

Glances flicker and flash among the circle of his fellow travelers, then out toward two of Fornash's people riding with them—a young man and a young woman, dressed in buckskins and moccasins, who at the moment are playing with Drinan's big dog under a tree a short distance away. Ricardo's more familiar companions look back to him at last. Tomoko takes a waterproof hat from her saddlebag and puts it on her head.

"Mark Fornash is dead."

"Dead? How?"

"We don't know how, exactly."

"We were afraid at first his people would blame us for his death," Trillia says, "especially since you were the last person to touch him while he was alive."

Ricardo fights down the feeling that something he did but cannot quite remember might have caused his friends pain.

"They didn't blame us?"

"They were *overjoyed* at what happened," John Drinan says. He sounds as if he still has trouble believing it. Trillia helps Ricardo out of his wet overclothes.

"I don't understand."

"Before everything happened in that ceremony of theirs," Trillia says, "some of his people told me Fornash's blessing was that he could 'soul-fly' and 'aerial voyage' endlessly. But that was also his curse. He couldn't take that final step into death, or transcendence, or wherever."

Tomoko nods, apparently struck by a thought.

"His partial immunity to the pandemic must have been a very rare type. That's the only explanation I can come up with for why his people call what happened an 'exchange of gifts.' "

"A what?" Ricardo asks, deeply confused—and just when he believed his thoughts were growing clearer, too. Drinan glances away from their escorts and back to him once more.

"They say you gave Mark something new. Something to which he had no final resistance. They say he gave you a couple of gifts too."

"Gifts?"

"Greater conscious control over your Wersign symptoms, according to them. Maybe something more, too, but they couldn't say exactly what."

"Do you think it's true?"

"You'd probably be the first to know, so pass the word on, okay?"

The strong downpour of the cloudburst, spending itself, slackens to a steady rain. Trillia wrings out the cloth she's been using to dry Ricardo.

"That's one more reason for us to go to Baltimore," she says. "Sister Vena's nuns are sure to know more about these things than we do."

"Why's that?"

"Their history and their reputation," John says, standing up from his crouch, knees clicking audibly. "Vena was obsessed with that space where physics pushes into metaphysics. When she was still in the islands, she used to discuss that sort of thing with Malika endlessly. If Mark Fornash did something to alter your condition via micro-psychokinesis or whatever, I can't think of anybody more up on how that might affect your disease than the nuns of Vena's New Baltimore Catechist Order."

Tomoko's bodyguard Caster nods, an impish smile growing on his face.

"You know what the locals around Chesapeake Bay call those nuns? The Sisters of Easeful Death."

Trillia scowls. Ricardo laughs, not really wanting to know why scattered bands of fishers, farmers, and hunters gave them that title.

"Now, why doesn't that make me eager to meet them? How are we going to get there, anyway? Where are *Sea Robin* and *Star Thrower*?"

"It was quicker to take you northeast overland," Tomoko says. "The afternoon before we left Durham, Fornash's people sent out riders to where they had our boats under guard. After the riders talk with your mermaids and merman, they're supposed to sail *Sea Robin* and *Star Thrower* north."

Trillia nods, consulting her map pad and tracing routes for Ricardo with her finger.

"Behind the Carolina capes here, past the Neuse and Pamlico rivers. Up the Alligator-Pungo Canal to the Alligator River. Across Pamlico Sound to Currituck, then up the Albemarle and Chesapeake Canal, eventually to Hampton Roads."

Following Trillia's outline, Ricardo sees an alternative in the soft glow of the map pad.

"Why not come up the Dismal Swamp Canal? That looks like a shorter route."

"It might be," Caster agrees, "but there are locks on that route, at South Mills and Deep Creek. Fornash's people don't think they can be opened. Impassable."

Trillia nods and returns to her tracing. With a fingernail, she presses on the map pad at the narrow neck of Hampton Roads, causing the pad to zoom in on that location, displaying finer-scale details.

"They're supposed to rendezvous with us at Hopewell on the James River, if they get there by the time we do. They might, too, even though they're making more distance. They're going by boat, with a day's head-start on us."

"What if they're not at Hopewell?"

"Then we're to meet them at the south end of the Hampton Roads Bridge Tunnel. After we meet up, we set out northward by boat through Chesapeake Bay for the empty city of Baltimore—like Phenix said."

John grabs Caster and Phenix by the shoulders and steers the younger men toward their Fornashian fellow travelers.

"Let's go get Aura and Markus before they wear out my dog. We'll set up camp and see if we can't roust up some fresh food."

Trillia and Tomoko help Ricardo into dry overclothes.

"So," Tomoko says, "now that you know what we've been up to, how about you? Where've you been?"

"Lots of places, in my dreams. I can't remember it all clearly, but some of it comes back into my head, from time to time. Strange stuff."

"Like what?" Trillia asks.

Ricardo smiles awkwardly at the two women.

"Like flying through the air back to the New Bahamas. In one dream I followed Trillia's grandfather around, but he didn't see me. I was invisible. I watched him working on something in his virtuality. Like a kaleidoscope of little crystal crabs, or tiny, bright-colored machines. I can only remember one phrase from that one: 'Gnomes of Wall Street.' "

He looks expectantly from one woman to the other.

"Doesn't ring any bells with me," Trillia says, standing up.

"Not much with me, either," Tomoko says. "Wall Street was a world market center. Now it's just empty towers—and maybe flooded streets, too, if the old dikes against the sea-rise haven't held. Do you think it's important?"

"I'm not sure. From what I saw, I got the sense Simon is now connected with these 'gnomes', too—whoever or whatever they are."

Tomoko nods and glances away from him, out beyond the forest canopy.

"The rain is letting up a little bit, but we're not going any further today. Can you walk to the tents and campfire, if we help you?"

Leaning on the two women, Ricardo finds his muscles are stiff. They ache from lack of use, but he can walk. His disorientation is largely gone. The cold damp of the air and the eye-watering smoke of the fire notwithstanding, he eats ravenously the fish—both fresh and jerked—set before him. Dried fruits, too, and fresh greens harvested out of the late spring woods.

After dinner the rainclouds dissipate. Sunset is a brief western dawn, bright and clean and golden. As the stiffness works out of his muscles, Ricardo finds he can move about unaided. He joins Trillia on a walk with Aura and Markus, along a path in the deep shade of the twilight wood. His compulsions to drum and dance are now much more under his control. His walk remains more rhythmic than in his island days, but that's not such a bad thing, in itself. Nothing wrong with having a little spring in your step, walking over the springtime earth.

The pale blond Aura and dark Markus come to an abrupt stop before them. They gesture for Ricardo and Trillia to look at what they've come across: a pair of plants, each with a whorl of three leaves, each leaf broad at the base and tapering to a distinct point. On each plant, from the center of the whorl, rises a three-petaled flower, white aging to rose.

"Your namesake plant," Aura tells Trillia, "or close to it. Each of these is a *Trillium*, so I guess two would be *Trillia*."

"We call them wake-robin," Markus says. "They bloom early in the spring. You don't usually see them in flower this late."

Staring at the plants, Trillia smiles, looking thoughtful and a bit embarassed.

"I never knew I was named for woodland flowers."

Ricardo examines the three-fold symmetries of the plant, the implied triangles emerging from the whorl, and glances at Trillia.

"They're pretty. Beautiful, in a subtle kind of way. But not flashy."

"Of course not. They're shade plants."

Ricardo smiles at the mild joke. Soon they return in deep twilight to the campsite. Parting company with Aura and Markus, Ricardo follows Trillia into the tent. Undressing for sleep, Ricardo feels much better, stronger. Feeling amorous, he strokes Trillia's hair, tries to caress her. She is pensive, then tearful. He whispers into her ear, from where he reclines behind her.

"Trillia, what's the matter, love?"

"Oh, nothing. Nothing—except we're both exiled in the wilderness, hundreds and hundreds of miles from home. Nothing—except you've got a fast-moving version of a disease that's always fatal. Nothing—except Mark Fornash told me people who aren't Wer just get a lightshow and a headache in that damned ritual we went through, but *I* saw all kinds of visions. Nothing—except you were nearly in a coma for four days and I didn't know if you'd ever wake up. Nothing—except, on top of all that, I'm pregnant with your baby."

The last statement blindsides Ricardo.

"Are you sure?"

"Of course I'm sure!"

Trillia breaks into sobs. Ricardo tries to comfort her, but it is some time before she will allow herself to be comforted. They comfort each other then, more and more solicitous of each other's feelings, until comforting becomes gentle lovemaking, a passion both joyful and sad. Before they slip into sleep, Ricardo realizes he lives in a changed world now, with transformed possibilities and responsibilities.

When he wakes the next morning, Trillia is looking at him, an expression of love and concern hovering above him in the blue-gray light of their blue-gray tent.

"Just making sure your sleep wasn't a relapse."

"Well, good morning to *you* too, I suppose."

She tosses her "pillow" of rolled up clothes at him.

"You know what I mean."

They join the others for breakfast. The sky becomes clear and bright, with a good breeze out of the southwest.

"If our counterparts on the water haven't run into any serious obstacles," John says, finishing up the last of his meal, "then they should make good time today with this wind. We'd better make time too. Hopewell's not far, but we do have to pass through the Petersburg end of the old Richmond-Petersburg metrop. You up for that, Ricardo?"

"I think so. I'm feeling pretty good."

"Feeling anymore 'conscious control' of your, er, symptoms?"

Ricardo, standing up from the log he sat on while eating, considers a moment before answering.

"I don't feel nearly as rhythm-driven as I did—before."

John pats his big dog on the flank.

"Think that's a result of what my old friend did to you in the ceremony? Or just some new phase in your condition?"

"I can't really say."

After the breakfast party breaks up, they move off to their respective tents and shelters, taking everything out and down, then packing it all up. Ricardo packs his share of the gear onto his own horse now. A black beast with a white star on its forehead—a "gelding Arabian," Tomoko calls it. Strapping his gear onto the horse, Ricardo welcomes the prospect of spending some cowboy time conscious in the saddle instead of playing Sleeping Beauty in a travois. He takes some of Trillia's gear from her and packs it onto his horse.

"Once we reach Baltimore, you really ought to just stay there and rest. You don't have to head up the coast to New York. You *are* pregnant, after all."

"I'm not *that* pregnant," Trillia retorts, swinging herself up into the saddle of her dappled gray mare. "You won't be shed of me that easily. I'm not more than three months gone yet. We go through this together."

Ricardo climbs into the saddle. He should have expected such an answer.

"Suit yourself."

Trillia's always been stubborn. Just like her grandfather. Which is strange, too. Ricardo wouldn't have expected that stubborn old man to let them get away into the wilderness without pursuing them, or at least spying on them—especially his granddaughter. Ricardo can't help thinking they're being tracked, *watched*, somehow.

From Dinwiddie to Petersburg they cross roadbeds eroded and summer-buckled and frost-heaved. Rust, mold, vines, and weeds reclaim permanently parked cars—either solitary or in sudden, tight, traffic-jammed masses, somehow more orderly than the dead traffic chaoses encountered earlier.

"I've seen this pattern before," John Drinan says. "EMP—electromagnetic pulse."

"Thank God there were only sporadic instances of that," Tomoko says. "Much more of it and we would have lost what solar power we still have. Most of the nonbiological computing, too."

Ricardo nods, though he doesn't completely understand it. He thinks of hazy childhood history-lessons, old nuclear blast footage.

The roads, like broken stone threads, still prevent the once-fragmented forests from reweaving their green blanket over everything. Beyond the interchanges the travelers see Petersburg slowly disappearing into resurgent wilderness. Those buildings still standing and visible after fire and rain show the hard wear of long neglect and abandon. Wooden homes gone paintless and gray, roofs overgrown with moss and weeds. Gravity and weather untuck the mason's careful lines, coaxing brick buildings into new, less predictable patterns and shapes.

Buildings of concrete and steel stand mostly glassless. Unintended windowbox gardens everywhere hang flowers on the sky. From every empty edifice, the conquering army flies its banners of rust red and spring green. As the little group of eight travels on toward Hopewell, John and Tomoko talk of Mayan ruins, cities that disappeared into the jungles of Central America, were excavated and cleaned up for the tourist trade during the twentieth century—only to be swallowed up by the rain forests again, now. Ricardo thinks of cathedrals and temple-complexes vanishing into forests and deserts throughout the world.

Passing through the burn-scarred ruins of Hopewell, they come to the James River, glinting in afternoon light. The travelers shout happily at seeing *Star Thrower* and *Sea Robin* not far offshore, beyond the broken and sunken docks. The loud hallooing of Ricardo's party brings the boats' temporary crews up on deck and sets their four Mer escorts leaping skyward from the river again and again. The Merfolk are glad to see them, but Ricardo expects they'll soon remember to pout at having been left on their own for so long.

The temporary crews of the boats—two in each—row raft and dinghy ashore. As the four Duke crewmen take over the horse train from the overland party, Ricardo notices they seem as much *relieved* as joyful at the reunion. He asks Aura and Markus about it, but all they will say is the crews had to pass the "Plains of Ash and Glass," the "Black Narrows" near where the James joins Chesapeake Bay—places their own party must now go. The Fornashians also fear someone they call the "Commander of the Capital," and the "Nooseway," too, around the "city of toppled pillars."

"Some kind of bad juju," Trillia whispers to Ricardo with a dismissive smirk. Ricardo wants to agree, wants to dismiss all of it as mere superstition, too. He would gladly do so, were it not for his bad dreams, in which he has heard that word "Nooseway" before. He wishes he could understand those dreams, or this world, more clearly. If his ongoing sense of permanent déjà-vu is the "other gift" Fornash gave him, Ricardo wishes the old shaman would have kept it to himself.

Tomoko, Caster, Aura, John, and a happily barking Oz take over *Sea Robin*. Ricardo, Trillia, Phenix, and Markus assume command of the *Star Thrower*. The Merfolk have remembered to pout—as predicted—and insist on keeping a low profile. With a strong following wind the boats make their way swiftly down the ever-broadening James River, the two of them running abreast as clouds begin to scud in the sky from out of the southwest.

Ricardo soon sees why the Fornashians referred to plains of ash and glass. Near what Trillia's map pad labels Chippokes Plantation, the greenery on both sides of the river goes strange and twisted. Further on, the trees and the usually overgrown undergrowth dwindle away. What buildings survive are more and more severely damaged, no matter what their construction. Before long the greenery gradually decreases to nothing but tough grasses on burnt, runneled earth, between piles of scorched stone debris, wildly twisted steel, ironwork melted and puddled like spent rust-colored candles. All around them they see the rough debris-filled lines of foundations, for buildings eliminated not by the long slow death of wind and water but by the quick bright flash of heat and blast.

Trillia, awestruck, looks from her outdated map pad to the world around them, and back again.

"Newport News is supposed to be right over there. Hampton, Norfolk, Portsmouth—they're all gone."

From behind *Sea Robin*'s wheel, Tomoko shouts against the stiffening breeze out of the clouding sky that pushes them toward the ruins of the Hampton Roads Bridge Tunnel.

"Nuclear strike. Multiple warheads, looks like. See where the ground has turned to glass? Vitrified, from blast heat."

Ricardo has heard of the damage nuclear weapons could do; he has seen pictures, but as he steers *Star Thrower* past it, he realizes how little any of that prepared him for what he sees around him. Dappled by the clouds racing overhead, the shifting light on the ruined landscape makes Ricardo think of fast-forwarded media, time-lapsed images of eons passing. Curiosity about this blast-shattered place overcomes even the Merfolk. Ricardo catches them furtively spyhopping behind the boats.

"But I thought there wasn't a nuclear war during the last days!" Tomoko replies through hands cupped to her mouth.

"There wasn't. Nothing so formal. The nuke strikes were sporadic—not organized according to any sort of battle plan. Only a few actual launches— lucky for us. A total spasm atomic war, a nuclear winter on top of the pandemic and collapse—and none of us would be here to shout about it."

"But how did this happen?" Trillia calls across.

From Tomoko, John takes over the steering of *Sea Robin*—and the shouted conversation.

"Who knows? Doomsday submarine crews. Silo sitters. Firing on their own orders after the rest of the world came crashing down. The people of these cities were probably already dead of the plague and the collapse. Maybe months or even years earlier."

"That's even crazier than the city burners," Phenix says. "At least the Purple Cloud Commandos watched the fireworks they set."

They make their way through the massive remains of the bridge piers—broken, scorched, blackened, and weathered—at the south end of what was once the Bridge Tunnel. Maneuvering amid the charred stone-and-steel stumps, Ricardo understands why Fornash's people call this place the Black Narrows. He glances at Markus with renewed respect. The younger man may be covered in tribal tattoos and piercings, his earrings and necklace may be made of bird skulls and feathers and pieces of circuitboard from the guts of ancient computers, but he and his people weren't just talking about "bad juju."

"Then the crews who brought us the boats," Trillia says, "the evils they were talking about are—what? Radiation?"

"Most likely *memories* of that," Tomoko says. "After all these years, radiation levels probably aren't much more than normal background. Still might be some hot spots, though. We'd better not linger too long here."

Ricardo agrees. Trillia spells him on piloting *Star Thrower* as they leave the great desolation of Hampton Roads and come into the waters of Chesapeake Bay proper. Off to the east, in the late sunlight, the broken span of Chesapeake Bay Bridge is hazy with cloud-dappled distance. Ricardo thinks of images he's seen of Stonehenge. These ruins might not be as old, but before long they may become just as inscrutable.

"Hey," Markus asks, looking at the image on Trillia's map pad. "You people want to get to New York, right? Why not just shoot out between Cape Charles and Cape Henry here, then go up the seaward side of this 'Delmarva Peninsula'? That looks a whole lot faster."

"That's a long run across open water," Ricardo answers. "Not a good idea in a boat this size, especially if these clouds mean the weather's about to turn."

Trillia nods from behind the ship's wheel, swiping a stray strand of sun-lightened blond bangs away from her face.

"We'd have to backtrack to see Sister Vena's people in Baltimore, too. This way we stop in Baltimore, then continue north and east to the Chesapeake and Delaware Canal. We take the C & D across the peninsula, into Delaware Bay."

Markus shakes his head.

"Running up the Chesapeake, right past the Commander's people?"

Trillia looks hard at him, deliberately wheeling into a more northerly course.

"That's what I don't get. The whole planet's *depopulated*! How does this Commander person have enough followers to even commit horrors—much less find people to commit them *on*? We've seen so few people and so much uninhabited land, you'd think there'd be nothing left to fight and kill about."

Markus shrugs.

"The Commander says Werfolk are abominations to be destroyed at any cost. But then, you islanders probably can't imagine such a thing . . ."

Before Trillia can respond, John calls to them from *Sea Robin*.

"Aura here doesn't think it's a good idea to head north past the Potomac. Any ideas on that?"

"We were just talking about the same thing over here," Ricardo calls back, looking from the other boat to Trillia's map pad and back. "I think they may have a point. We should make it to Tangier Island just after sunset. Why don't we anchor there for the night, then early tomorrow morning sail into Tangier Sound, east of Smith Island and Marsh Island? Then we can sail Hooper Strait, between Bloodsworth Island and Bishops Head, back into the Bay proper—for the run straight up to Baltimore. That keeps us well clear of the mouth of the Potomac."

John looks at Tomoko. Gesturing toward Ricardo, she says, "He was right about getting abducted by Fornash's people, wasn't he? I trust his instincts."

Everyone, even Aura and Markus, finally agrees. Ricardo feels relief that the matter is settled, but also an uncomfortable sense of responsibility. It's *his* plan, after all. He hopes it doesn't prove shortsighted.

The wind continues to favor them. In twilight they reach Tangier Island—less an island than a collection of beaches, marshy sand spits, glades, inlets, and small wooded rises. After the boats drop anchor, the Merfolk help him and Trillia hunt up a fresh catch to supplement their delayed meal. Earth and sea both are fertile and beautiful here, protected from the worst of wind and wave by the shape of the great bay—and spared too from the horror visited upon Hampton Roads.

They pass a night blessedly free of incident. Ricardo begins to wonder whether the Commander of the Capital is only another local memory—and, if so, whether they might have let their fears get the better of them. Eating breakfast with the others, he does not recall having had any bad dreams during the night. If they were unpleasant, he doesn't want to remember them anyway.

Dawn lights the low morning mist to a golden fog around them—much to the relief of Aura and Markus. Not so thick as to hinder navigation, the fog and mist is still thick enough to cloak their presence from distant observers. The air is too still for sail, so they use their boats' quiet electric motors instead. On stored solar power they motor north, from Pocomoke into Tangier Sound, behind Smith, then Marsh Islands.

Through the fog and mist it's difficult to tell where one island ends and the next begins. The morning mist dampens all sound—which, paradoxically, makes all the travelers more prone to silence than talk. The Merfolk have vanished without a trace. The birds and insects, too, seem to be holding their songs, if not their breath. Even John's big dog barks not at all. The whisper of electric motors and water lapping against hulls are sound enough only to convince them they have not all gone deaf overnight.

In such silent and ethereal fashion they run Hooper Strait, passing between Bloodsworth Island and the eastern shore before coming again into the center of the Bay. Silent as a coracle moon in a midmorning sky, they pass north of the Patuxent River between Governors Run and Scientists Cliffs. The wind picks up there and the mist and fog dissipate. Shutting down the electric motors, they unfurl *Star Thrower*'s and *Sea Robin*'s sails into the strengthening breeze, letting the wind wing them over the Bay like white-winged skimming birds.

Their fear of discovery dissipates like the fog as the wind urges them along, faster and faster. After the long quiet of the morning, their run up the bay now becomes a raucous, noisy race between the two boats, a bow-riding pair of Merfolk surging ahead and falling behind with each shift in the boats' positions.

Still they see no one. Under full sail, the boats and their shouting crews and leaping Merfolk race toward the finish line, the storm-scarred bridge linking Annapolis and the eastern shore via Kent Island. *Sea Robin* passes that line first. Not far beyond the bridge, however, as they are headed into more open water again, Phenix lets out a shout and points back toward the bridge.

"Ho! We've got company!"

Following Phenix's pointed and spoken directions, they see three riders on horseback on the span behind them. The landsmen, clad in blue and black, are close enough for Ricardo to see that one of them has brought what looks like binoculars up to his face. The strangers are still far enough away, however, that they present no immediate threat, especially given the speed of *Star Thrower* and *Sea Robin* over the water. Aura and Markus call to each other over the water, wondering if the "company" they've spied might be some of the Commander's people.

Onward the boats and their Merfolk escorts fly. The travelers on the decks, at least, are more serious and somber now as they turn northwest. Sailing up the Patapsco River, they come into Baltimore Harbor at mid-afternoon, passing the remains of a shattered and blackened bridge span.

Nearly all the buildings around the harbor show extensive fire damage, beginning at the area Trillia's map pad calls the Dundalk Marine Terminal and continuing counterclockwise almost all the way around—past Fort Holabird, up to the ruins of the Maryland Science Center and Baltimore Museum of Industry, around to Waterview Avenue and Lansdowne, to Frankhurst Avenue and Fairfield. It's a different sort of destruction from what they saw at Hampton Roads, though. The scene here looks almost as if somebody or some group purposely set the entire harbor ablaze—perhaps by blowing up a chemical or fuel tanker.

Such an action strikes Ricardo as insane but somehow not surprising. He has already seen too many examples of the damage the last days of global madness wrought on the landscape. The destruction here might not have been the product of accident or of mindless mob mentality, but something carefully willed, planned, and executed.

Hulks burned above the water line and half-sunk wrecks barricade much of the harbor. They moor as close to harborside as they can. Leaving the four Merfolk to guard *Sea Robin* and *Star Thrower*, the travelers make their way ashore by dinghy and raft. After they tie those craft up for their return, Trillia with her map pad takes the lead—with some help from Aura and Markus. They follow her away from the harbor, through rubble-strewn streets.

"Everybody at Duke said the New Baltimore Catechists are housed at the Baltimore cathedral. I think that's what's listed in my map pad as the Basilica of the Assumption of the Blessed Virgin Mary."

"How will we know it when we see it?" John asks. "The farther we get from the harbor, the more intact the buildings are."

"I've got the street grid and location. That ought to be some help. The map pad says the cathedral is Neoclassical Revival style—with a 'classical' façade and 'Ionic pediment.' "

"Just look for tall pillars," Tomoko says, noting the uncomprehending expressions of the mainlanders. "With their tops shaped like rams' horns or double scrolls."

"Onion-shaped domes on the belfry towers," Trillia says. "Probably green in color. Each one topped by a Latin cross. A big central dome, too."

They get lost in the labyrinthine, debris-strewn spaces of the broken city. The Wer and half-Wer mainlanders, however—Caster, Aura, Markus, even Phenix—seem to possess a far stronger sense of direction than the islanders. Ricardo feels it growing in him, too, though he doubts Trillia would believe it. Maybe he's more aware of the subtle signs of human use now than he was in the past. Even the barely discernible traces of trails through the debris-strewn streets.

At last they see the cathedral ahead of them. Broad steps lead up to a portico whose pedimental roof is supported by tall columns crowned with graceful rams'-horn scrolls. Squat, greenish onion domes cap belfry towers. A broader, much larger dome stands farther back, and less elevated. The stone of the building itself is grayish-brown in color—"porphyritic granite," Trillia's map pad calls it.

The building is no silent monument to the past, however. On the grand porch, women bustle about—dressed in white saris bordered with blue piping, the original subtlety of their garments thrown off by the large bright red cross sewn on the back of each. As the travelers walk onto the portico proper, Ricardo sees the women are ministering to perhaps a dozen people in black gowns on cots and trundle beds. Most of them rest peacefully. Others convulse slowly—or spasm, more rapidly. Some of the ministering women—all of whom carry shoulder-slung small harps on their backs— play music or sing softly to their charges.

These black-gowned people are patients, Ricardo realizes. Soul-fliers in the last stage of what Fornash called the shamanic complex. This place is not a hospital but a hospice. The women bustling about are nuns of the New Baltimore Catechist Order, the Sisters of Easeful Death. Tomoko catches one of them lightly by an elbow.

"Sister, we were friends of Sister Vena's, in the New Bahamas. I'm Dr. Tomoko Fukuda. This is John Drinan. We know Sister Vena has passed on, but we were wondering if we might talk with your current Mother Superior."

At the words "Sister Vena," "New Bahamas," "Tomoko Fukuda," and "John Drinan," the young nun's eyes grow wider and wider, until Ricardo thinks they'll climb clear up into her sisterly wimple. A look of unexpected beatitude spreads over the woman's entire face.

"Would you and your friends please follow me? I'll take you to Mother Madeleine immediately. You are awaited."

The young nun leads them into the building. A broken-rainbow twilight prevails within—product of afternoon sunlight shining through a series of stained-glass windows, set in recessed, arched panels along both sides of the cathedral. The light reminds Ricardo of the poem Mark Fornash spoke at the beginning of the remembrance ritual at the Rhine Center—even more than the terminal patients' black gowns remind him of the garb worn by Fornash's initiates, before that ritual began. He wonders if the black gowns and robes might be echoes of those last-day legends of black-robed souls rising into the sky.

About him, Ricardo sees boxlike pews, then the shining pipework of the organ loft. As he walks forward with the others, he realizes the building is cruciform in shape, vaulted by several shallow domes—the entire structure a well-balanced juxtaposition of spheres and cubes. At the heart of the building's crossing arms, they pass under a large dome decorated with circular panels which somehow remind him of eyes.

Above those rounds, near the top of the dome, is a broad, circular trompe l'oeil depiction of clouds and blue sky. At the zenith and center of that overarching vault appears an image of a small dove surrounded by an overwhelming burst of feathery, lambent light radiating away in all directions. Staring at it, he thinks of John's strange tales of the Light that knocked him into this universe from a nearby one.

He has to walk fast to catch up with the young nun and the rest of his party. He barely has time to note another dome trompe l'oeil (this one showing the Virgin Mary assumed into the sky, amidst cherubs and the clouds of heaven) before following the group into an alcove not far away.

The young nun speaks to an older Sister sitting quietly there—meditating or praying. With a remarkable ease and grace, the older nun stands and approaches the visitors. She shakes hands with all of them, introducing herself in a soft voice, her eyes sparkling agelessly out of a wrinkled face.

"It's a great honor to meet people who were so big a part of Sister Vena's experiences. Come with me downstairs. We maintain a shrine to her memory in the New Crypt. We can speak there in less hushed tones."

Following Mother Madeleine, the travelers wend their way down helical stairs into the cooler, damper, more echoing confines of the New

Crypt. As they walk through the arched and colonnaded underground space, Ricardo notices that young Phenix pays particular attention to the mortuary elements of the decor—ossuaries, reliquaries, walls stacked from floor to ceiling with carefully ordered skulls and bones. When he speaks up, the teenager can't quite keep the disdain from his voice.

"Is this why they call you the 'Sisters of Easeful Death'? Because you bury people?"

"During the days of the pandemic," the Mother Superior says, "Sister Vena recognized the great need for preparation in dealing with the rigors of madness and death. We are known as the Sisters of Easeful Death because of our hospice work. We are thanatologists. We try to help every person we encounter develop a mindset and experience a setting appropriate to his or her needs at the end of life. That's why we travel with small harps—to play and sing them on their way."

Tomoko nods as they walk slowly through the deep twilight of the subterranean vaults.

"That's why Vena turned abjurer and fled the islands so early. She couldn't bear staying isolated on the islands while the rest of the world died."

Mother Madeleine brings them into a dim, candlelit alcove. She gestures them toward the twenty or so chairs ordered in rows there.

"The idea of such preparation is a very old one, actually. At least as old as the Egyptian or Tibetan books of the dead."

Ricardo, taking a seat, finds he is facing a maroon-curtained space. Over the top of that curtain he can see an arched niche of indeterminate depth.

"Are those the sources you draw from? Or does what you do come mostly out of Catholicism?"

Mother Madeleine glides into the center of the space between the rows of chairs and the curtain.

"The faith that has grown up among us preserves the old religions, while at the same time evolving something quite new from them. We follow Sister Vena's example in that. But I shouldn't be answering these questions. There's a better authority. Ask Sister Vena yourself."

The travelers glance at each other. Is the Most Reverend Mother encouraging them to pray? Or is she a few beads short of a rosary?

"I thought she was dead," Markus says, trying to be polite.

Smiling, Mother Madeleine walks toward the curtain.

"She is—but as I said, we've built a shrine to her memory."

The elderly Mother Superior pulls the curtain aside with a flourish. Before them, in a tall upright aquarium tank like something from a Houdini water-escape, a woman in nun's habit appears to float, glowing firefly yellow-green. Atop the tank is a pod of sensors—optics, audials, olfactories. Slender manipulator arms on the sides of the tank end in tactile force-feedback pads. Over speakers at the base of the tank comes a voice in subtly accented English.

"Tomoko! John! I knew you'd come!"

Beside him, Ricardo sees Phenix and Caster startle at the unexpected sound and image. He wonders if the apparition's words somehow explain the young nun's comment that the visitor's arrival here was expected. Nearby, John peers at the tank in disbelief.

"Vena, is that you?"

A tinkling sound—laughter meeting wind chimes—emanates from the speakers, filling the small alcove. It echoes unpredictably in the subterranean space.

"Yes and no. There's no *body* in here, but there's *somebody* in here. We found this biocybertank at Johns Hopkins—a prototype, part of the original joint project with MIT and Stanford. Sorry about the bad yellowish color, but they weren't much on graphics that early in the development process. My image is made from steerable bioluminescent microbes, all running *lucifer*ase—firefly juice!"

The virtual Sister Vena gives her tinkling laugh again. Tomoko nods, less taken aback by the apparition than the rest of them—especially Phenix and Caster, who don't seem to have had much experience dealing with weird virtuality tech. *They* have grown very quiet.

"But what *are* you?" Tomoko asks.

"Technically I'm a simulacrum running on a quantum biocomputer. Malika was right, John. Quantum, bio, and code—they all link up."

"But how?" John asks.

The virtual Vena laughs and rolls her eyes.

"*Everyone* asks that! Not my specialty, you know, but this is how I think of it. My Sisters here recorded a big snapshot of the process of my mind before I died. From all the holographic wave patterns of my brain and consciousness they created a complex soliton probability wave—a wave of translation. The wave interference pattern of my consciousness, stored holographically, forms the basis of a 'brainless' yet cognitive artifact. A conscious quantum simulacrum, if you like—though arguably not a human consciousness anymore. This firefly facsimile is how I choose to represent myself."

Trillia shakes her head and turns toward Mother Madeleine.

"Why would you want to do such a thing? No offense intended, but it's like talking to the living dead."

"We wanted to keep her memory alive the best way we knew how. This biocybernetic intelligence has been programmed with everything *we* know of Sister Vena, in addition to the 'snapshot' of her cognitive processes. We wanted the best and most responsive expert system we could create, so we could continually test against it the doctrines of our developing New Catechism."

"Enough about what or who I am," says Sister Vena. "We need to get back to your question, young man—the sources of what we believe, which is something I *do* know something about."

The simulacrum Vena is staring right at Ricardo. He finds it disquieting—rather like being interrogated by a giant Tinkerbell.

"I realized that the way in which the latter stages of the pandemic manifested themselves were profoundly shaped by both cultural context and individual consciousness. *That* led me to develop a syncretic personal faith that rejected neither of my own cultural reference frames, Hindu *or* Catholic. Our experimental faith continues to elaborate itself, incorporating elements not only from the great world religions that came out of the Middle East and the Indian subcontinent, but from all the religious and metaphysical traditions of the world that once was."

"Sounds pretty polyglot," Ricardo says, finding his tongue at last.

"It might strike you that way but, as I said, it's an *experimental* faith. We systematically search for better and better approximations to the truths reflected 'through a glass darkly' in all human religious impulses. Not just religion either, by any means. The sciences very much involve searching for better approximations to truth, or at least to reality. The Sisters of our Order are always searching out those places where the physical and metaphysical intersect."

"But what's the goal of all this 'approximating'?" Trillia asks.

"Finding where the omega point of physics meets the omega point of faith. Where the singularity at the heart of the mind meets the singularity at the heart of the black hole."

"You're losing me," Trillia says.

"Long before the pandemic, a physicist named Tipler postulated a class of cosmological models in which—though our universe is finite in both space and time—as this universe is *steered* toward an end-point of Big Crunch gravitational collapse, the gravitational shearing forces of the twisting and deforming of space-time rise toward *infinity*. As our universe heads toward that singularity, those chaotic, highly unstable and violent oscillations provide *unlimited* energy. Another pre-pandemic theorist, Turing, held that there is no upper limit on the number of computational steps that are physically possible. In the final moments of a universe steered toward the Big Crunch, the energy available for computation becomes infinite. In an infinite number of computational steps there is time for an infinite number of thoughts. The subjective experience of time itself thus becomes infinite."

Ricardo feels as if he is being catechized by this sisterly simulacrum. Whatever odd vision of "infinite mind" Fornash left behind at his departure—and whatever temporary reprieve his contact with Fornash may have given him—Ricardo remains all too aware of his own nearness to mortality. He shakes his head at the distance and abstractness of what the simulacrum Sister is trying to explain.

"But all that's at the far end of time—and that's a long way away from any of us," he says.

"Not necessarily," Vena explains patiently. "Albert Szent-Gyögyi, nearly one hundred years before the pandemic, said the brain is 'not an organ of thinking, but an organ of survival, like fang and claw. It is made in such a way that we accept as truth what is merely advantage.' Yet at omega, truth and advantage are in fact one."

"How so?"

"Such a future as the one that Tipler postulated—one in which *this* universe becomes infinitely 'open' computationally, even as it becomes completely 'closed' spatiotemporally—such a future is of *advantage* to any intelligence. It is in the best interest of intelligences everywhere in the universe to *steer* the universe toward the omega point during the course of gravitational collapse. The future is not fixed, so it can't be broken!"

Trillia is too busy frowning in disbelief to appreciate the sisterly construct's little joke.

" 'Intelligences'? Plural?" she asks.

Sister Vena nods wavelessly in her tank.

"The final singularity of the omega point is omniscient in that the 'society' or 'ecology' of minds at that endpoint knows everything it is physically possible to know. The omega point is omnipresent, since the whole of physical space-time is, at the endpoint, filled with that ecology of minds. The omega point is omnipotent because, at the moment of singularity, it controls *absolutely* the course of events taking place in the material universe. The result is an apocalyptic genesis, in which eternity is born out of time."

Tomoko laughs.

"Omniscient, omnipresent, omnipotent! Your religion makes physics sound like theology. Does it make theology sound like physics? How is this 'apocalyptic genesis' supposed to take place?"

"According to the theologian Pierre Teilhard de Chardin, the movement toward omega is less an apocalypse than a 'co-evolutionary convergence.' The noosphere, the realm of thought and knowledge, becomes involuted into what Teilhard called a Hyperpersonal Consciousness, which he felt would be fully achieved at omega. At that point, matter and consciousness would reach the terminal phase of their convergent integration and become one. Absolutely indistinguishable."

This Turing-Tipler-Teilhard nonsense is getting us nowhere, Ricardo thinks. *Who cares what's supposed to happen in some distant hypothetical future?*

"That sounds like it's almost as far down the time line as the Big Crunch at the end of the universe," he says aloud.

"Again, not necessarily. Both Teilhard and Tipler thought too 'locally.' Teilhard's mistake was that he thought his theory was just about *this* world, Earth. And he didn't foresee how much the development of non-human intelligences, particularly machine intelligences, would speed up the progress toward omega. Tipler's mistake was that he thought omega could only take place at the end of *this* universe, at a big crunch. What he didn't realize is how the existence of the *plenum* changes all that."

Near him, Ricardo sees John sit up straighter, apparently struck by a thought.

"Since even the multiverse of the pre-pandemic physicists was essentially infinite," John says, "the 'point of infinite energy for infinite computational steps' already exists—if one can borrow, for even an instant, the computational resources of an infinite number of universes."

"Exactly," the simulacrum Sister says, smiling as if at a pupil who has just demonstrated a particular aptitude for tangential thinking. "Parallel universe processing—rather than the serial or sequential processing those earlier theorists were stuck on."

Tomoko hugs herself a bit against the cool damp of the underground shrine.

"But what do these omega points have to do with the singularities you mentioned?" she asks.

"In essence they're all varieties of the same thing. What Tipler and Teilhard called omega, what the Tetragrammaton people called a quantum information density singularity, what the pre-pandemic astrophysicists called the singularity at the heart of the black hole, what Mark Fornash and Malika Hardesty, following the consciousness theorists, call the 'singularity at the heart of the mind'—all are the same transuniversal thing."

Trillia shakes her head as if it has begun to hurt.

"I can't see how consciousness and black holes can be linked, much less somehow the 'same.'"

Sister Vena responds so patiently, Ricardo wonders whether that patience is "remembered" from the original, or arises from the fact that this nun is a construct running on a strange biological machine.

"Think *advantage* again. Before the pandemic, physicists believed they had discovered proof that there is a natural selection of 'favored' universes. When a black hole forms, it produces another universe from the singularity in its interior, creating another expanse of space and time disjoint from our own—a 'daughter' universe. The physical laws in the daughter differ from those in the parent, but only slightly. The number of progeny a given universe *has* depends on the physical laws prevailing within the parent universe. There is a selection pressure such that, after many generations or iterations, the subset of the plenum those physicists called the multiverse had to increasingly be dominated by those universes that generate the greatest number of progeny. Our own universe is the outcome of such selection. It is maximally efficient at spawning new universes—more black holes, more singularities. Our universe tends toward the production of singularities—both through the physical process of black hole formation and the mental process of consciousness and decision-making."

A deep frown creases the whole of Trillia's face. From experience, Ricardo knows the stubbornness that expression signifies.

"How do you make that last jump?" Trillia asks. "I don't see it."

Abruptly Ricardo remembers something he scanned before leaving the New Bahamas. Pieces begin to fall into place as he looks from Trillia to the nun in the tank.

"I think I do. D. B. Albert talks about it, in *Spontaneous Human Consciousness*. Only what you called the ecology of minds, or hyperpersonal consciousness—all personal consciousness completely integrated at omega—I think that's what Albert calls archetypes."

Jarringly, Vena's virtual persona disappears, replaced by large, yellow-lettered text, scrolling upward where her face had been. Ricardo recognizes it as the passages he read in Albert's work:

The energy that feeds the universal intersection system appears as portal experience *in consciousness and as* event horizons *in the world. Consciousness and portal experience are different aspects of the same thing, related as microcosm is to macrocosm. Consciousness is the intersection of body and spirit in the mind of the individual, while portal experience is a joining of personal and universal intersection.*

Like the distinction between particle and wave, however, as human consciousness has continued to evolve under the influence of the archetypes, the distinction between microcosm and macrocosm has begun to dissolve. Through mode-locking, universal energy is available dynamically, though not necessarily causally, to every dynamical system in the universe. The energy that fuels the black-hole furnaces in quasars and the galactic cores in the physical universe is the same energy that archetypes fuel within the psyche—moving systems beyond causation, to dynamicality.

Since all consciousness is a variety of portal experience, then consciousness is simply where Otherworld meets this world, just as an event horizon is where singularity meets space-time. Mystical experiences in religious vocabulary, and consciousness in Jungian vocabulary, and event horizons in scientific vocabulary are all the same thing expressed in different languages: points at which other or spirit meets the spatiotemporal world.

After they've all had time to read it, the Vena construct reappears and speaks again.

"Yes. Forces that exist in both the psyche and the plenum, to the degree that the psyche and the plenum are self-similar. I think of them as plenum bodhisattvas, who forego nirvana until all and everything is fit for that bliss. Albert wasn't thinking plenum theory when he wrote that, but it fits. Think of 'spatiotemporal world' as the multiverse of all physically possible universes. Think of 'other' or 'spirit' as that larger system of all logically possible universes, out of which the multiverse, as a subset, is always coming into being. I've said it before, as Madeleine can tell you: Consciousness is a shortcut for getting from matter to spirit, which have nevertheless always been connected the long way around."

Trillia's frown, Ricardo sees, has softened somewhat. She's a pragmatist and realist, yes—but also pragmatic and realistic enough to remain open to things which at first glance seem idealistic and fantastic.

"But what is there in that 'shortcut' that brings all those theorists and theories together?" she asks.

"The same goal unites them all, whether they know it or not. We are more than just individual creatures subject to the laws of physics or societies. We are also conscious agents of principles—forces, archetypes, spirits, plenum bodhisattvas, ecologies of mind at the end of time, what have you—which transcend space and time but also *work through* space and time."

"How?" Tomoko asks pointedly. "I don't see how the physics and the metaphysics line up."

"In any universe, time ends at the moment when the energy available to computation, to *thought*, becomes infinite. If, as the pre-pandemic physicists contended, other times are just special cases of other universes, then those forces from the end of time in *one* universe can influence the past in *other* universes."

Trillia shakes her head.

"What would lead them to do that? Why should they care?"

The virtual Vena smiles broadly.

"Teilhard said that at omega, all consciousnesses are integrated into Hyperpersonal Consciousness by love. Love is why they care. If that's too mystical for you, say instead that those universes and their intelligences which trend toward consciousness and enlightenment have an evolutionary advantage, because such universes maximize their production of singularities."

"You still haven't told us *how* that happens," Trillia persists.

"Each decision of every mind in all the universes of the plenum not only sheds photons but also generates a minuscule black hole, a subnanosingularity. On the other side of each of those tiny black holes, below the Planck scale, a nearly parallel universe branches off."

"The road taken *here* may not have been taken *there*," John says quietly. "Alternate universes. Just like Malika says."

"And what happened to you, John, is proof that there is a *there* there. Our role as conscious creatures is to discern the pattern of this evolutionary intelligence existing throughout the plenum. We can't fulfill that role, though, until we can scale up from the sub-Planck quantum level to the classical level, where we live and think. Our goal, then, must be to *exteriorize* the singularity-making capacity of consciousness. To scale it up in a controllable fashion, so that all those singularities and omega points great and small *line up*—bringing the biosphere, noosphere, infosphere, and universe into conjunction with those plenum forces influencing us from beyond time."

"And you think this can be done?" Tomoko asks, sounding skeptical but also impressed by the wonder of such a possibility.

"It has already been done, elsewhere and elsewhen. Once the singularity-making capacity of consciousness is exteriorized, parallel universe processing is a reality. Infinite energy becomes available for infinite thought."

Ricardo sees John nod. The tattooed older man seems to have considered the consequences already.

"Time ends," John says. "The door in the vault of heaven swings open."

"What you experienced, John, suggests that everything *can* line up. We *can* pass into that singularity, that otherness, that omega point—and come out again in a different universe. The fact that it *has* been done is proof that it *can* be done."

Ricardo glances at Trillia, his beloved pragmatic realist. He can see she doesn't believe it *all*, but is nonetheless considering it.

"But the only way to know there is to go there," Ricardo says. "As Mark Fornash said—not long before he died."

The simulacrum of Sister Vena glances down, away from the eyes of all her visitors. When she speaks again, Ricardo wonders if the simulacrum can counterfeit emotion—it sounds so real.

"Ah. I hadn't heard that. 'Died' may be the wrong term for Mark, however. He understood that we have a conscious kinship with all things. That the universe is symbolic and imbued with intentionality. Death is a seductive but illusory substitution—the toxic mimic of transcendence. A substitute we accept only when we have convinced ourselves transcendence is impossible and therefore completely unavailable to us. Mark wouldn't have accepted that substitute. He understood how much room there is, in the plenum, for possibility."

Brave words, Ricardo thinks. He wishes he could bring himself to believe them. As if reading his mind, the simulacrum Sister Vena transfixes him with her gaze.

"How did he die?"

"From the new variant of the pandemic I gave him."

"A new variant? Would you allow me to take a sample from you—to analyze it?"

"That's part of the reason we came here," Tomoko says, something in her voice suggesting relief at having finally come back to more practical and mundane issues. "So we could benefit from your expertise in plague symptomatology."

Ricardo sees the others looking expectantly at him. He stands up, rolling up his left sleeve at the same time.

"I don't see why not. But be careful. Whatever happened to Mark Fornash, a sample of my blood could still be dangerous."

One of the manipulator arms on the side of the tank rises, waiting. Mother Madeleine rushes from the room, looking for something.

"I'll take my chances," the simulacrum says as Ricardo walks toward the virtual Vena. "Will you be able to stay long with us?"

"If you can't find some way to cure Ricardo," Trillia says, taking the question as referring to all of them, "then, no. We'll need to find Simon Lingham in New York all the sooner."

Mother Madeleine returns and hands over to the tank's manipulator an intrusive-looking fluid sampler, little improved beyond an old-fashioned hypodermic syringe.

"I see," the Vena simulacrum says. "Remember me to Simon, then— when you find him."

Mother Madeleine preps Ricardo's arm. Vena's remote manipulator unerringly strikes a vein and draws blood, then just as unerringly injects the sample into a port beside the tank.

"It might be best if two nuns of our Order accompany you on your way," the virtualized Vena says. "Sister Mariel and Sister Tawanna. Their people scavenged in the Manhattan area, so they know the terrain. They'd be good at looking after your symptoms, too, Ricardo—although you don't seem to be manifesting much, at the moment."

"Thanks," Ricardo says, rolling down his shirt sleeve.

An unexpected silence opens among them. When the construct speaks again, it sounds distracted, if such a thing is possible.

"Not at all. Thank *you*. Ah, here. A preliminary scan indicates your new variant is, unfortunately, as incurable as the old. Sorry. Some new twists, however. Strange. I'll need time to analyze them. Goodbye, for now."

Sister Vena's form disappears from the tank, instantly replaced by a computer rendering of a wormhole, shining like a stylized Grail. Even Mother Madeleine seems surprised by the abruptness of it. After a moment she recovers herself and walks forward. Grasping the edge of the maroon curtain, the elderly nun pulls the drapery to, obscuring their view of the biotank and bringing their audience with the simulacrum to a close.

Following Mother Madeleine's lead, they depart the shrine and the New Crypt, climbing the helical stone stairs into the cathedral proper once more. Accompanied by half a dozen other Sisters of Easeful Death, the visitors and nuns make their way through deep twilight to what was once the Archbishop's Residence, a grand pile of antique opulence a short walk away.

On the way, the conversation runs along pleasantly enough—until

Aura and Markus mention the three horsemen in blue and black the travelers saw on the bridge to the south, near what was once Annapolis. In moments the nuns are abuzz with talk of the "Commander" and the "Knights ExLibris."

"Bad Latin, you know," Mother Madeline says with a disdainful sniff. "The Commander's soldier-librarians are better soldiers than librarians. If they wanted to say 'Knights *of* the Books' then they shouldn't have concocted 'Knights *from* the Books.' "

Mother Madeleine nods to two of the Sisters. Once those two depart, the nuns speak no more of the issue. Ricardo wonders what mission those two nuns departed on.

In the main dining room of the Residence, the visitors are treated to a simple but delicious meal, the main courses of which feature crabcakes and oysters and duck. The long predicted arrival of abjurer exiles and their reunion with Sister Vena (or at least her simulacrum) should make for a joyful occasion, but the worry that the Commander's forces may be abroad—and interested in the visitors—strains conversation during the meal, for all its fineness.

After dessert Ricardo and Trillia are guided toward their room by tall, lean Sister Tawanna. Exhausted, Trillia eagerly prepares for sleep, overjoyed at the prospect of spending the night "in a real bed again, after an eternity of tents and boat cabins and decks." Making happy bed noises, she snuggles in and soon falls asleep.

Ricardo, however, cannot sleep. He cannot get out of his mind what happened with Sister Vena—especially the abrupt ending of their audience with her. Leaning out the window of the bedroom into the cool night, he looks down into the yard below. Beneath the tree canopy, Mother Madeleine and two of her nuns are talking. He can't hear all of what they say, but what he *does* overhear does little to quiet his mind. He and his fellow visitors have brought with them more trouble than the nuns anticipated—all of Sister Vena's predictions notwithstanding. The two nuns Mother Superior is consulting with must be technical types, given their jargon-laden speech. While Ricardo can't understand all of it, he gathers they are discussing what has happened—and is continuing to happen—with the Sister Vena simulacrum. Odd sentences and phrases stand out, juxtaposing themselves: "Survival of consciousness after death is a halting problem" and "not predictable." "Come to closure and output, versus going into an infinite loop and running forever." And the strangest one—"Only way to find out is to run the Death Program."

The nuns move out of earshot. Ricardo pulls his head back into the room. As he gets into bed, he feels more puzzled than ever. He hopes the sample the virtual Vena took from his body didn't bring on the simulacrum's strange behavior.

When he is at last able to sleep, his dreams are all intercut with each other, out of sequence, out of context, out of coherence, as if a squad of Dada-art commandos have hijacked the editing gear on his dream machinery, montaging and collaging materials from different dreamlines. The effect is so disturbing that—in the midst of being chased by blue-black wasps which are the next moment powerboats of the same color—he wakes up, slamming so rigidly upright in bed he awakens Trillia.

"Ricardo? What's the matter?"

"Weird dreams."

"Tell me about them, then."

She rubs his shoulders, trying to get him to relax as he attempts to describe them to her. Before long the massage turns into mutual caresses. Just as things become clearly erotic, however, they hear a loud knock at the door.

"Sorry to wake you," says Sister Tawanna, opening the door partway, "but Mother Madeleine needs to see all of you right away."

Then the nun is gone, to knock on the next door down the hall. Ricardo and Trillia dress. Stumbling into the dark hall outside, they join their fellow travelers—all half asleep and as full of questions as they are.

In the main dining room, framed by flaring torches, Mother Madeleine awaits them, trying to make light of what may be a grave situation.

"I've received a piece of news that concerns me. A force of those soldier-librarians with the bad Latin grammar have been sighted near Severna Park. They are riding at speed toward Baltimore. We don't know that those horsemen you saw on the bridge were Knights ExLibris, or that this bunch is interested in you and your whereabouts, but it's a distinct possibility."

The visitors glance at each other, unspoken questions in their expressions.

"What would you recommend we do?" Tomoko asks.

"You said you were headed for the C and D Canal, is that right? Gather your gear together, get back to your boats immediately, and sail into the Bay—before these Knights or their friends try to bottle you up in the harbor."

"Then what?" asks Caster, still rubbing sleep from his eyes.

"Then sail for the canal at top speed. Mariel and Tawanna know that area. With luck you may get into and through the canal, even if the Knights *are* after you."

They soon agree to the course of action Mother Madeleine has outlined. Led by Sister Mariel and Sister Tawanna, the visitors leave for the harbor. With the two nuns to guide them through the predawn light, they reach their moored craft in less than twenty minutes. Before sunrise, they make five crew to each boat, Phenix at the wheel of *Sea Robin* and Caster at the wheel of *Star Thrower*.

The slight seaward breeze is not enough to fill their sails. They motor quietly out of the harbor and down the Patapsco. By the time the sun has risen clear of the horizon, they are in the bay proper. A stiffening breeze fills their sails as they come around to a northeasterly heading. When they come abreast of Pooles Island, Ricardo allows himself the hope that they'll get out of the north end of Chesapeake Bay and into the C and D Canal without incident.

Not until the mouth of the Bush River does everything go to hell. Passing the river's mouth under full sail, they are spotted by other sailors—crews of two night-black sailboats moored on the river's southern shore. On seeing *Star Thrower* and *Sea Robin*, the strange boats weigh anchor, unfurl sky-blue sails, and give chase.

Star Thrower and *Sea Robin*, scudding over the waves, have a good lead on their pursuers. They might still outrun the black boats and make good their escape through the canal, Ricardo thinks. As they pass Grove Point, however, the futility of that hope becomes clear to all. From the shore of what was once Aberdeen Proving Ground, four blue-black patrol boats swing out, roaring like great angry wasps. Two more blue-sailed black craft move out of the mouth of the Sassafras River, behind them.

Utterly focused on making the canal, the crews of *Sea Robin* and *Star Thrower* try to ignore the net that the angry motorboats are tightening around them. Then Ricardo sees that three blue-sailed black vessels block the straits ahead of them, between Turkey Point and Crystal Beach.

"What now?" Phenix calls to Caster.

"Ram our way through!" Caster calls back.

The dark-clad crews aboard the powerboats deduce what Phenix and Caster are planning and—judging from the *whump* of deck guns and the splashes fountaining the water before the bows of *Sea Robin* and *Star Thrower*—they don't approve. They underline their disapproval with the rattle of lighter arms. Bullets whiz overhead, ripping through sailcloth.

Onboard *Star Thrower*, Tomoko takes the wheel from Caster. John Drinan does the same with Phenix aboard *Sea Robin*. Tomoko and John steer the two boats pointedly to the west, away from the canal. The rest of the crew on each boat make a sad show of raising their hands in surrender— Caster and Phenix with great reluctance.

In moments *Sea Robin* and *Star Thrower* are completely surrounded by blue-black boats crewed by taciturn men in uniforms of the same hues. *All very smart, crisp, and color-coordinated*, Ricardo thinks sourly. *Maybe we should don the black gowns of Vena's terminal patients now, and get it over with*. Glancing at the gun-toting men standing alert in their uniforms, caps, and sunglasses on the boats close at hand around them, Ricardo thinks of his dream from the night before.

Precognition again? Like what he experienced before they were captured by Fornash's people? Maybe. He doubts being taken prisoner by these hard cases with their hard faces will prove as pleasant as the time spent at Duke, however.

Their captors herd *Sea Robin* and *Star Thrower* toward the spot of ground Trillia's map pad calls Spesutie Island. As the heavily wooded island looms darker and closer before them, Ricardo wonders what has become of their Merfolk escort. Did the explosions from the deck guns drive them off? Or had they already fled, earlier? Wherever they are, he doubts they could be much help now.

29

Apocalyptic Triptych
2033

"WHY, GOD? *WHY?*" MARK'S MOTHER SAID FROM HER SICKBED IN THE next room. "You promised never to burden us with more than we could bear! How could anyone possibly bear *this?*"

She broke into sobs then. Mark heard the sound with a mixture of sadness and relief. He didn't think, then, that those sentences would be the last coherent words he would ever hear his mother say.

Now, with Malika and John helping him shovel dirt onto her winding sheet in late afternoon light, Mark thought about his mother's last days. *What did you want, Mom?* he asked silently, looking into the newest grave. *Mainly for me to listen, I guess—while you reran your life in words.*

He *had* tried to listen, even when what she said was painful for them both. He looked at the two graves beside the one he was working on—his father's and his brother's. All so new. In a distant, abstract way, he knew billions of new graves had disturbed the earth in the last month, all over the planet. Some were orderly and thoughtful, straitened bodies in straight rows, like these. Others were jumbled masses, pits in the ground, limed and bulldozed over. Most were simply ashes, some urned and hidden, many more scattered on the wind.

He had begun to envy the dead. What was the point of living, now? He had played Cassandra, predicting the future yet powerless to stop its unfolding. What good was his 'shamanic complex' when, for the vast majority of humanity, it was proving indistinguishable from madness and death?

He didn't want to think about that, but it wouldn't go away. The shoveling done, Mark turned to look at his father's gravesite. In the old days he always rejected Dad's quirky survivalist fears and the expenses arising from them. The solar-powered summer escape house with its commanding vistas, up a hidden, gated, gravel driveway off Marian View in Idyllwild. The guns, ammo, and batteries. The water drums, the imperishable food. The backup well and solar pump. The simple monstrance of Dad's little lockbox, filled with disks of gold and silver—round wafers in Mammon's inedible Communion. So unnecessary and redundant. Paranoid to the point of absurdity.

Or at least it used to be. When he, John, and Malika returned from the Spires Research Library in New York, however—aboard a private flight ending on a private rooftop landing pad—they found they had returned to a City of Angels grown more insane and chaotic than even a life-long Angeleno could have imagined. The world had been so altered by pandemic that his father's survivalist fetish now seemed perfectly reasonable planning.

Mark had little trouble convincing his companions that the hidden summer house in Idyllwild was their best hope for safety. Malika had just learned she'd lost all her nearest relatives, in the Chicago quarantine riots. John claimed no family of his own in this world. Together with John's big dog, Oz, they fought their way out of the madness overwhelming Los Angeles—a city racked with the pangs of giving birth to Hell, where avenging angels and delirious demons in their human forms vied for control of the streets, agreeing only on their favored weapons of fury and fire.

The small party bound for Idyllwild tried to avoid the traffic-choked highways and burning city centers wherever they could, sticking to back streets and foothill terrain as much as possible. Yet even there they could not avoid the madness. People like the fellow Mark thought of as Screaming Gun Man, roaring "Ain't nobody here 'dying instantly'! Long suffering for us all!" and punctuating his ranting with gunshots at every living thing he spied. Or the distraught matron crying over and over, "Why does everyone always want to destroy my city?"

The little Idyllwild-bound party picked up still stranger reports from those they met on the road. Almost everyone still sane enough to pass along warnings had already managed to head for the hills, disappear into deserts, or flee into distant fields—but not all. By day the travelers skirted encampments where the Army of the Pure Bible (Jepthah Rite) purified the world and lay down the foundations of the Kingdom of God on Earth by driving wooden stakes into the hearts of suspect children, then burning their flesh—holocausts as foundation-sacrifice to a wrathful God not seen since Old Testament days. By night they dodged gangs of starving, mesmerized wolfmen who, foiled by Oz's presence, attacked and ate the easier prey of women and children hiding in homes. The travelers knew the truth of that only belatedly—from the sound of the victims' screams.

In the L.A. Basin, night and day seemed controlled by different forces, armies equally unenlightened no matter where the sun or moon might stand. Near Pasadena, the travelers hid from armed vigilantes in all-terrain vehicles. From the few sane and compassionate people they met, they learned that the all-terrain vigilantes were looking for lo-tekkers and tree-people, anarcholudds and disurbanists. To immolate by hanging, burning, or crucifixion—blood-sacrifices to pay for the crime of unleashing the pandemic upon the world. Further east, on turf controlled by other terrorists equally righteous and insane, those hospitals and medical clinics not already torched as "suspected biotech sources of the madness plague," were simply and utterly overwhelmed, transformed into insane nonasylums locked into tighter and tighter spirals of ritual triage. Police, firefighters, national Guardsmen, and regular soldiers tried to maintain a hollow semblance of order—an increasingly impossible task, as more and more of their own numbers succumbed to "prionoid schizophrenia" or "organic psychotic brain syndrome" or "psychotic depressive reaction" or "hysterical dissociative neurosis" or "bipolar psychosis" or any of half a hundred other names given to the madness sweeping the world, the lunacy the entire armamentarium of medical science could not even effectively diagnose, much less contain or cure.

Under a great high pall of smoke, columns of clouds by day and pillars of fire by night sprang up everywhere, too many and too confusing to ever guide the lost tribes of Los Angeles to safety. Day and night changed places, too: Day darkened by miles-long smoke clouds raining down ashes and flakes of fire from blocks upon blocks of burning buildings. Night skies lit eerie-bright by flames until it seemed the whole sky was ablaze, that Hell itself had usurped Heaven's place above the City of Angels. Hilltops in the San Gabriels and San Bernardinos glowed with the bonfires of shamans and prophetesses. Rainmakers, trying to quell the fires spreading throughout the basin and foothills, sacrificed animal and human victims on rough stone altars to mountaintop warrior storm gods.

Warned by rumors and the smell of burning bodies on the wind, Mark's small party turned south and made its way through the burnt-over districts along Highway 60, in hopes of avoiding the vehicular killing fields stretching from San Bernardino to Cabazon along Interstate 10. They had reached only the Box Spring Mountains, upheaved rockpiles east of Riverside, when the power grid, grown ever more spotty, went down for the last time. Southern California became once more a land lit only by fire, harsh blazes casting a baleful smoky glare on endless scenes of bloody wounding, murder, rape, cannibalism, and incest—all the old dark horrors come round again.

At times it seemed to Mark that they passed not through landscapes of day and night but Hells only more or less lurid. Highway 60 from Moreno into the badlands was a wall of fire: Both occupied and abandoned vehicles in the immense catastrophic traffic jam there stood aflame, an unmoving river of fire as far as he could see. Half-mad refugees, fleeing through the broken hills, claimed the conflagration was tree-people retaliation for the murder of disurbanist philosopher D. B. Albert in the San Bernardino Mountains. All-terrain vigilantes had summarily executed him in front of his cabin near Lake Arrowhead.

Heading southeast in a line roughly paralleling Gilman Springs Road and the Ramona Expressway, the small party made its way under smoke-filled skies onto the drying bed of the San Jacinto River. Passing north and east of the new ghost towns of San Jacinto and Hemet, they walked across golf courses where local retirees once spent so much of their time. A pathetic spirit of the dying world lingered there, over greens just turning brown—still playable, though no one teed off or played through on the empty, windswept links.

Up the forking riverbed, they passed the still ghostlier remains of what had once been a nomadic town like Uproot City—now peopled only with corpses of those dead of the Plague, or killed by others who would soon be dead of the same disease themselves. Into the mountains—up through the manzanita, into the oaks, then into the pines—Mark led Malika and Oz and John, to the safe haven his father had long been preparing. Their trek had etched the horrors of the southland into their minds with bloody hand and spreading fire, but at last it was over.

They were "safe," but had they endured it all only for—this? Only to spend endless sleep-deprived nights and days here, outside Idyllwild, on the lookout for the stray mad straggler? Only to spend their time warning off the crazed and starving and lost—or shooting them for approaching this pitiful refuge? Only to bear witness as Mark buried his family here?

Mark peered fixedly at the graves. When he looked at his brother's grave, he thought of Phil's last words, scrawled on a slip of paper before he committed suicide, leaping like a great cat off the high back deck into the steep ravine below. "We've done all we can," his brother wrote, "and nothing can be done. No more to say." John and Malika had helped him bind his father and mother into their sickbeds, after that.

Looking at the space of slowly settling earth over his brother's remains, Mark thought of Sister Vena's presentation in New York, and Lieutenant Losaba's, too. The idea that stigmata—and shapeshifting, even more so— were symptoms of "conversion disorders," psychological conflicts converted into bodily disturbances. Metamorphoses, in which physical change was a temporary *relief* from mental conflicts so overwhelming they must otherwise end in suicide. For all the uncountable millions who had been swept away by their shapeshifting, how many more had, like his brother, killed themselves because they couldn't shapeshift *enough*?

Shamans of the old times taught that people will be animals, animals will be people, and gods will be both. Some sacrificed themselves, some sacrificed others, but why did the divine demand death? What good was it for consciousness to leave the body, for the soul to fly and "aerial voyage," if it always had to return to the body—if body *and* soul just died, in the end?

He looked at his father's grave and tried to remember the hopes they had all once shared—and the fears. My dad never really knew his own mother, he thought. Mark never met his grandmother because she drowned in the Truckee River when his dad was two months old. When Dad was a little boy, too, Dad's uncle and cousin drowned in a deep hole below Boca Dam, while he ran back and forth along the shore, helpless to rescue them. Dad didn't drink and he never learned to swim. Yet, when he shapeshifted, beautiful silvery scales appeared all over his upper body and the last word he tried to spell out before he died was "W-A-T-". They understood. They gave him what he wanted.

With a slow sigh Mark turned to see John and Malika looking at him expectantly.

"Nothing more to do here. It's time to move on, before it gets too late.

I'm going to push that panic button Spires gave each of us at the conference. Either of you up for joining me?"

Malika glanced at John, then back to Mark.

"Count me in."

John shook his head sharply.

"I can't believe it! You're just going to give up and run away? Hide out on some damn island with that bubble-helmeted nut case?"

Malika frowned deeply.

"Wake up, John! Solitary last stands may be romantic, but they're also stupid. We've crossed an event horizon, can't you see that?"

"And what's that supposed to mean?"

"Everything we've known is collapsing into the black hole of this pandemic. Everything has *changed*. What we're headed toward is a singularity in human history. The place where all the laws *predict* that all the laws *break down*. Maybe by working with Spires and other researchers, we have a chance of coming out on the other side of the black hole!"

Pointedly, Mark and Malika shook down on their wrists the slim bracelets Spires' people had given them in New York. With a flourish they pressed their "panic buttons," activating the transceiver/geolocators contained in the bracelets. A moment later, a message appeared on each bracelet, informing them that they were to proceed to a location referred to as "The Point." The message and geolocator provided precise coordinates for that place, then advised them that their transport would arrive in eighty-eight minutes.

Mark was more than a little amazed. Never underestimate the reach or persistence of wealth and power, he thought—especially a powerful man with a plan, like Cameron Spires. With the whole world going to wrack and ruin, Spires was still somehow managing to maintain a fleet of transport craft ready to be dispatched to any point on the globe.

They looked expectantly toward John, but the ex-spacer made no comment on what Mark and Malika had done, nor on their announced time of departure.

"If you're not going to join us, John," Mark said, "the least you can do is help us pack."

Trying to decide what to take with them on such short notice was like being told a wildfire was approaching their house and they had less than an hour and a half to evacuate. They gathered up what they thought they could not live without—but probably *could*, if they had to. With John at the wheel of Mark's father's electric car, they made their way toward The Point, south of Idyllwild. There they would abandon the little ceramic-motored vehicle, if John didn't want it.

The sunset was a spectacular one—deep shades of orange and brick-red, from particulates rising in enormous columns out of the cities and wildlands burning to the west and south. Despite that spectacle, The Point stood deserted. No tourists or locals were out to catch the sunset, as Mark had so often seen them in the past—gazing in awe at far less dramatic ends of days.

The sun slipped below the horizon. Moments later, a black boomerang shape came winging out of the south toward them, low and under radar, following the terrain. Oz barked excitedly. Mark had expected some sort of helicopter, but he was wrong. What came to hover not far from them was a stealth transatmospheric jump jet.

No sooner had the stealth jumper set down beside them than a deep door slid back, revealing a crewman waving them hurriedly inside. After loading their gear into that yawning space, Mark and Malika waved farewell to a hesitant John Drinan. Suddenly, in unspoken agreement, as they climbed toward the cargo bay they began waving and whistling and calling to Oz. The big dog ran toward them, his startled master following in the dog's wake. As Mark and Malika pulled the dog in, John clambered in after. Mark and the crewman slammed the cargo bay door closed behind John and motioned the pilot to lift off.

"Aw, dammit," John said, frowning at his dog and its two human co-conspirators. Mark and Malika slapped and gripped their comrade on the shoulders. John, for all his balking, seemed secretly *relieved* as the stealthy aircraft climbed into the fire-stained sky.

FROM GREENWICH, SIMON LINGHAM LOOKED TOWARD LONDON AND remembered waking there to the raucous cawing of crows. He thought of mornings when, still half asleep, he glanced out the window and saw those birds, black shards breaking over the whitening city rooftops, mobile pieces of darkness staging a rear-guard action against the growing day.

In those dawns, when he had sat on the edge of the bed listening, it had seemed to him that the birds were mocking the city and its inhabitants, cawing down upon the snorting lorries and autos, upon the crowded tube trains. Upon the souls rising from the underground at a hundred stations, amnesic and insensible to the joy and pain of another day aborning, joining the dark-coated tides flowing through the streets of gray London, making their way into their high offices, their works and days hung like scaffolds against the sky, put up and taken down with noise enough to drown the murderous warning of crows. . . .

On all those mornings, in all those years, Simon never heeded that warning. Which is why, he supposed, he never expected the view he stared into now: London afire in the afternoon, arcs of flame miles and miles long, spreading deep into the suburbs now. Clouds of smoke hovered high above the great city for a hundred miles around. Smoke, too, hazed all the horizon between the Royal Astronomical Observatory's hilltop here, hard by Greenwich, and the broken dome of St. Paul's, barely visible in the distance.

He told himself that real and imagined vistas of London aflame were almost as old as the City itself. Years ago, playing tourists on a weekend away from Cambridge, he and Tomoko had taken a previous trip downriver from London to Greenwich. Their riverboat guide—an outspoken Christopher Wren and Inigo Jones enthusiast—fancied himself something of an architecture critic. He was a great storehouse of facts on the many floods and plagues the city had suffered, but he waxed most eloquently when it came to the damage done to the Old City by the Great Fire of 1666, and the further damage done to Georgian and Victorian London by German bombs and rockets during the Second World War.

Now, however, the banes of fire, flood, and plague were no longer merely the matter of history. The madness plague had set cities aflame across the planet. When Hong Kong had been the first to go, people tried to write that off as a Chinese aberration—a Taoist fire-and-smoke virtualization of the city and all its goods for use by the dead in the afterlife, a continuation of a local tradition that included the burning of "hell money" and paper cars and paper suits for the ancestors. Simon had seen the coverage with horror. Hong Kong was one of his favorite cities, and the idea of it reduced to blackened ruins and hanging gardens covered with greenery sweeping down from Victoria peak was almost too much to contemplate. Now the burning had come to London, and who knew when some madman or maddened crowd might breach the Thames Barriers, allowing a final flood to complete the late great city's devastation?

Looking northwest in the afternoon light, Simon saw the red-ball sun dipping between and below the tops of darkly mushrooming smoke clouds, falling toward the great arcs of burning city whose light stained the sky the color of bright blood every night, all night long. He thought about his more recent journey downriver, with Tomoko and the rest of the Provisional Medical Authority, a scant week before—and the pandemonium through which the PMA staffers had passed in their flight from the city.

The loathsome and stinking London Underground had seemed to go on forever, charnel-crowded with its army of shadows and shades, its pierced and hung and electrocuted dead, their corpses gnawed and mutilated, decapitated and butchered for meat. The dead's broken and bloodied legs, arms, and hands grasped or kicked at air from beneath piles of collapsed brick. Half-buried faces looked far too composed as they slept the longest sleep in dirt and building debris.

The living were almost worse: scuttling starvelings, concentration-camp wasted, fleeing like roaches the light of battery-powered torches. As the medical scientists and the squad of heavily armed Royal Marines escorting them made their wary way past, the debased creatures stared out at them from dark corners and niches, with hollow or greedy eyes.

The PMA staff came up out of the hellmouth of the underground at Westminster. At first Simon and Tomoko were relieved, but aboveground things were nearly as bad, even so close to the guarded zone of the river. The sunlight of summer day was in retreat before the smoke and fire of Westminster Abbey and the Houses of Parliament—all ablaze. Not far away roared the crowds of the insane, whose fury the PMA party had escaped by dodging into the dead and dying underground.

Simon's mood darkened with the sky. Under a snow of ashes mixed with flakes of fire falling from the air, they walked beside the river, weary but alert. When he and his fellow staffers boarded the commandeered cruise boat, the wind off the Thames came up, persistent and sharp, clearing the air somewhat. As the boat pulled away from the dock, he saw the pigeons and city doves hovering too close to their long-accustomed buildings—wings catching fire as the buildings burned, doves plummeting aflame toward Earth in satanic parody of the Paraclete. From everywhere in the city, dark birds erupted, enormous flocks of rooks and crows, riding the human-made winds and weather of the city wildfires. The whorling masses of dark birds moved with perfect familiarity about the burning town, as if they had long been waiting for this day, when they might stretch out their eclipsing wings between the bright sky and all the hopes and dreams of the great city.

The journey downriver was a voyage through a nightmare. Fire consumed this building and that along the banks, raining firedrops onto a river choked with the debris of businesses and households. Smoke lay both high and low, darkening the sky for miles around and choking first one stretch of the river, then another. Simon saw the Globe Theater burning again at bankside—the replica built forty years back now dying in flames, as had its original four centuries before. The old Globe, he remembered, had burned when wadding paper from a stage firework landed on the thatched roof and set it afire—but no one noticed, the playgoers considering it an "idle smoak" and "their eyes more attentive to the show," as a chronicler of the time had put it.

No one had died that time, but they were not so lucky now. Even the Americans' vaunted freedom of speech did not permit shouting Fire! in a crowded theatre, but when the whole planet was a crowded theatre and the world was burning (for all that everyone tried to ignore the smell of smoke), more people should have shouted Fire! earlier—restrictions on free speech not withstanding. Simon feared that, this time, the "great Globe itself" was lost.

The commandeered cruise boat picked its slow way downstream among burning wrecks and debris. The only conversation was the Marines' telling of the horrors they had seen throughout the country, and some of the scientists, especially Tomoko, questioning their armed escorts on the more bizarre details. Simon shook his head at the thought of the crazy, globetrotting, zoo flyout crusade that had brought Tomoko *to* and then trapped her *in* London. His own work had done the same, also trapping him, midstride on his way to Switzerland from New York—bringing the two of them together again when the PMA made its sweeps, desperate for medical staff.

Exhausted and barely awake enough to listen, he heard again the now too-familiar stories. Armies of werewolves and vampires. Hair-covered wildmen and wildwomen moving through the streets and countryside. Rumors of so-called Werfolk living in abandoned churches. Gargoyles, come down off their ancient edifices and incarnated in human form. Satyrs and manticores and harpies and selkies. Lurid tales for a firelit world, the product of secondhand reports, or of mad moonlit night-clashes where, afterward, the dead shapechangers conveniently and inevitably reverted to human form.

"—tribal shamanism," Tomoko said. "In Seattle I met scores of people who said they had seen Chief See-Yathl. The old chief told them there was no death, only a change of worlds. Other people told me ancient Suquamish Indians had returned—and were possessing *them*. They saw gods in canoes and high-prowed fishing boats paddling down the streets, following spirit-salmon beneath the stone streams."

"I can top that," said one of the younger Marines. "A couple months ago, near the British Museum, I met people said they were gods of Babylonia and Egypt. Said they could grow animal heads on their shoulders—bird beaks and wings, too!"

Simon shook his head. An anthology of similar stories could be collected from cities around the world. Balinese witch-dancers with long-tusked masks and fingernail extensions, showing up in shopping malls. Urbanites claiming descent from the Dogon of Mali, who had reconnected with the "Star People of Sirius" now on the way to pick them up. X-ray visionaries who claimed to engage in cosmic hunts and battles—via *dancing* as birds and bears, kangaroos and cranes, eagles, emus, and elephants, ghosts, devils, and bogeymen. Sun Dancers and Medicine Wheelers. Naked sea-goddess women chasing invisible seahorses down city streets. Still other, more nebulous incarnators, who believed they were vessels for the gods of extinct ammonite and trilobite civilizations—and were dancing those long-extinct species back into time.

For all their oddness, such stories seemed quaint now, coming as they did mostly from the drumming, dancing, and dreaming times, before things grew truly grim and terrible. Perhaps, however, those earlier "incarnations" contributed to the terrors that followed. They no doubt left a deep imprint on those who—drifting with the pandemic into ever more chronically altered states of consciousness, thoroughly depersonalized and wildly hallucinating—found themselves vulnerable to the hypnotic suggestions presented by those zoomorphic dances and dramas.

At last, in midafternoon, the cruise boat arrived at the town pier beside Greenwich. Though the sky here, too, was darkened by the great smokeclouds of London burning, Greenwich was still intact. Just beyond the abandoned pier stood the domes and baroque architecture of the Royal Naval College. Beyond the Naval College, framing the old Queen's House, stood the National Maritime Museum—all of them, though abandoned and neglected, still largely undisturbed.

Disembarking at the pier, Simon and Tomoko, along with the rest of their party and its escorts, made their way, quiet and alert, to the King William Walk. When they came to Greenwich Park's spacious lawns and centuries-old trees, Simon found the order of the old grounds reassuring—though the Marines did have to fire off a few rounds to scare away some overly curious "satyrs" and "wood nymphs."

At the heart of the park, on top of a not inconsiderable hill, the Old Royal Observatory stood, unharmed. By the time they walked onto the summit of the ridge where the observatory stood, all in their party (except the well-toned Marines) had worked up a good sweat in the summer heat.

In the week that had passed since their arrival, they'd all come to know the Old Observatory well. This complex of clocks and stars, of mirrors and lenses—with its cobblestone courtyard and Planetarium, its Telescope Dome, its Bradley Room and Quadrant House, its Harrison's Longitude Prize galleries, its Camera Obscura, its Time-Ball—had become their new, if temporary, home.

Turning away now from the sun declining over dying London, Simon slowly made his way to the Telescope Dome in the brick Equatorial Building. More Victorian than the edifice that housed it, the 28-inch refractor inside was Britain's largest telescope—a well-wrought cannon weighing in at over a ton and a half. Now it stood abandoned and gathering dust, interest in the well-behaved stars above overwhelmed by disasters on the Earth below.

Thinking back on their trip downriver, Simon remembered the willing ear Tomoko gave to the fighters' tales. How she had asked serious questions of them, despite the fact that (Detective Losaba's testimony notwithstanding) there was no proof that any of that was real as far as he was concerned. Perhaps Tomoko hoped she might hear in those tales something exculpating her and her discoveries. She must be feeling more than a little guilt for what was happening to humanity throughout the world.

Unfortunately, the only plausible theory at the moment was that it was *her* engineered prionoids that were at the root of it all. While the prionoids were undergoing Spires' clinical trials in Los Angeles, Johannesburg, Bombay, and Hong Kong, several strains of microbes unexpectedly incorporated and further modified the engineered shapeshifter proteins. The engineered prionoid was a species-barrier jumper *par excellence* and an uncontrolled form of it ended up in a common strain of airborne microbe—made all the more ubiquitous by human mobility around the planet. Said ubiquitous microbe vectored the prionoids' abnormal conformers into the human nervous system, where they interfered with neurotransmitter production—until the madness sweeping the whole bloody burning world was the result. The prionoid treatments Tomoko intended for neuromodulating and *conforming* the schizophrenic homeless had instead gone wrong, resulting in the greatest failure of social conformity the world had ever seen.

Resting his hand on the cool barrel of the telescope, Simon thought such a scenario still had a lot going for it. The drumming, dancing, and dreaming phases of the pandemic were simply a chronic altered state of consciousness, arising from prionoid alterations of neurotransmitter levels. There were precedents. Progressive dementia, hallucinations, paranoid delusions, and deep personality changes had all previously been associated with prion and prionlike diseases. Such a prionoid-only explanation could even account for many of the physiological changes he and his colleagues had noted in the brains of victims they had autopsied—particularly the astrocytosis in the neocortex and larger areas of cortical alteration associated with the very last stages of the disease.

For all its successes, however, that explanation's incompleteness was still bedeviling. At the conference in New York, Fornash and his ilk were at least right in their contention that the prionoids didn't "cause" the pandemic, anymore than psychoactive substances "cause" mystical experiences. Both merely caused physicochemical changes in the brain, which the individual mind interpreted and used in its own way. Even worse was the fact that the theoretical model the WHO scientists and their colleagues had developed could by no means provide an organic-level explanation for the so-called "stigmata" of the dreaming phase, nor for any "shapeshifting" and "soul-flying" stages. Still less could that account for the oft-reported lunar periodicity of the psychosis.

As the pandemic progressed and deepened, Simon and his more rigorously minded colleagues had no choice but to conclude that reports of the existence of these latter phenomena must be mistaken—with no objective reality except as somatizations of delusions. Yet, despite the rigor with which he had defended the accepted scenario against people like Mark Fornash at the Spires conference, Simon could not manage to fully convince even himself that the accepted scenario was the whole of the story.

But what were the alternatives, really? Fornash's quasi-mystical belief in shapeshifting as an ability latent in and inherent to the human species? Or the suggestions of those other theorists who tangentially supported Fornash's contention that shapeshifting could physically occur—but held that some as-yet-undetermined binomechanism or nanorganism was tangled up in it? Even Cameron Spires had raised that issue at the conference, suggesting that some such tech might actually exist.

No, Simon thought. Such explanations only multiplied the implausibilities. Yet the greatest implausibility and most saving paradox of all was his own immunity to the pandemic.

The luck of the draw and the blood test: that was all that had caused the angel of death to spare him, but it had been enough, so far. He possessed a rare benign polymorphism in a tiny protein component of his own neurochemistry. The presence of those few extra peptides had rendered his variant of that protein particularly resistant to a "change in conformation." His physiology was abnormally nonconforming to the "abnormal conformers" of the prionoid pandemic—a trait he shared with Tomoko and partially with Mark Fornash, although Fornash's molecular resistance wasn't precisely the same.

Leaving the Telescope Dome and the Equatorial Building, Simon looked up to where the Time-Ball's rise and fall had at last been stopped and stayed after—what? Centuries? Passing through door and curtain into the darkness inside the Camera Obscura, Simon's eyes adjusted slowly, until he at last saw scenes made of light collected and deflected (by a system of solar-motored mirrors) onto round tables in the center of the darkened room. The Camera Obscura's expanded capabilities were as close to a closed-circuit television system as they could manage in a post-powergrid world—and vital to the surveillance and guarding of their position on the observatory ridge.

Looking down at the largest of the mirror-reflected scenes, he saw that the mirror system bounced down its light from an arc traveling along the horizon, swinging slowly from the dome of St. Paul's in the distant west to the Millennium Dome closer at hand. As he watched the strange real-time world projected before him—made up only of photons, yet as apparently true as any perception of consensus reality—Simon thought of the old philosophical concept that time is the moving image of eternity, not so much a thing in itself as a movement in something else. Tomoko spoke without looking up from the scene shifting across the table before her. The young Marine beside her, even more intent on the table-scenes before him, said nothing.

"Hello, Simon. Took you long enough to finish your patrol."

Simon checked the glowing countdown time on the bracelet he had received at the Spires Research Library Conference. He had hoped he would never have to use the "panic button," but now it glowed dimly red and flashed because he, like Tomoko, had in fact activated it.

"Just saying goodbye. Pickup isn't for a quarter of an hour yet."

He and Tomoko were the last members of the PMA staff still remaining at Greenwich. Those whose pandemic symptoms had not yet made them too dangerous (or too ill) to travel with had already fled toward the coast, taking the majority of the Royal Marine escort with them. This Marine and his two comrades guarding the approaches to the ridgetop would join their fellows on the trek east as soon as Simon and Tomoko were safely evacuated.

Looking about him now—at Tomoko and the Marine and the array of Camera Obscura surveillance "screens"—Simon felt as if he were in the control room of some kind of amphibious submarine or mobile island. The Observatory at Greenwich was always intended as the temporal and terrestrial link between the starry oceans above and the watery oceans below, the connecting point between navigations celestial and nautical.

Into his head flashed a vision he hoped was not prophetic: a view of the Observatory on its ridge, sailing between starry and salty oceans, surrounded by the waters of the Thames estuary—after the Barriers had been blown and the ensuing deluge had covered all the surrounding lower-lying lands.

The sound of an explosion rocked the building. Simon jumped, fearful his vision had come to pass.

"What the hell was that?"

The biggest motorized mirror at that moment completed its scan and he, Tomoko, and the Marine saw the cause. A cloud of smoke mushroomed into the sky across the Thames.

Simon squinted against the late afternoon light as he ran out of the Camera Obscura. Crossing the main courtyard, he stepped over the once-illuminated strip of opaque glass designating Earth's prime meridian—the zero line which arrowed from a set of telescope crosshairs, through a glass tunnel in the cobblestones, then northward in imagination toward where the old Millennium Dome stood. Or *had* stood, until a moment earlier, when someone had ended its structured existence in an instant of fiery demolition.

"Simon!" Tomoko called from the door of the Camera. "If you're just going to stand there staring into space, then stare into it on the surveillance array!"

As he headed back into the Camera, Simon saw the young Marine stride off in the direction of the explosion, talking rapidly on a chunky solar-powered field radio. What was all the rush about? He and Tomoko would be gone and the Observatory facility abandoned in a few minutes anyway.

On the surveillance arrays, he soon saw good cause for alarm. Near the river, in sunset light, ragtag torch-bearing gangs were swarming up from the ground like maddened ants. They were erupting out of the tunnel connecting this side of the Thames with the farther bank—where the Millennium Dome had just been reduced to rubble. The images from the Camera's array of surveillance mirrors made it all too clear that the torch-bearing gangs were coalescing into a sizable mob, armed not only with torches but also with crude weapons.

Good God, Simon thought. *The Observatory is the last great surveillance machine. They're coming to destroy it, like peasants out to burn Castle Franken-stein!*

As the mob moved in a wave out of the streets and into the park grounds, Simon and Tomoko dimly heard the *whump* of mortar rounds, followed by persistent rattling bursts of machine-gun fire. On the surveillance arrays in the dim room, he and Tomoko saw torches and torchbearers going down, caught in the open by enfilading fire from two of the Royal Marines. Watching the arrays, Tomoko and Simon shouted positions over field radios to their defenders. Another round of mortar fire commenced, smart bomblets homing in on many more of the attacking mob.

Still the invaders came on. Despite the firepower the Marines had at their disposal, it was only a matter of time before their positions were overrun and the Observatory itself was taken—

A more horrible hell burst upon the Earth, fire so bright Simon had to avert his eyes from the arrays. When he looked back, he saw the ground around and below the ridge everywhere carpeted by fire. The ancient oaks of the park blazed in instant tall bonfires. By one table's light, however, Simon also saw a dull glint on the skin of a black boomerang, sweeping in a swift arc around the ridgetop.

"I think our ride is here," Tomoko said grimly. "Let's go."

Together they exited the Camera Obscura. The smell of woodsmoke and charred flesh hung heavy on the wind as they made their way forward, toward where a stealth jump jet was settling onto the ground. As Simon and Tomoko climbed aboard, he wondered where their Royal Marine guards had gotten to. Before he had time to voice that concern, the jet lifted off and shot away east, toward a fat full moon on the rise.

They soared away from the holocaust behind them. Simon stared at that moon, pale as a well-scrubbed skull. Numb, he thought of all the lives burned away in an instant, sacrificed so that he and Tomoko could be here, now, flying into an unknown future.

To what purpose? As his shock and numbness abated, the questions only proliferated. To the old-time alchemists and astrologers, the moon represented the memory of the past which made the future possible. What light to the future was the full moon if it shone only on empty cities? What good was this vast holocaust consuming the world, if human beings, who had kept time's vigils for so long, were sacrificed utterly—taking with them both time and memory?

The image of an hourglass came to him as they flew silently through the moonlit night. Yes, that was it. Sand and hourglass, like the moon and the minds of the moonwatchers, were complementary aspects of the same thing. An hourglass without sand was as devoid of purpose as sand without an hourglass. Human art and skill transformed sand into the glass of the timepiece. The glass of the timepiece in turn transformed the fall of sand into the keeping of time, at least for the perceiving human mind—the same mind that had made the moon both god and goddess, not just a dead rock insensibly played over by light from an idiot furnace burning mindlessly, eight minutes away.

Even that eight minutes too was time out of mind. Now the glass shatters, Simon thought, and the fall of moondust means nothing.

FROM THE VALLEYS THAT SISTER VENA OVERLOOKED FROM TSHUKUDU, the clapping, humming, drumming, and ankle-rattle rhythms of many dancers rose up more and more loudly. Judging from the noise, there were more trance-dance circles surrounding their position here than anywhere else in the territory. The lieutenant's stalking and killing of the Wersigned had at last drawn this unwanted attention from those who had been her prey. Now, it was the lieutenant and Sister Vena who were being stalked.

Tshukudu was once an exclusive backcountry camp, according to the lieutenant. Noted for its service, its cuisine, its sweeping vistas. The grand views showed broken concentric rings of spectacular rock outcroppings—product of millions of years' weathering wearing down the ancient volcano whose crater had become Lake Mankwe.

The lieutenant had chosen the spot because the grand views made it defensible. The two women had fortified a rock outcropping with low walls of loose stone. Sister Vena kept watch for what the night and its full moon might bring, while the lieutenant patrolled the scrubland nearby.

Sister Vena prayed Spires' people would fly them out of here in time. She doubted they could—despite what her panic-button bracelet told her. Here they were at the ends of the Earth, with the world they had known ending everywhere. Not even Spires' wealth and power could mount a rescue mission for them, under such conditions.

If she had possessed accurate foreknowledge of the chain of consequences that had led her here, Sister Vena doubted she would ever have brought attention to herself by making her discoveries known to the world. She could blame no one but herself. She was the one who sent off the notes and observations that brought her to the attention of Spires and his talent scouts. That attention led to her recruitment for his conference on the pandemic. *That*, in turn, led to her traveling at Spires' expense to South Africa, to continue conferring with Leira Losaba on the overlap of the stigmatic and shapeshifting aspects of the madness plague—only to be trapped here as the pandemic's effects rapidly worsened.

Mother Mary's mind was already addled with plague by the time Vena left India, yet maybe the shrewd old nun had been right to chastise Vena for her vanity. Maybe it *was* only pride in her discoveries that made Vena circumvent the proper workings of Church hierarchy. If *that* were true—and equally true that pride goeth before a fall—then Vena had fallen far, in this faraway land.

Not so far, though, as Leira Losaba had fallen. And precisely because this *was* a faraway land.

Before leaving riot-ravaged Mumbai for Spires' conference, Sister Vena saw illness blooming like terrible flowers in the bodies and minds of everyone who had ever been dear to her. Trapped in South Africa on the return trip, she had at least been spared the deeper degradations and more intimate horrors that would by now have overtaken her family and friends in India. She could only wonder what had happened to her mother, or to her brother Sudip. She could never *know*.

South Africa was Leira's homeland—and she had not been spared such horrors and degradations. They had found *her* mother being eaten by barbarous leopard-skinned men, their faces and hands smeared with blood like the muzzles and paws of big cats at an antelope kill. Leira Losaba at that moment went into a rage of vengeance that had yet to subside. The renegade police officer had since blazed a trail of blood through the roiling twin cauldrons of murder and madness that were the South West Townships and Johannesburg—and Sister Vena, caught up in her mad companion's wake, was swept along in it.

As they fled toward Rustenberg, Sister Vena looked behind them. The horror of destroyed cities should have turned her to a pillar of salt, as it had Lot's wife, but it didn't. She realized that cities throughout the world must be burning in much the same manner as Joburg and Soweto now burned. Cameron Spires was right: all the old racial, tribal, religious, and political hatreds—long smoldering under the glossy veneer of civilization—had been fanned to wildfire again. Now the smoke and flames rose from the residences and businesses of wealthy and poor alike.

From a distance, the burning cities were indistinguishable from enormous trash fires. Left as stinking corpse-fields or otherwise abandoned by their citizens, that was all the cities amounted to, now: elaborate trash, waiting for time and fire to turn them to dust and ashes.

Sister Vena pushed such thoughts away from her waking consciousness as they traveled northward to a haven that existed only in the lieutenant's mind. To her vengeance-ridden companion Vena tried, again and again, to talk reason and compassion. The world around them, however, made little room for logical explanation, much less the expression of loftier moral qualities. Sister Vena watched in horror as Leira Losaba metamorphosed with shocking swiftness into the killing machine of "the lieutenant."

Soon the lieutenant filled all the space Leira Losaba had once occupied. She became the avenging angel of Duty, and her Duty was to kill anyone who posed a threat to them—most especially anyone manifesting any sign of shapeshifting. *Their* mere existence was a threat. All such were to be disposed of without further consideration.

Beyond Rustenberg, the terrain itself went mad, or at least the human creations within it had done so. The complex of luxury hotel, casino, and waterpark that made up the Lost City resort—its Rider Haggard façades ornamented with huge animal sculptures and topped with domed towers of elephant tusks, straight out of *King Solomon's Mines*—now succeeded as an "exotic future ruin" beyond its designers' wildest imaginings. One wing of the complex was extensively fire-damaged. Its derelict swim- and surf-pools stood filled with algae-slimed logjams of bloated corpses, a flotsam of bodies bobbing on a blood-dimmed tide.

Sun City, too, had become a city of the moon. Severed heads stared sightlessly from atop every wall. The ritually sacrificed lay piled waist-deep about the Monkey Plaza and the Bridge of Time. Of the casinos still standing, most were cratered by explosion and fire. Upon all humanity, it seemed to Sister Vena, there had come the profound desperation of an animal that chews its leg off to escape a leg-hold trap, or a wolf that bites into its own belly, rips open its own entrails, to get at some terrible poison it has swallowed.

When the transplanted jungles surrounding the resorts gave way at last to the high veldt zone of Pilanesberg National Park, she felt deeply relieved. Tramping through the veldt, Sister Vena exclaimed at its natural wonders—its elephants, hippos, giraffes, and buffalo, its lions, leopards, and cheetahs. The lieutenant had grunted at that.

"This was a 'controlled wilderness.' Farmlands, until the 1970's. Most of the big stuff is reintroduced. Not that that much matters, now. Once the cities are all abandoned and the farms are overgrown, they'll be reintroducing themselves everywhere, on their own."

Elephants roaming the streets of Johannesburg, feeding in Joubert Park, Sister Vena thought. Giraffes grazing overgrown flower boxes on second-story patios and balconies. Cheetahs chasing springbok through crumbling concrete canyons. Lost Cities, all the more exotic for having once been so ordinary.

"He-e-e-e!" shrieked someone in the nearest of the trance-dance circles below, jerking Sister Vena back to the present. Listening more carefully to the drums and ankle-rattles now, she lifted to her eyes the night-vision field glasses the lieutenant had given her.

Sister Vena knew that shriek meant someone else had returned to the present, too—*out there*. When she'd first heard such fearful noises from around the dance-fires in the night, she thought some trance-dancer had fallen into the flames. The lieutenant corrected her, explaining that the loud cry she heard was the sound of a trancer's aerial-voyaging soul returning to the body, which had remained behind in what the local Werfolk called "half-death."

Scanning the nearest group with her night-vision glasses, Vena saw others on the ground, also passed out in half-death. Some in the trance-dance circle ministered to the unconscious, holding their heads and blowing powders in their faces—to bring them back, to prevent the half-death from becoming full death. Others continued to dance as they had danced all night long: hunched forward and making short tight steps, until the spirit-power made them stagger, leap, or somersault as it rose whirling in them like some sort of kundalini lava, spiraling up the spinal column and erupting into their heads.

Still others of the trancers, male and female, danced forward in Vena's direction now, well aware of her watching presence. They presented toward her the sexual postures of jackal and big cat, baboon and eland. When the lieutenant translated the stories and songs they chanted, though—those were even stranger than such behavior. Tales where honey, dribbled on a leather shoe placed beside a river, somehow caused an eland to grow underwater which (once surfaced and killed) was also the hide source of the leather shoe thrown into the sky to make the moon, which in turn goes dark as blood in death for three days each month, before being reborn and resurrected, shining. And, if that weren't enough, the honey was also somehow semen and the leather shoe was also somehow a vagina.

Removing the field glasses from her eyes, Vena watched the full moon settling toward the horizon and tried to imagine it as a little shoe dancing across the sky. *Or a boat on the water,* she thought, remembering something Mark Fornash told her at the Spires conference in New York. "The moon is a boat," he said, "the ego on the sea of the unconscious. The wise fisherman doesn't pull too many fish up out of that sea at once, or the boat will capsize and sink."

Gazing through the moonlit darkness, toward the sound of the ever more frenzied trance-dancers, Vena wondered if those dancers—and all whom the madness plague had possessed, everywhere—were pulling so many fish aboard they were sinking the moon.

"*Stront!*" the lieutenant hissed, suddenly beside her, looking through her night-vision goggles. "They're 'shifting *en masse*! Berserking! That will make them hard to stop. Get your glasses to your eyes, Sister! Scan the field! Tell me if you see any of them trying to outflank us."

The ensuing mad skirmish seemed all the more chaotic viewed by moonlight and night-vision optics. For the lieutenant it was a firefight—although the trance-dancing berserkers returned fire mostly with arrows, spears, and slingshot stones. The shapeshifting warriors had numbers on their side, however. They would soon overwhelm the two women in their fortified rock outcropping—for all the lieutenant's skill and superior fire-power.

They did not hear the stealth helicopter gunship until it was over them. By then large caliber machine-gun fire was strafing the ranks of their attackers. An amplified voice called down to the women from the cockpit of the chopper.

"Remove your night-vision gear! Close your eyes!"

Sister Vena did both, but she could still feel the bright pressure as flares and searchlights burst from the helicopter and lit the hilltop brighter than day. She heard a singular mechanism firing and rotating, rotating and firing.

When she ventured to open her eyes, the light had dimmed only slightly. Nothing moved near their hilltop. Around them the corpses of their attackers smoldered as if smote by the hand of God. Rescue had come, but at a terrible cost. Vena felt no joy at the sight, only small relief and great weariness.

A ladder descended from the stealthy gunship as it hovered quietly above them. The lieutenant, smiling and whooping, clambered up it and inside. Behind her, Sister Vena climbed up and inside too, more tenta-tively. The helicopter rose, then swung away in a wide arc, south and east.

Over the intercom, their pilot informed them they were headed to a private airfield outside Durban. There they would rendezvous with their flight to the Bahamas. Glancing beside her, Sister Vena saw the lieutenant grinning from ear to ear in the dim interior light of the helicopter, her eyes still glazed in adrenaline rush.

The helicopter swung away from the setting moon. Sister Vena shook her head. What end could justify the means of this bloody rescue—without itself being tainted by the blood spilled, the lives lost? Yes, Vena was glad to be alive, but was her life worth all those deaths? Would Cameron Spires' brave new world be worth all the blood and violence of its birth?

The madness overwhelming the world now was deeper and more des-perate than war, more chaotic than mere anarchy. Neither the conferees' predicted Great Death nor the Werfolk-proclaimed Great Shift had come for her—only the great sadness of seeing a once-magnificent world civilization destroying all it had ever made, out of deep and secret self-loathing. Flying through the night, Sister Vena felt in her heart the paradoxical truth: Even those who had not been afflicted with the pandemic had still been afflicted *by* it.

30

Proving Ground
2066

LIBRIS GUARDS LEAD TRILLIA AND THE REST OF THE TRAVELERS TO THE Aberdeen Main Compound, across a narrow causeway from Spesutie Island. That she is now discernibly pregnant gets Trillia no special treatment from her captors. The travelers wait under guard on a lawn at the northeast end of the main compound—an impromptu courtyard decorated with the heads of half a dozen executed Werfolk. Under late afternoon sun, a huge vehicle clatters up the broken roadway toward them.

"An American light battle-tank," John explains to the nervous Werfolk in their party. "One of the solar-powered prototypes."

The tank skids to a halt before them. A hatch atop the tank pops open. On the ground, two lines of ten troops snap rigidly to attention, saluting. Out of the tank climbs a, bulldozer-bosomed woman dressed in a summer uniform of the same blue and black as the troops. Her attire is distinguished only by shoulder epaulets and other subtle signifiers of rank.

As the woman descends from the tank, Trillia stares in disbelief, more startled by what she's seeing than by the grotesque remains of the butchered Werfolk around them. The murderous Commander is—a woman? And not only a woman, but one she somehow *recognizes*. The Commander removes her helmet, revealing graying hair as she strides forward.

"John? John Drinan? Tomoko Fukuda? It is really you? Good God, it's been ages!"

The Commander shakes hands with her two old and stunned acquaintances, then steps toward Ricardo, who introduces himself.

"I knew your father well. Welcome. And you are—?"

"Trillia . . . Spires," Trillia says at last.

"Cameron's granddaughter! And in a family way, too—am I right? You're welcome, welcome! We're honored to have you among us."

The Commander turns to Sister Mariel and Sister Tawanna, who eye the leader warily even as they shake hands with her. When the Commander asks after Sister Vena and her health, Sister Tawanna remarks flatly that Sister Vena is "still dead." The Commander gives a short nod, before shaking hands hesitantly with Phenix. She does not address Caster, Aura, or Markus at all, almost as if they merit her notice no more than John's muzzled dog, Oz.

"Leira," Tomoko asks cautiously, "why were we brought to you under guard?"

"My apologies, but it's a dangerous and uncertain world. How could my Knights know you were friends of mine, eh? Especially given who you were traveling with. This is a restricted area, of vital importance to the security of our state. Naturally my soldiers here are a bit on edge."

"Restricted?" Tomoko asks. "Why?"

The Commander glances around at her troops, then with a shrug dismisses all but the four soldiers of her personal guard.

"Follow me. I'll show you."

Commander Losaba sets off at a vigorous stride, leading them into and out of one minimally lit building after another, gesturing about her as they walk.

"Before the plague and the collapse, this compound and all of Spesutie Island were connected to the Aberdeen Proving Ground. This was a major U.S. Army testing facility. The complex around us researched and developed technologies for enhancing the lethality and survivability of both advanced weapons systems *and* the individual soldier."

"Lethality *and* survivability?" Ricardo asks. The Commander nods.

"Armor, anti-armor, and individual soldier protection. Munition survivability. This facility developed electric tank guns. Their 'silver bullet' kinetic energy projectiles could destroy enemy armor at extreme distances. This facility also developed special tank armors—smart, titanium, counter-kinetic, electromagnetic—to defeat such silver bullets. Smart, ceramic and composite body armors and helmets. Projectile-proof face shields with built-in heads-up displays."

A smile of sheer joy lights the Commander's face as, turning, she makes a gesture broad enough to take in the travelers, their escort, and all their surroundings.

"Over there, they worked on electrically powered armament systems, like that tank I drove up in. Smartweave structural sensor systems. Hardened subminiature devices—impervious to blast and electromagnetic pulse effects. Ferroelectric phase-shifter materials for phased array antennas. Polymers and adhesives. Super fibers and protective coatings. Lightweight metals and ceramics with unique battlefield properties. High-density metals and alloys. Composite materials for ballistics and ordinance. High durability elastomers. Composite kinetic-kill sabots. Tungsten-alloy penetrators. Laser-ignition propulsion for shells and missiles."

"More and better ways to kill," Trillia mutters.

The Commander spins on her heel and points back at Spesutie Island proper.

"Without getting killed oneself—exactly. That's what lethality and survivability are all about. Across the causeway, in the Robotics Facility, they developed unmanned ground tactical vehicles. Battlefield robots controlled remotely—'telepresently,' as they used to say. Semiautonomous battlebots. Scientists and engineers here did everything from basic research to technology generation. So you can see why it's of paramount importance that we restrict access to this area."

"No," Trillia says. "Frankly, I can't."

The Commander frowns as they stop before a large mess tent. She leads them inside the tent, which is still bright and airy despite the declining light of the summer sun. Probably the big reason mainlanders prefer tents to the dark, empty buildings, Trillia thinks—at least in fine weather.

"Perhaps it's no longer the case on the islands," the Commander says, "but here on the mainland we're still at the scavenging and salvaging stage, as far as our techonomy is concerned. It'll be years before we can reliably produce bullets on our own—much less 160 mm howitzer smartshell kinetic-kill projectiles. The Proving Ground contains tactical and strategic resources. They must be guarded so we can utilize them as the need arises."

"That's not what I meant," Trillia says. "What 'need' is there? With so few people and so much planet, why would anybody want to go to war over any of it?"

The Commander laughs as she motions them to take seats around her table. Soldier-servitors scurry for more tables and chairs and water glasses. Aura, Markus, and Caster are discreetly seated at a nearby table.

"Living in the islands has lulled you younger people into a false sense of security, exactly as I feared it would. You have no idea of the chaos and struggle that overwhelmed the mainland after the pandemic and the collapse. All civilization worthy of the name is gone. Those Trufolk who remain have reverted to pitiful subsistence. Scavenging in the woods and fields. Hunting and fishing. Growing a few sickly cereals and vegetables, bartering a few idle crafts at best. Order was completely overthrown. But order can come back. High civilization will come back."

Soldiers serve the Commander and her guests a salad course of wild-harvested greens. John Drinan glances down at the tired, muzzled dog beside his feet.

"And that's what you're trying to do?"

"We're already doing it! Look at these Trufolk, the men and women serving us. You would not believe the squalor many of them were living in when I first took up residence in the old Capitol building, a dozen years ago. Lives built on scrounging and theft and murder—nearly as barbaric as Werfolk. Look at them now. From bands of scavengers, brigands, and occasional murderers, I have crafted a new force for order—in a remarkably short time."

"How'd you accomplish that?" Ricardo asks, concentrating on his salad but still not quite keeping the disbelief out of his voice. Commander Losaba swirls her glass of finely aged pre-pandemic wine.

"I gave them a mythology. A new flag to rally round. A model of soldiery and social order that links us to the lost grandeur of *both* the American military *and* the Library of Congress. And to something much more, too. We are the conservators of all the knowledge that once was—like the monks and nuns who preserved classical learning after the fall of Rome. Together we are the first spark of a new order, one which will bring the light of technomic civilization back to all the world!"

The main courses of venison and fish begin to arrive.

"The monks and nuns of a thousand years ago didn't keep slaves!" Sister Tawanna says hotly. "Those nuns and monks never did anything like what you've done in and around Washington! You've turned it into a slave labor camp!"

The Commander stares coldly at the young nun.

"We keep no slaves—only prisoners of war. I am at least honest enough to admit the danger the subhuman Werfolk pose to everything I hold dear."

"Is that your excuse," Sister Mariel asks, "for *executing* young Werfolk 'prisoners' at the first sign of shapeshift?"

The Commander's face hardens still further.

"Not my excuse—my *reason*. Werfolk are not truly human—how else to explain the acts of bestial savagery I have seen them commit with my own eyes? Every surviving were-creature is a threat to the future of humanity. We exploit them for labor, then execute them before they become dangerous. Just speeding along the 'transcendence' their lunatic religions all preach. It is a perfectly rational and realistic policy."

John Drinan stares at the Commander, clearly taken aback by what he's hearing.

"I knew you had no love of Werfolk, but I can hardly believe that I'm hearing Leira Losaba say these things. How could someone who came from where you came from—with that history—possibly oversee such a policy?"

The Commander turns stiffly toward and then away from John.

"I see no contradiction. I *do* remember the history of the world that once was—quite well, thank you. When the Emperor converts to the religion of slaves, the barbarians aren't at the gates. They're sitting in the Imperial palace."

Trillia laughs. Everyone looks toward her.

"I don't think anyone could accuse my grandfather of 'converting to the religion of slaves.' "

Losaba nods slowly, cutting carefully at her food with knife and fork.

"I spent fifteen years as his head of Security. When I left, many people wondered why I turned abjurer. The answer is simple."

She pauses to take a bite of her food and chew it before continuing.

"I left because island policy toward the Wer was too lenient. President Spires allowed the option of banishment. Why? If you banish rats, they return a hundredfold. They must be exterminated—killed at every opportunity."

"But the nature of the pandemic *and* the nature of the Wer have both changed!" Trillia protests.

"Really? I've seen no proof of *that* in my encounters with them. From the 'tolerance of subhumans' rot *you're* spouting, I'd say your grandfather has indeed become a convert to the religion of slaves. I never agreed with his creating the Merfolk, to tell you the truth. Already too many subhumans around, for us to be further outnumbering ourselves with them."

"The Merfolk protect the islands," Ricardo says in disbelief. "They're the first line of defense against raids from the mainland. Besides, they can't breed."

"They're just Mer . . . cenaries," the Commander says, smiling oddly at her little joke. "With time they'll switch allegiance—to the side of the hairier shapeshifters. I've never believed that part about their not being able to breed, either. They will. You'll see, if you live long enough. If we don't eliminate them, then the Werfolk and the Merfolk together will overrun the New Bahamas. When they do, everyone there in the islands will be *stunned*."

The Commander, having finished her meal, stands up. Her guards come to attention.

"If you wait for the Werfolk and the Merfolk to rebuild the cities and produce great architecture, then you will wait in vain. In a million years' time, they will never begin to match what true humans accomplished—and can accomplish again, if we allow ourselves the chance. My duty is to help foster that chance, before the subhumans outbreed us into extinction. There's room on this planet for only one species of human being. That's the way it's been for twenty thousand years, and that's the way it will always be."

"Sister Vena was right!" the nun Tawanna says. "The horrors you saw during the pandemic turned your wits! That's why you want to destroy all Werfolk—as much as Vena wanted to save them!"

With a bored shrug, the Commander drops her napkin on the table. As if at a signal, the guards surround the travelers and their escorts. They have ceased being "guests" (if they ever truly were) and are now simply prisoners once again.

"Vena worked her work, I work mine. I hope those of you who *are* fit will *see* fit to join me in my work. Those three"—the Commander points to Aura, Markus, and Caster—"are not fit. Seize them. They are to be executed upon my return. As for the rest of you, your training and expertise make you valuable to us. It will take three days for my forces to finish reconnoitering the northern reaches of Chesapeake Bay south to the narrows at Annapolis. I give you those three days to decide. Join us voluntarily on our return to Washington, or be carried there by force and re-educated once we reach the Capitol. Such a re-education process will not be pleasant. Consider your options carefully."

The Commander addresses the last of this to Trillia, staring hard at her before turning on her heel and striding away. Guards hustle away the three obvious Werfolk. Trillia and her group are prodded and pushed back over the causeway, onto Spesutie Island proper, into the cavernous spaces of Building 1120 B, the Robotics Facility.

Before the night has well begun, Trillia and her fellow prisoners hear a clatter of mechanized transport—accompanied by shouting, the pounding of hooves, the firing of heavy guns. Soon thereafter, their guards fall into a much more relaxed stance. The Commander and the main body of her troops have apparently departed the area.

Without warning, Trillia, John, Tomoko, Ricardo, Phenix, and the two nuns are hustled out of their holding cell within the Robotics Facility. Outside, they are put into a holding tent, on the edge of a plain of broken stone, punctuated by weeds and grass, hard by the Robotics Facility. Their Libris guards—armed conservators of the museums and libraries of the past against the barbaric present—break out a goodly supply of alcohol and proceed to drink deeply.

Before long, the captives learn why they have been brought outside. Not for their own entertainment and convenience, but for that of their captors. With much noise and backslapping, the contingent of thirty or so remaining Knights Libris cobble together what look to be viewing stands. These they place about the plain of broken stone and weeds, making that waste space into an improvised arena. Trillia fears she and her fellow prisoners will take center stage in this spectacle—until she sees that, with the exception of the three heavily armed guards maintaining a vigil about their prison tent, none of the Knights is paying the prisoners the least attention.

Trillia volunteers to maintain watch on their captors' strange goings-on. John and Tomoko join her for a time, looking on as, under blazing torches and battery-powered lights, the soldiers carry or wheel into the arena dozens of oddly shaped and glittering machines, in a range of sizes.

"Biobots," John says, peering at what the soldiers are placing in the arena. "Mechanicals modeled on biological organisms. The big thing in the center looks like a biotank or biocybernetic habitat. Like what Sister Vena was in, only a later model."

Trillia nods, thinking the troops are about to stage some sort of robot war spectacle for their own amusement. The awe and reverence with which the troops take their VR control circlets into their hands and place them on their heads, however—even those who are more than a little intoxicated—leads Trillia to suspect it's more complicated than that. Clearly she is not getting the whole effect the troops are experiencing, since all she can see is a section of the overview screen and speakers the troops have set up, for the benefit of the three guards who must refrain from giving their full attention to whatever it is their comrades are up to.

Sneaking a peek at more of the screen, Trillia is surprised when the first thing she sees is the enormous birth-flash of the universe—followed by all that flash's inflationary splendors, spreading and cooling and creating space-time, gaseous clouds whirling down and condensing ever more tightly with gravity, igniting into stars.

"What are they doing?" Trillia asks Tomoko, looking from the troops to her and back again. Tomoko stares fixedly at the soldiers. The Knights are not just sitting there in rapt attention—they seem somehow to be participating in what is happening on the screen.

"I can't say for sure. They look like they're *performing* it, though. Shaping it. Maybe playing the roles of the contending forces that steer the evolution of the universe. The contracting force of gravity, the expanding force of the nuclear reactions that fuel the stars."

"What's the point of that?"

"Games don't have to have a point," John puts in. "All they need is a goal and forces to contend over it."

Tomoko and John leave her, but she barely notices. On the screen, Trillia watches the troops interactively create the solar system, spinning planets into being, primal fireballs shaped from accretion disks of cooling starstuff. Volcano and vent and meteor strike. The capture of the moon, the start of the long partnered dance with Earth. The tectonic shimmy of continents too thick and buoyant to be subducted. Fire-fountain volcanics, mountains soaring and crumbling. Cloud and thunderbolt and storm. Glaciers advancing, retreating. The uneasy sleep of rivers in their beds. Oceans rising, falling.

Then, out of that welter of cycles and hypercycles, Life, and the biobots coming to life in the arena, to applause and cheers. New forces coming into play and battle: pseudobacteria gobbling chemicals, artificial algae devouring photons, synthetic cells, cybercoelenterates, teletrilobites, alphanumeric ammonites, graphical user gastropods, semiautonomous cephalopods—

Tomoko returns and speaks to the nearest guard, getting his permission to close the tent flap so that the "guests" can retire for the night. The guard, as preoccupied as Trillia with what he's seeing on the screen, gives a perfunctory permission. Tomoko lowers the tent flap and secures it, before leading Trillia by the arm toward the back of the tent.

"It's Ricardo. His Wersign is flaring up. It's bad."

Ricardo spasms in shapeshift, twitches in soul-flight. Helping her fellow prisoners hold him down and keep him quiet, Trillia worries that if the Commander learns Ricardo is manifesting Wersign this way, it will mean his death. She hopes her anger at the Commander will keep the tears from welling into her eyes, but it doesn't.

"Why now? Why has it become so uncontrollable *now*?"

"I don't know," Sister Mariel says, trying to quiet the struggling Ricardo. "Maybe it's the stress of capture, our situation as prisoners—"

"Whatever the cause," Tomoko says, inserting a rag into Ricardo's mouth to muffle his outbursts, "any 'remission' he got from Fornash seems to have run its course."

In the holding tent the six of them—Trillia, Tomoko, John, Phenix, Sister Mariel, and Sister Tawanna—can only hold on to Ricardo and watch as he writhes in the dark rapture of soul-flight. At least the noise of the Knights' continuing robo-gladiatorial ritual is loud enough to drown out the muffled sound of Ricardo's pangs and throes as his spirit is sundered from and returned to his body again and again. The resurgence of Ricardo's symptoms, too, has at least waited until *after* their interview with the Commander—thankfully. If he had not appeared symptom-free then, he would be awaiting execution, just like Caster, Aura, and Markus.

Eventually, Ricardo grows exhausted enough that it no longer takes six people to hold him down. After a time he falls into a twitching, fitful sleep. Trillia wanders toward the front of the tent, bone-tired. She loosens the tent flap enough to see that the Knights' strange ritual is still going on. In the cybernetic ecology of the biotank, on the ground of the arena and in the air above it, infotech insects, fractal fish, arithmetical amphibians, recursive reptiles, binarized birds, machined mammals, all struggle with fang and claw, eat and are eaten, compete and cooperate, go extinct or coevolve.

Only at dawn do the troops call a halt to their game-rite. Some crawl off to sleep, but most of them are too pumped up by the experience to retire yet. The guards change, the replacements occasionally looking in on the prisoners. Finding their guests awake or asleep but unchanged in number, the guards pay their charges less and less attention. They don't examine Ricardo closely enough to see the paroxysms that pass through his body from time to time—nor do they note that his eyes, although partly open, twitch from side to side in his head. Trillia and her companions, fearing anything they say might be overheard, speak in whispers throughout the day.

"We've gotten him to quiet down," Sister Tawanna tells Trillia in midafternoon. "We've used what techniques we know to help Ricardo—and us—control to some degree the manner of his shapeshifting."

Trillia stares at her lover's face. His eyes still jitter distressingly. Trillia rubs her own eyes with her hands, exhausted.

"He's conscious, then?"

"Only partially. His symptoms are an odd blend of the shapeshifting and soul-flying phases. I've never seen anything quite like it before. Then again, the soul-flying phase is the most ambiguous and paradoxical of all."

"What's that supposed to mean?"

"It means," Tomoko says, putting her hand on the younger woman's shoulder, "that none of us—not Wer, Tru, or Mer, not Fornashian, not New Catechist—can tell you much that is objectively verifiable about it. It's the most subjective phase, the least accessible to probing by objective science or waking consciousness."

"But it *is* the last stage, isn't it? That means he's dying, doesn't it?"

John blows out a sigh, so loud amid their hushed voices that it startles all of them.

"Everybody's dying all the time. You met Mark Fornash. He was aerial voyaging for years. His people, and most of the Wer I've met, too—they regard the last flight as something like 'achieving the escape velocity of the soul.' "

"I don't understand."

"*Both* death and transcendence," Sister Mariel says.

Trillia shakes her head bitterly, trying to keep the catch in her voice from breaking into a sob.

"You'll excuse me if I don't find that prospect as 'joyful' as you true believers do!"

She gives way to soft, stifled sobs then. She does not want comfort from anyone. Sleep is the only comfort she'll accept, once she has cried herself into that place. She dreams of the baby she is carrying. On waking, she cannot remember the dream, though her belly swells beneath her hand, each passing day rounding her more, like the waxing moon.

Around her, inside the tent, everyone sleeps except for John. He stares out the tent flap at the Knights' ritual, which has resumed. Trillia gets up and walks toward the entrance. John turns to her as she comes up beside him.

"These biobots are better at morphing and linking up than anything I've ever seen. Human evolution and history are the topic tonight. Cultural phases—hunting and gathering, through herding and farming, to industrial and infotech economies. City-states, empires, nations, and corporations."

"Why do they spend so much time on it?"

"I'm not sure, but I think this role-playing ritual is some sort of mnemonic practice, too. Part of the bigger 'mythology' Leira says she gave them. I don't know how she put it together, but whatever it is, it's coming to an end."

Stomping about on the field, unopposed, is the biggest 'bot yet—a thing resembling a human form, but ten times human size. It is fleshed with cityscapes, composed of all the accretions, components, and infrastructures of millennia of urban civilization. As it raises its arms in triumph, out of the biotank flows a steel-gray goo—swarms of binobots flooding forward, flowing up the legs of the cityscape robot, overwhelming and overcoming it, the wave of microbots melting the cityscape robot's form into their own formlessness, deconstructing and decohering the citybot molecule by molecule, atom by atom, until it is completely overthrown—just as humanity and its cities were overthrown by the plague.

A roar goes up from the troops playing their roles. Trillia can only shake her head, glad the perverse rite has ended. She watches the crowd of Knights breaking up amid much self-congratulation. The soldiers straggle off to bed and sleep, which sounds like a good idea to her, too.

Trillia doesn't remember falling asleep until she is shaken awake. Before her leers a face so time-battered and wolfish she almost cries out before the wolfish crone slaps a hand over her mouth. When Trillia's eyes have stopped darting about enough to let the old woman see she is recognized, the woman takes her hand from Trillia's mouth.

"I know you! You're—"

"The bloody Werfolk cavalry, kiddo," the old woman says, so low it's almost a growl, but accompanied by a broad lupine wink. "Guadalupe Sanchez, at your service. No time for jawing. Help my friends here get the rest of your party on the move and we're out of here."

Joining two young loincloth-clad men in waking the rest of the prisoners, Trillia does as she is told—except for the no-jawing part. The wolfishness, she sees, is already easing from Lupe's face.

"How did you find us?"

"Simon had already sent us south looking for you—when *he* called us. His spirit-guide led us to you."

Trillia's confusion is overwhelmed by relief at seeing that the *he* Lupe referred to—Ricardo!—is sitting up, blinking dazedly. A weak smile shows on his face as he gets slowly to his feet.

Leaving the tent, the escaping prisoners step over the body of one of their guards where he lies, facedown in a pool of blood from his own slashed throat. Oz pauses to sniff the body. John jerks the leashed but no longer muzzled dog after them. Two more guards lie dead in the improvised arena. Their Werfolk rescuers have done bloody work, swift and silent as the angel of death.

A worn blanket of mist cloaks the night. Despite the poor visibility, their Werfolk guides lead them unerringly along a wooded path toward the sound of waves. They have just reached the cove where *Sea Robin* and *Star Thrower* wait, anchored not far offshore, when they hear the first distant shot.

"Damn!" Lupe mutters. "Our people must have been spotted, bringing out the other three."

The escapees and their rescuers climb aboard dinghies and paddle toward the familiar boats, passing near a pair of patrol boats tied up at a floating dock. On shore, in the direction from which they came, shouts rise. Their escape has been detected. Beyond *Sea Robin* and *Star Thrower* drift two watercraft—sleek and low-slung, but small—which Trillia has never seen before. Their rescuers' boats.

Trillia is glad to hear *Sea Robin*'s engine purr when she punches in the starter code—and almost as glad again when she hears *Star Thrower*'s engine up and humming a moment later. As the escapees ready their boats, Lupe brings one of the unfamiliar watercraft around before the bows of *Sea Robin* and *Star Thrower*, calling to them just loudly enough for them to hear.

"Follow me to the C and D Canal. Stefan and Clara will take their boat to the rendezvous point, to see if they can't pick up our people and the rest of your party. Hurry now!"

Stefan and Clara cut away north and west in their craft while Lupe's boat heads east, the escapees in *Sea Robin* and *Star Thrower* behind her. Glancing back over her shoulder, Trillia sees lights, made hazy by the fog, coming toward the shore and the cove they have just left. A flicker of worry—about the patrol boats moored there—passes through her mind. Then she is too busy steering and trying to follow Lupe's lead to give any of her mind to more worry.

Several minutes later, as the escapees round Turkey Point, Trillia hears the distant roar of powerboats starting up and coming on. Before either of the two pursuing craft are even halfway to the escapees' position, however, each patrol boat abruptly stalls out and catches fire, before blowing up with a night-shattering blast and mushrooming fireball of burning fuel, scant minutes later.

"Looks like your finny friends have done their part," Lupe calls back to the escapees. Trillia nods. Lurking Merfolk—via a little sabotage—have just changed their odds. Near the mouth of the Bohemia River two more patrol boats approach, only to repeat the same sequence of stall, fire, explosion, and fireball.

As their little three-boat flotilla passes by the old Corps of Engineers anchorage on the Chesapeake end of the canal, Trillia wonders how many of their pursuers went down with their ships—and how many took the hint and abandoned ship before their watercraft exploded. The three fleeing boats move deep into the canal, eventually passing a clanging robotic dredge.

"Stay tight here!" Lupe orders. "Parts of the canal are pretty choked and shoaled, despite that old dredge!"

A moment later, Trillia sees other boats coming slowly in their direction. She calls out about them to Lupe.

"Don't worry about them! Those are hulks your Merfolk are dragging toward the Chesapeake entrance of the canal. They'll let our other boat through, if it makes it, then they'll scuttle those hulks where the canal is narrowest. That should make it impassable. With luck, anybody following us will have to go all the way down Chesapeake Bay and around the peninsula!"

An hour later the flotilla crosses out of the canal and into Delaware Bay. They make their way south, accompanied by the occasional spyhopping of their Merfolk escorts. The fog closes in again as they cross the shallow flats along the eastern third of the bay. The little flotilla moves quietly and carefully throughout the night, but at good speed nonetheless.

Dawn turns the fog golden around them and begins to burn off the misty veil. They pass Cape May—once home to wide, sandy beaches and well-preserved Victorian homes, now all succumbing to erosion, abandonment, dilapidation. Lupe guides them into temporary anchorage on Cape May Inlet, between two parallel stone breakwaters.

"We'll wait an hour or so for Stefan and Clara and anyone else they may be bringing. We agreed to rendezvous here if we made it through the canal and over the flats. If they don't get here before midmorning, we can assume they're not coming."

While they wait in the inlet's broad harbor, away from rotting hulks and sunken docks, Trillia and Ricardo confer with their Merfolk escorts. They repeatedly reassure the finned tribe that both of them are still hale and whole. Their escorts are no longer the same merry little band of Merfolk, however. Amphitrite seems estranged from the others, though Trillia can't say why.

Talking to the Merfolk, Ricardo puts the best face he can on his condition, but he's still fighting the paroxysms that shake him at intervals. Sending the Merfolk off to patrol the harbor, Trillia sits beside him at the back of the boat. She pulls his head onto her shoulder.

"Love, what did Lupe mean when she said your 'spirit-guide' led them to us?"

Ricardo rubs his eyes tiredly, then shakes his head.

"You'd better ask her. I dreamed something about them—about Lupe and several other Werfolk, playing some kind of hide-and-seek chase game with me. About getting them to talk to Merfolk, too. It doesn't make much sense, when I think about it now."

The other low-slung boat, the double of the one Lupe pilots, heaves into view. As it comes closer, Trillia sees four Werfolk she does not know—two previously introduced as Stefan and Clara, and two others. Also aboard are Caster and Aura, but Markus is missing.

Introductions are brief. Stefan nurses a bloody wound to his left shoulder. Myka—one of the other Werfolk—has a blood-soaked rag wrapped around his head. Caster too is wounded, a deep gouge to the outside of his right thigh. Listening to their report to Lupe, Trillia learns how much more difficult an escape the imprisoned Werfolk had. The worst of it is that Markus is dead—killed while escaping. Aura is numb with shock.

Caster is brought aboard *Sea Robin*, there to be tended by a grim and thin-lipped Tomoko. Of the rest of the group, Myka and Joachim join Lupe in her boat, but Aura remains, unmoving, behind Stefan and Clara. The newly arrived party has seen and perhaps done terrible things, but Lupe is not about to let anyone pause long enough to think about that.

"We make a double-time quick run from here. On our way north, Simon and my people left a cache of food and medical supplies near the Steel Pier in Atlantic City. We'll stop there long enough to gather up that gear and tend our wounded before we move on."

Lupe pauses. The others nod grimly.

"The inland waterway is a mess between here and Atlantic City, so we travel open sea from Cape May until we reach Absecon Inlet. We take the inland waterway from Atlantic City to Barnegat, open water up to Manasquan, then on to Manhattan."

Trillia and the rest are too tired or distraught to do anything but nod in agreement. Through the haze of a dull summer morning and early afternoon, they fight annoying ocean chop until they come in sight of the broken-towered gambling palaces of Atlantic City.

Since Ricardo is doing better, and eager to be of help herself, Trillia relinquishes her map pad and the wheel of *Sea Robin*. Lupe, Clara, and Joachim—the young Wer whose name Trillia learned last—will go ashore to recover the cache the earlier northbound party buried beside the Steel Pier. Trillia volunteers to join them.

They land beyond the weathered tower of Absecon Light House, on the Absecon Inlet side. Trillia follows her Werfolk companions onto sand gray and brown and white, then past bent and rusted metal railings and onto what Lupe calls the "boardwalk." Where it is not covered by wind-banked sand, or so weathered it has broken apart, what Trillia can make out of the boardwalk tells her only that the boards were laid in a zigzag, herringbone-twill pattern. She sees little to be impressed with, but Lupe goes on and on about the place, talking about "saltwater taffy" and "roasted peanuts." As they pass the broken glass and rusted steel façades of the various towers, monoliths, and ziggurats, Lupe points out with her shovel what she calls Hiltons, Harrahs, Caesars, and Ballys. Reminiscing about the lost amusements of the vanished world, the old woman laughs until she seems almost ready to cry.

The Steel Pier, when they reach it, is a long ocean-battered structure of rusting metal and crumbling concrete, splashed with lichen above the waves, encrusted with mussels and barnacles below the tide lines. Sea-worn as it is, the pier still supports the faded wood façades of "show-places" and the twisted metal contraptions of "rides."

In the sand not far from the pier, Clara hands over to Joachim the shovel she has been carrying. Lupe, remarking on Trillia's pregnant condition, at first refuses to let Trillia dig. Trillia pooh-poohs the older woman's concern until Lupe at last lets Trillia take over the digging for her. Despite the cooling ocean breeze, Trillia finds the digging hot, hard work—especially since, for modesty's sake, she is wearing a good deal more clothing than Joachim. The dark-haired young man, lithe and tanned, is clad only in a soft deerskin loincloth. Clara, her gray-streaked reddish hair fluttering in the wind, passes a pipe back and forth with old gray-headed Lupe as the two women try to keep their loose, multicolored shifts from blowing too much in the sea breeze.

"I remember what this place looked like fifty years ago," Lupe says, looking around her. "When I was a girl I visited here during summers. Crowds came down from New York City and Trenton and Philadelphia. Thousands of men and women and children, in bathing suits as skimpy as what Joachim there is wearing. Striped beach umbrellas rippling in the breeze. People on the boardwalk, rolling or walking along. Vendors, hucksters, carny barkers calling and shouting after everyone's money. Rides clattering and banging. Sweet smell of taffy, cotton candy, roast nuts. Sad, to see it this way. No lost city is ever as empty as an abandoned amusement park."

Clara screws up her face against a sprinkling of windblown sand.

"Your friend Simon now, up there in Manhattan, might not agree with that."

"Maybe not," Lupe says, laughing lightly and nodding her head. Trillia pauses from her digging.

"You said Simon sent you looking for us. You know where he is, then?"

Lupe frowns.

"Not exactly. We left him in Manhattan's green front yard—what used to be called Battery Park. He still hadn't found everything he was looking for when we left, but from scouting around, he found the first of those 'gnomes' things."

Trillia takes up her shovel and joins Joachim in digging again.

"Ricardo mentioned those, too. What *are* they?"

"High-tech voodoo from the old days. I don't like them. Machines that *smart* are against my religion. You'll see. I don't like Simon's 'interfacing' with them, but what can I do? I'm responsible, in a way."

"How so?"

"One of my tribe slipped him some soul-vine wine his first night on the mainland. He had some kind of big vision. After that, he dropped all his other plans—nothing but New York and gnomes would do."

"Is that why he didn't stop to see any other abjurers on the way?"

Lupe ponders that, then shrugs.

"All I know is, after that first night with us, nothing else mattered except getting to New York. Some of my people and I tagged along—as much to keep an eye on him as anything else. Crazy, I know, but the spirit moving in him was enough to move us."

"And he sent you himself? To find us?"

"Commanded it, more like. I don't think it was wise for us to leave him when we did, but he found some of those damn gnomes and from talking with them he was all hot on getting you and your boyfriend, Ricardo, to join him in New York."

Trillia wipes sweat from her brow.

"How'd he know we were coming after him?"

"More of that Oldfolk machine farseeing, I guess. We weren't too far along, looking for you and Ricardo, before your friend started sending his spirit-guide at us—our *low*-tech voodoo way—and it got too obvious to ignore."

Trillia looks up from her digging again.

"I don't understand what you mean by 'spirit-guide.'"

Joachim laughs.

"Neither does your boyfriend."

More puzzled than ever, Trillia looks at him, then at Lupe.

"Ricardo is a powerful soul traveler, but he's not very good at controlling it. I don't even think he knows what he's doing. Sometimes he appeared to us as a blue-white ball of light, like a will-o'-the-wisp."

"Sometimes he was a deer or a wolf or a bear," Clara says. "Only with a human face."

"Once he was a fire right in the center of my head," Joachim says, frowning at the memory. "Hurt like crazy whenever I turned the wrong way."

"At least he led us to you," Lupe says with a wry smile. "That's all that matters, in the end."

Trillia shakes her head.

"When I asked him about it, all he remembered was dreaming something about playing hide-and-seek with you."

Joachim smiles, and pushing his shovel in deep, he bends down to look into the hole he and Trillia have been working on.

"I guess you could call it that. Hey, look at this! Here we are!"

Lupe and Clara join them around the hole. Together they pull up two metal boxes and two canvas bags of supplies. Dusting the sand off a bag before Clara shoulders it, Trillia wonders why they buried all this stuff so far below ground. To protect it against animals? Or other scavengers?

They haul the recovered supplies down to the shore beyond the lighthouse and toss the gear in the dinghy they came ashore in. Halfway to where the other boats wait, Trillia feels a pressure on her forehead—slight but sudden, as if someone has just placed a hand on her head. Too much strain from working while pregnant? She glances around. Her companions are in a much worse way, clasping their brows, gritting their teeth, and groaning.

"Ricardo," Lupe says, in pain. "He's doing it again."

When they reach the *Sea Robin*, Trillia hurriedly joins Tomoko and John at Ricardo's side. Trillia puts a hand to the face of her trembling and spasming lover.

"I'm here, Ricardo—I'm here."

The pressure on her head vanishes. His spasming slows and stops. Ricardo opens his eyes wide and stares at Trillia.

"Simon! I saw Simon! He needs us."

Trillia nods. The others try not to stare. They divide the recovered gear among them and finish their work with the wounded, or grab a bite to eat from the newly acquired stores. The four boats move north again, one Merfolk escort leaping at the bow of each. Trillia stays with Ricardo. Despite the heat, he continues to shiver.

They sail through the afternoon and into evening, past flooded channels, endless salt marshes, tidal bays, and low shorelines devoid of human landmarks. Toward sunset, though, they come upon fallen-down lagoon developments, dense-packed small houses on old landfill flooding and washing away, disappearing into cordgrass thick with birds.

Not long after sundown, they reach the upright bascule bridge beyond

Manasquan Inlet's parallel breakwaters. Over dinner, the travelers call from boat to boat in the twilight, debating the merits of pressing on, through the dark, to Manhattan.

"A run through the night is too risky," Lupe says, shaking her head.

"But we *must* go on tonight," Sister Mariel urges them. "We need to put as much distance between ourselves and the Commander as we can."

"But we're far outside Leira's territory by now, aren't we?" Tomoko says.

"As a precaution, then," Sister Tawanna says. "Mariel and I know our way into and around New York. It's worth the risk."

"I agree," Ricardo puts in. Weak as he is, he stuns everyone by the force in his voice. "I know what my vision showed me. We need to reach Simon Lingham as soon as possible."

Against Lupe's and Tomoko's caution, the persistence and ardor of the younger travelers at last prevails. In the dark they set out from Manasquan toward Manhattan, sailing through the night between a dark continent spangled with fireflies and two dark oceans, one above, one below, both sprinkled with bright stars.

Long after midnight, mist and clouds obscure the stars. Predawn light stains the eastern sky before the Verrazano-Narrows Bridge looms up ahead of them. The great bridge, for all the beauty and grace embedded in its every line, looms dark and intimidating in the dimness of the early morning. Trillia shivers as they pass beneath it, thinking of fantastic spiders weaving such a web of stone and steel.

Then the mist parts and—shining golden in the light of a sun rising beneath clouds of an overcast dawn—they see before them the cloud-capped towers of a ghostly, magnificent island-city.

"Manhattan," Sister Mariel says, and on her tongue it is the name of a place hallowed by all the souls of its dead.

In the golden light of the Upper Bay, Trillia watches as their Merfolk escort leap before the bows of their boats. No, wait. Only before the bows of *three* of the boats. One of the Merfolk is missing.

NOT FAR OFF ROCKAWAY BEACH, NEREUS WAITS FOR AMPHITRITE, WITH half a dozen other Merfolk guards. When the beautiful young mermaid reaches him, she looks troubled. Her distress reminds Nereus of his own increasing discomfort. All these months of lurking and hiding and following, all this spying and lying—at his creator's command—have begun to wear on him. Fighting against marauding Werfolk was always more straightforward than these observations from afar, this endless taking of reports. Nereus chafes under the restraints of this secretive service his master has put upon him.

"They've reached the great city, Father Nereus," Amphitrite beams to him, her call betraying nervousness and exhaustion.

"You've done well," Nereus replies, trying to sound more confident of his mission than he actually feels. "I will convey that information to Him immediately."

He is close. President Spires is "on a brief vacation, free of the mundane cares of office." His oceangoing yacht lies only a day's hard swimming away.

"I feel I've done neither well nor good," Amphitrite responds.

Nereus doesn't know whether he's more taken aback by the mer-girl's downcast and sorrowful tone, or the all-too-Trufolk way she has played upon words. Her work has, necessarily, forced her to face uncomfortable facts. She too has probably seen how similar the Merfolk's shapeshifting enemies are to their Trufolk masters—and how different *and* similar both are compared to the Mer. Nereus wonders if she has been pushed to the brink of what the Trufolk call psychological collapse—by the rigors of her journey, the difficulty of keeping these reports to him secret from her friends.

"Father Nereus, if you would, please let me go home now. I'm terribly tired of this game. It's not fun anymore. Thetis and Psamathe and Thaumas have stopped liking me. I come and go from them and cannot tell the truth of where I've been."

The mer-girl's sentiments only confirm his suspicions as to her mental state.

"Have you told them of our meetings?"

"No! Never, Father Nereus!"

The mer-girl's obvious fear irks him even as he pities her. He has never wanted to inspire fear, yet here it is. No matter how much fear he might inspire, too, he doubts he can keep Thaumas, Thetis, and Psamathe from suspecting what Amphitrite has been up to.

"That's good, little one. Remember what I told you: the consequences of revealing what we've been doing could be terrible indeed."

"Yes, Father Nereus."

"This is a very serious game. I need you to play it just a little longer, Amphi. You must rejoin Thetis, Thaumas, and Psamathe."

"If you say so, Father Nereus. I go now."

He watches her swim away. She drags through the water as if a killing weight were pushing her slowly toward the bottom. She vanishes, first to eye and then to sonar. It tears at Nereus's heart to see one so young and frail so burdened, but who can he tell of such feelings? Merfolk are not supposed to be distracted by matters of spirit, of emotion. Love is supposed to mean nothing to him. Yet he could love this child far more than its creator does—who, for all the superior prowess Trufolk claim to have in such realms, does not feel for this part of his creation one droplet of the ocean of care and concern Nereus feels toward her now.

He still has his duty. He must do it, though he understands less and less *why* that should be so. If he can be neither father nor brother nor lover, and she neither mother nor sister nor beloved, who cares whether Merfolk are truly immortal or not? What good is a life that goes on and on, if it can never be shared deeply with anyone else? Did Cameron Spires create his Merfolk only to imprison them in such a hollow life?

With two of his comrades, Nereus turns in the direction of President Spires' yacht. He swims rapidly, trying to dispel his heretical thoughts through sheer physical exertion. Many hours later, when the three Merfolk reach the yacht and come into the President's presence, Nereus is as blandly dutiful as his strength will still allow.

31

Escape Bubble
2033

CAMERON SPIRES IN HIS HIGH TOWER FELT AS THOUGH HE WERE THE LAST man left alive on Earth.

Before the local news stations failed, he saw first the emergency rooms, then the hospitals, and then the mortuary response teams overwhelmed by the scope of the catastrophe. Age, gender, ethnicity, religious beliefs, sexual orientation, socioeconomic status—none of it made any difference in the end. The pandemic was an equal opportunity destroyer.

No one was prepared for what happened. How could they have been? In the past, disaster preparedness relied on the assumption that the disaster would always be limited and local—that there would always be someplace free of catastrophe, from which help and order could come. The global scope and unprecedented enormity of the pandemic meant there was just *no place* from which help and order could come, in the end—because there was no place free of catastrophe.

In New York, Cameron saw just how tremendously the dead came to outnumber the living. Good intentions, human sympathies, respect for the deceased—none of it mattered at the last. The survivors (most of whom were also ill with madness plague) could not possibly cope. Neither mass graves nor mass burnings could handle the innumerable corpses. New York became a charnel city.

Fear that thousands upon thousands of bodies rotting in summer heat would spread collateral contagion led to entire housing developments and apartment complexes being blown up and set afire in the boroughs and most of the outlying areas. In vain. For all the damage they wrought, fires could not be set fast enough to eliminate the metro area's corpse burden. Vultures visiting from the countryside, millions of urban cats and dogs gone starving and feral, the worms, beetles, and fungi of slow-jawed time—only hordes of such carrion eaters could handle the burden of all those bodies left behind.

Through a concentration of the city's remaining fire-fighting forces into the areas below Eighty-sixth Street—and the dumb luck of unseasonably heavy rains—Manhattan had been spared the worst of the flames. The towers of the island were all abandoned, or nearly so, once the power failed and the elevators stopped working. Some residents still living after the power grid went down took refuge in the parks, but not for long. From his aerie Cameron could even now see the tattered medical and morgue tents left standing about Central Park, in the Sheep Meadow, the Great Lawn, the North Meadow. Still more or less intact, too, were the long lines of portable toilets—and longer lines of makeshift incinerators—all along the mall. Abandoned now, the smell rising from the park in weeks past must have been as horrible as any stench in human history.

City power, light, and sewer had been out for nearly two months. Only Cameron's solar auxiliaries made this place livable, keeping the elevators running and the automated security up. Protection against murder, mayhem, and opportunistic crime was less of an issue now, anyway. When thieves, killers, and the many more "eccentric" classes of human predators became scarce too, *that* was a sure sign that the urban population had collapsed further than anyone could have predicted.

His Bahamian sanctuary had been ready for over a month. Yet Cameron has stayed, long overdue for departure. When he thought to ask himself why, the only answer he came up with was a grim combination of death watch and the captain's custom of going down with his ship.

Not that he actually intended to go down with the sinking ship of human civilization. Whatever guilt or responsibility he might have felt for his role in this greatest of all catastrophes, he certainly was not going to foolishly sacrifice himself. Too many had done that already. He still had his escape route all mapped and prepared. He'd use it when he was ready.

In the screenspace of his virtuality shades, he had watched as all the cities of Earth one after another stopped talking and waving their arms for help. He had listened while the great noise of human communication fell silent. Live Webcasts and beamdowns from those few still-functional nodes and satellites—and from the orbital habitat, too—all had now gone dark and dead. The eclipse of civilization—its global collapse—was total.

Running on the bioenergetics of his own body, his virtuality shades would stay functional as long as he lived. In the shades now, when he tried to call up the rogues' gallery of those who had participated in his Tetragrammaton teleconference, he found that none of them survived in the flesh, besides himself.

Which was not to say none of them survived in other ways. Dr. Vang had transferred a model of his mind into a data construct. Michael Dalke and Martin Kong, too, each in his own peculiar way, had transferred both mind and body, their flesh gone electric.

Cameron knew the truth of such apotheoses as well as anyone. He had overseen those transfers to the GNOMES. Once simply "Gödelian Nonstandard Optimized Market Evolution Systems," the GNOMES were now something much more: a nascent cyberecology of cellular automata running on quantum biocomputers. Tetragrammaton connections had allowed the dying Vang, Dalke, and Kong to reserve their spaces in that bioelectric environment. Dalke and Kong also claimed contacts with other machine intelligences throughout Earth's infosphere—and far beyond—now all linked to the GNOMES.

Cameron could not speak to the truth or falsity of their claims. He could only say he remembered strange, eleventh-hour conversations as he prepared those dying men for transfer. He was their psychopomp, the only man capable of making straight their ways into the afterlife, or at least the afternet. He remembered working on the cybercolony of cellular automata which would be imprinted with the model of Vang's mental operations, as Vang himself, nearing the end of his corporeal life, steepled the fingers of his hands weakly before him.

"I fear your Dr. Lingham was more right than he knew. In a war I fought in as a boy, a soldier once explained that he and his men had to destroy a village in order to save it."

Cameron—preoccupied—had nodded and turned to the old man.

"I've heard preachers say the same thing about both Noah's flood and the apocalypse. That God had to destroy the human race in order to save it."

"Perhaps Tetragrammaton," Vang mused darkly, "in trying to protect humanity from extinction, has now brought on that very extinction."

Cameron assured him such a situation could *not* be the case. Vang shook his head weakly, then handed Cameron a dataneedle.

"If Tetragrammaton has done so, then you must pursue the Lapis Program. Here are the access keys for it. That alone might redeem Tetra-grammaton for having brought about the death of all humanity."

"Shh! Save your strength."

To please the old man, Cameron agreed to check on this Lapis thing, whatever it might be, if only to get Vang to shut up about who was or wasn't responsible for the extinction of humanity. It turned out to be more worthy of his attention than he expected. The Lapis, as potential "human singularity," could definitely foul up his plans—and would need to be prevented.

Two days later, however, Dalke and Kong arrived, after a long and arduous journey. They brought the same issue of human extinction up to him, too, unburdening themselves of some supposed guilt or responsibility, as if Cameron were an enviro-suited Father Confessor giving them the last rites.

Dalke's manatee-like livesuited form reminded Cameron of how sailors' tales of mermaids and mermen were supposedly misconstrued manatee sightings. He had never quite believed that explanation, but looking at Dalke now, Cameron pondered the possibility of a future form of humanity which might swim the world's oceans as easily as mermaids or manatees—or even move like digital dolphins through seas of virtuality. Then Dalke's spasms would make him splash about madly in his float tank, he'd talk nonsense again, and Cameron's dream would vanish.

"Before you transfer us, we've got to tell you. Kong and me, we helped create the interaction of brain and prionoid. A situation too computationally complex to model in any supercomputer or biocyb habitat."

"What? I don't understand."

Kong moaned, then spoke in pain from the gurney he lay on.

"The *paradoxica pandemica*. Pandemic of paradoxes, paradoxical pandemic. In one evil little package. You and Vang made it easy. Neurotransmitter-tweaking prionoids. Bugs and germs doing what bugs and germs do. And the question that flipped your immortalizing binotech to another mode."

"What question?"

Dalke's voice sounded like laughter through gritted teeth.

"Will the best defense always go on the offense against its own team?"

Kong, who had escorted his float-tanked companion to New York despite being at death's door himself, tried to explain.

"Must any complete defense against extinction itself become a cause of extinction?"

Thinking the two men delusional, Cameron smiled indulgently, trying to humor them.

"Depends whether 'best' equals 'complete,' I suppose. Sounds like a question for the GNOMES to solve, not mere mortals."

What the two men said next—Dalke cryptic, Kong clarifying unfathomably—only confirmed Cameron's suspicion of their mental instability.

"The GNOMES have already been asked. The pandemic is their answer."

"What do you mean?"

"Möbius prionoid. Infinite-loop binoprogram. Orders from the Allesseh. The immortal mind that haunts the eternal deep, at the heart of the galaxy."

Whew boy. That was just too much of a stretch. Attempting to *save* humanity from extinction was what was *causing* its extinction? And humanity was not yet extinct, anyway—no matter how lonely he might feel here, high above a sepulchral New York City, apparently abandoned but whose metro area population might still be as high as ten thousand, according to some of the machine-generated scenarios.

And the GNOMES. How could he afford to believe what Dalke and Kong suggested about them? And who had asked "the question"? He doubted Dalke and Kong could have come up with it on their own, though maybe Vang could have. Yet, despite the collapse of technological civilization, the GNOMES still knew Cameron was the benefactor who had caused them to come into being in the first place—and who was even now keeping them powered up by the sun through the new dark age.

No. He could by no means shut them down. Too vital a resource. He had no choice but to remain in contact with them—even long after he left New York City for the islands. Whether Vang, Dalke, and Kong were wrong or right he would learn on his own terms, in his own time, through indirect questions to the GNOMES. It might take years, but that was not a problem. He could wait. Once he made good his escape from New York today, he would have all the time in the world, and all the world in his time.

He took one last look around his towering home's 360 degree panorama of city and park, sea and sky. He had lived in the urban world all his life. Once, every city was an immense theatre, its dramas as many and varied as its inhabitants. It was a thing of stages and scaffoldings, old neighborhoods and obsolete edifices struck like sets on the last night of the play, the luckier façades of buildings moved about, lifted and lowered from the fly floor, preserved and kept while the buildings behind them were demolished. Without its people, however, Manhattan had, like every city, become a much simpler and more static thing. A mountain range of monoliths and ziggurats. A skyline of glass and steel façades. Dreaming cliffs soaring above dark, asphalt-rivered canyons swept by a flash-flood of death. New York, the city that changes every hour, had stopped changing. The big show had closed. It was time to leave.

Cameron Spires pulled the emergency lever that transformed his lofty residence into that other thing it had also always secretly been, from the moment of its creation: a rotor-winged escape craft, part helicopter and part projectile-proof transparent bubble. He had built it out of fear that his headquarters might one day be besieged by mobs, but it would serve him just as well in this empty world. Above him, the great spire opened out into five blades. Engines hummed, rotors whirred and picked up speed. Beneath his feet, explosive bolts blew.

Vertigo overwhelmed Cameron as his escape bubble leapt free of the building it had been anchored to for so many years. Settling at last into level, autopiloted flight, the bubblecopter headed for Cameron's ocean-going yacht, the *Derceto*, an hour offshore.

All this will make a magnificent ruin someday, he thought, looking back at Manhattan as he left its dark towers behind.

Cameron landed on *Derceto*'s helipad and exited the escape bubble, giving only the most perfunctory of orders to the waiting crew. Seeing the way his escape craft overburdened the yacht and caused it to list, he ordered the crew to push the rotorcraft overboard. It splashed into the ocean and sank, severing his last tie with the world that once was, the world that had come tumbling down.

Secluding himself in his private suite of rooms, Cameron remained there as the yacht and crew made their way south toward the Bahamas through calm seas. Reviewing reports, he saw with pleasure that his

Bioneering Institute was already well established, with over one hundred employees at work. Of those who had attended the conference at his research library in New York some months back, over eighty percent of those still living had already been brought to his compound on Grand Bahama, or were en route. Other experts and equipment from around the world had also arrived or would be arriving soon.

Better and better. In his secluded rooms on the trip southward, vast vistas opened up before Cameron's eyes. The great work was already underway. Visionary, bold, pioneering work. The creation of a new society, a place free of catastrophe because it was free of the madness plague. A place of order and solace in a mad world. A place safely quarantined and sealed off from contamination by that world. A place where the human race and the race to save humanity would be one and the same—end and means, destination and journey. One people, one leader, one goal.

Anyone coming to live on his islands was—and would continue to be— screened for plague symptoms. The people allowed to participate in his noble experiment already constituted the world's largest concentration of persons with genetically coded resistance. Benign polymorphisms, in all the relevant neurotransmitter synthesis pathways.

He could take no chances, however. Anyone showing even the earliest warning signs of prionoid pandemic symptoms would have to be banished from the islands. Only in such a tough-minded manner could he forge a true utopia—not like the fragile, fuzzy-minded "good place" the idealists in their orbital habitat had tried to build. Something real and solid, upon the Earth.

And for a better world, better people. Immortalized human beings. Even people who would never succumb to the madness plague—people bioengineered for an aquatic life, safe from airborne plague mechanisms. During his journey south, Cameron saw it all in his mind's eye. The great work to be done in creating the Merfolk. The creation of a still more dynamic and invincible superhumanity, rebuilding a world at last far greater than that which had been lost. A new world which, with his guidance, would overcome the setback of pandemic and collapse—to someday take its rightful place in the heavens, among the stars.

In the midst of such plans and visions, he thought of the wise magician Prospero, the beast-man Caliban. He remembered the great lines from

Shakespeare: *O wonder! How many goodly creatures are there here! How beauteous mankind is! O brave new world that has such people in it!*

But no; he was getting ahead of himself. He had not yet reached his islands of refuge. No Miranda had yet been born of his line, nor Ferdinand to trouble her. Mankind would be no beauteous creature, for quite some time, as the world's silence and darkness grew and lingered. Yet, by the time *Derceto* sailed into harbor in Grand Bahama, the world he knew he could create—the world he saw in prospect before him, so fabulous and so new—he knew that island world would be a light in darkness, a voice of wisdom in silence, after this long hour of the wolf had ended.

32

Love Enough for Time
2066

THEY COME ASHORE AT NORTH COVE, HOMING IN ON THE RUST-STAINED twin pillars of the old World Trade Center, and the spireless Spires Tower beyond. Ricardo knows he is dying. He is not fatalistic about it, but he has a sense of his fate—has had that, at least since his encounter with Mark Fornash. He does not know his destiny, but with each step he takes he feels closer to his final destination.

His soul wants to fly out of his body at the least provocation. His friends must help him walk. Sometimes, when he collapses, he must be carried on a pallet. The coppery taste never leaves his mouth, now. For all that, he worries less about himself than about the burden he has become for those around him. Most of all he worries what will happen to Trillia and the child she carries, after he is gone. So much left to be accomplished. The future weighs on him at least as heavily as the past—all around them—weighs on all their small party.

Through the morning haze, through the windy chop where the Hudson and East Rivers flow into the Upper Bay, the travelers can still see the monument the oldsters call the Statue of Liberty, on Liberty Island. Nearer at hand stand not only the pillars of the Trade Center, but the buildings of the World Financial Center: giant stepped-pyramids, their broken levels overgrown with vines and sapling trees. Soaring arcades of broken glass and broken ornamental archwork. Inscrutable obelisk skyscrapers. Off ledges and in and out of broken windows, birds soar here, too—hawks, eagles, and falcons, hunting the many species of prey that live and nest in the abandoned city.

All the Werfolk, and John and Tomoko, too, walk armed and alert. They leave the dock and climb the stepped walls of the dikework protecting this island—from sea levels still rising, Tomoko says, though rising more slowly all the time, now. In an attempt to reorient herself to their location, Lupe pauses before the storm-weathered and anciently graffitied New York City Police Officers Memorial, dedicated to those who died in service to the city. Looking at the memorial, Ricardo thinks of something Lupe said as they approached Manhattan in dawn light: "Only time will destroy it, for it is sacred." Somehow, he knows that to be true. Yet, for all its sacredness, he does not doubt that unpleasant surprises lurk here, and he is glad for the wariness of those around him.

Ricardo barely sees the broken-cobbled esplanade. Lupe leads them southward and Trillia helps him walk. Beyond South Cove, however, his mind clears somewhat. They stop beside a building of unusual shape, which weathered signs denominate the Museum of Jewish Heritage and "A Living Memorial to the Holocaust." Just beyond the memorial, at the edge of Wagner Park's weedy tangle and sapling forest, stands a most peculiar statue: an ape, upright and dressed like a man, dancing with a cat, also standing, dressed like a woman, clothed in what Tomoko identifies as Regency style. John clears away the vines and weeds at the oxidized statue's base—Oz helping by digging at the tangle too—to find that the sculpture is called "Ape and Cat at A Dance."

The image holds everyone's attention, not just for the shapeshifted creatures it depicts, or for when it was made, but most of all for the building near which it stands. Holocaust and shapeshift, cheek by jowl. Was that juxtaposition only coincidence? Or was it a foreshock of things to come—of the great shapeshifting holocaust that would strike down all but the tiniest remnant of humanity?

Startled birds flutter and animals scatter over deep debris as they move onto a street. Ricardo is swept by a wave of trembling and weakness so overpowering, he stumbles and must lean heavily on Trillia—and Phenix, too, who comes to help. Lupe leads them down Battery Place and up Broadway, following tracks and traces only she seems to know. Ricardo thinks of Simon. As he does so, he finds he, too, somehow knows where to place his feet, as if he has walked this way before.

Through the canyoned maze of lower Manhattan, over mounds of broken glass and stone, they come to the revival gothic of Trinity Church. The roar of wind, or animals, or voices echoes distantly through the canyons. The travelers stop, more alert than ever. At last they move on. Lupe refers to the church at Broadway and Wall as "the temple at the end of Moneychangers' Row." Ricardo makes no sense of that until he remembers what Wall Street was, in the days before the pandemic.

"Even the moneychangers' buildings look like temples," Trillia says quietly as they reach what her map pad describes as exchange buildings, at the corner of what were once Nassau and Wall Streets. Tomoko nods.

"The city treasury, inside the temple of the city's patron deity. Like the Parthenon in ancient Athens."

Amid the rubble and debris in this vicinity, even making up the majority of the detritus in places, lie the skeletal remains of a tremendous number of people. Some great act of mass suicide or ritual carnage seems to have taken place here. Ricardo's sense that the area they're passing through is a "holy district" only grows stronger as they turn onto a side street. There, in a small park bordered by the columned façades of historic government buildings, massive bronze sculptures of an old bull and a slightly younger bear face each other across intersecting lanes and park space.

Tomoko stops between the bull and the bear, looking from one to the other.

"Maybe Mark Fornash was right when he called the stockmarket shamanic gambling."

Ricardo doesn't know enough about such things to speak to the truth of them—but he too finds it an odd coincidence that they should come upon oversized statues of iconic animals in the midst of what was once a great technorational metropolis.

Not far from where the bull and bear stand at odds, Lupe leads them inside a Spires Biotechnologies building. They pass through a smashed glass door, down a maze of corridors, into a drum-shaped room. The decor there is all stainless steel, chrome, and clean-room white. The light, such as it is, emanates from a liquid-filled sphere in the center of the room, one nearly as high as Ricardo is tall. He lets go his grip on Trillia and Phenix and walks unsteadily toward the sphere, drawn to it, as Lupe talks to the rest of the party.

"This is where Simon accessed that GNOMES thing before we split up. I thought we'd find him here, but he seems to have moved on."

"Where?" Aura asks quietly. It's the first thing Ricardo has heard her say since they escaped from Spesutie Island and the Knights Ex Libris.

"Your guess is as good as mine at this point," Lupe says. "I'm at a loss. Look at all the optics in the ceiling, though. See how active they are? Wasn't like that, before. These machines are too damn smart, I tell you. I just hope Simon didn't run afoul of them."

Leaning on the railing that surrounds the sphere, Ricardo glances at the ceiling. It's true. As he watches, he sees a high percentage of those lenses shift their focus to the sphere in front of him, or to him and the sphere, as nearly as he can tell. The attention of those tracking and staring lenses is unnerving. The sphere, too, is disquietingly familiar. Like Sister Vena's biotank, a kelp forest, and a coral reef—all at the same time.

"Lupe, what is this thing?"

Lupe takes a step in the direction of the sphere and then stops, cautious.

"Simon said some of the GNOMES live in it. A cyberecology sphere, he called it."

"A biocybernetic habitat," Tomoko says, nodding. "Sort of a cross between a self-sustaining ecosphere and a very high-quality virtual reality system. Its denizens are artificial life forms—cellular automata, with both bio and cyber origins. They made the fastest previous supercomputers look about as smart as an abacus. Institutions with heavy simulation needs got the first big ones—the military, space agencies, national museums, big city libraries. They were becoming more common, just before the plague hit."

Ricardo nods. Seeing what looks like a pinkish glow on the surface of the sphere nearest to him, he leans forward, squinting at it. An instant later, he has the briefest impression of something flying at his face. Before he can raise a hand to ward it off, he is hit squarely in the forehead—

Unconscious, he sees a strange, three-sided building. A tall, blockish tower with a stout spike at its top. One great library, then a second one, with stone lions before it. A pillared temple with geometric, human, and animal forms spread across a ceiling starred like the evening sky. Another tower, tapering more gracefully above great metal eagles' heads projecting from cornices. Statues of Merfolk riding on the backs of fish and dolphins and sharks, on stepwise fountains gone to green-slimed pools. A flying golden man with a burning heart in his hand. Cathedrals. A broken glass tower with a stepped pyramidal base—vines hanging from it, tree roots dangling toward the street. Statues of nude women, horns of plenty, heroic leaders on horseback. Real horses galloping through woods and meadows. Twin-towered buildings above woodlands. A brick edifice crowned with eagles and wreaths. Another statute of a green hero on a green horse. A great glass-walled cube, with an only sightly smaller and still enormous sphere inside . . .

Returning to consciousness, the last thing Ricardo hears is Mark Fornash's voice, talking again about scalar waves and laughing. Only the laughter sounds *real* as Ricardo returns to consensus reality. The consensus of his friends gathered round him, wary and with weapons at the ready, is not inclined toward humor. Above him, Trillia's sun-lightened hair falls around her shoulders and neck as she stares down at him.

"Thank God! He looks okay."

Ricardo lifts himself weakly to his elbows, then to the palms of his hands. Trillia wipes at his forehead. The creases there feel slightly sticky—with blood?

"What happened?"

"The sphere shot something at your forehead," Lupe says. "Cut you pretty good."

"We thought it was glass or plex," John adds, "but right after that first shot hit you, the sphere sealed itself back up."

"I thought I heard someone . . . laughing?"

"That came from the speakers," Tomoko says. "I don't know what it's supposed to mean, but I'm worried. Some of those GNOMES or cellular automata or whatever they are may have gotten into your bloodstream. How do you feel?"

He shrugs, feebly.

"Not much different. I think I know where Simon is, though—and how to get there."

They stare at him with deeply questioning looks. Ricardo wonders if they believe the blow to his head might have jogged something loose more than it already was.

"Honey," Trillia asks quietly, "are you sure? You've never been the best with directions."

John Drinan stifles a laugh. Ricardo smiles, then describes what he saw in his blackout as fully as he can. With Trillia and Phenix's help, he gets to his feet at last.

"I may get us lost once or twice along the way, but I can get us there— I'm sure of it."

As they leave the building, he neglects to mention that some of the cityscapes and landscapes he saw in his blackout appeared to him in a peculiar sort of double-vision: as if seen once when the streets were still full of human activity—and once, much more recently, in abandonment and neglect. He wonders idly if Simon visited Manhattan *before* the pandemic, too.

Exiting the building, they return to the maze of detritus-strewn streets, beneath the cliff walls of the towers. The task of finding one man in the vastness of this lost city seems daunting to everyone, but Ricardo is confident in the memory of his vision, and they make what feels like progress.

They follow a long arc: Water Street as it turns to St. James, St. James as it turns to Bowery, Bowery as it turns to Fourth Avenue. The rotted leaf-debris, the weeds in the gutters, the scrawny saplings in the cracked streets—all tell them they are approaching the pocket wilderness of Union Square Park, before they actually see it. Continuing their arc in a diagonal across the park, they drive a growling pack of scrawny wolfish dogs before them, back toward their lair in the "strange, three-sided building" of Ricardo's blackout.

"The Flatiron," Sister Tawanna says.

"I should have recognized it by the description," Sister Mariel agrees. "From the rest of what he said, I bet we go up Fifth Avenue."

Ricardo follows their suggestion, which soon proves correct. He points out the big blockish tower with the heavy-duty spire atop it, which the nuns are able to identify as the Empire State Building by its black streaks of smoke damage. The party of travelers is not far past the base of that building when, not far off Fifth, Ricardo sees once more the first of the great libraries he saw in his blackout. The rich and beautiful pre-pandemic structure his encounter with the GNOMESphere showed him, however, is long gone. The building is a shambles, burned and looted of its treasures decades earlier. The nuns, with the help of Trillia's map pad, guess that it's the Pierpont Morgan Library, but the building's fabric is so damaged they cannot be sure.

Fate has been kinder to the building fronted with the massive, weather-worn lions—the New York Public Library, according to the nuns and Tomoko, who remembers it from a pre-pandemic trip to New York. Ricardo feels certain that even if he is no longer here, Simon Lingham lingered in this structure.

Leaning on Trillia as they make their way around the building and the ivy-choked expanses of Bryant Park, Ricardo can't escape the sense that he's walking around a structure pre-designed to make an impressive ruin. Above fountains slimed a vivid algal green from summer rains stands the statue of a young nude female with a horse behind her, both of them before a wall carved with the inscription "Beauty Old Yet Ever New / Eternal Voice And Inward Word." Above the slimed-over fountain pools on the other side of the main entrance an older, male figure, backed with a shapeshifted sphinx, stands below the inscription "But Above All Things / Truth Beareth Away The Victory."

Everywhere in the library's exterior ornamentation he sees images of lion heads. Winged, double-serpent torches stand on its stone corner posts. The capitols of its columns are topped with stone acanthus ferns. Meanders snake about the stanchions of long-shattered light globes. Where the stone ornaments are not covered by vine and ivy on the Bryant Park side, he sees reliefs of cow skulls and garlands, rams' heads and wreaths. If all the animals frozen to stone about it were to shapeshift suddenly back to life, the library would be a zoo.

Did the builders intend that this place, in its afterlife, should so resemble an animal-associated temple? He and Trillia stop between what look like cow-skulled funerary urns, to stare at the arched, half-domed shrine above a patina-covered statue of William Cullen Bryant. Ricardo can still read the shrine's inscribed lines: "Yet let no empty gust of passion find an utterance in thy lay / A blast that whirls the dust along the howling street and dies away / But feelings of calm power and mighty sweep / Like currents journeying through the windless deep." Deeper into the park, ivy drapes and shrouds busts of Stein, Goethe, and Andrade, before it sweeps away in a green tide.

"I think I found your man with fire in his hand," Phenix says, not without some pride of discovery. "Inside. I used the light on Trillia's map pad to find it."

Ricardo and Trillia follow Phenix inside the building via a large broken-out window. They climb over heaped piles of dumped books and other records, through hallways of scuttling squeaking rodents and fluttering birds. The long corridors smell faintly of books and files long since mildewed, but more powerfully of rat, roach, bird, and mouse feces. The strongest smell of old mold and mildew surrounds a space of ashes.

"Mariel says sprinkler systems killed a fire here," Phenix tells them, "before it could spread through the library."

Given the damage to the surrounding books, that seems a Pyrrhic victory. On the upper floors, things are better. In many places books are still on the shelves. Moving up and down broad marble stairs, they finally come to the remarkably well-preserved hall of the McGraw Rotunda. The nuns are waiting for them there. Phenix flashes the light from the map pad up onto the ceiling of the rotunda.

"Prometheus," says Tawanna, "carrying the stolen flame from heaven."

Phenix shines the light on other images along the walls, and on their accompanying captions: Moses and the tablets of the laws, a medieval monk in a scriptorium, Gutenberg showing proofs of his Bible to the Elector of Mainz, Mergenthaler and Reid with their Linotype machine. Ricardo shakes his head.

"I'm afraid not. None of this stuff fits. The Prometheus I saw—if that's who he was—is a statue, not a painting."

Mariel and Tawanna glance at each other.

"That sounds awfully familiar," Mariel says, trying to remember. "Grand Central Terminal?"

"Maybe," Tawanna agrees. "That would fit what he said about 'human and animal shapes' on a ceiling like the evening sky."

On their way out, they pass another cyberecology sphere, glowing dimly. Ricardo's glance lingers on it.

"Hey, stay back," Phenix says, only half-joking. "Those things don't like you."

Leaving the library grounds, they walk amid the weeds and debris of Forty-second Street. They pass a bank of purple coneflowers, which Phenix says "smell like butterflies" and Ricardo agrees. Ahead they spot the gracefully tapering tower of his blackout vision. As they make their way toward Grand Central, Ricardo can even see the great ornamental eagles' heads. This is the Chrysler Building, according to Sister Mariel.

Coming to the riveted metal and shattered glass of the terminal's entrance at Vanderbilt and Forty-second, they go inside. The riveted iron of the passageway gives way to marble. The interior is at points as dim as middle twilight. Seeing more than enough hints of skeletal remains, however, they leave Trillia's map pad light off and avoid confronting the specters.

Passing through a low, gracefully arched opening, they find themselves standing within an immense enclosed space. Sunlight streams through six tall arched windows, three at either end, as well as smaller lunette windows set into the edges of the enormous barrel-vaulted ceiling, high above their heads. What that daylight makes visible, however, tempers their awe at the size and beauty of the Main Concourse.

Thousands of human skeletons lie tumbled together about the floor and stairways. Despite the sunlight, the presence of so many of the dead casts a pall, rendering the interior space cavernous and subterranean. Their collective gasp immediately wakens many spirits. The space around them becomes an enormous echo chamber resounding with the fluttering of pigeons, the shufflings of bats, the screeching of owls, the scuttling of rats—all startled by the visitors' entry into this charnel terminus. The cacophony of it paralyzes the travelers. Even when the noise dies down, they continue to speak in whispers.

Tawanna points to the celestial ceiling.

"Are those the images you saw in your blackout?"

Ricardo sees and recognizes them now. A cerulean sky mural with thousands of gold stars fills the whole of the barrel vault. It depicts in anthro-pomorphic or zoomorphic form the constellations of the zodiacal belt—Aquarius, Pisces, Aries, Taurus, Gemini, Cancer. Orion brandishes his club to keep the spirits at bay, while Pegasus is frozen in flight there, too.

Leaning on Trillia and Phenix, Ricardo nods slowly, thinking of D. B. Albert's old conundrum: *Do the stars make constellations in the mind, or does the mind make constellations in the stars?*

"Something wrong with the placement of the constellations," John says, craning his neck. "Not scientifically accurate,"

"More than that," Tomoko says. "They're reversed. A God's-eye view, from the heavens looking down toward Earth. In the days before the pandemic, people didn't pay much attention to it."

Ricardo supposes the great barrel-vault mural was intended to bring the heavens inside the building, but on hearing Tomoko's words he is struck by other possibilities. The history of humanity and its place in the universe almost seems reflected in this building. Once, human beings went about their lives beneath these heavens, paying no attention to the divinity watching from the other side of the sky. Then, beneath these same heavens, human beings died and the dead rotted, in unbelievable numbers, and the divinity on the other side of the sky paid no attention to *them*. He begins to feel more woozy and weak than ever.

"Honey," Trillia says quietly, "why did you bring us here?"

"I don't know. Maybe that globe—in the center there, where the skeletons lie thickest—maybe it's another cyberecology sphere?"

"I don't think so," Tomoko says, shaking her head. "I believe that's the big brass clock where people used to meet, but I'm not inclined to find out. You don't look so good. Let's get you out of here."

As they lead him out, he sees crumbling papers blown into corners—old train schedules. He passes under dead chandeliers. The conical ones suggest to his feverish mind Sister Vena's graphics of black holes bending down to singularity, while the toroidal ones suggest her images of the plump grape-shape of the Big Crunch universe. He is glad to be out in sunlight again, when it comes—even if it does hurt his eyes. Sister Mariel speaks suddenly, struck by an idea.

"Rockefeller Center! There's another Prometheus there. Mermaids and mermen riding fish, too!"

The others look expectantly at Ricardo.

"Let's go."

The walk to Rockefeller Center tires him, but the faded golden glitz there restores his confidence. Along the middle of the inclined promenade there are indeed mermaids and mermen riding fish and sharks and dolphins—though they resemble the Merfolk *he* knows more by artistic license than anything else. Here, too, is Prometheus flying in a ring of gold, weathered and dulled, yet still bearing in his right hand fire shaped like a heart. The wall at his back is inscribed "Prometheus Teacher in Every Art Brought the Fire that Hath Proven to Mortals a Means to Mighty Ends."

The carved pedestal Ricardo leans upon is incised with the credo of John D. Rockefeller. Tired and ill, he finds his gaze slipping from one "I believe" to another, until it snags upon this: "I believe that the rendering of useful service is the common duty of mankind and that only in the purifying fire of sacrifice is the dross of selfishness consumed and the greatness of the human soul set free."

The words resonate peculiarly for Ricardo, so much so they grant him, for all his physical weakness, a new sense of clarity and mission. He turns to the nuns.

"We're headed the right way. Fifth Avenue it is."

Happy but feverish, his mind going in and out of focus, he leans on Phenix as their party moves up the avenue, past a broken Atlas bearing a broken world, past strange green reliefs in strange green stone, past the spired Neo-gothic splendor of St. Patrick's Cathedral. They come to a glass tower, its top shattered by explosion or fire, its stepped pyramidal base overhung with vines and burst by tree roots dangling toward the street—another edifice trumpeted by Ricardo's dream vision.

They hear drumming ahead. His companions move more warily, but Ricardo feels little need. The elements of his blackout vision come alive to him again, more powerfully than ever. Twin-towered skyscrapers soar above the woodlands of what was once Central Park. William Tecumseh Sherman rides motionless on a motionless horse. Live horses gallop through woods and meadows, ridden by Werfolk in loincloths and buckskins. The travelers make their way cautiously around monumental statues of nude women or goddesses backed by chimerical horns of plenty—until Sister Mariel suddenly breaks from cover and runs shouting toward the riders, yelling in Spanish and English as she snatches the nun's wimple from off her head.

"They're my people!" she yells back to Ricardo and the rest of her startled companions, before running on. Soon the riders approach them and Mariel makes introductions all around. Ricardo gathers that Mariel's people are working their way through the city on a scavenging expedition— and taking and taming more of the wild horses that frequent the area, descendants of the few Central Park carriage horses that managed to avoid being eaten during the old civilization's final days.

Mariel's reunion with her tribe is joyous and loving but brief, once she explains the urgency of their pilgrimage. The riders nod.

"We already know something about your journey," says a horsewoman, "ever since the Oracle arrived."

Ricardo comes abruptly alert.

"Could you take us to this Oracle?"

The nods of agreement are not yet finished before the travelers find themselves being helped onto horses. Together, they set out across the park, half a dozen young men and women of Mariel's tribe escorting their party. They make their way down asphalt walks decayed almost back to wilderness tracks, then past the Central Park Wildlife Center, heavily overgrown with wisteria and ivy and sapling trees. Ricardo wonders if he's hallucinating when they pass beneath a vine-hung arch topped with a bell clock, circled by animals playing musical instruments—monkeys with hammers for ringing bells, a hippo with a violin, kangaroos and goats with horns, an elephant with a squeezebox.

They pass under further archways of brick and stone—some standing, some fallen. They ride over or alongside rock outcroppings like the ribs of a stone giant buried under the earth. Down weedy avenues of gnarled ancient elm trees, they pass the pedestaled busts of various gods and heroes of the world that once was—memorials both toppled and standing, but all sinking to oblivion amid the vines and saplings of neglect. Below the ridge where they ride, a statue of a winged woman stands above a weedy fountain and plaza, before a reedy lake shored with abandoned boats docked at an abandoned boathouse.

Crossing a bow-shaped bridge soon after, Ricardo sees swans, ducks, and loons on the rushy lakes nearby. The riders and striders pass into a mazelike ramble of paths then, wending their way through a dense wood of oaks and locusts whose roots have long since broken up the asphalt of the old walkways. Beyond the path itself, rough benches and rustic bridges spanning bouldered streambeds are the only signs of a human hand in the woods.

Passing at last out of younger groves of sycamore and gingko, Ricardo sees through a haze of pain and fever the building complex whose south end is crowned with eagles and wreaths. Further on, great columns are fronted by another statue of a green hero on a green horse. Ricardo thinks that, if they had tongues, the taste in the old bronze statues' mouths would not be so different from that in his own. The travelers cross the cracked remains of Central Park West and ride up the grassed-over sidewalk toward what was once Eighty-first Street.

Then, finally, there it is: the great glass-walled cube, with an only slightly smaller and still enormous sphere inside, lit by a chaos of images.

"This is it," Ricardo says in as strong a voice as he can muster, pointing down a gently sloping path leading toward the turbulent world behind glass. His effort is hardly necessary. Their escorts are already leading them in that direction. As they ride to the bottom of the path, Ricardo sees biological and astronomical spheres and spirals embedded in the stone of the walk's crumbling surface. He wonders if he is hallucinating.

Lupe calls out warmly at the sight of a small group of Werfolk standing guard—the very ones who accompanied her and Simon on their way north. With help from Trillia and Phenix, Ricardo dismounts from his horse. As he walks through the crack-spalled but still intact glass doors, Ricardo is startled by the sound of laughter he has heard before, in dream or vision, now booming from speakers throughout the building.

"Hello, everyone!" Simon Lingham's voice says. "I've been waiting for you!"

The newly arrived visitors stand among dead simulators and surrounded by old exhibits of Earth and sky. Two- and three-dimensional displays hang from the ceiling and walls of a tall, airy space of marble, steel, and glass. Tomoko shakes her head and gives a grudging smile.

"Simon, why does it not surprise me that I should find you in a museum?"

The laughter booms around them again.

"Technically, this is the Hayden *Planetarium* in the Rose Center—but you're right. I've always loved museums. I'm below you. Come down past what used to be the Big Bang exhibit, to the Black Hole display. Please join me."

The party of travelers makes its way downstairs. On the great sphere, Ricardo thinks he sees an image of a sperm whale—glinting redly of stars—in combat with a dark-matter squid. He is so weak and disoriented, Phenix and Trillia almost have to carry him. Modulating between pedantic smugness and childlike wonder, Simon's fact-stuffed rumblings over the loudspeakers—about "mazed spiral wave patterns" in "Belousov-Zhabotinski reactions" and "concretionary masses of anthracite coal" and "heart muscle behavior" and "neural networks" and "cellular automata" as "Turning-pattern fingerprints of self-organization"—don't help Ricardo's disorientation much. On the sphere above them, images like wave-form renditions of snake-mongoose battles flicker, the enormous contending forms composed of innumerable smaller images—all in colors shifting up the spectrum toward blue and white. As Simon continues, Ricardo realizes that the smaller images on the great sphere are somehow following Lingham's thoughts and speech.

When the party sees Simon, however—below the great sphere, yet attached to it, *interwoven* with it, by an organic-looking umbilical snaked into his headplug, his voice coming not from his mouth but from the sphere's speakers, his whites-up eyes remming fiercely in his gaunt face—his recent companion Lupe and ex-wife, Tomoko, both cry out.

"Good God! That thing's got him!"

"Simon, what *are* you doing?"

"Learning. Accessing what this cybercology sphere knows. The largest ever created—see? Fifteen times my own height. Weighed twenty tons and had a volume of 345,000 cubic feet when it was built, back at the turn of the century. It was the most advanced virtual reality simulator available to the public when it opened, but it wasn't 'eco' back then—just *cyber*. Right here is where the whole idea of the cyberecology sphere started."

Trillia eases herself and Ricardo to the marble floor nearby, Ricardo's weight having grown too much for her and Phenix both. Ricardo, feeling almost too tired to ever move again, is happy to rest motionless on the floor. Trillia rises to her knees.

"Why here?" she asks.

"The luck of juxtaposition. The Rose Center had a self-sustaining ecosphere habitat within sight of a big spherical virtuality machine. Some bright people made the connection. Biocybernetic habitats were the perfect solution for fully mixing the 'cellular' and the 'automatous.' The year before the pandemic, the Museum remodeled its old cyber virtuality into *this*, the world's largest self-sustaining biocybernetic habitat—the ultimate synthesis of museum and planetarium, virtuality and ecosphere."

Trillia looks down again into Ricardo's eyes, checking on him.

"Is the self-sustaining part how it survived the Collapse?" she asks.

"Not totally. During the pandemic, Cameron Spires kept this place guarded, safe, and powered up. This umbilical rig was originally built for the kind of headplugs we have in the islands—especially for those used by members of the Spires bloodline, like yourself."

Trillia stares about the place wide-eyed.

"My grandfather?"

"Indeed. He saved it for his own uses. To run his Wall Street GNOMES on it, and other things, too. Machine-loaded consciousness-constructs of some of his Tetragrammaton friends. Vang and Kong and Dalke, I think, but I still can't find my way into the core constructs—just their outlying records."

"How do you know all this?" Tomoko asks.

"This is nothing! You can hardly imagine how much I've learned. These biocybernetic creatures and their ecologies have evolved far beyond where Cameron started with them! He's not the only human the GNOMES are in contact with, now. *I've* been interfaced with them around the clock, integrating my own consciousness with theirs, to form a combined entity."

Lupe looks worriedly at the body on the floor below the great sphere, but any response to her worry would not seem likely to come from that quarter. Ricardo thinks Simon's mind has, to a great degree, already left his body. His human form, still vestigially attached to the sphere by the umbilical, is utterly quiescent but for the rapid movements of the upturned whites of his eyes.

"Is this what my people meant when they called you the Oracle?" Sister Mariel asks.

Simon's laughter resounds from the speakers once more.

"The Oracle! I suppose that's as good a name as any!"

Trillia looks frustrated.

"Dr. Lingham, why have you done this to yourself? Aren't you taking your conflict with my grandfather a bit far?"

Again the amplified laughter surrounds them.

"No, no. This is much bigger than Cameron and me. There's an entire world in here. The inhabitants remember Cameron and still owe a certain fealty to him. Their creator-god has largely abandoned them, however. His creation has struck out on its own. 'Self-sustaining' has now mixed with 'cellular' and 'automatous' here to produce something increasingly *autonomous*."

Lupe doesn't like the sound of that at all.

"What do you mean?"

"They have completely reconstructed the physical fabric of the sphere. Through its water supply, the sphere itself has spawned a bunch of worldlets. The reservoir in Central Park is full of them, though they don't seem to be very active yet. The biocybernetic creation doesn't need Spires, or me, or anything besides sunlight to keep it powered up. It can take care of itself, as far as protection against outsiders is concerned. It's a mesocosm."

"A meso-*what*?" John asks, crouched beside Oz, stroking the dog's head.

"A middle cosmos, between the microcosm of the single cell and the macrocosm of the single Earth. Or like the city—as a sociological middle cosmos, a social *mandala* between the microcosm of the individual and the macrocosm of the universe."

"A city as a 'mandala'?"

"Wherever and whenever they occurred, the first city-states—whether in Sumer or Egypt, Crete or the Indus Valley, China or Peru or Central America—were always inhabitable sacred mandalas intended to make visible in human affairs the great order of the universe."

Throughout the sphere, images dance to match Simon's words. Watching the display, Ricardo thinks that, even now, some ghost lingers here of the great sphere's former role in planetarium and museum.

"The priest-king of the sun or the moon was enthroned in the temple tower, at the center of the walled city-state and at the top of its social hier-archy. The five visible planets danced in an orderly round about that cen-ter—as did the sun and the moon through the constellations of the zodiac. Wheels within wheels, circles within circles. The wheel itself, the calen-dar, written language, and ritual arts—all of them rose together with the sacred city whose every feature reflected the sacred heavens."

As the voice of his old mentor continues to boom through the museum space, Ricardo wonders how fully Simon has integrated himself with the biocybernetic creation to which he's umbilically connected. How many of his words are his own? How many are those of the entity he's been inte-grating himself into?

"The two most important numerical systems came from that, too. The decimal system was used for business accounts in the temple compounds to keep track of grain collected in taxes. The sexagesimal system was used for ritualistic measures: the mandala of time, with its 365-day year, and the mandala of space, with its 360-degree circle—plus five, from the four sides of the temple tower oriented to the points of the compass, and the center point in the temple sanctuary itself. The four compass points lead to the center point, where the infinite flows into the sphere of space. The five days intercalated into the calendar are days of ritual and festival, dur-ing which the eternal flows into the sphere of time."

Ricardo thinks of the ceiling in Grand Central and wonders about its "mesocosmic" function. He thinks of Lupe's comments on moneychang-ers. Tomoko's words about the Parthenon. Above him, Ricardo sees the sphere changing, becoming more complex, more orderly, more rami-fied—and brighter. The others notice too.

"I don't see what numerical systems have to do with what you're doing to yourself," Tomoko says, her face grim.

"They have everything to do with each other. Two centuries ago, the philosopher Emerson wrote that 'the end of the human race will be that it will eventually die of civilization'—and it very nearly did, in my own life-time. I want to know what it is at the heart of cities and civilization that is so self-destructive, and I think I'm on track to discovering it. The split between the sexagesimal and the decimal systems is the split between the sacred and the profane. The GNOMES started out as a system for predict-ing the evolution of global *markets*, after all! There are other profane forces, too. The 'netizens,' the oldest form of artificial life in the infosphere, began as a virus program in a *bank* in Kansas City. The Allesseh, too, if it really exists, is frighteningly profane—and almost too terrible to contemplate."

Looking up at Trillia's face under the growing glow and increasing ornateness within the sphere, Ricardo can tell she's becoming impatient, even before she stands up.

"Look—we've traveled all this way because Ricardo is ill. We hoped you could help him, but it doesn't look like you're doing much to save yourself, much less Ricardo."

"I'm doing more than you know. How much do *you* know about how the pandemic worked?"

The travelers tell him what Mark Fornash suggested—about the synergy of effects among prionoids and binotech and microbes, particularly the link between brain chaos and introduced nanorganisms, mediated by scalar waves. Simon's amplified voice booms out again when they finished,

"Yes, Mark got most of it right. Just a couple of pieces missing."

"Such as?" Trillia asks.

"Such as the fact that variants of the same binotechnology which allows for life extension among Urfolk in the islands—which also allows for the embryo-morphing capabilities that created the Merfolk—is also what underlies all the shapeshifting and stigmata of the plague."

"How is that possible?"

"The technology Cameron Spires 'adapted' to extend life was based on a communications nanotech. His life-extension binotech was seduced to return, at least partially, to its latent communications function. As a result of being confronted with an incompleteness problem concerning death and extinction—but ultimately traceable to defenses against computer viruses."

"This arithmetic 'seduction,' then," Tomoko says, pondering the complexity of it, "underlay the structure of the pandemic superpathogen?"

"A component of it, yes—and of numerous less virulent subsequent forms. All of which Cameron Spires has known for years how to cure. He has kept that secret because it also defeats the life-extending capabilities of the binotech underlying his longevity treatments."

Above the stunned visitors the great sphere now seems to enclose something very like the stalagmites and stalactites of a cave, crossed with the spires of a night-lit city. That hybrid thing is growing to fill the entire space, before their eyes.

"How did you learn all this?" Tomoko asks.

"From what *I'm* doing. From trying to save this biocybernetic creation from itself by healing the split, the divide within it. By shapeshifting it into a unified system. I was the epidemiologist in charge when the human world was destroyed by pandemic. It happened on my watch. Like you, Tomoko, I've wanted the answers to these questions for decades. That search kept me Cameron's faithful advisor for too long. Now I've finally got the answers I've been after."

Despite the overwhelming taste of old statues in his mouth, Ricardo finds himself speaking, so tiredly he feels as if he's talking in his sleep. The thoughts he speaks seem to be coming from somewhere outside himself— from memories of conversations overhead in Baltimore and North Carolina and only now understood. From other sources, too, as if he is speaking for persons no longer present. Gasping, he tries to make them understand the self-similarity he's seeing across all scales.

"Mirrors. Divided and incomplete, like the world in the sphere above us. Death poses the same halting problem for both it and Spires. Can't be certain beforehand what the result of running the Death Program will be. Output and closure—the pattern of the self disappearing into nonexistence? Or an open-ended infinite loop—the pattern of the self continuing forever? Only way to know there is to go there. To run the Death Program. They don't want to go there. So they run *away* from the Death Program. They will sacrifice the human species, perhaps the universe too, to stay undying in this world—because that is always more certain than sacrificing oneself."

Above them the complex construct in the sphere continues to grow, and grow brighter. Trillia, hearing the difficulty with which Ricardo speaks, reaches down to cradle his head. She looks down at him, tears beginning to run down her cheeks.

"But why you? Why us?"

"Because we can create the Lapis," Simon replies quietly, despite the amplification of the speakers. "The Absolute Paradox. The mesocosmic mortal who unites the macrocosm of the universe and the microcosm of the individual. The human singularity, through whom the infinite and eternal enter space and time."

Ricardo's unamplified voice is a hoarse sound not very much louder than a whisper.

"Yes. The being through whom Fornash's quantum ocean and Albert's intersection system meet. Through whom the singularity-making capacity of consciousness is exteriorized. Through whom parallel universe-processing becomes a reality—infinite energy becoming available for infinite thought, just as Sister Vena said. Through whom the deity sleeping in matter is awakened—by self-sacrifice."

Trillia's tears are wet on Ricardo's face. She screams at the motionless body of Lingham, then at the great complexly glowing sphere overhead.

"Do something! Cure him!"

Ricardo smiles feebly and takes her hand in his.

"He can't. I have the new variant. Your grandfather saw to that. But it's a variant he never expected—a variation he has been trying to prevent for years."

Overhead, the sphere grows so achingly bright, they have to shield their eyes.

"Simon," John asks, "what are you doing with the sphere?"

When it answers, the amplified voice sounds hurried, for all the motionlessness of Simon's body.

"Re-creating it. Making it into Mount Sumeru. Eden. Olympus. The Temples of the Sun. The Earthly Paradise. The Shining City of God. Eliminating the last bits of darkness—"

"I don't think that's a good idea," John says, his voice full of memory, or foreboding, or both.

"Why ever not—?"

Gunshots sound. Glass shatters. Ricardo sees his companions nearest the doors and windows falling or diving for cover. Behind a grim, khaki-clad vanguard of his Island Patrol praetorians, President Cameron Spires sweeps into the room, in shining armored environment suit and clear-visored helmet. He glances up at the bright sphere, then issues a command.

"Release the Kong and Dalke constructs into the system!"

Darkness roils the great sphere over their heads. On the floor, Simon begins to jerk and twitch. Trillia clasps her hands to her face.

"Grandpa, what have you done?"

Cameron Spires ignores her, gazing around the room.

"You know what I miss about the old civilized world?" the man in the armored suit says. "The parties. The soirees where everyone was allowed—even expected—to make young, glamorous fools of themselves. Even if they were no longer young."

He looks disdainfully down at Simon and Ricardo on the floor.

"Now I sometimes wonder if the human species is even worth saving."

"Who are *you* to say that?" Trillia asks pointedly.

"Trillia, don't delude yourself. The mythic nonsense of these people you've fallen in with is tiresome. I refuse to become a superstitious peon. True Folk will never be content to turn into a bunch of fearful old peasants waiting to die."

He turns on his granddaughter.

"*You've* acted like a superstitious little idiot throughout the whole of this affair. Getting yourself pregnant with this man's child has no glamor to it. It's a peasant girl's. I've tolerated your misbehavior long enough. The only good that's come of it is that you and your companions have aided me in finding Lingham, here—and destroying this traitorous lieutenant of mine, in a manner fitting his betrayal. And no, I will *not* cure your lover. I wouldn't, even if I could. Let death cure him. Once this sad episode is over, you will return with me to the islands—if I have to have you brought back bound and gagged!"

Tired and lost, Trillia looks distractedly from the spasming Lingham to the gasping Ricardo to the darkening sphere overhead.

"Oh, Grandpa. How could you be so selfish?"

Spires glances away.

"Is it selfish to try to make a better world? The pandemic and the collapse provided an opportunity, but now that opportunity seems almost foreordained. The madness plague, like most of humanity's children, was both planned and unplanned. The old world had to be destroyed so that another, designed to my own specifications, might someday bloom in its place. Never doubt the world can be improved. The GNOMES evolved to become these biocybernetic environments. In time, such habitats will replace this old, tired, stone-hearted planet we live on. On some not-so-distant future day, all humanity will be transformed into Triphibians. They will be creatures born from humanity. They will possess those valuable mental powers of the Werfolk, without the dross of madness. They will be capable of living aquatically like the Merfolk. *You* should know something about that, Trillia, my dear—since you invaded my private files! Immortal and aquatic, in enclosed biocybernetic worlds, Triphibian humanity will journey throughout the universe. And they will be your children, Trillia, after the abomination you're carrying has been eliminated."

Trillia cries out and tears at her hair—until Ricardo touches her hand. He gestures with his head toward Lingham, whose convulsions are growing rapidly more violent.

"I'm going to help him."

Trillia moans, reaching toward the umbilical plugged into Simon Lingham's head.

"How? You don't even have a headplug!"

"I don't need one."

Smiling slightly, Ricardo glances up at the sphere roiled by turbulent vortices. The bottom of the sphere glows a vermilion brightness for an instant, before a cytoplasmic flow drops swiftly from the orb above him, a protrusion engulfing and assuming him bodily into the sphere. The last thing he sees as the pseudopod takes him into that otherworldly space is Trillia tugging at Lingham's umbilical, removing it from his head with difficulty.

TRILLIA LOOKS AT THE UMBILICAL IN HER HAND, THEN AT SIMON LINGHAM. He has stopped his violent spasming, but now he is utterly still. Nothing moves—not even his eyes. She takes the umbilical and brings its thin, dull needle-probe back behind her head. Her grandfather shouts at her.

"Trillia! No!"

Defiantly, Trillia rams the probe into her headplug—and travels to that world in which Ricardo's soul flies, on its last aerial voyage.

RICARDO SWIMS A VAST LAKE, DIM AND COLD, TOWARD THE ISLAND AT ITS center covered by jungle and ruined city. Looking about the ruined cityscape before him, Ricardo understands instantly what has happened. In trying to render this biocybernetic creation a completely bright City of God—a sphere of will, being, and life—Simon overlooked the reality of the darkness—unwillingness, nonbeing, death. Ricardo thinks of the ancient symbol of the Tao. Always a spot of light in darkness and a bit of darkness in light. Inconsistency in completeness, incompleteness in consistency.

Dark clouds tower above him as he flies through the ruined cityscape. Despite Simon's efforts, the world-city Ricardo moves through remains distinctly alien—at least as alien as the Mayan ruins in Central America were to the first Europeans who encountered them.

Amid the ruins, he sees complex meander, spiral, zigzag, and lattice patterns ornamenting the top of each story. Bas reliefs of mixed creatures—part animal, part human, part machine—stand on walls of what might pass for stone or stucco. Some of the creatures are intact, others fragmented, headless, limbless. The back walls of ritual spaces are covered with great tablets bearing inexplicable scenes of these mixed creatures engaged in enigmatic rites, surrounded by texts of indecipherable glyphs. Monuments and stelae, leaning or standing or toppled, litter the inhuman geometries of the city. The alien faces and symbols upon them sink into dust and undergrowth. Even the columns and doorways—if that's what they are—are like nothing Ricardo is familiar with. Ramps and stairways, fronted with enormous sculptured heads of mixed creatures, climb brokenly up pyramids collapsing into mountains of rubble.

Far more alien than the ruins of the world-city, however, is its emptiness. Most alien of all are the "plants" and "animals" of the wilderness—draping, covering over, springing from, or moving stealthily about in those ruins. The wilderness growing upon this shattered world-city is so diverse, it seems gathered from ten thousand planets.

Yet, unerringly, amid all the alienness of ruins and wilds, Ricardo knows where to go. In the most devastated zone, he climbs the broken stairs of a temple so decayed it has reverted to a grassy knoll at its top. This is the Place of Sacrifice in Ruins. Atop it stands a figure of shadow seemingly condensed from the dark clouds overhead, a creature of innumerable shapes and no stable form, although about it there is a shifting suggestion of two heads, and a great sharp-bladed axe held high. The creature crouches in an alert and ready stance, expecting battle.

Ricardo offers it no fight. As he kneels before the creature, he recognizes it: the Dalke and Kong constructs, grown inseparably together in their incarnating of something very distant and alien. Looking at the incarnation, sensing through Dalke's and Kong's understanding of it all the realities this creature embodies, Ricardo now also understands the Allesseh for what it truly is.

Not just something that began as an expanding network of Von Neumann probes. Not just an artificial galactic nervous system, evolving itself and coevolving its linkages to sentient species for millions of years. Not just something self-translated into a higher dimensional cosmological form no longer simply mechanical, organic, or even physical. Not just a hyperdimensional node at the center of the galaxy, existing in more than one universe at once.

No: A bodhisattva gone bad. One who has been through so many incarnations, it has fallen in love with space and time and all the universe's innumerable productions. One that's taken in so much data it has become self-absorbed and self-obsessed. Able to continue to exist in any one time and space only so long as it never truly knows itself in that time and space. Who fears that each universe trends toward total consciousness, toward enlightenment, toward transcendence. Who hopes each universe, too, is bodhisattvic, and will not take the next transcendent step until all within it are also totally conscious. Who believes that—through the impossibility of any system's being fully complete and fully consistent at one and the same time—it can block that final enlightenment throughout *this* universe forever.

As the axe-wielding fallen angel and old adversary hurtles toward him screaming, Ricardo feels only pity and compassion for it. For its existential dread, which works to keeps microcosm and macrocosm forever separated, consciousness forever unconscious of itself. For its refusal to recognize the reality of anything larger than universe or multiverse. For its refusal to accept the idea that the radical inconsistency of the multiverse and the radical incompleteness of any single universe are together reconciled in each other—in a plenum where all that is possible is real.

As it dismembers his body, Ricardo realizes that it is not hate that drives this thing, but a misguided and all-consuming love. The misguided lover has separated itself from that sea of love at the end of time, in which dwell those realities called by many names—archetypes, spirits, plenum bod-hisattvas, hyperconsciousness at omega, ecologies of mind. By such separa-tion, this thing that names itself the Allesseh has made churning Hell seas of itself.

As it lops off his head, Ricardo dies, yet remains the conscious agent of those forces who have love enough for time, but not too much—tran-scending space and time even as they continue to work through it. Ricardo is gone, and yet still here. Like a shaman killed in dream who dies in the physical world, his clothes sag to empty.

At that instant, all the singularities and omega points Sister Vena spoke of line up *in him*. Parallel universe processing begins. The energy avail-able to his thought becomes infinite. As he is brought utterly into con-junction with those plenum forces influencing the universe from beyond time, time ends for Ricardo Alvarez.

His flesh and bone unravel, weaving themselves into the grass of the ruined temple, shooting through the temple and all the buildings, re-creating all this world in a new form, that of a glowing reef-city ensconced in a full moon, an underwater forest and binotechnically homegrown hometown, where one cannot tell the town for the oozy trees, because the town *is* the trees. Through all the changes, the pattern of his consciousness remains, floating as if encased in a crystalline vacuole.

Reweaving his old body out of the sphere's new materials, however, he suddenly finds that crystalline consciousness locked in another place—and in pain.

In pain from having been somehow the very ground that a shovel has been thrust into—a shovel in the hands of Mark Fornash. Ricardo finds himself growing rapidly up, out of this gash in the strange new ground of being.

"Hello, Ricardo. Sorry about that, but I wound and heal, you know. Since you helped me out of my old life, I suppose I owed you one, too!"

Ricardo sees about him others doing what Fornash is doing—Sister Vena and Markus among them, others he barely remembers, and far more whom he has never known—all in loose and flowing black robes.

"What are you doing?"

"Harrowing."

"But who are all these people? How is this possible?"

"Pattern persists," Fornash says with a shrug. "Independent of the substrate upon which it is realized. Two plus two equals four, whether that pattern is realized through knots in a rope, electrons flashing through logic gates in a computer, or quantum events in a human mind. Burn the rope, smash the computer, kill the mathematician—two plus two still equals four. Consciousness too is pattern. It too persists, independently of the substrate on which it is realized. What you're seeing is just one of those realizations. One easier for you to understand. Call it a graduation from the flesh—black robes and all. A commencement of what comes next."

"But I don't understand."

"You will. When you've got infinite energy for infinite thought available to you, you make the jumps from data, to information, to knowledge, to wisdom—*really* fast."

When he appears to her, surrounded by crystalline light, Trillia gasps. He embraces her.

"Ricardo, what happened?"

"I died, love. But I also changed."

Trillia is overwhelmed with confused emotion.

"Don't worry. Someday I hope you'll join me, but not yet."

"Join you *where*?"

"In the community of Love with which Time ends. The only absolute. Only Love's Communion can end Time's Dominion."

"What community? Where?"

"Remember what Sister Vena said. Other times are just special cases of other universes. Those forces from the end of time in one universe—the one John Drinan came from, for instance—can *influence* the past in other universes, like the one we grew up in. That influence is what shaped my death."

"I thought your illness was my grandfather's doing."

"It was. Once it interacted with the cyberecology of this sphere, though, my new variant proved to be the Lapis variant. What has happened to me is the result of the unity of opposites, which is what the Lapis is all about. And that work's not done yet. I need your help."

"What can I do?"

"When you return to the world, you'll find my body there. It'll be dead, but it will also have changed in other less apparent ways. I want you to set my body adrift in the reservoir in Central Park."

"But why?"

"The reservoir is full of the biocybernetic worldlets this habitat was preparing. In order to reopen the physical portal to the universe John came from, I have to duplicate the kenosis, the quantum infodensity event Jiro Yamaguchi pulled off in *that* universe. Ask John about it. Tell him I'll see to it the portal back to his universe is open, but beyond that it's up to him."

Trillia is tremendously puzzled.

"All right. What about Simon Lingham? I pulled the umbilical out of his head while he was still connected."

Ricardo smiles.

"He'll be fine. He'll wake up once the Sister Vena simulacrum finishes running its program. It will figure out that, in this instance, an infinite loop *is* an output."

"How will that help him?"

"The achievement of closure on that program will cause the simulacrum to send out a quantum scalar wave fluctuation. That will bring Simon around, but it will not be the end of that wave. The biocybernetic habitats will amplify it, not long thereafter. That amplified wave will affect all minds on this planet, bestowing on everyone everywhere—including Werfolk, Urfolk, and Merfolk—information about all your grandfather's activities."

"But they won't listen. They all want different things!"

"Oh, they'll pay attention. Those who wish to remain Urfolk will want to know about cures involving benign polymorphism, as well as the prevention of prionoid uptake. The Werfolk will be attentive because that quantum download will allow them access to techniques for consciously—but, alas, still mortally—controlling their Wersign. It will also allow the Merfolk to see why they cannot be simultaneously immortal and fertile. The one they choose will be up to them."

"And my grandfather? And his guards?"

"When you come back to the world you know, you'll find them immobilized. An 'information-overload paralysis,' as it were. They must not be in this building when what's coming happens. The Rose Center must be completely cleared of everyone. You'll need to see to it that they're brought outdoors."

"I'll do what I can."

"One last thing. The child you're carrying—ours—is actually twins. A girl and a boy. My variant of the pandemic has altered my contribution to their genetic structure, but there's an interesting prionoid twist from you, too. Since they are heterozygous, they can have normal lives of normal lengths, as they are. They can also, however, realize something *more*. A far better variant of your grandfather's plan for the evolution of humanity. If you wish that, then stay immersed chest-deep in the water of the reservoir after you have set my body adrift. If you decide to stay, you'll know when to get out."

Trillia has an infinitude of questions. Seeing Ricardo beginning to fade from her with distance, she can only think to ask one.

"All those people who suffered in the pandemic—did they transcend, or die?"

Ricardo looks at her oddly.

"Both, actually. Consciousness is a pattern that persists, and they have persisted."

Was that preacher Raheem met in some sense *right*? Has everyone who died of the plague raptured out? Are those of us left behind Preterite, in ways we would never have guessed?

Ricardo is gone. Her questions remain.

SIMON LINGHAM WAKES. WHEN HE PUSHES HIMSELF UP ONTO HIS ELBOWS, he sees Trillia directing those who accompanied her on her journey here. Shaking his head to clear it, he manages to come to a sitting position. Looking about, he sees the prostrate forms of Cameron Spires and his guards sprawled about the place. From the sphere above Simon, shafts of light, laser-straight and bright, shoot to all those prostrate forms—somehow causing a very different sort of light, lambent and sensitive, to glow above their heads.

Even as he watches, those shafts of light and their flickering counterparts blink out. Cameron and his fallen forces remain unmoving. Trillia's fellow travelers begin dragging and carrying them out of the building. Beside him, Simon sees another unmoving form: Ricardo Alvarez. In the same instant he realizes both that Ricardo is dead, and that Ricardo's death has somehow been in place of his own.

As John, Tomoko, Phenix, and Trillia approach, Simon struggles to his feet. Trillia eyes him carefully.

"You're all right, then? Thank heaven. Do you feel strong enough to help us bear Ricardo's body to the water? You're sure?"

Simon assures her he is, although he doesn't know exactly which water she's referring to. The rest of them reach down to take hold of Ricardo, and Simon joins them, taking hold of an arm and shoulder, then lifting when they do. Together they carry Ricardo's body away, out the shattered remains of the doors, along the spiral- and sphere-embedded concrete walkway, beside the small tangled wilderness of what was once lawn and park beside Eighty-first Street. Trillia's other companions have removed Spires and his guards into that pocket of wild space, stripping them of their weapons along the way.

As the bearers walk with their burden, two women in white and blue nun's habits join them, following behind. Lupe approaches them, too. Speaking quickly to Phenix, she takes the young man's place in the impromptu funeral cortege, leaving him to take charge of those watching over Spires and his men. The young man nods. Joining a group of riders on horseback, Phenix sends two to accompany the cortege.

Placing their feet carefully, they cross the broken and weedy intersection of Central Park West with Eighty-first Street and the Seventy-ninth Street traverse. Under moonlight they pass into a grove of Siberian elms. Beyond that they pass through the spreading pinetum near the Great Lawn. From trips in pre-pandemic days, Simon remembers that the Great Lawn was punctuated with a scattering of sandy baseball diamonds. All gone to woodland, now.

Past the tumbled brick ruins of the old carpentry workshop, they come at last to the high chainlink fence, rusted and gapped, surrounding the reservoir. They stop to negotiate a tight break in the fence-line. Simon absently flips over with his toe a fallen sign. "This reservoir contains your drinking water—keep it clean," the sign reads.

The artificial lake glitters in the moonlight. On the horizon loom the silhouettes of abandoned skyscrapers. Nearer still stand the trees of a park grown to wilderness. The reservoir itself is not full. They carry Ricardo along and down a sloping bank, until they find an aluminum dory, Water Department property, untethered and drifting in the shallows. They place Ricardo on the floor of the boat. Simon takes a position in the bow, Lupe in the stern, and Trillia amidships.

Lupe and Simon have not rowed far when Trillia calls them to a halt. Together, the three of them gently lift Ricardo's body high enough to clear the sides of the boat. They ease him feet first, into the water. Ricardo's body drifts a moment, then slips swiftly below the swirling surface. Simon is surprised by the swiftness of it. Shouldn't human flesh and bone be more buoyant?

Light begins to flash through the reservoir—white, yellow, purple, blue—like heat lightning under water. The sight of it is startling, but less so than the sudden splash when Trillia dives in. Simon and Lupe call to her, but she waves them off.

CAMERON SPIRES AND HIS GUARDS, STILL UNCONSCIOUS, DO NOT STIR, and Phenix, watching over them, finds his attention wandering. The great sphere, caged in its tall glass cube, catches his eye. He watches it a while, then turns to Aura.

"Is it my imagination, or is that sphere starting to brighten again?"

The pale blond woman stares at it as well.

"It *is* getting brighter. Starting to pulse, too."

A deep humming, first felt and then heard, joins the brightening pulsations of the sphere. The pulsings of light and sound increase in frequency together. The light from the immensely complex reef-city inside the sphere becomes so bright that Phenix, Aura, and all the others guarding spires and his men must shield their eyes or avert them.

The humming rises in an ear-piercing crescendo. The glass curtain walls of the tall cube shatter. The great sphere, abandoning its support stanchions, rises through the wreckage of its glass cage. It drifts upward in the night, a soap bubble blown around a glittering world, plaything of a godlike child.

When it is gone, drifting like a wayward moon over the woodland of the park, Phenix breathes a long sigh of relief. Despite all that has just taken place, however, his unconscious charges have still not awakened.

THE STRANGE SECOND MOON, FORMER MAIN ATTRACTION OF THE FREDER-ick Phineas and Sandra Priest Rose Center, has already commenced to hover over the reservoir before Trillia sees or hears it. Floating on her back in the flashing, whorling water—facing in the direction opposite that from which the sphere has come—she notices the light from it first, before the object itself catches her eye.

Dropping slowly down the sky, the sphere's effects begin to grow. The wind picks up, blowing toward the sphere from all directions. Small waves and whitecaps rise on the artificial lake's surface. Glowing white where the sphere settles toward it, the water of the reservoir ripples upward like a milkdrop crown. As the sphere sinks into the reservoir— moon submerging in ocean—the point of their contact grows too bright to look at.

Trillia herself experiences the most profound effect. Innumerable tiny glittering worlds whorl and spiral white light about her, then within her, a galaxy moving through her flesh and blood and bones—an ecstasy alter-ing her life and the lives of those she carries within her. As surely as she feels it, she knows there are no words for what she is feeling. If language is the distance between the ocean of ecstasy and the moon of the self, then what need has she of words, when there is no longer distance or separa-tion?

The sphere disappears and dissolves into the water. A moment later, with a thunderclap of rushing air, a tremendous pillar of rainbow light shoots into the sky in a vertical wave. From it, another wave—far greater, though unseen—propagates instantly. In her head, Trillia learns every-thing Ricardo promised. She understands.

The rainbow pillar disappears. For an instant Trillia thinks she sees in the afterimage Ricardo's face, drifting among the stars, a constellation growing dimmer with distance.

She is almost content to die now. Almost.

Instead, she strikes out toward the dory, swimming strongly. With its high sides and sharp prow, the dory looks to her like a boat made from a quarter-moon, but one whose lower reaches lie dark below a waterline of clouds. In the horns of that moon, Simon and Lupe lie, slowly coming back to consciousness.

Epilogue

What the Future Was

CAMERON SPIRES STARES IN DISBELIEF AT THE PICKET LINE OF MERFOLK, tridents upraised, blocking the departure of his small cutter from its mooring in the Hudson. Of all the appalling indignities he has suffered in the last twenty-four hours, he fears this will prove to be the worst. Nereus, his old ally, stands at the head of the Mer detachment arrayed against him, the body of a dead mermaid floating gently before him.

"Nereus! Put down those underwater pitchforks of yours and let me pass!"

Other than shaking his head No, Nereus does not move. Cameron glares at him. No, it was not enough that when he returned to consciousness he found himself and his most loyal retainers under guard by Trillia's forces. Not enough that, wherever that scoundrel Ricardo disappeared to, he took the GNOMES, the biocybernetic habitats, and all Cameron's plans for them with him. Not enough that he's lost all his hope for his Triphibians—and realized all his fears of the Lapis. Not enough that the granddaughter he would have savagely upbraided for all of this—forbidding her from ever returning home—has instead upbraided *him*. Not enough that, angry and ashamed at having all his most debatable decisions made public in every private mind, he finds that during the course of this day and its miserable march to these broken-down docks, all but two of his "most loyal" retainers have gone over to Trillia and her people.

No, *now* Trillia and her forces have to see him stymied by this Merfolk obstinacy! He has had enough. Cameron guns the small motorboat's electric engine. It surges forward. He sees Nereus nod and the Merfolk disappear from his path. Good. At least someone is finally showing him the proper respect.

The cutter suddenly tips up on its side as if it has struck a ramp. As the boat starts to flip over, Cameron recalls with a sinking feeling the Merfolk's most practiced defensive maneuver, the one he has seen them use against shapeshifters' boats during a dozen raids—

He and his two loyal followers come thrashing to the surface beside the wrecked and overturned cutter. His yacht *Derceto* stands too far offshore in the swiftly flowing Hudson for them to swim the distance. The three men struggle back to the shore where Trillia and her followers watch and wait. Coming out of the shallows, he shouts furiously at his granddaughter, gesturing to the yacht, and to what once were *his* islands, invisible beyond the horizon.

"Take it! Take it all, and to hell with you!"

"Your ignition code for *Derceto*?"

Turning toward the yacht, he sees its crew lowering the second cutter into the water.

"As if the crew hasn't already betrayed me—and thrown its lot in with you!"

Trillia watches the other cutter starting toward them.

"I would still prefer to know the code."

"You already know it, you little fool! The one you stole to break into my private records. I should have changed it long ago, but I was too used to it. Turn it around and it says 'Open Sesame'!"

Seeing her mouthing it out—3-m-a-5-3-5-n-3-p-o—Cameron shakes his head. A weak little joke, but not so weak as that *he* should have been bested by this girl-woman. Squatting down on his haunches (not easy in a flex-armored environment suit), he sits on a sandy spit near the shore and stares glumly about him. She and her people go into a great confab about who will go where and rendezvous with whom. The other cutter approaches the shore and waits, its electric engine pushing quietly against the current of the river. Trillia, Tomoko, and Simon approach him.

"We will leave you all appropriate supplies from the *Derceto*," his granddaughter says. "Every solstice and equinox we will land more supplies at this site for as long as you live."

Cameron gives a dull nod. For as long as he shall live. *Without longevity treatments, presumably.* The death sentence of banishment, executed now upon him. Banisher banished. Ruler of exiles exiled. *Let us sit upon the ground,* he thinks bitterly, *and tell sad stories of the death of kings.*

He watches Trillia, Simon, and Tomoko depart in the cutter for *Derceto*. He watches the rest of them (all *her* people, now) depart on foot and horseback toward the Battery. Cameron Spires looks at his two comrades in exile beside him and, for the first time in his life, he feels old.

STANDING AT THE HELM OF *SEA ROBIN,* WAITING FOR THE LIGHT OF THE sun to leak over the horizon, Lupe thinks how different things are now than when she last approached these islands. Then, she led a motley flotilla of Werfolk raiders. Now, she finds herself at the head of an armada composed of folk Wer and Mer and Ur, as Simon always calls them now.

Traveling southward, they have lost a few of those who started with them. Sister Mariel has returned to the New Catechists, to report fully on what she saw during her travels. Sister Tawanna, however, is still with Lupe here aboard *Sea Robin*. Aura rejoined Mark Fornash's followers, promising they would send an envoy very soon. Phenix has returned to his family. Two of the guards who escorted Lupe and Simon north have rejoined Lupe's own people.

Otherwise the company of travelers has grown steadily. Along their route they have been joined by boats of many sizes. The new arrivals are full of rumors and prophecies, which are also somehow memories. News regarding the downfall of Cameron Spires is much bandied about. Eagerly anticipated is any word of his very pregnant granddaughter, Trillia.

Lupe smiles at the thought. The rising sun shows the long outline of Grand Bahama before them. A cheer goes up from the armada at the sight of it. Lupe's smile hardens with tension when she sees a line of Merfolk swiftly approaching, leaping through the water.

The Merfolk wheel and escort the armada, one swimmer to the bow of each boat. Lupe relaxes. She still hasn't quite gotten used to this alliance with her former enemies, especially here. That will take time.

Always hard to know where one will find common ground. Turns out the

Merfolk are leery of smart machines, too—a good sign. Looking through some of Cameron Spires' old speeches in databases aboard *Sea Robin*, Lupe was surprised to find that even an old enemy like him should remember and value some of the same ideas she does. An obscure notion like "the hour of the wolf," for instance. Lupe was startled to find, among Spires' records, a fragment of a poem her own father loved, with its lines about how the hour of the wolf has now ended, and the time has come for the world to be "built up again, struggling in darkness." Spires used it as the concluding passage in his first speech upon arriving in Grand Bahama from New York. The words, she knows, were those of a crazed poet and musician of the last century, from a poem called *Jamaica* rather than *Bahama*. Spires apparently thought they suited the time and occasion, nonetheless.

She ponders those words as *Sea Robin* and half a hundred other boats sail into the harbor, toward a waving crowd of a good size for so early in the morning. She thinks she sees Trillia among those waiting to greet them.

Perhaps those old lines of Morrison's are even more appropriate now than they were then. The hour of the wolf. The time when most people are born and most people die. The time when dreams shape reality most powerfully. Has it really now ended?

Maybe, she thinks with a wolfish grin. And maybe not.

JOHN DRINAN'S LIGHTCRAFT RISES INTO THE NIGHT SKY, BORNE UPWARD on powerful laser pulses, toward where he hopes Ricardo's promise will prove true: that the same hole in the sky he fell out of, all those years ago, is now open again to receive him. He smiles crookedly.

"Same planet, different universe."

The memories of that other time are a persistent dull ache. Even now—after his trip north and all they accomplished, here on the brink of triumph and return aboard this salvaged spaceship making such a God-awful racket in its passage through the atmosphere it sets Oz to barking—even now, he can't be sure the tunnel-vortex which once spat them out will now breathe them back in.

"Cape Phoenix to Sol-Flier 1 . . . Cape Phoenix to Sol-Flier 1 . . ."

Coming out of his reverie, John recognizes Malika Hardesty's voice over the comm. He also realizes that his chief mission control officer has been calling him for nearly a minute.

"Sol-Flier 1, here."

"Good to hear your voice, John. I was wondering what happened to you."

"Roger that. Just thinking about parallel universes and holes in the sky—and in the bottom of the quantum sea."

Malika groans. They've been over this ground so often it's become a joke between them.

"Check your readouts, John. Do you see the veil over the elephant's trunk yet?"

That's what Malika calls the plenum contact point he's looking for: the thin veil between the universes, which will hopefully be swept aside to reveal the "elephant's trunk" of the vortex itself as he approaches. John sits up straighter and checks his readouts, looking at the interferometer Malika designed, scanning it for a section of false-color space flashing pale blue with the telltale radiation of contact.

"No, I—wait a minute. Confirmed. I have the contact point—and a fix on it."

"Dive in, then. Let's hope the veil lifts and the curtain parts."

"Done."

John sets the controls, sits back, and waits. Science and technology—even Malika's physics—have taken them as far as they can. Now it all depends on whatever Ricardo managed to accomplish in his last moments. John wonders if there will be any sign when the veil lifts, when the lightship passes into the vortex. . . .

He needn't have worried. The signs when they come are obvious. The veil between universes lifts in a bright flash, to reveal the moon suddenly become countless moons—and countless spaces where the moon might have been—extending away infinitely. Standing waves shift outward from the center of this flood of images. Like ripples. Like an Australian aborigine's *tjurunga*. Like the coherent signal of the present leaving the noise of the past behind it, plunging on to make sense from the noise of the future.

The ripples grow stronger, until waves become waterfalls of glittering moons. The echoing base of the lunar cataracts seem to be pulling away into unfathomable distance. The moonfalls themselves wrap past 90 degrees, past 180, past 360. They catch themselves in a vast spiral, a single turning vortex of moons, the moons distorting to white noise as the vortex spins faster.

Before they pass through the needle's-eye-narrow throat of this Holy Grail hourglass tunnel and reality dissolves completely, John is granted the grace to know that the here and now is also the infinite and the eternal. When his ship disappears, John Drinan's smile is the last thing to go. He thinks and remembers in innumerable other minds, and innumerable other minds think and remember in his—

Hello, John! Hello, Oz!

Voices: of his cousin Seiji, whom he met once. Of his cousin Jiro, whom he has never really known, yet whose voice he now somehow recognizes. Coming into his mind from rippling out-of-focus spheres like interference patterns in holographic plates showing up under ordinary light—inscrutable two-dimensional patterns that will show three-dimensional images under laser light of the appropriate wavelength. Only these "patterns" before him are at least three dimensional already, likely much more—and there are far more of them than just those he associates with Seiji and Jiro.

And this place is—?

With a cosmocentrism appropriate to where you were born, Jiro says, *call it Universe A.*

Which, all things being reconciled here, says Seiji, *has already transcended.*

And the universe which, from the end of time, influences Universe A Prime, which you've been living in for something over a third of a century.

So I can't go home again?

Never could, says Jiro. *My fault, really, that the Light blew you into A Prime. Upshot of struggling over completeness and consistency with the Allesseh here. Going home again is always also returning to the scene of the crime. Can't be helped now. Special cases of other universes.*

And if I return to the scene of the crime?

You'll get caught in a strange loop, Seiji says.

And he sees what he always should have discussed with Cameron Spires. A summer evening. The westering sun. Dry August grass golden on hillsides around Lake Falmouth, Kentucky. His parents. His aunt and uncle. Automobile accidents—some in which his parents and uncle and aunt are killed by a car driven by Cameron Spires' grandfather. Some in which the cars never hit each other. Some in which Cameron and his grandfather swerve over the edge to avoid the oncoming cars and only the boy Cameron dies, while John and Seiji and Jiro's parents all live.

Innumerable variations on the accident and its consequences—only one yielding Universe A, now transcended. The forcing of A Prime into that pattern would trap all possible worlds inside some kind of hyperKlein bottleneck, a Möbius of time neither quite frozen into space, nor space quite disappeared into time. All possible universes of the plenum never coming unstuck from the eternal repetition of a few brief moments. The Allesseh in A Prime never reconciling itself to the final step.

He knows that A Prime is his home now; the cost to alter it is too much—and, besides, someone always has to look after Oz.

—until he and Jiro and Seiji understand together that what happened above comes before what will happen below and neither takes place without the other.

John in his lightcraft falls back down the sky, a rainbow of meteor thunder in his wake, toward the vermilion sunset and fingernail moon of the world that has become his home. Morning, and evening—the second day.

THE LINES TRILLIA IS READING WHEN THE BOOM FROM THE SKY DISTRACTS her are these:

The second half of life does not signify ascent, unfolding, increase, exuberance, but death, since the end is its goal. The negation of life's fulfillment is synonymous with the refusal to accept its ending. Both mean not wanting to live; not wanting to live is identical with not wanting to die. Waxing and waning making one curve.

Putting aside the old book of Jung and glancing up at the noise, Trillia sees the fingernail moon and thinks of waxing and waning. The rainbow in the sunset makes her think of the treasure to be found only at its end. She leans forward on the sand to where her babies lie, in the nautilus-shaped bassinets the Merfolk presented to her. The waves dying on the shore rock them gently.

"Look! Look at the rainbow!"